But there were easier ways to get the information he wanted, weren't there? What was the point of being a sorcerer if you couldn't use a little magic to smooth out the bumps in your path? ...

He stabbed his thumb, let a few drops of blood patter on to the pile of Civil Service stationery, and described a complicated sigil in the air with the tips of his fingers. A faint sensation of static electricity stirred the hairs on the backs of his hands, then earthed itself ...

He picked up the first file. One of the midge voices swelled, overwhelming the others, pressing against the inside of his skull. Loric closed his eyes, listening; then, suddenly he knew ...

Shared World anthologies from ROC/Midnight Rose

TEMPS
EUROTEMPS

THE WEERDE
WEERDE II: THE BOOK OF THE ANCIENTS (forthcoming)

VILLAINS

EUROTEMPS

EDITED BY ALEX STEWART

DEVISED BY
ALEX STEWART AND NEIL GAIMAN

A ROC BOOK

PENGUIN BOOKS

Published by the Penguin Group
Penguin Books Ltd, 27 Wrights Lane, London W8 5TZ, England
Penguin Books USA Inc., 375 Hudson Street, New York, New York 10014, USA
Penguin Books Australia Ltd, Ringwood, Victoria, Australia
Penguin Books Canada Ltd, 10 Alcorn Avenue, Toronto, Ontario, Canada M4V 3B2
Penguin Books (NZ) Ltd, 182–190 Wairau Road, Auckland 10, New Zealand

Penguin Books Ltd, Registered Offices: Harmondsworth, Middlesex, England

First published by ROC, an imprint of Penguin Books, 1992
1 3 5 7 9 10 8 6 4 2

Typeset by DatIX International Limited, Bungay, Suffolk
Filmset in 10/12 pt Monophoto Melior
Printed in England by Clays Ltd, St Ives plc

CONTENTS

IF LOOKS COULD KILL   *David Langford*   5

A VIRUS IN THE SYSTEM   *Christopher Amies*   27

HIDE AND SEEK   *Jenny Jones*   55

LE GRAND MOANS   *Anne Gay*   75

EL LOBO DORADO IS DEAD, IS DEAD   *Liz Holliday*   89

PLAYING SAFE   *Marcus L. Rowland*   129

SORTILEGE AND SERENDIPITY   *Brian Stableford*   149

PHOTO FINISHED   *Molly Brown*   191

MONASTIC LIVES   *Graham Joyce*   209

THE FOREIGN POST   *Colin Greenland*   229

A PROBLEM SHARED   *Tina Anghelatos*   243

TOTALLY TRASHED   *Roz Kaveney*   261

THE LAW OF BEING   *Storm Constantine*   309

Additional material by Alex Stewart.

It was long after midnight before Loric pushed the swivel chair back from his polished oak desk, and yawned loudly. His study, once the servants' parlour of his Chelsea town house, was a cosy room; warm yellow firelight flickered from the spines of his books, the spiders and curios housed in glass cases, and the backs of the curtains bracing themselves against the last chill of winter. Warm and secure, seldom visited by anyone else apart from his housekeeper, here most of all he felt at home.

Except tonight. He walked around the desk, stretching the cramps from his back, sparing the heap of files no more than a glance of distaste. The few he'd read so far were stacked neatly on an occasional table to the left of his chair; the rest, far greater in number, overflowed the blotter in an untidy heap, lapping around Madeline's photograph to the left, swallowing the pen tray to the right, as they sprawled towards the yellowing human skull next to the paper-clips. Some were stamped in red: DEPARTMENT OF PARANORMAL RESOURCES. DO NOT REMOVE. Others belonged to the Home Office, and a handful to other agencies, which would have been extremely upset to discover they were missing.

Loric yawned again and poured himself another cup of Earl Grey from a teapot which seemed far too small to contain the amount he'd already drunk. His body clock was still on Brussels time, his flight had been delayed, and he was tired from the relentless round of public receptions and private diplomacy that dealing with the Commission always required. And now he had to brief the Minister in the morning; another of Orpington's little legacies he could well have done without.

Ministerial briefings had always been Philip's job, before his abrupt departure from the Department; now Loric had to deal with virtually everything himself. It was bad enough having to sweep the wretched man's misdeeds under the carpet, he thought; getting stuck with his workload as well was adding insult to injury.

'Oh, well.' He took a sip of the tea and returned to his desk. The sooner he finished, the sooner he could get to bed. The cup clinked gently against the saucer as he set it down, easing himself back into the chair.

Mechanically he selected the next file from the stack on the blotter, folding it open to scan the typescript inside. The words danced on the paper, blurred with fatigue. He yawned again and let it fall. This was hopeless.

But there were easier ways to get the information he wanted, weren't there? What was the point of being a sorcerer if you couldn't use a little magic to smooth out the bumps in your path? He knew he'd pay for it later, in headaches and dizzy spells, but aspirin would see him through the briefing, and an early weekend would take care of the rest. Probably. He rummaged through the papers for the letter opener.

Are you sure about this?

'Yes.' He stabbed his thumb, let a few drops of blood patter on to the pile of Civil Service stationery, and described a complicated sigil in the air with the tips of his fingers. A faint sensation of static electricity stirred the hairs on the backs of his hands, then earthed itself.

Loric slumped back in the chair, disorientated. The

stack of files tugged at his attention, the mingled whine of a dozen mosquito voices echoing behind his eyes.

Drink some tea.

'Oh. Right.' He sipped again at the rapidly cooling beverage. The familiarity of the action brought him back to himself, left him feeling stronger, more in control. The subliminal whine lessened but failed to fade entirely. He replaced the cup and pinched the bridge of his nose.

'You may have been right,' he said after a moment. 'I'm more tired than I thought.'

One at a time, then?

'One at a time.' He picked up the first file. One of the midge voices swelled, overwhelming the others, pressing against the inside of his skull. Loric closed his eyes, listening; then, suddenly, he knew . . .

IF LOOKS COULD KILL

David Langford

The law relating to the paranormal is almost incomprehensible, except to those who have studied it
from their cradles, and even for them it is a labyrinth of uncertainties, of false clues, blind alleys,
and unexplored passages.

        A. P. Herbert, *More Misleading Cases*, 1930

'This is rather a curious kind of tower,' observed
Father Brown; 'when it takes to killing people, it
always kills people who are somewhere else.'
G. K. Chesterton, *The Wisdom of Father Brown*,
        1914

'Sir, I have no Talent. I have genius or I have nothing.'

Caligula Foxe inhaled a firkin or two of air and glared
across his desk at our visitor.

'I'm afraid, Mr Foxe, that you'll find that the question
is for Committee B2 to decide.'

'It is a confounded impertinence.'

Certainly it was quite a job keeping my hands where
they belonged, on the smaller desk and scribbling ostenta-
tiously in the notebook. I kept wanting to hug myself.

When this Seyton Cream of the Department of Paranormal Resources had asked for an appointment, I'd booked
him in on general principles, since it was guaranteed to

5

annoy Foxe. Half of my pay is for being a gadfly, after all: he signs the cheques and he said it himself. Also there was at present a certain coolness between Foxe and yours truly. Thank goodness my holiday break was a mere three days off.

Cream swivelled in the red leather chair we kept reserved for clients, and brought his bony face to bear on me. 'I would greatly prefer this discussion to be private.'

The corner of Foxe's mouth twitched invisibly. 'Mr Goodman is privy to all my affairs.' Anything that got on a pin-striped civil servant's nerves was okay with him. But then the world's biggest detective remembered his little dispute with me, shifted his one seventh of a tonne irritably, and added: 'Nevertheless, Charlie, on this occasion we shall dispense with the notes. Your transcriptions have been less than satisfactory of late.'

I felt a hot flush just behind my ears. The fat old windbag. He knows damn well that I can outperform a cassette recorder for flawless playback, notes or no notes.

Cream said, 'Very well. I would now like to come to the point.'

'A truly astonishing declaration from a professed Eurocrat,' murmured Foxe. 'Sir, I believe I can approximate to your point without further aid. Your wretched Brussels committee has wallowed through eighteen months and more than a million words of legal verbiage, addressing the definition of paranormal Talent. You now intimate that deductive and inferential genius, such as I choose to hire out for pay, might soon be so classified. You imply that in the vilest governmental tradition of compulsory purchase, I myself could be placed on the DPR register . . .'

He shuddered involuntarily. He never left the old house in Westbourne Terrace if he could possibly help it.

Talents have to report in at the DPR's slightest whim: I pictured Foxe edging his bulk sideways through the shabby door of their Praed Street office, and sternly suppressed a twinge of pity.

'I did not say –'

'Pfui. You unmistakably implied.'

Cream fiddled with the regulation bowler hat on his lap. 'Perhaps I have approached this matter in the wrong way.'

'Indeed, yes. The carrot is customarily dangled in plain view before any tactless allusion is made to the stick.'

'I stand corrected. I've suffered through Committee B2 sessions for so long that I begin to forget how to deal with human beings. Sometimes it seems the thing will never end. You know how it is with the EC.'

Foxe inclined his head politely.

With a visible effort Cream started talking to the point about his outfit's problem, which had nothing to do with committees. It seemed there was this guy Xaos who might or might not be running a foolproof murder bureau. After a minute I let my attention slide a bit, thinking of a certain upcoming trip to Provence with Lila, a very good lady friend. Maybe when I got back, Foxe would have seen sense about that antiquated typewriter that had caused all the coolness.

Clearly there was no chance at all of him accepting the DPR commission that was taking shape. A foregone conclusion. Foxe hates being a second choice, and part of the spiel was that the Yard's Odd Squad had already dead-ended on this one. He hates following orders, and Cream was issuing him a complete plan of action. He hates government work, and need I say more? Above all, he *really* loathes being coerced. No chance.

So it was a sudden cold shock when I heard him say distinctly, 'Yes, I believe I shall be able to accept the case, at a fee to be determined by mutual agreement. Mr Goodman himself will be pleased to carry out the entrapment precisely as you suggest. I assure you that he is reliable, discreet and loyal . . . indeed he will be giving up a long-planned holiday to work uncomplainingly on this very inquiry.'

Cream was not visibly impressed. Me even less. As I said, a definite coolness.

This rift had started with the typewriter I use for all Foxe's reports and correspondence . . . not to mention his damn plant records. Once upon a time an IBM Selectric 82c had been super-duper luxury; in 1992 it was a rattle-trap and a pain.

'A great detective needs the best,' I'd explained in courteous and reasonable tones, covering his desk with glossy brochures of word processors, laser printers. But Foxe decided to get on a hobby horse.

'Charlie,' he'd declared, opening his fifth bottle of beer that morning, 'there is a high dignity in words. You well know that I employ them with ceaseless care and respect. I consciously choose not to have my sentences agitated in some electronic cocktail shaker or capriciously re-arranged at – as you remark – the merest touch of a key. Call it obstinacy, call it Luddism . . .'

I didn't call it anything, not out loud, but I'd privately opened up the Selectric and done things to the motor bearings. Now it made a noise like a two-stroke engine with asthma. I was planning to wear Foxe down.

After I showed Cream to the front door, I thought bitterly about the Provence trip and wondered if I'd worn him down too far. We discussed the case, very politely. I'll just pick out the highlights of the dossier.

Item: the corpse was a minor parliamentary cog called Whittle, secretary to some Junior Minister's assistant.

Item: there was a villain, the man called Xaos, who advertised a personal service for 'removing obstacles' to a happy life, nudge nudge, know what I mean?

Item: there was a tearful confession, from Whittle's wife Diane, who had wanted a divorce, wanted it a whole lot. He hadn't. She closed out their joint account and went to pay a call on Xaos.

Item: there was no evidence. The Met had played pass-the-parcel with the affair. Forensic said flatly that there was nothing to show Whittle hadn't simply popped off from natural causes, immediate cause heart failure. Even the Odd Squad admitted that although the death was, quote consistent with attack through psychic attrition unquote – the Evil Eye to you and me – the guy Xaos showed no sign of that Talent and anyway had apparently never got close enough to the victim. Maybe there was an accomplice, even if no one could trace one? But hey, this could well be something new and paranormal and therefore the DPR's pigeon. Pass-the-parcel. Exit Scotland Yard, chortling and washing their hands.

Item: I checked our file of current papers and found the *Eye* ad was still running. *OBSTACLES REMOVED. Clear the path to happiness. No satisfaction, no fee. Xaos, 071 022 3033.* Enough to set anyone thinking and wondering. Cream's dossier included the guy's address, a flat in Pimlico, but even this was no big secret. When I tapped in the number and made an appointment for 3 p.m., the chirpy voice at the other end told me just how to get there.

Foxe had further instructions. Our freelance colleague Paul Sanza, the best private operative outside Westbourne Terrace, was going to play the victim in this charade – the obstacle to be removed. 'The bleating of the kid excites the tiger,' Foxe murmured. And my part was to follow in the tracks of the embittered wife and consult Xaos.

'No doubt a circumstantial story will occur to you,' said Foxe blandly. 'For example, some attractive woman with whom you are besotted has chosen with the fickleness of all her sex to transfer her favours to Paul. Might this not constitute sufficient motivation?'

Paul is a skinny runt with an oversized nose and ears like satellite dishes. I have my own views of my personal attractions and was not best pleased.

'No,' I said with feeling. 'I thought I'd say he was a boss who'd stumbled into the kind of government work he never takes on, and totally screwed up my holiday with some attractive woman with whom I am besotted. And from whom I expect a sock in the eye tomorrow when I break it to her.'

'Charlie. If I am to counter Mr Cream's grotesque implied threat of the Temps register, I require leverage. It is necessary that we involve ourselves this once in their affairs.'

I didn't believe a word of it and was composing a short, pointed speech, but then our chef Franz came in and announced lunch. His very own *beurre de cacahouète avec confiture* is not a dish to keep waiting. Foxe demonstrated leverage and was out of the chair faster than you might think.

He allows no discussion of business at his table, and a week ago he'd decreed that all talk of typewriters and word processors counted as business. I wouldn't work for anyone else but by God he could be trying. Today, between huge mouthfuls, it was language-lesson time. 'Charlie, you will undoubtedly have recognized Xaos as a Greek name or pseudonym. The X is of course the letter *chi* and so the word corresponds to our term "chaos". A contemporary Greek translator would anglicize the name as Haos, with an *H*, since . . .'

Talk about respect for the dignity of words. He's never

happier than when he's slamming them against the ropes.

The weather was fine. I decided to walk through Hyde Park and stretch my legs on the way to the appointment. It also gave me more time to practise the story I planned to hand out to Xaos.

His place turned out to be nothing impressive, a dump above a seedy grocer's. 'Mr Xaos?' I said, as he peered over the door-chain. 'I'm Bill Durkin.' That was a safety measure. Charlie Goodman, brilliant assistant to Caligula Foxe, was occasionally mentioned in newspapers.

'Just Xaos, Mr Durkin. Can I offer you some coffee?'

I said no thanks, sat down and looked him over. You couldn't call him striking or sinister: chubby, light-haired, thirtyish, about five-six. But something in his very pale eyes made me wonder whether he needed any accomplice for whatever games he got up to.

He said cheerfully, 'The usual thing is for you to tell me what you think is getting in the way of the life you want to lead. Then I tell you whether it's something my personal Dyno-Rod service can clear. I turn down a lot of people I can't help.'

That had been in the dossier too. The Yard had located and interviewed some of his rejects. A man who wanted Lord Heseltine offed for political reasons. Another with a grudge against the Warden of All Souls for trying to change his sex via laser beams from UFOs. A woman whose husband had cut and run, she didn't know where but she wanted to know for sure he wouldn't come back. Foxe had pushed his lips in and out and eventually said, 'Suggestive.'

My avowed problem was of course Paul Sanza. It's best to cram as much truth as you can into a story like this, so I told Xaos several warranted facts, at length:

that Paul was a private snoop but had otherwise been a pretty good pal, that I played poker with him and the gang three times a week, that he won too often for my liking, and that he knew all about my lady friend Lila.

'But now the bastard fancies her himself,' I lied. 'He's good at ferreting things out, and he's dug up stuff about me. Never mind what. Just let me say she wouldn't like it one bit. So I'm to lay off Lila or he'll leak things to her, maybe even to the police. I should never have trusted a guy in his slimy line of work.'

For the duration I believed in it enough to produce a light sweat on my forehead. Give the man an Oscar.

'Yes,' said Xaos. 'I can see that you must really hate this Sanza now. Him and no one else?'

I thought of asking whether he offered a wholesale discount, but just nodded.

'Now you might be thinking, how does the Xaos service work and why did I pick this name? And I'll gladly tell you. There is absolutely nothing up my sleeve. I don't even ask a fee in advance. You pay only when fully satisfied. Of course, by then you'll also be satisfied about the measures I could take if you changed your mind . . . but let's not go into that. Now: have you ever heard of chaos theory?'

'I read the colour supplements sometimes,' I said cautiously.

'Then I expect you'll know the example they always give. The tiny beating of a butterfly's wing starts a chain of ripples which in the end affect the course of a hurricane on the far side of the world. A sensitive dependence on initial conditions. This is where I work, at a level that doesn't even register on instruments. A paranormal gift, you ask? No, I have no Talent in the usual sense . . .'

You and Foxe both, I thought. Me, I went and took the DPR tests like a good boy and was relieved when they classed me dead normal.

'But I do have an extraordinary sensitivity to the minute fluctuations of chaos. I see its patterns running through the world. Getting up in the morning, I might clearly sense that delaying one further instant in, say, pulling on a sock would set up a significant eddy in history. One that in the end could sway the political balance of Indo-China.'

'What doesn't?' I said sourly. Was he just a common or garden loony after all? Were his successes just a few natural deaths that sort of happened by coincidence in a much longer roster of failures?

'I offered a deliberately far-out example, Mr Durkin. More to the point, if I choose to stay aware of some person's identity – someone such as your "friend" Paul Sanza – then I can sense things about the flow of chaos as it relates to that person. By tiny choices I send out butterfly ripples. I turn the luck of the world against them. Perhaps it will be disease, perhaps accident. In all my waking hours when I'm on the job, I steer my actions with that in mind, and compel disaster. See, I twiddle this pencil *so*. Air currents move and propagate. Hours or days later it could mean the last straw for a particular party in Solihull or Dublin.'

'Well, don't twiddle that thing at me.' I usually manage a better class of repartee, but in his weird way Xaos was sort of impressive. His eyes got to you.

I offered him a Polaroid snap of Paul. He glanced at it and nodded. 'Thanks. Since you've interacted with him so much in the past, my sensitivity has already picked up the feel of his pattern. It's important, by the way, that you don't deviate from your own routine. Keep going to those poker games with Sanza, and so on.'

His casual attitude gave me a feeling of being somehow wrong-footed. Xaos didn't even seem specially interested in Paul's address. Foxe had been speculating after lunch about a repeat of the bluff someone had worked back in 1961, with witches and pentagrams and death spells as window-dressing to distract everyone from the strictly mundane planting of a lethal dose in the victim's larder. You needed an address for games like that. If there was any chance that he was on the level . . . Those eyes!

'Well, Mr Durkin,' said Xaos, 'I'd be pleased to make a small bet with you. If this obstruction to your happiness has not disappeared in, let's say, two weeks, I'll gladly pay you five thousand pounds. And, of course, vice versa.'

Of course it was okay and perfectly in character to agree with a tremor in my voice, but I wished it had been one hundred per cent an act. We shook on it.

'But don't you get a lot of unwelcome attention?' I asked, hoping to start a crack somewhere. 'The ad could mean anything, of course, but the rumour I heard was pretty clear about what you offer.'

A thin, knowing smile. 'Believe me, I'm safely beyond the reach of the law. I cannot be prosecuted. Goodbye.'

Back at street level I signalled unobtrusively to Terry Carver, our second-best freelance after Paul himself. His job was to keep watch and tail Xaos if he took it into his head to go visiting. Then I located a Mercury callbox and keyed in the Sanza home number. He sounded cheerful enough.

'The curse has come upon you,' I warned. 'Have you got Sally Cole babysitting you there?'

'All according to plan, Charlie. She sends her best.'

Sally was a reliable witch-smeller on loan from the Bonner agency, hired to blow the whistle if there really was any weirdo attack. Anyway, the textbooks insisted that while evil-eye merchants didn't need actual eye contact, they could operate only at fairly close range. Our other regular operatives were watching Paul's flat in

Haringey around the clock. Nothing could get to him without being spotted. Surely.

As usual, between four o'clock and six, Foxe was pottering in the plant rooms at the top of the house when I got back. I climbed three floors to report as instructed, but he was in a cantankerous mood, blowing hot and cold: 'I am not altogether happy with this involvement. I might yet reject the commission. Bah. Please type a full transcript of your conversation with the man Xaos, making three carbons. They may be required.'

I pronounced a word under my breath and left him alone with his babies. Why any grown man should want to cultivate paranormal saprophytes ... They were no big thrill to look at, and you could spare only so much admiration for the way they rooted in weird surfaces. One grew on armourglass, another on Teflon, a third sucked its nourishment somehow from hard vacuum. Foxe's star item was a sport from Nevada that made out quite happily on a polished slab of depleted uranium, which would personally worry me if I lived in Nevada.

Six and a half pages into the transcript, Foxe moved majestically across the office, settled in the one chair in the world he really loves, and rang for beer. After a pause he looked hard at me. His index finger moved in tiny circles on the desktop, which is usually a sign that he's bottling something up.

'Charlie. Am I correct in believing that the infernal clatter of that machine is worse than customary?'

'Pardon, sir?'

His eyes narrowed. He picked up one of the completed sheets I'd laid on his desk, and felt it between finger and thumb. 'To the best of my knowledge, the system of embossing print on paper was made obsolete by the six-dot alphabet published by Louis Braille in 1829 and elaborated in 1837.'

'Gosh, it must be the dedicated energy I put into it, sir, struggling with weakening fingers against antique machinery.'

'Pfui. It is an electric typewriter. You have turned up the impact setting with intent to annoy.'

He had me there. You can't fool a detective genius. But I was still mad about the holiday, and escalated things by typing on for another paragraph as though I hadn't heard.

'Mr Goodman!' This time it was a full-throated bellow. My eardrums twanged. 'Let it be known that I have not the slightest intention of investing in the puerile gadgetry to which you are so attracted.' He inhaled deeply, resenting the effort of bellowing, and went on in whiny, sarcastic tones: 'But what is this? It was four carbon copies that I required, and not three. You must have misheard me, Mr Goodman. You will need to retype the six, no, the seven pages already completed. I do hope it does not make you late for your *important* appointment to play poker tonight.'

I pronounced another inaudible word, with feeling.

Dinner was not a happy meal. It was *doigts de poisson 'œil d'oiseau'*, another of Franz Brunner's great specialities, but Foxe was distinctly off his food. In spite of its impressive size, any little thing could turn his stomach. I made bright conversation about chaos theory and butterflies. It didn't seem to help.

Afterwards Foxe conscientiously endured the racket of the typewriter as he dipped into a book, *Chaos*, by James Gleick. Conceivably he was working. From his bilious expression and the way he dog-eared the pages, I deduced that he wasn't enjoying the style. In all the time before I finished he only said one word. Looking to and fro between a page of my transcript and something in the book, he stated: 'Untenable.'

Nor was the poker game at Paul's a wild success. I was late after all that retyping and took some chaff about devotion to duty. So did Terry, ringing in hourly to report that he was half frozen and Xaos still hadn't budged from home. The rest of the hired help were mightily pleased to be getting paid for attending their regular card session, but they didn't have a genius to live with. Paul came out ahead by forty pounds, most of it mine. I passed certain remarks about how it was hard to play and bodyguard at the same time, and how I preferred to go easy on a doomed man, but my heart wasn't in it.

Next morning Foxe evidently felt the same. He declared a relapse.

Relapses take him in various ways. Sometimes he shuts himself in the plant rooms for a week, fiddling with unlikely cross-pollinations. Other times he shoves Franz out of the kitchen and camps there obsessively, cooking *lapin pays de Galles* in fifty different styles. This one, though, was just plain malingering in bed.

What it always means is that his brain is going on strike. Here we were in this damn stupid case, for no better reason than Foxe wanting to needle me, and with nothing to do but sit on our bottoms waiting to see if Paul toppled over and died. No dangerous errands for intrepid Goodman. No spicy little facts for the genius to work on. The closest he'd got to actual thought was claiming that my dialogue with Xaos contained 'interesting and suggestive points'. I couldn't see them myself.

Foxe was laying it on with a trowel today. At nine he skipped his regular two hours with the plants, and stayed in bed, wallowing in self-pity. At ten he called Dr Wolmer, and I groaned at the thought of the cheque I'd have to draw because Foxe never chose to walk three doors along the road to the surgery. At eleven Wolmer came down from the bedroom, looking non-committal.

'Tell me straight, doc,' I asked earnestly as I showed him out. 'Are they baffling symptoms of a kind unknown to science?'

'You could say that,' he said. Of course he was too polite to suggest the great man might be, ahem, imagining it all.

Towards noon my desk phone buzzed. 'Come to my room at once,' said Foxe. Maybe now he wanted a lawyer and a priest.

He is an awesome sight in bed, a vast expanse of yellow silk pyjamas like the endless prairies of wherever it is they have endless prairies. Doc told me once that a human being eats his own weight of food every fifty days, and seeing Foxe like that makes me wonder how he can ever find the time. I studied him critically. He looked more unhappy than ill.

'Charlie, I am entertaining a conjecture. The possibility is remote, yet ... Since yesterday evening have I felt ... less and less well. I invariably distrust coincidence. Could the man Xaos have penetrated your deception in some fashion ... turned his weapon, whatever it might be, against not Paul but myself?'

'Anything's possible,' I said, humouring him. 'With funny eyes like that, he might do all sorts of odd things.'

'You will proceed ... no. I may require you here. You will telephone /Terry and instruct him to break cover. He is to enter the flat and render Xaos unconscious. Paul or one of the others will go to him with a syringe and a supply of pentothal, to keep him so. If Xaos is to be ... taken at his own face value, he cannot maintain his influence while kept insensible. The conjecture will be tested.'

I have omitted the distracting grunts and gasps. Foxe was really hamming it up. It was pathetic. My own professional pride wouldn't let me believe for a moment that Xaos had seen through the story – he'd have had to be a telepath *and* a damn good actor. All the same, I disliked him on principle and approved of action, any action.

'I'm betting that you're wrong, sir, but here goes,' I said, and sprinted downstairs, hoping Terry had remembered to pack his cellphone.

He had.

I cooled my heels for twenty-five minutes, flipping through much thumbed brochures of Provence and once again growing increasingly irritated with Foxe. If I couldn't take my rightful holiday, why the hell couldn't it be me who burst in and socked Xaos on the jaw?

Then Terry called. He'd worked it better than that. 'I just went up, told him a friend had recommended me to consult him, said yes to coffee and slipped him a Mickey Finn when his back was turned. Dead to the world. He was easy meat, Charlie.'

'Right,' I said. 'Foxe will tell me to say "satisfactory" and so I do. Be seeing you.'

I buzzed the sick room and passed on Terry's message. 'And do you feel a sudden surge of relief and well-being, sir?'

'No,' said the theatrically feeble voice.

Which was exactly what I'd expected. Imaginary illnesses are real toughies to treat, I thought to myself.

By now I dare say you've guessed the secret of how Xaos really worked his tricks. You're probably thinking I'm dumb not to have deduced it for myself. Let me just say that I'm not the genius in this household, only the legman ... and puzzles are a million times harder to solve when you're close to them, living through them.

I lunched off a glass of milk. That didn't bother Franz,

but he came down almost in tears when Foxe refused the tray carrying a light, eleven-course invalid snack. I had begun to get the creepy feeling that something was going on right under my nose, that I was missing the obvious.

Around then Ron Cohen of the *Eye* rang to remark that, according to the whispers of little birds in his ear, our favourite fatso was now pulling chestnuts out of the fire for the Department of the Preternaturally Ridiculous, and what about an inside story? I bandied words with him, not referring to small ads.

Seconds after I'd hung up, Paul reported in. Xaos continued to sleep like a babe, he reckoned they could keep him that way for another twenty-four hours solid, and to pass the time our gang had made a fine-tooth search of the dump. No voodoo props, no death rays, no written records of the obstacle-removing business. No news: of course the Yard had done the same and drawn a blank, though their dossier kept sort of quiet about it.

Mid afternoon, and I heard the whir of Foxe's private lift. His idea of exercise is to go up and down twice. I wondered if he'd pulled out of his goddam relapse and started making plans for the new problem of our court appearance when citizen Xaos gave evidence on charges of assault, conspiracy, actual bodily harm with a hypodermic . . .

Then I saw something I'd never seen before. Foxe was standing in the office doorway in his vast yellow pyjamas, swaying ponderously, looking shrunken, greenish and three quarters dead. Great drops of sweat stood out all over his big face. It was a hell of an impressive performance.

'Charlie. An alternative conjecture. Please . . . obey me without question. I instruct you to order the word-processing equipment of your choice, for immediate delivery. Use the agency credit card. I . . . also wish to apologize for the cancellation of your holiday ... shall make amends. I ...' He closed his eyes and leaned hard against the door-frame.

My God, I thought, he's actually delirious. He really was ill now, in such a state that I wouldn't have been surprised if he'd started splitting infinitives or using 'contact' as a verb. It truly was sort of touching to think our little rift had been so much on his mind that he'd staggered down like this for a deathbed repentance scene.

'You should be in bed, sir,' I said, and sincerely meant it.

'Mr Goodman. Kindly carry out my instructions at once.' There was enough of the old snap in his voice that my hand dived straight for the telephone.

'Black Mountain Systems? I have an urgent order.' I knew by heart what I wanted, of course. I mean, what the office wanted.

When I turned, Foxe was sitting behind the big desk in his pyjamas, mopping his face with the wrong handkerchief (it was a souvenir of the Ballard case and still had the original blood stains) and breathing heavily. His colour was a little better now.

'Kindly fetch Mr Cream at once. I will instruct Paul to bring the man Xaos here. My alternative hypothesis has been fully confirmed. Thank heavens.'

I have to confess I still hadn't the faintest idea what he meant.

By the time I'd hauled a strongly protesting Cream from his Ministry (lucky he wasn't off committeeing in Brussels again), Paul had arrived and decanted Xaos into one of the yellow leather chairs. He looked thoroughly groggy, and so would you. Foxe had dressed, shaved and – I'd bet – eaten his head off. I steered our client to the red chair.

Foxe looked at him with satisfaction. 'Mr Cream, I would like to introduce you to Mr Xaos.'

'Just Xaos. No Mr. And you won't believe the lawsuit I'm going to hit you with when I get clear of your goons.'

'Be silent, sir. I shall be brief. As we agreed, Mr Cream, my operatives carried out a decoy manoeuvre. Mr Goodman approached the gentleman sitting there, who in effect undertook to ensure for a consideration that a certain man died within a fortnight. Several points about the reported conversation struck me, such as the nonsensical smokescreen of part-digested chaos theory, the seeming lack of interest in personal details of the proposed victim, and the emphatic remark that Mr Xaos himself was safe from prosecution. Indeed he is.'

'If they can't prosecute, then you haven't earned your fee,' said Cream sharply.

'We shall see. May I continue? Frankly, I know little of the pesky ways of paranormal Talent, but nevertheless I formed an interesting conjecture to account for this assurance of immunity. The Yard searched in vain for a murderous accomplice. What occurred to me was the notion of an unknowing accomplice.'

Cream said, 'That sounds like a contradiction in terms.' Xaos chuckled uneasily.

'Mr Xaos, I speculated, is the possessor of an interesting Talent. He cannot himself wield, but can temporarily confer, a power of malignity akin to what is commonly known as the Evil Eye. To test this conjecture after visiting him,' Foxe said through his teeth, 'Mr Goodman undertook to act out spurious feelings of resentment and dislike towards myself, pretending for the purpose to be discommoded by an obsolete typewriter. A small and seemingly childish pretext, but Mr Goodman's powers of theatrical self-deception are remarkable. The result . . .'

A cold shock like a bucket of ice-water had hit me in

the stomach. If I'd been any madder with Foxe ... My eyes were popping with sheer rage at what Xaos had so goddam nearly made me do. The bastard, the absolute bastard. For a moment I couldn't speak, only glare.

'Charlie!'

Xaos had slumped sideways in the yellow chair. Paul Sanza was at his side straight away. 'Heart, I think. My God, he's gone. No, he seems to be picking up again ... That's odd. Pulse went and came back again. Yes, he should pull through now, I think.'

'Which would tend to confirm my hypothesis,' Foxe said silkily. 'Have Franz bring brandy. Charlie, my apologies. I inadvertently goaded you into anger, forgetting the extent of your loyalty and devotion.'

He takes a lot for granted, does Caligula Foxe. I fought for calm and worked away at swallowing the lump I'd never admit was in my throat.

Foxe's shoulders lifted a tenth of a millimetre, which for him was an expansive shrug. 'You see, Mr Cream? Of course in the Whittle case it was the wife Diane after all. Following Mr Xaos's treatment, a period of serious hating at close range would have put paid to anyone. (One sees, does one not, why he refused customers who wished the deaths of people in remote or unknown locations?) You can't prosecute him: he didn't do it. You can't prosecute her: she acted unknowingly and the evil gift will have faded away, leaving no evidence. I deduce that it must fade, because, otherwise, even the Yard would have detected her unwitting Talent.'

No wonder Xaos had insisted I should carry on playing poker with Paul. Good grief. That, if only I'd had a real grudge, would have handed him the black spot for sure.

'H'mm,' said Cream, scratching his jaw and pointedly ignoring the weak, catarrhal noises from the body in the yellow chair.

'I am pleased to release the man Xaos into your custody. In all justice the DPR should lock him away as a social disease, but no doubt you will prefer to place him on a meagre stipend and make some dubious use of his ability. Meanwhile, I shall ask no fee but require an assurance that your pestilent Committee B2 will in future regard deductive and intuitive genius as falling outside the scope of the paranormal.'

'Nonsense. How the devil can I commit the Department to a stance like that?'

'Consider the alternative,' said Foxe dreamily, wiggling a finger at him. 'Mr Goodman occasionally publishes records of my cruder and more sensational cases. If the Xaos affair were made public, then so likewise would be the hitherto unremarked fact that temporary Talents can be induced. I rather imagine this would mean starting again, *de novo*, on Committee B2's legalistic definition of the paranormal. Eighteen months' work, do I recall your saying, and a million words of draft regulations?'

Cream had gone twice as pale as his name. 'Jesus,' he said. 'I mean, how extremely inconvenient that would be. I . . . Very well. On behalf of the Department, I accept your terms.'

'Satisfactory. Would you care for beer?' Foxe rang the bell.

'No, thank you.' The civil servant issued a constipated little smile. 'I suppose the DPR are getting off lightly. I've heard a great deal about your exorbitant fees and, frankly, am somewhat surprised that you don't want money as well.'

'But I do,' murmured Foxe, indicating the chair where, under Paul's and my tender care, Xaos was groaning and spluttering into his brandy. 'A certain bet was made with an authorized representative of this agency. Assuming that Mr Sanza can contrive not to die before the end of the stipulated fortnight, Mr Xaos will owe me the sum of five thousand pounds. I intend to collect.'

The ex-obstacle remover snarled feebly at Foxe. If looks could kill . . . But of course *his* couldn't.

Later I struggled hard to master the new word processor, as Foxe pretended to read his evening paper and gave me the occasional cynical look. It was a damn sight more complicated than the ads had claimed. Don't let him say anything, I thought, as for the umpteenth time the machine beeped rudely and flashed ERROR. In five or six days, according to Xaos, the curse would wear off and I'd be able to risk getting mad at people again. For now, just don't let him *say* anything.

He said, 'Tonight, at my request, Franz is preparing *crapaud dans le trou* in a sauce of his own invention. An excellent conclusion to the case.'

It was a recipe he knew very well I could get along without. 'I'll try my best to enjoy it, sir,' I said with false eagerness, 'but of course it could discommode me in some small and seemingly childish way. I might have to struggle to control my temper, you know, as brutal feelings of hatred rise up in me at each fresh mouthful . . .'

Foxe's eyes narrowed dangerously. I felt a huge, death-cold wave of sickening weakness crash through me and realized that Xaos had left him with a parting gift. By gum, for the next whole week we'd *both* have to be incredibly calm and polite. Somehow.

We discussed it.

Nothing to concern him there, Loric thought. *Cream was safely back in Brussels, keeping a discreet eye on Bennett, and what the Minister didn't know about potential loopholes in the system wouldn't hurt him.* He settled back into his body with the familiar vertiginous lurch, and added the file to the stack on the occasional table.

His tea was stone cold by now. He warmed it with a passing thought, and sipped at it as he selected another file.

As he lifted the folder, something about the midge voice that rose from it disturbed him; fleeting images of bright sun and sea, hard-edged Mediterranean shadows. Ripples of memory blew across the surface of his mind.

'Greece. Hell.' He'd never gone back there; even after all this time, it would have been too painful.

After more than twenty years. I'm touched.

'I always said as much.' Funny how they still fell back on half-serious bickering when things got too intense. But it always worked. His hands steadied, and, before he could change his mind, he let the voice well up around him.

A VIRUS IN THE SYSTEM

Christopher Amies

———————

Every corridor in Swanley House is exactly the same. Same dingy colour, same Civil Service décor innocent of any design innovations since 1950, same redolence of obscure b & w movies about the Men from the Ministry. There are miles of them.

And after ten minutes I'd seen quite enough.

I pushed open the door to Room 527, and heard Marcia Jones chattering on the phone to one of her two hundred alter egos. I wondered if killing off all the Marcias would only result in one rap for murder as they are all the same person.

I stood there just inside the doorway, admiring the décor (cheap Civil Service desk, wilting pot plant, micro-computer, poster of Torremolinos, Marcia), while Marcia ignored me and went on chattering about her Dick's willy, or was it her Willy's dick?

I thought, there's a customer here.

'There's a customer here,' Marcia said eventually, when she could be bothered to put the phone down.

'Exactly,' I said languidly. 'My name's Sarah Jamison. I've an appointment with Dr Warburton-Smith.'

'Really,' said Marcia.

'Yes, really. Can I see him?' As usual with Marcia, this was getting me nowhere.

Just then the inner door opened and Hugh Warburton-Smith came into his outer office.

'Hello, Sarah,' he said, extending a firm hand. I shook it. 'Do come in.'

This is more like it, I thought. Dr Warburton-Smith reminded me of a country GP, all amiable manner, tweed suit and confident competence. He wasn't a Talent, though; just a career Civil Servant, a Doctor of something unmiraculous. His office was lined with huntin' and fishin' posters, and on the desk was the portrait of a large, handsome woman cradling a tiny baby. I took a seat opposite him and sat back in expectation.

'Tea?'

'Oh, yes, please. It's very hot out.'

'Milk and sugar?'

'Milk, no sugar, thanks.'

I took the mug and Dr Warburton-Smith smiled reassuringly at me. I smiled back. Being called in by the DPR usually meant me getting my arse in gear and being sent off somewhere I had no desire to go, but there was no need to be offensive about it. There are enough people walking about quite prepared to do that.

'Sarah,' said Dr Warburton-Smith, 'what do you know about the Dark Avenger?'

'It's a computer virus,' I said. Like Monty Python almost said, you have to know these things when you're a weirdo.

'He,' Warburton-Smith corrected me. 'He is Keith Bingham, commonly known as the Dark Avenger. He's a rogue Talent. British, but living in Greece.'

'Oh, yes,' I said, and thought, I've heard something about it in the papers.

'In the papers,' Warburton-Smith concurred. 'He's causing trouble, Sarah. Bringing Talents into disrepute, as though they could have a lower public esteem than they already do.'

'That's a shame,' I said.

'To be exact,' Warburton-Smith continued, 'he is behaving like a Talented lager lout. He goes around breaking up bars and beating people up. Being able to move around unseen is a great help. He's been going after the gangs of youths who beat up tourists, and after drug-pushers and so on . . . up until now.

'Trouble is, we think he may now be on to something bigger, and the Greeks have suddenly sat up and taken notice. They say it's our pigeon; he's British, and, due to European Harmonization and all that, we have to pull his chestnuts out of the fire for him.

'Sarah, we want you to go and bring him back.'

I sat and pondered.

'Don't look so worried, Sarah,' Warburton-Smith said, 'you're getting a free holiday out of it.'

'Why me?' I asked.

'I think you know very well,' Warburton-Smith said. 'Your Talent could come in very useful. Auto-suggestion should do the trick. Besides, you've been to Greece before, haven't you?'

'Well . . . to Mitilini with Club Med, five years ago . . . but it was only for a fortnight . . .'

'Fine. You're just the girl for the job.'

I pondered some more. My immediate idea was to leave the Dark Avenger to stew in his own juice, but for one thing the dictates of the DPR have to be obeyed, and for another, why should he do as he likes, when I can't? Besides, I've heard Greece is pleasant at this time of year. Up until then DPR assignments had usually landed me in places about as appealing as a head cold.

'Okay,' I said. 'I'll go.'

'Fine,' Warburton-Smith said. 'I thought you would.' He handed me a manila A4 envelope. 'In here is documentation on Keith and his whereabouts, habits and so on, a return ticket to Athens, and a single ticket from Athens to London. It's valid for two weeks, but don't take too long. Also you have an appointment to see Nikos Kallinikos at the Dorchester at eleven today. Go for it, Sarah.'

I took the envelope and left. As I went into the passageway, Marcia sniffed loudly in the middle of her conversation with another of her duplicates.

My my. The Dorchester. The doorman only deigned to look at me when I flashed my DPR pass, and I'm sure he sniffed as I went in to the lobby. Well, fuck you, not that I'd give you the pleasure. I thumped the lift button and, in a while, up I went.

Kallinikos resembled a toad. Fat, unhealthy, a big round mouth and an expensive cigar drooping from it (Toad of Toad Hall!). He had a whole suite of rooms in the hotel, dark wood furniture and gilt-framed paintings. I stood facing him across a very big teak desk.

'Ah, Miss Jamison,' he said. His accent was so sugary that I felt my teeth would rot listening to it. 'So pleased you could coming.' He extended a flabby hand and I shook it. It was like masturbating a dead fish, not that I'd know. He took the opportunity to look up and down my body, then asked me to sit. 'Did you having a pleasant journey?'

'Very pleasant, thank you.'

'Good. I do not like to leave my room while I am here; more comfortable that you should coming here, I think. We are going to having words together.' He made an expansive gesture. 'Regarding the Dark Avenger. Do you knowing him?'

'Not personally, no.'

'Pardon me?'

'No,' I said, thinking, Jees, this is going to be a one-word answer session. The guy only speaks English. He doesn't understand it.

'He is your trouble. British trouble. He is making a nuisance of him in Athínai, just like lager louts and football hooligans. Po po po po po.' He shook his head sadly, trying to make a show of sincere emotion. I felt that if he had ever felt any genuine emotion, it was probably greed.

'So,' he went on, 'you will go and talking to him.'

'Yes,' I said.

'Bringing him back,' Kallinikos continued.

'Why,' I said, 'don't the police just arrest and deport him?'

'What did you saying?' said Kallinikos.

'Why don't the police not arrest him?' I said, sighing.

'Not good for international relations,' said Kallinikos. 'Talents are supposed to working in harmony together. But our Greek Talents, in our Greek IPP, are hard-worked without sorting out the English drop-outs.' The way he said it made it sound like 'English' and 'drop-out' were synonymous. I decided to actively dislike him.

'I am assigning you,' said Kallinikos, 'one of our own Talents, even so. Miss Zaprou will meeting you off the plane. You will staying with her. You will flying tomorrow, yes?'

Fine, I thought. A Greek paranorm. I hope she speaks English.

I showed myself out, and headed for the tube with my personal stereo playing. On the way home only two people yelled 'fucking freako' as they passed me. Believe me, that isn't many.

The shop let me take a few days off without too much fuss. I can be useful there, selling old books to people who just might be thinking slowly and carefully enough to let me put words into their mouths; nothing exploitative, just tipping them towards parting with their money, as Mr Szasz, the owner, puts it.

On the flight to Athens I sat with the DPR dossier on my lap and read assiduously. The Dark Avenger (I read). Born Keith Philip Bingham, he refused the approaches of the DPR on several occasions, despite his ability to disappear from one place and reappear in another, with just a few seconds' delay. The only trace of his passage is a dark fuzz in the air in the place he left. Hence the name.

I don't mind that. Honestly. As far as I was concerned, the Dark Avenger could beat up as many hooligans as he liked. It's the not going along with the DPR's gentle requests that I do not approve of. I mean, when would these people do as they're told? When there's a gun at their heads? Do me a favour. When the Department says 'frog', people hop. Even Captain Croak.

I arrived in Athens and dragged my bag off the conveyor belt in the late afternoon. It may have been late, but it was still pretty hot. Just as I cleared customs, a short Greek with a wide brown grin came up to me and asked, in execrable English, where I wanted to go. I told him I'd get a taxi. He seemed disappointed and wandered away muttering, 'Pretty lady. Po po po po po.' I took up my bag again and headed for the arrivals hall. As I walked into the concourse, bag in hand, a young woman strode towards me: a small girl with lots of tangled black hair, round glasses and a red-and-yellow flowery dress.

'Hi, Sarah,' she said merrily. 'I'm Maria Zaprou. Welcome to Greece!' Her accent was resolutely American. Unlike Kallinikos, I decided to like her; I just had to. I felt definitely in need of a friend.

We headed back into Athens in Maria's little Japanese car, which she drove with what was either tremendous skill or a lot of luck.

'Don't worry,' she said, ' I know when things are about to happen. I'm a very minor Talent, but a Talent all the same.'

I spent the journey looking for signs of Ancient Greece. I can report that there isn't much of it left. There was the Parthenon, up on its hill above the smog, looking like a picture postcard; and there were streets and streets of vile grey and brown houses crowding the slopes that once bore vineyards where philosophers strolled.

Maria's apartment was full of chrome and steel, like a 1950s American movie, or a 1950s American car for that matter, with a video jukebox and a wide video screen. Dark green foliage spread out of pots and crept down towards the smooth stone floor. Around the walls were pictures of well-known singers and American super-heroes. Zeus (very appropriate here) was pictured carrying a railway locomotive through the air. Kid Spectrum was only half visible against a multicoloured backdrop, half a grin on his face like a Cheshire Cat by Dali. And there was our very own Dark Avenger, leaving behind him a dark hole in the fabric of space-time.

We sat on beanbags and drank Amstel Beer.

'Sure,' said Maria. 'I was shown your photo. Knew you were coming. Did old Kallinikos try to get you to fuck him?'

'No,' I said.

'Mm. You do surprise me. He likes blondes. Maybe you didn't give him the opportunity.'

'I'd rather die painfully,' I said.

'You probably would if you upset him too much. He, kinda, belongs to the organization that doesn't exist, if you follow my meaning.'

'Exactly, I said. As in "Mafia? There is no Mafia!"'

'So, then,' said Maria, 'we get to work together.'

'Pooling our Talents,' I said.

Maria smiled happily.

'My only minor ability,' she said, 'is perfect timing.'

'It must be very useful.'

'Oh, yes. I used to think it was just coincidence. Then the IPP noticed me and I got dragged before the Lizard King himself.'

'Kallinikos?'

'The same. He is quite the big noise. Still, I don't mind. It pays the rent, such as it is. This apartment is my brother's.' She drew out the word 'brother' and momentarily sounded more Greek than American. 'My invariable knack of falling on my feet means I just happen to have a brother who is into real estate, even dinky little bits of Plaka like this one. Bits that just happen to be on the up and up. You ever read that Avram Davidson story, "The Sources of the Nile"? Like that. Being in the right place at the right time. But only in small ways. Nothing big.'

Maria took a long mouthful of beer.

'Anyhow,' she said, 'I guess we have to talk about Subject Number One. Keith Bingham, the Dark Avenger. Hero to the Greek kids and fearless fighter against the drug-barons.'

'If he's that big a hero,' I said, 'why do the cops want him out?'

'He's a hero to the kids. That automatically means a villain to the cops. And because he's a liability. The cops are working up their case against the heroin bosses, trying to get a legitimate arrest or two. Then along comes this dickhead who can vanish into a personal Black Hole, beats up a few of the small fry, and alerts the big fish. You see?'

'Also he could be in danger,' I suggested.

'There is that,' said Maria. 'Assuming the barons give a good godsaddamn about their couriers – which I doubt – he could well get his toes roasted.' Given what Maria had said about Kallinikos's connections, things began to slide into place.

'So, Maria,' I said, stretching, 'what do we do?'

'Do?' Maria echoed. 'We go meet him, of course. What did you expect?'

So we met him. Maria took me to the Kalapothaki, a taverna on a fairly touristy street, and let me by the hand through leering Greeks to a quiet table. Quiet, in this context, meant not having to talk to a face framed by tourists' denimed bums.

'He'll be in,' she said. 'We have enough time for one drink and then he'll be here. Just wait and see, okay?' I liked Maria's smile. Very engaging. We sat and drank beer, and around us the din of the Greek evening went on, people calling and clapping, trying to drown out the sound of a jukebox. A youth came and stared at both of us for a minute at least. I gave him a time-honoured two-fingered gesture which he didn't understand; the hand signals are different here. He actually thought I was being encouraging, and sat down with his legs wide apart. Don't these guys realize what a tempting target that makes for a well-aimed foot?

'Do you speak English?' he said.

'Not to you, no,' I said. He looked at Maria, who said something in Greek. The boy got up and wandered off, swinging his key chain.

'Where I come from', I said, 'that means you swing the other way.'

'Not here,' Maria said. 'It's actually Greek official policy that no Greeks are homosexual. How very macho, which you'll see when you meet the Avenger. Here he is now.'

I guessed she knew by the raised voices, but it could have been her Talent in operation. The Avenger was in mufti: jeans, Nike trainers and a Dead Kennedys T-shirt. I had to admit he was a muscled little flicker, all brutal blond get-up-and-go-ness. Eyes scanning the crowd like a predatory bird. People greeted him, clasped his hands, his arms. Maria got up and moved like a snake through the crowd, pushing softly, seeming to climb through people, until she got to the man. From where I was sitting it looked like they knew each other. Maria kissed him on both cheeks while he held her by the waist. Then the two of them headed back towards me. The Avenger smiled warmly at the sight of me, and I smiled happily back.

'Hi,' he said, 'I'm Keith. Pleased to meet you.' I offered my hand, and he bowed over and kissed it. Most chivalrous.

'No cloak this evening?' I said.

'Cloak? Oh, I get it. Only when I'm Fighting for Truth and Justice,' he said.

'And the American Way?'

'I s'pose so. You really are very pretty.' He raised his bottle of Amstel and drained half of it, then turned to the bar and yelled for more beer for all of us. I ignored his last comment but looked into his eyes for a moment as he turned back to face me. I don't think of myself as pretty. Sexy maybe, but not pretty. But if he thought so, fine. I mean, I'm a Talent, in a society dominated by people who regard Talents as morally unsound or just plain freaky. I need reassurance now and again. You might otherwise wonder why, with my Talent, I'm not the richest, most admired woman in Britain. It's 'cos I'm a weirdo, dear.

'I've heard of you,' I said, touching his fingers with mine. 'You're making quite a name for yourself.'

'Well, yeah,' said Keith. 'Can't do it in England, of course. It'd rain, and people wouldn't take me seriously.'

Take seriously a guy who can do weird things to space-time? I thought. Sure they would. But probably in a way he wouldn't like.

'You like being in Greece?' I asked.

'Damn right!' Keith tilted his chair back, pulled a packet of cigarettes from his jeans pocket, and offered them around. I declined, but Maria took one, accepting fire from Keith's antique Zippo lighter. The barman came along and put down beer.

'Is free,' he said, smiling. 'On the house.'

'You know,' said the Avenger, 'I'm a hero around here. Vigilantism is against the law in England. Here I'm cool.'

'Isn't it dangerous?' I asked, all ingenuous little-girl stuff.

'Sure,' Keith said, puffing out his chest, 'that's the fun of it. Last month I chased a nasty little pusher across Syntagma Square until he had an unfortunate accident. That's the trouble with these people. They're quite prepared to have sex, but show 'em a little bit of violence and they go all mingy on you. Sort of calling the tune but folding up when you tell 'em to pay the piper. It wasn't my fault he ran under a trolley-bus.'

'It was in all the papers,' Maria said.

'Don't they ever try to get even?' I asked. 'Family vendettas and the like?'

'They would if they could,' the Avenger said, 'but I'm careful where I go. This place may look peaceful to you, but the owner has a pair of shotguns behind the bar, and he's used them before now.'

'You mean,' I said, 'this place is dangerous.'

'Nah,' said Keith, 'you're safe.'

'I'm pleased to hear it.' If anyone is going to be waving guns about, I'd rather they were on my side. Men, of course, may see things differently.

'I know,' Keith said. 'Why don't you come to the beach with me tomorrow? We can go swimming.' And, I thought, you can see me in a bikini, which is clearly what you want. Even just bikini pants, if I feel like showing myself off to you. Okay. Fair enough.

'Sure,' I said. ' Good idea!'

Maria told me the Greeks never discuss the weather because they know what every day is going to be like. So; the next day was the 17th of July, and we sat on the beach while around me the summer went on. Keith lay beside me, telling me of his exploits since he'd come to Greece. If only half of it was true, it was pretty impressive. According to Keith, he had practically stopped the Greek youths' sport of casually beating up tourists on beaches and at camp-sites, and was well on his way to putting the crack trade to flight.

'Usually,' he said, 'I run rings round these people for a while, close in on them, beat them up a little, and then call the police. They are only too glad to oblige, and the suspect only too pleased to give himself in. Anything for a nice cell with a floor, four walls and a ceiling.'

'But why do you do it?' I asked. 'Why not leave it to the police? I mean, the Greeks have a reputation for being pretty hard on drug-dealers . . .'

'There's too much for them to handle,' he said. 'Besides, the police have gone soft except where foreigners are concerned. Most of them don't care any more, and those that do sort of let me get on with it. Me, I do care. It's 'cos of my brother . . .'

'What happened to him?'

'Ian took a tab of LSD one night at a party, when he was nineteen. He used to smoke a joint or two before that, but I think he reckoned he'd try something stronger for a change. It sent him very strange. He never got off the stuff, and now he's on heroin. It's killing him. That's why.' I reached out and stroked Keith's chest. He took my hand and pressed it in his.

'I was arrested in London,' he said, 'for vanishing and reappearing in front of people in Oxford Street. I'd walk up to someone, do my trick, and then appear beside him and tap him on the shoulder. I especially used to like doing it to tourists.'

'Why?'

'Something to do. Haven't you ever wanted to just shake people up a bit?' He looked at me closely. I shook my head, very slowly, but I wasn't convinced.

'Oh, Sarah,' Keith said, sitting up. 'They have to die, you know. The whole fucking lot. They have to die, or what's a heaven for? Who cares what they want? I mean me, I want to be tied to a chair and beaten unconscious, but who cares?' He looked at me with a leering grin, then looked away again and stared out at the sea.

'Listen,' he said quietly, 'you know where I got the name, don't you? The Dark Avenger? I am a virus in the system. What else can you be if you're a Talent? Do you understand?'

I murmured something non-committal, but I understood all right. For all we were on different sides, we had lots in common.

'Okay,' Keith said. 'Watch this.' He stood up and ran towards the restless sea. I sat and watched him, a hand shielding my eyes. As he came to the waterline, Keith bounced on his toes, then disappeared. Against the blue of the sea, the mark of his passage was a ragged black shape fading quickly into the background. Keith reappeared a few yards away, waved to me, then did the same trick a few times and finally appeared by my side. I started, then shook myself and smiled as he lay down beside me.

'Neat, don't you think?'

'Very neat,' I said, and rolled slightly towards him. He wasn't even sweating; I wondered what happened to him while he was moving in and out of reality.

He leaned over and kissed me. Very softly, lips to lips. The look he gave me as he moved away again said, yes?

I wasn't sure. Maria wasn't even looking, which I didn't think was very Greek of her. From what I could tell the Greeks stared at everything.

That afternoon Maria got a phone call from Kallinikos, calling her and myself into his office at six. We presented ourselves to his secretary, who rolled her eyes heavenward when we mentioned we'd come on IPP business. I think the gesture was one of humorous resignation, but it might have been something else.

Kallinikos was no prettier in shirt-sleeves. Here he seemed to rejoice in his fat arms and ample belly, sitting in his leather executive chair and sipping Perrier, letting it all hang out.

'Have you finding him?' he asked me.

'Oh, yes,' I said.

'Good,' he said with an avuncular smile, though I'd hate to be his niece.

'Is most important,' Kallinikos said, 'that you stop him stirring up trouble. I have not speaking to him, but I must knowing where he is. So that the IPP can keeping an eye on him, yes?'

'Yes,' I said.

'Maria,' he said, and went on to her in Greek. The conversation seemed to start off reasonably civilized, and then got gestural later on, lots of handwaving going on. Maybe they were having an argument, or else they were just making a point. I don't follow the current idea that says you have to wave your arms about to have a conversation. Where did we get that from? Probably the same people who think it's all right to be noisy in public. Go to the West End of London any Saturday evening and you'll see what I mean. Especially if, as in my case, they pick up anything you think and start yelling it at you. But then, Greece is Greece. All those gestures are part of the way of life.

'So,' Kallinikos said eventually, 'if you do not making him stop, we are having trouble. We are making him stop ourselves, and is not pleasant. Is not pleasant for us, is not pleasant for you. Are you understanding?'

'Completely,' I said. I thought, we're being threatened. Fine. That's in character.

'Good,' said Kallinikos, with that vile smile again. Finished with engines. The interview was over.

'It's all bull,' Maria told me on the way home. 'Kallinikos has already threatened the Dark Avenger in the press. We know Keith's been attacked in bars by neo-fascists, and when that happened Kallinikos knew about it very quickly; too quickly, if you ask me.'

Neo-fascists? I thought. I didn't think our Keith was as bad an egg as the press made out.

That evening Keith came round to Maria's flat, bearing bottles of beer. Maria had to go out to work, so Keith and I had some time to ourselves. It was a warm evening and outside the noise of the city faded to a murmur.

We talked about ourselves, our paranorm abilities, our pasts, our hopes for the future. He was clear as to what he was doing. I became less and less sure of myself.

'Don't get in the way,' Keith said gently. 'You might get hurt. You're too nice to be hurt.'

'Don't be so sure,' I said.

'Oh, I mean it. I'll give up when I'm ready to. But not yet, Sarah. Not just yet.'

I went to stand by the window and looked out. As I'd hoped, he came to stand beside me and put an arm around my waist, drawing me close into him. After a while he turned me to face him, now with both arms around me. He looked at me with that same look, asking, yes?

Yes, I thought. So.

'Yes,' he said. Then his mouth was on mine, our tongues swarming over one another like avid living creatures. I pushed myself against him and let him draw our bodies together.

Finally I led him into my room.

'They want you to bring me back, don't they?' Keith asked afterwards, as we lay side by side, my head cradled in the crook of his arm, my hands playing idly over the hard planes of his body.

'That's right,' I said.

'Knew it. I know who Maria works for, and why else would she have a British Talent staying in her flat?'

'But you're not going to go back?'

'No. Why should I? I like doing what I do, and I like doing it here, thanks very much.'

'Mm. What are you going to do?'

'I'm going to Fight Crime,' he said. 'As though you couldn't guess, Sarah my love.'

'I knew I shouldn't have come along,' I said.

'Not even for the ride?'

'The ride was fine. I should never have listened to Nikos Kallinikos.'

'Kallinikos. Now there's a name to conjure with.'

'Sure,' I admitted, 'but would you want to?'

'Oh, Christ, no,' Keith said and rolled over. 'He's one of the old guard. Just being foreign is a crime against humanity to those guys. He does not like me one bit.'

'But will you give up and come back?' I asked, never quite giving up. Yes, I will, yes, I thought, like Molly Bloom in *Ulysses*.

'Y. . . wait and see,' Keith said. He smiled and kissed me. 'Not that easy, sweet love.'

*

42

At midday the next day we all went to Kalapothaki. We drank retsina and ate *mezes*, and Keith and I became happier and happier in the Mediterranean sun. Meanwhile Maria was beginning to fidget, and looking more and more edgy. She was looking out of the corner of her eyes at a man standing across the street, smoking. He had the look of the professional loiterer so completely that I was sure he was just a lottery-ticket seller, or some such.

'I've noticed him,' said Keith. 'Don't make it so obvious.' But Maria wasn't leaving it at that. She fidgeted some more and was quite unable to eat or drink.

Finally she said, 'Let's go.'

'What?' said Keith.

'Now. Quick!' She stood and turned round, faced the patrons of the bar, yelled something in Greek. 'Get down!' was probably the gist of it.

She left at a run, out of the doors, Keith and I behind her. A gust of hot air hit us as we piled out into the noon sunshine and kept running. As far as I was concerned, we'd carry on running until Maria stopped. Keith had vanished; I could guess the direction as thin air. We were only a block away when there was the dull crump of an explosion, followed by the watery crash of breaking glass and a cacophony of screams and car horns.

We turned to look. People were wailing. A woman in a white dress soaked red was wandering round and round in circles. A man lay facedown on the pavement, his outstretched hand opening and closing rhythmically. People were standing about, gibbering, gesturing. Then I saw Keith, at the edge of the crowd, flickering in and out of vision until he finally grabbed a man by the collar and bore him crashing to the ground.

'So much for "you're safe",' I said, shivering.

'We'd better get outta here,' said Maria. We turned to

go but found our way blocked by two large and imposing figures in uniform.

'You,' said one of them. 'Come with us.'

It was the cops.

Maria and I were in a small, windowless room, sitting on hard wooden chairs. The policeman questioning us tapped on his notepad with his pencil and occasionally whistled. It was driving me nuts, as was no doubt the intention. He looked as though he was longing for the return of the Generals' regime: black glasses, .45 at the hip. His English was actually pretty good; maybe he was used to dealing with British and American trouble-makers. And just as likely he was sick and tired of them.

'So.' The cop and Maria talked Greek for a bit, with Maria giving her version of just how we knew when to get out of the bar.

'She says she knew that you all had to leave. And you followed her?'

'Yes,' I said. 'She's precognitive. A recognized Talent. Check with the IPP if you don't believe me.'

'Oh, I have,' said the policeman. 'That checks out, all right. But even assuming I was to believe that story, that Maria Zaprou just happens to know when things are about to happen, this leaves us with another question.'

Don't tell me, I thought. *I know.*

'The question of Mister Keith Bingham,' said the cop. 'Or should I say, the Dark Avenger. Do you know if anyone wants to kill him?'

'Kill him?' I said.

'Sure. He is a vigilante. So far it's been little criminals, hasn't it? Thieves stopped, tourist-thumping gangs and small-time drug traffickers nicely brought to bay. But now, this Petros Argyrios he chased under a bus ... I wonder who he might have been working for?' The cop shrugged expressively. 'I wish Mister Keith would do us a favour,' he said, 'and keep out of our police business. You're lucky that bomb only blew out the window, and nobody was killed. Me, I don't think it was meant to kill anyone. It was a warning, you understand?'

'Like in *The Godfather*,' Maria said. '"This time it's your horse, next time it'll be you."'

'Exactly,' said the cop.

The telephone rang. The cop picked it up and uttered a few monosyllables into it. Whoever was on the other end seemed to be having a one-sided conversation. Eventually he put it down, and said, 'You have a visitor.' The door opened and in came Nikos Kallinikos.

'Well, well, well,' he said, raising his hands palm-upwards and shaking his rubbery jowls. 'What a sad day. Maria Zaprou, Miss Jamison, you are supposed to be keeping an eye on the Dark Avenger. We are going to seeing him. Now. He is going back home to resting. Yes?'

Maria and I looked at each other, puzzled.

'Good idea?' I asked.

'Sure,' Maria said. 'I can lead us there. At least this way we have him almost red-handed.'

I felt suddenly wistful. Keith didn't really need to go to those lengths to prove himself, did he? Be careful, Sarah, I thought. You're getting fond of him.

'Well?' said Kallinikos. 'Let us going.'

We headed up narrow streets, bordered by tall ochre houses with balconies swarming with plants, past ruins of ancient walls that the newer houses had been built on and around. Trapdoors opened down into dark basements; I should not have liked to walk those streets drunk and alone late at night, for the risk of falling into a cellar and breaking a leg. Little *yiro* shops pumped a smell of roasting lamb and yeasty bread into the street.

Children ran between us, shouting. My dress was sticking to my shoulders, and my underwear was beginning to chafe.

'Is it much further?' I asked.

'Not much,' said Maria. 'But it's all uphill.'

'Oh, fine,' I said. Kallinikos did not appear worried. Perhaps he was fitter than he looked. Perhaps he was just used to this kind of thing. At one point he exchanged greetings with an old man sitting outside a café. From inside came the *thwack* of backgammon counters.

Keith's lair was in an old Turkish house, flaking white walls baked in a century of sunlight and an old blue-painted door. Maria knocked and there was a sound of scraping from behind the door. Keith opened up and stood there with his face expressionless.

Then I saw the man standing behind him.

Several inches taller than Keith, he was either strangely disfigured or wearing a bone-white mask like the face-paints of ancient Greek heroes. I couldn't tell. The face was entirely expressionless, but the slanted eyes shone with a strange yellowish light. He was wearing some kind of metallic shellsuit, bright white.

'Go in,' said Kallinikos from behind me.

Something was very definitely wrong. I just hoped that whatever it was, wouldn't hurt.

Maria and I went in. The mask-faced man walked slowly backwards, keeping all of us in his sight. As he backed away, I saw the gun in his hands. Oh, shit, I thought. How very melodramatic. Why can't we let the Greeks get on with being foreign?

When we were all inside, Kallinikos shut the door behind him and stood with his back to it.

'Allow me,' he said, 'to introduce Takis Theokratis.' Takis said nothing.

'We are going to be instructed,' Kallinikos said. The atrocious accent and grammar had all but vanished. 'Or more precisely, you are.' Then he giggled. Oh God, I thought. Oh God, oh God, what did I sign up with this lot for?

'Now,' Kallinikos went on, 'the Dark Avenger will remain where he is.' Takis handed Kallinikos the gun and bound Keith's wrist behind him. 'I do not think the Avenger's skills extend to emulating those of Houdini.' He giggled.

I looked around. The house was open on one side, where it gave into a vacant lot full of rusty machinery; on the other three the ancient walls were shored up by equally ancient furniture. There was a sudden sharp line of division where shadow gave way to sunlight.

'I have researched,' said Kallinikos, 'into Mr Bingham's Talent. It appears to work over distances of five metres or less; not very far, really. Mr Bingham will be on a race against time. Either he outwits my friend Takis over the obstacle course for the time I require, or he gets killed. Is that understood?'

He waved the gun, and we went outside. What good was my power going to be just now? I couldn't argue with a gun, and I needed optimum conditions to work in. Kallinikos leaned on the wall and gestured for us to stand against it, at the other end. Takis followed him, tied our hands behind our backs, and made us sit down against the wall. It was hot, and rough, and it was the least of our problems.

Kallinikos had opened a bottle of ouzo and was drinking affably from the bottle. Even so, he never let go of the gun.

'This,' he said, 'is the scene where the villain explains his plan to the hero who is about to get killed, isn't it? Well, I shall oblige you a little.

'Basically, your friend here, Mr Dark Avenger Bingham, has been making a few enemies among my friends. People who have a little trade going on, making sure they make money, while keeping the young people of Greece supplied with enough drugs to keep them from the idea of making trouble. Greece is a turbulent country, and trouble could lead all the way to revolution. Revolution would be a terrible thing for us, you know. After all, who wants to lose their power in the land? Or their justly made wealth?'

'Justly?' Maria exclaimed. 'You wouldn't know justice if it bit you. Which it will, some day.' She spat a torrent of Greek at him. I didn't understand the words, but I could tell what she meant. Takis leant down and backhanded her in the mouth. She spat blood.

'Fuck you,' said Keith.

'Not at all,' said Kallinikos, aiming the gun at Keith's groin. 'You're going to do your trick for me, English boy.'

'And if I don't?'

'Why, then you get dead, don't you?' He drank again, deeply. He was keeping all three of us covered with the gun. The rope was beginning to chafe into my wrists. 'I might even see to your friends as well.'

'Bastard,' said Keith.

'You really do mean to keep it up,' said Kallinikos. 'I hate to say, "resistance is useless", but I'm afraid it is. Watch this. Takis?'

Takis picked up a brick from the debris-littered floor, tossed it up in the air, then punched it. The brick disintegrated into orange splinters.

'Iron Hands Theokratis. He would have boxed for Greece,' said Kallinikos, 'except that Talents are outlawed.'

'Fucking melodrama,' Keith sneered, but I could tell he was a little disconcerted. Me, I was peeing my pants, if not literally then very nearly. Takis undid Keith's bonds and pushed him into the courtyard. Keith stumbled and nearly fell, then recovered himself and the contest began.

Keith flickered out of vision. Takis tried to second-guess the Avenger and flung himself at a place a few yards to the right. Keith rematerialized behind him and threw a punch at the back of the Greek's head. Takis grunted, turned round, and slammed his fist into the space Keith had occupied. Keith had already vanished, leaving only the familiar dark closing space. Then he reappeared behind a pile of old machine parts.

As Takis reached it and a spray of old cogwheels and piston rods exploded into the air, Keith vanished again, and reappeared behind the belligerent Greek. He double-handed Takis in the back of the neck. Takis grunted and poked a fist over his left shoulder. It caught Keith on the cheekbone. Keith fell backwards, rolling in the dust and springing to his feet again, as Takis charged towards him. Takis kicked at him, with a kick that would have taken Keith in the groin if he'd still been there. Keith dodged to one side and kicked Takis in the ribs. Takis just grunted. Keith vanished.

Stop stop stop, I was thinking, making myself look at Kallinikos to see if I could make him say it. His jowls worked once or twice, but he seemed to be enjoying himself too much. Then Keith appeared on the wall and flung himself down at Takis, hands around the Greek's neck from behind. Takis twisted like a fighting bull – this was a labyrinth, and he the Minotaur – and threw Keith to the earth. There was an audible thump as Keith's head hit the ground.

Keith faded out, then faded in again. He was having trouble, by the look of it; maybe the use of his Talent was tiring him, and he couldn't keep it up much longer.

Keith stood, just in time for Takis to deliver a vicious kick to the side of his stomach. Keith roared and sat down.

That's it, I thought. That is Keith finished. Oh God, oh God, that's it, that's it, this is the end. My Keith, my Keith, my l. . .

Kallinikos looked to be on the point of orgasm, watching Takis standing over Keith and sneering through that vicious mask. The white-faced Greek wasn't doing anything, though. He seemed to be hesitating. Keith was trying to stand up, and flickering in and out of vision, replaced by a veil of darkness, then reappearing.

Kallinikos gestured to Takis: get in there! But Takis was simply standing, saying something in Greek.

I just knew what it was. Even if Kallinikos was too clever or obsessed to pick up on my mental radiation, part of Takis's mind had been listening in.

Then Kallinikos brought up the gun. If Takis wouldn't finish the game, he would.

Maria screamed. Her Talent: just to know exactly when things were going to happen. Her scream was enough, at that precisely correct moment, to put Kallinikos off his shot; the bullet missed and hit Takis, who was standing in front of Keith. It took half of Takis's chest away. He was not going to need the services of a doctor. I swallowed very deeply.

'*Dead* Takis,' said Maria with deep satisfaction. But she too looked a bit pale.

Kallinikos was gaping in horror and the pain of a sprained wrist, and staring at the gun that he'd dropped on the ground.

Keith vanished. Then he reappeared in front of Kallinikos and kicked the fat man in the belly. Kallinikos doubled up. Keith stood over him, dripping with Takis's blood, and pushed him away from the gun. Watching him carefully, Keith untied us.

'That's the end of the line,' he said. 'Okay, fatso, get ready for a life of sewing mailbags. Your prints are on the gun. Oh, and Takis was giving himself up when you shot him. Or maybe you knew that.' He shook his head sadly. 'How will you live with yourself, fatso?'

That was when I threw up.

When the police arrived and arrested Kallinikos, they wanted to interview him about secret contributions to the Tory Party. Murder was a bonus. Like Keith said, they threw away the key.

'And now?' I asked, hours later. Keith and I were in bed again, in his room, listening to the endless roar of traffic in the night. Too much hard work and excitement, I thought drowsily. I'm retiring.

'Now, I'm retiring,' Keith said. 'I'll do as you want.'

'You're kidding me!'

'Not at all. I'm coming home with you. That was the last call for the Dark Avenger. The Talent has its limits. What you don't know is how close I was to being an ex-Talent, when you and Maria saved the day.' He smiled and kissed me again. It was a long kiss and I almost forgot what I was going to say.

'You mean,' I said eventually, 'you'll turn yourself over to the Department?'

'Now who said anything about that? Not me. But I know when things are getting too hot.'

'Too hot? I'll give you hot. I'll . . .' Give up, I thought. Then we can all go home.

'You do already, Sarah. More than you know. I can see how you persuade people to give up.'

Told you, I thought. I poked him softly in the ribs. He was right, though. Like I said, I am persuasive. I still don't know how much use my Talent was in the final showdown, but Keith believes it worked. Why else would Takis give up when he was winning? And like I always said, it does need optimum conditions. Being tied up and held at gunpoint isn't one of them. Being in bed with a lover is.

Mark Antony gave up the arts of war for the arts of love, and the gods of war deserted him. Keith was heading home on a one-way airline ticket, paid for by the DPR. He'd abandoned the gods before they got a chance to do the same to him. Our Gods, of course, were a different matter. It didn't bear thinking about what they might want done to him. But I hear their clemency can be as great as their powers.

And me? Mission fulfilled.

No wonder I fell asleep smiling.

Loric exhaled slowly, returning to the familiar surroundings of his study. It hadn't been so bad. But then his own memories weren't of the mainland, of city streets and tourist traps. He discarded the file, digesting what he'd learned.

Bingham discreetly retrieved, and high-level corruption exposed in one of the DPR's European counterparts. Something he could claim as a success, and, more importantly, by the right degree of understated disapproval, divert any awkward questions about Orpington. Most satisfactory.

Almost your old self again.

'Thank you.' Invigorated by relief, he called the teapot from where it kept warm on the flagstones. It hovered over his cup, poured, and returned to its perch, while Loric picked up the next folder.

HIDE AND SEEK

Jenny Jones

September 1973. They'd known each other for two years, and it seemed longer.

'But I don't want to know where *you* are every second of the day!' he shouted. 'Why can't you leave me alone? Why do you have to spy on me?'

'I can't help it . . .' And indeed she couldn't. She stared at him helplessly, and wondered how they were ever going to part.

At first it had been fun. She had been nineteen when she had first fallen in love with David Earnshaw, in his role as herald in Verdi's *Otello*. She had loved his black hair and bright eyes, his high, passionate tenor voice. Backstage he was rather older than she expected, but this was no disadvantage.

He belonged to a repertory company, singing a succession of roles that depended more on looks and voice than on acting ability. Most often he was in the chorus, a soldier, a courtier or peasant, and only occasionally achieved soloist status. Neither his memory nor his theatrical skill would support a leading role.

Much of his life was spent on the road. He had been cheered to discover how much Isabel Bradley loved him. He called her his most faithful fan, at the start. Loyal and true, never failing, never wavering . . .

She had turned up all over the place, when he was least expecting it. He'd find her waiting in strange bars, smiling hopefully. She welcomed him off trains, joined him in restaurants.

David Earnshaw had been flattered by these unexpected visitations, although he was used to the admiration of women. He was well aware of the power of his textbook good looks. It had seemed to him reasonable that she should be obsessed with him. It was appropriate that young women everywhere should want to spend time with his dramatic and elegant person.

He was intrigued and amused that she was prepared to follow him all over the country, that she could find him wherever he went. It all seemed rather delightful. For a while.

Their affair was brief and claustrophobic. Cheap boarding houses, hostels and guest houses . . . Fattening meals in shabby pizza houses and smoky pubs.

Their love-making was uninspired. He was too egotistical to consider her pleasure a priority, and she was too immature to know it could be different. Their conversation was not much better. She liked to read, to dream. To listen to music, to talk about ideas. He said he had enough of music every day. What he wanted to do was to watch videos or sport, and drink, night after night.

They were singularly ill suited. Without much regret they parted.

That was when the trouble really started.

Isabel Bradley woke up the morning after her farewell to David with a feeling of great relief. She was free at last, and could get back to her job in the bookshop. She could stop dashing all over the country, and start enjoying an ordinary life.

As she showered, she idly considered what he might be doing. By the time she'd finished breakfast, she knew he was still in bed, his arm thrown casually over someone else.

Already?

For a moment she was diverted by a painful jab of jealousy, but it was soon subsumed in a far greater worry. Apparently part of her was still attuned to David Earnshaw. She knew where he was. The White Lily Guest House, Cardigan Road, Cheltenham . . . She was horrified to discover that he was still the centre, the focus, of her thoughts. Something in her revolved around him all the time.

She went to work and tried to pick up the threads of her life. She put books on shelves and dealt with customers and took her lunch hour with friends, and she always knew where he was. Night or day, near or far, she could pick up a map of Britain and pin-point the exact place.

'I suppose it's a Talent,' she grumbled to Janey, who worked with her in the shop, 'but it's a remarkably useless one . . .'

'Oh, I don't know. I think it's rather romantic, rather like the Lady of Shalott or something . . .' Janey was laughing at her.

'No, it's not, it's tatty and inconvenient.'

'Will you report it to that Department? The one that deals with all the weirdos?'

Isabel sighed. 'I suppose so. That's what they tell you to do, but what use could it be?'

Janey shrugged. None the less, two days later, Isabel Bradshaw went to the local office of the DPR and registered with them the unusual and irritating fact that she always knew where David Earnshaw was.

Six months later she woke up one morning and felt that her mind was free. She looked at the map on her kitchen table and felt no jolt of recognition, no instant of knowledge.

Somehow or somewhere, David Earnshaw had disappeared from her life. She was released. She did not speculate about what had happened to him, she just felt that she had recovered from a painful and debilitating illness.

Two weeks later she received a postcard from Italy.

'Wonderful news – job with Italian Opera in Verona. Wine, women and song – heaven! Tan progressing nicely. Great weather, glad to escape at last! Love, David.'

She wondered why he'd sent it and sat staring at this tactless missive for a while. Vanity, she thought. Showing off. He just wants to impress.

A flicker of amusement crossed her face. Well, perhaps it was romantic, after all. Like a ghost, her little Talent was imprisoned by sea-water, cut off by the English Channel . . .

It didn't matter any more. She wished him well, peacocking away to all those excitable Italians, singing his heart out under a foreign sun. And while he was abroad, she need never think of him again. She shrugged and threw the bright postcard away. David Earnshaw was part of the past.

November 1975. She was working in the travel department of a large bookshop in the city centre, and there were signs that her Talent was developing.

It was trivial enough. She restored to their parents children lost between the picture books and the café. She watched them peering among the dictionaries and the guidebooks and asked, 'Have you lost someone?'

And then, with varying shades of anger, worry or irritation, they would describe their errant offspring. It was easy. She enjoyed their gratitude, and occasionally wondered if she might be of more use elsewhere. She considered getting in touch with the DPR once more, but it didn't seem urgent.

October 1977. Isabel and Janey joined a ramblers' association. Most weekends they went walking on the North Downs. Isabel enjoyed the exercise and the undemanding companionship. She grew to love the wide-open spaces and hidden valleys.

Once, when the mist came down unexpectedly, she helped look for a young couple who had become separated from the rest. It was cold and late by the time they were found, and she knew that, with training, she could have managed it better.

Next morning she contacted the DPR.

Within the year she was on almost permanent assignment to the Department.

August 1978. A convicted rapist on the way to Broadmoor went missing when the van escorting him broke down.

Within three hours Isabel Bradley had been summoned. Her contact with the DPR, a man called Peter Marsh, took her to interview the rapist's mother.

The woman, untidy and distressed, spoke of her son with bewildered affection, protesting his innocence, blinking at Isabel through eyes watery with anxiety.

Isabel looked at a map of the area and traced him almost immediately. He was picked up half an hour later, still handcuffed, wandering disconsolately through a deserted industrial estate.

'How do you do it?' Peter Marsh had asked her later. 'How does it work?'

She had laughed, slightly embarrassed. 'Even rapists have mothers ... I identify with the object of love,' she said, as if it didn't matter. 'Affection will do, sometimes just friendship. It doesn't work if the lost person is a loner. If no one knows them at all . . .'

They became known as medians, the people interviewed by Isabel Bradley. The people who made friends, or had children, or became lovers . . .

1978, 1979, 1980–84, 1985. A succession of cases, for Scotland Yard, the Salvation Army, Mountain Rescue and the Military Police. She found children who'd run away to London, she found known criminals and careless mountaineers. She found deserting lovers and defaulting tenants. Occasionally she found a kidnap victim.

Sometimes she was too late.

It was like a drug, a fatal addiction. Being needed. Isabel Bradley's life was patterned by champagne successes and belladonna failures. She lurched from search to search, and the years went by. She was too wrapped up in it to make much of her personal life. There were few lovers, no children . . . She was only peripherally aware that there were flecks of grey in her hair, that her eyesight was increasingly unreliable.

Peter Marsh was her immediate superior and her only colleague. He arranged her frequent absences from the bookshop where she still nominally worked. He ferried her all over the country, wherever she was required.

Sometimes he brought clients to her. He was like a pimp, she told him once, savagely, at the end of a case when everything had gone wrong. When he had called her in too late, and the girl had died from an overdose . . . A slow, stupid pimp, worse than useless, who made her prostitute herself to futile causes . . .

'Don't get so involved,' he said. 'It's only a job.'

He was patient with her, humouring her occasional depressions, cushioning her from the tangled emotions of so many of her clients. She never even realized that she was becoming distanced from the major human passions.

Peter Marsh shielded her from publicity and smoothed over her relationship with the DPR, even to the extent of allowing a rather unorthodox clause in Isabel Bradley's contract with the Department.

It was that she should not be required to work overseas.

'It doesn't matter why,' she said to Peter Marsh. 'I don't like going abroad, the food makes me sick. This is my home. So put it in print, please.'

It didn't often arise, anyway, he knew. The odd crook, the nervous student, an abducted child here and there. Most people who wanted seriously to disappear – politicians, terrorists – went far afield, South America, Indonesia . . .

There were other seekers in the country, she was not unique. But because she was a star, swifter than any other, she was allowed this small eccentricity.

March 1992. Isabel turned off the television. There was no need to sit by the phone, waiting for the call. No little kid abducted by a nasty pervert, yet. It would take time for the wheels to turn, the floodgates to open.

Open they would. It had been the last item on the news. A small footnote at the end, where they put the jokes. The Home Secretary, shaking hands with various grey-suited figures in Brussels. Funny how politicians always look like fish, she thought, not paying much attention. Those sincere eyes, and mouths gobbling and gabbling . . .

A new era of international co-operation. Welding together the peoples of Europe in harmony and understanding. She barely listened. A special relationship, they said, to everyone's benefit, and then the catch. The great and good of the paranorms to be shared round ... To help in each other's fight against crime, to combat terrorists, to reinforce stability and order. To assist each other wherever possible. Quid pro quo, etc., etc.

I'm going to be busy, she thought. Think of Mafioso kidnaps, climbers in the Alps ... all those missing children in Paris, in Amsterdam ...

I'll have to forget the shop. I'll have to travel, I'll be jet-setting all over the place ... Isabel sat very still, and stared at the wall.

David Earnshaw. Somewhere still in Italy, she assumed, because Italy would suit him, all that sun and song, but it could be France or Germany ... She had heard nothing from him since that bright postcard. She thought, if I go abroad, I might find him again when I start seeking.

The conviction grew the more she thought about it. Whatever I do, wherever I go, if we're not separated by sea-water, I'll find David Earnshaw again. My Talent would not exist without him.

Two weeks later there was a briefing in Peter Marsh's office. Details of an Italian kidnap, of the family situation and the political implications of the whole case.

'It's a real crisis,' he said. 'The family is wealthy and powerful. The father's in the cabinet, the mother's an ex-film star. The DPR want to put on a good show, before the tabloids get their knives out. There's a committee under way at the moment.' He leaned forward across the desk towards Isabel. 'It's a question of funding, Bella,' he said confidentially. 'You know what they're like.'

Isabel paused over this. 'Who's the median?'

Peter Marsh sighed. 'The mother's under heavy sedation and the father's refusing to talk to anyone. Heavy Catholic, suspicious of paranorms ... The nanny's in intensive care, having taken the best part of a bottle of sleeping pills. The grandparents have never even seen the baby. They were going to come over from the States for the christening next month.'

'So there's got to be a miracle?'

'So there's got to be you. We've found one of the maids, who used to help out on the nanny's day off.' His voice was complacent. 'There's a flight in two hours. We can be there by dinner.'

'You've booked seats for the other seekers, I trust?'

'No. Just you.'

'What a shame. I won't be using it. I get airsick.'

'Well, there's an overnight ferry –'

'Take someone else, Peter. I'm not going.'

'It's in your contract –'

'Look carefully, Peter Marsh. Read the small print. Right after where it says about holiday pay. There's an escape clause, and you agreed to it at the time. No visits overseas.'

For a moment his face was livid. She thought he was going to hit her. 'Why, Bella? Why be so bloody neurotic?'

She smiled. 'Nothing to do with you, Peter.' She stood up, reaching for her coat. 'Give my love to the Colosseum.'

Three days later Peter Marsh was in his superior's office. He was not happy.

'She won't budge? No result?'

Peter squirmed.

'This may get awkward, you realize. Embarrassing, even.'

Loric had never looked less embarrassed. Indeed, it was beyond the realms of fantasy to imagine him even slightly disconcerted. Peter Marsh shifted to the other foot and remembered with depression that Marcia was making coffee.

This was one of the worst mornings of his life. He should never have agreed to that clause. For a moment he wondered whether he could disappear too, do the proverbial runner, take off in a puff of eldritch smoke.

'No,' said Loric. 'It wouldn't work. I'd find you straight away.' He paused, his eyes clear and guileless. 'I know you so well, you see.'

She was sick with fury, shaking with rage. She looked at the bald paragraph, the addenda to the contract, at the words 'unless instructed by the Head of Department'.

'I'll call the union in.'

'There's no case.'

'This is not the contract I signed!'

'You've no way of proving that.' Peter was eyeing her nervously, as if she might explode.

'Damn you, I will not go abroad!'

'Refusal will be taken as an offence under Section 48. There's no way round it, Bella. You've got no choice.'

Three hours after her interview with Peter Marsh, Isabel's bags were packed. Clothes, money . . . She took with her only two books, *The Oxford Book of Twentieth-century English Verse* and a pocket atlas of Britain. She left no notes, no messages, no forwarding address. She locked the door of her flat carefully, and permitted herself a grim smile at the thought of Peter Marsh's dismay. She hoped never to see him again.

She was running away. Isabel knew how people managed to lose themselves, none better. She was Isabel bloody bloodhound Bradley, after all. She knew what people did to elude those who sought them. Essentially, you make no friends, you encourage no confidences. You remain faceless in people's lives, neither shy nor confident. You do not ask for money, you steal only when it's easy. You go where the crowds go, and avoid lonely places, small villages, corner shops in residential areas.

You live on your nerves, and you never relax.

She was acting strictly outside the law, breaking her contract in every way. She was in a blue funk with nerves, jumping at shadows, watching every passer-by with suspicion. She thought, this is what the rest of my life will be, at best. If I keep a low profile, and never become ill or make friends, and find a low-key job with a casual employer, I might just get away with it. I might just avoid being sent overseas, where David will mess everything up . . .

She decided to look for casual, seasonal work. With any luck, no one would require a P45 or references. She made her way circuitously towards the coast, to the seaside towns she remembered from childhood.

It was harder than she'd envisaged. Perhaps she had lost the knack of getting on with people, perhaps they were put off by her greying hair and short-sighted gaze. Probably faces younger, prettier than hers, were preferred when it came to waitressing in cafés and guest-houses.

But the reason why Isabel found it difficult to find employment was nothing to do with her age. She was neatly dressed and quietly spoken. She looked healthy, sensible and reliable.

She was also self-contained, and this was the problem. An indefinable air of apartness hung around her. Her sociable smiles were that bit too guarded, her eyes were dark shadowed.

A lifetime of seeking had left its mark. She had played a crucial part in too many lives. All those people, the parents, the lovers, the friends, the lost . . . She had held herself separate for so long. There was no ease about her, no comfort in her presence. She was not quite like anyone else.

She would be disquieting over people's holiday breakfasts. Potential employers made their excuses and turned away.

Increasingly anxious, she travelled slowly eastwards along the south coast.

That week Peter Marsh's tie was not straight, not from Monday through to Friday. Friday evening, at five thirty, the toe on his left shoe was scuffed and his palms were sweaty. He was painfully conscious of all three defects as Loric stared at him.

'Gone missing? Have I understood you quite correctly?'

Yes, blast you, Peter thought. Of course you understand me absolutely bloody correctly, every word and thought. It's not fair . . . He coughed, trying to create a diversion for himself. It failed.

'Careful . . .' said Loric kindly. 'Now, what other seekers have you?'

This was easy. 'No one in that league. She's the best. The Italians want only her.'

'But I asked you about the others. Strive to pay attention. I want you to get the mainland seekers together. Put them on her trail.'

'What, *all* of them?'

Loric did not so much as raise an eyebrow. Peter Marsh blushed, something he only ever did in Loric's presence.

'All of them,' Loric confirmed patiently. 'As you so impetuously pointed out, they want only Isabel Bradley. And so, Mr Marsh, that is who they're going to get.'

He leant across the table towards Peter Marsh, and gave him his instructions.

*

MARASSO BABY KIDNAP – MAFIA STRIKES AGAIN!

The headlines jumped at her. Isabel bought one and read the front page. Little Carlo, she thought. Six weeks old, too young to know he was missing his mother and nanny. He would just feel uncomfortable, slightly on edge. He'd probably grizzle more than usual, and it would irritate those around him.

He would know nothing about the enormous police operation, about the questions being asked in parliaments throughout Europe. If someone fed him, and changed him, and gave him the odd cuddle, he'd be more or less all right.

The promenade was crowded with trippers and school parties. The noise was overwhelming, shouts and screams from the fairground on the pier, the disco blare from a ghetto blaster on the beach, the mid-Atlantic drawl of the man calling bingo numbers. The heady scent of fried onions and sun-cream blotted out the smell of the sea.

She had tried south of the pier that morning. After lunch she'd have a go at the north bay, but she was discouraged now. She looked at the line of fish-and-chip shops and hamburger stalls without enthusiasm. In the end she bought some prawns and a breadcake, and sat on a bench, watching the drifting, noisy crowds.

A woman sat down beside her, laden with bags of towels and vacuum flasks. She was sweating heavily, and wiped the back of her hand across her face, sighing. She did not lean back in her seat, did not attempt to relax. Her eyes were constantly scanning the crowds, her lips pursed with irritation.

'Are you looking for someone?' The eternal question.

'My youngest,' said the woman, still watching the crowd. 'Said he'd be here at one and no delay. And it's gone half past, and we've got a bus to catch. Little perisher, playing me up like this . . .'

'Is that him?' Isabel pointed along the pier to where a group of small boys was crowding round a fisherman.

'Garee!' The woman was off, waving frantically to her child.

Together they came back to the bench to collect the bags. Gary was now snivelling, the red fingermarks on his calf livid. 'You must have eyes like a hawk,' said the woman to Isabel. 'Must be useful, eyesight like that . . .'

'Trouble is,' said a voice behind Isabel, after they had gone, 'trouble is, you're blind as a bat without your specs, and anyway she never told you what the boy looked like . . .'

Isabel sagged against the seat. 'People don't think logically when they're worried,' she said eventually. 'You should know that.'

Peter Marsh moved round and sat beside her. 'Aren't you impressed?' he said. 'It didn't take us long, did it?'

'How many did you use? Three, four?' Her voice was calm. She would not show bitterness to him.

'You should be honoured. The whole crew was brought in.'

'And who gave it away?'

'An old friend, who wishes to remain anonymous.'

Janey? thought Isabel. Who else was there? She had known Isabel long enough to act as a median. She would have had no reason to refuse.

'I'm not going abroad,' she said. It sounded pathetic, even to herself.

'Aren't you?' He looked at her quizzically. 'Would you care to tell me why? The truth, this time?'

She looked at him, neat grey figure, reliable, unflappable. Treacherous. He probably knew her better than anyone else.

'You were the median,' she said with sudden knowledge. 'They used you to find me . . .'

He smiled gently.

'What's wrong with abroad, Bella?'

So she told him all about it.

She was not sick on the plane, although her stomach was tight with tension during the flight.

There were photographers at the airport, microphones thrust under her nose, a babble of voices in Italian and English on all sides, demanding answers from her.

Peter had her by the arm, clearing a path through the crowd to the waiting taxi. They were driven at lunatic speed through the city to a villa in the hills, and there, under the watchful eye of the Italian police and with the aid of an interpreter, Isabel interviewed the Marasso's maid.

A small child, she learned. Very slightly premature, and so a little underweight. His eyes cloudless blue and clear, his hands perfect, his skin shading towards yellow.

He rarely cried, the maid said. But when he did, he preceded the cry with a high scream, a banshee wail.

Just the thing to drive a kidnapper, already living on nerves, right over the edge.

'What was his smile like?' she asked, and the maid looked at her with surprise.

He wasn't smiling yet, she heard. Too young. In a week or two, or even a month, then he would smile ... But his eyes looked as if they might understand anything.

Isabel felt an impression arise, an identity emerge. The maid was standing with her shoulders slightly curved, as if ready to cradle the baby. Her hands were soft and loose.

Someone very new in the world, someone still half in a realm of warmly pulsing blood, of darkness and comfort.

'He drinks –?'

'Only liquids,' the maid said, 'warmed to the right heat, given in sterilized bottles . . .'

Unconsciously, Isabel found herself standing by the pile of maps Peter had brought with them.

She leafed through them, letting them fall on the floor, and all the time this strange new image beckoned to her.

Her hands paused, and flicked open one of the maps.

Northern Italy, Tuscany?

Without hesitation, her gaze was drawn to one place.

'There,' she said quietly, pointing.

The Hospital of St Catherine, she read. On the outskirts of Milan.

'Where else would you hide a small baby?' said Peter Marsh, smiling at her. 'But in a maternity ward?'

They were flown to Milan immediately. During the brief flight the area around the hospital was carefully and completely cordoned off. No one wanted to panic the kidnappers, no one knew if they were even there. Perhaps the child was being cared for by some credulous nurse, some innocent auxiliary.

The hospital itself was recently built, and vast, serving a large area of the suburbs. The wide doors slid back automatically.

There was a babble of noise, the continuous patter of feet on lino, the rattle of trolleys and the occasional ping from the lifts. The sunlight was blasting through the large window in the hall. Further along the corridors, shutters had been drawn.

Everywhere was crowded with people. Uniformed staff, neat-waisted nurses, white-coated medics, patients on crutches, in dressing-gowns, fully dressed, with slings, bandages, and all their relatives and friends, chattering and arguing and gesticulating . . . Women with bulging abdomens, trailing toddlers and prams and pushchairs.

Their interpreter spoke to the receptionist. She pointed to the lift.

'No ... not that way ...' Isabel was already drifting down one of the corridors of the ground floor.

'Maternity is on the third floor, signora.' The interpreter caught her arm.

'But the baby is down there,' she muttered, pushing past her.

He was calling to her, urging her forward, needing and waiting ...

She heard a shriek, a high-pitched scream, louder than she'd expected. Her quarry was very close.

She pushed through the double doors to the room where he lay.

Festooned by tubes, hung up on drips, surrounded by television screens and a bank of dials and controls.

As she stared at him, his mouth opened and made again that high-wheeling, dreadful sound. His skin was sallow, his figure emaciated. Baby-blue eyes looked straight past her face.

David Earnshaw, still calling her.

She had found him once more.

An Italian paranorm known as the Maestro found the Marasso baby, clean, well and much adored, in the home of a woman whose own child had been stillborn.

David Earnshaw lay unmoving and unknowing in the hospital, while they waited for him to emerge further from the coma. He never did, but it was some months before they turned the machines off. The driver of the car which had knocked him down had already been released.

Long before that final flip of the switch, Isabel Bradley had returned to England. She continued to work for the Department on a variety of cases.

They never tried to send her abroad again. The addenda to her contract vanished as if it had never been. But sometimes, when she heard Italian opera, she would cry.

Like so many other people.

'Hm.' Loric discarded the file, and stretched. Nothing to bother the minister with here either. But he was thoughtful, nevertheless. It always unsettled him, seeing himself through other eyes. 'Burns never knew the half of it.'

Wasn't he the one with the spider fixation?

'No.'

Pity. You'd have had a lot to talk about.

'That reminds me. I haven't fed the tarantulas yet.'

Yawning, he reached for the next report.

LE GRAND MOANS

Anne Gay

Hadrian Rumbold was ashamed of his aitch. Why couldn't he be plain old Adrian, like everyone else? Or more to the point, considering he'd been compulsorily summoned to the DPR for what was probably going to be the major bollocking of his life, why couldn't they all be like him? A child of peace and light, man. But it was the Nasty Nineties and nobody cared about Flower Power any more, or the saga of his hassles with the fuzz.

Especially that bourgeois bitch behind the desk who he was sure was secretly laughing at his *H*. Consequently he faffed and dropped things more than usual as the Marcia at reception fiddled with his files.

'H. Rumbold, did you say? We don't have anyone of that name here.'

Hadrian's eyes did a quick road-crossing drill: left, right, left. Then they did their best to settle into a super-cilious sneer, but it was hard work when their whites looked like crazy paving. Red rimmed, red veined, their pupils shrunk to microdots, they polkaed back towards Marcia while their one careless owner mumbled, 'Oh yes you do. Me. Only the Marcia who was on when I was registered in 1987 spelt my name *Rumbled*. Check on the computer if you don't believe me. Eurotemp HR/ 3759/D.'

She didn't believe him. But then she never did. Not even when her long, varnished nails clicked over the terminal and Hadrian's name came out just as he said it would. Like it always did.

'Now,' he begged, 'please, just as a favour to me, will you please change the spelling?'

'Oh, I couldn't do that, not for ever so. You've been Rumbled. It says so here, you've been Rumbled ever since you first arrived. You should have said at the time.'

'I did! Well, I might have done. I meant to. Probably.'

Marcia pointedly studied the display on her screen and said nothing.

'Well, can't you at least drop the aitch?'

'There isn't an aitch in Rumbled.'

Before he could protest, a firm masculine voice crackled over the intercom. 'Bis chat Crumbled, Martian? Bend him pin.'

Marcia smiled triumphantly. 'We've got no time to waste, Mr Rumbled. Mr Graves will see you now.'

Mr Graves wasn't much help. One phone crooked under his chin, he was shouting down another one. He was busy taking notes, but the government-issue biro was blobbing ink all over the place. Horrible grey bits of nicotine gum lurked in a metal foil ashtray under a no-smoking sign. Even as he spoke, he spat a masticated lump out and tried one-handed to force another out of its obstinate bubble-pack.

Covering the receiver – 'Security,' he mumbled – Graves aimed part of his squint at Hadrian.

GBH of the ear'ole time, thought Hadrian miserably. *But it wasn't my fault, not really. I couldn't help it.*

But it wasn't. Quite the reverse.

'I'm not going to say a word about your last cock-up, Rumbled. Not a word. Just don't do it again. Evidence belongs to the DPR, and don't you forget it this time, okay?

'Now, see that pack over there? It's your first lot of instructions. You're going to France to work with the Sûreté. It's a big job' – Hadrian grinned in a glow of sudden importance until Graves went on – 'but all we've got is you. Cut-backs.'

'Cheers, man. You really know how to make a guy feel good. What –'

The boss gabbled into one of the phones, then slammed it down. It began ringing again immediately. Graves dropped it in the waste-paper bin. Totally ignoring Hadrian's defunct question, he said, 'Oh, do stop moaning, Rumbled. Don't make contact with your contact. He'll get in touch with you. All you're there for is to lead him to the stash. And leave it well alone this time. We've had a whisper that it's just a sample. Some special stuff the dogs don't recognize, and once it hits water, it just breaks down into harmless goo.

'Don't forget you're an ambassador from the good old UK. Don't go hog-wild on the expenses because you haven't got enough money to do it. Don't screw up for once. Bring some evidence back for a change, hey? And don't forget your health-insurance number. You'll need it.'

It sounded ominous. A selection of nervous twitches arrayed themselves on Hadrian's thin face. He asked apprehensively, 'Why? Because of the water? Or the food? Are there poisonous spiders? Or . . . or . . . something else?'

Graves took a second to stop fidgeting and look as directly as he could into Hadrian's eyes. Hadrian didn't think things could get any more ominous than that. Then the boss trumped himself in ominousness. 'Just check out your blood type, Rumbled. It might save time.'

Hadrian complained to Marcia. He complained to the woman sitting next to him on the plane, even after she pointedly put her headphones on to watch *Airport '91*.

And after that he complained to the stewardess about air safety.

At least when he landed at the poky little airport by the Pyrenees, our hero from the Bureau found that the French customs man pronounced his name without the aitch. 'Monsieur' – the official checked passport, face, passport, face, in a kind of quadruple take which instantly gave the traveller a B. Sc. in guilt – ''Adrian Rumbled, hein?'

Hadrian nodded several times and said, 'Yes. I mean, oui,' in a voice like a constipated mouse. Not a single sniffer-dog leapt out at him. And there wasn't so much as a tug in his special sense – except for the faint echoes from his own clothes. It didn't stop him having a lifetime's accumulated guilt, though.

But the customs man merely nodded at the fraying hippie and said, 'Professional nose, hein? We 'ave been expecting you. May God go with you. 'Ave a nice day.'

Bemused, Hadrian walked out into the spring sunshine. He couldn't believe his luck. Off to the south the mountains were doing Heidi impressions, their snow-capped crests shining pink in the early evening light. The sky was going all out for blue, and wisteria dripped lyrically from the scattering of small white buildings. The roofs were made of crinkled red tiles and a bell from a church tower in the distance was sounding the angelus. There was a scent of Gauloises in the air. Even the cars the other side of the fence were helping: they were driving merrily on the wrong side of a road past brown and cream signs that said exotic things like RALENTISSEZ – TRAVAUX. Hadrian thought it was a hyphenated village. It never occurred to him that the beautiful South of France had road-works too.

'Bloody hell!' said Hadrian. 'I've finally cracked it! I've actually got a decent assignment from the DPR.'

'Quoi?'

It was a small, male taxi-driver with a wine-gut of Massif proportions. Hadrian hadn't realized that he'd spoken aloud. 'Er, um, eh?' he said in his best schoolboy French. It hadn't actually occurred to him before that the only people who spoke O-level French were other English people ritually tortured by the disciples of the great god Whitmarsh in classrooms with torn posters of the Eiffel Tower on the walls.

Luckily the taxi-driver seemed to have understood. 'Monsieur 'Adrian Rumbled?'

Aitchless, 'Adrian beamed and shook the taxi-driver's hand. *Is he my contact?*

'Taxi. Suivez-moi.'

It was only because the driver was now getting into his battered Citroën that 'Adrian knew what to do. But once he was actually on the way to his 'big job' with the French flavour of MI5, the undertow of nervousness started slurping its way through 'Adrian's being once more.

As the cosy darkness closed in around the Citroën, yellow headlights slanted across the road to Sète. 'Adrian had looked it up in an old atlas: Sète was by the sea. Well, more on a sort of lagoon, really.

All of a sudden he bounced up in his seat. Ballooned by excitement, he strained against the seat-belt and shouted, 'Look! Over there! Is that the Med? La Mediterranean Mer?'

A Gallic shrug. Well, there had to be one. After all, this was France. The driver mumbled, 'Bien Sûr,' and 'Adrian subsided sadly. But not too sadly. Even if it wasn't the Med, the Bien Sûr was pretty with moonlight sliding over its dark crumpled waves.

Thousands of white lights glittered out over the lagoon;

strings of fairy lights on anchored yachts competed.
'Adrian was entranced. The last of his anxiety was
drowned out by the midnight beauty of it all, and not
even the smells of fish and mud-flats could depress him.
When all was said and done, it was much nicer than
Dagenham in the rain. But then again so was pleurisy.

The driver parked with a heart-stopping flourish at a
back-street pension and haggled about the fare. Sharing
this quaint local custom made 'Adrian feel like a sea-
soned traveller.

'Adrian finally retired, stuffed with bouillabaisse and
anaesthetized with pastis, to the lumpiness of the bolster
on his bed.

I wonder when I'll get my next lot of instructions? he
thought. Then he recalled Graves's serious look and the
bit about health insurance and his blood type. And hadn't
the customs man wished him 'Go with God'?

The memories stirred his sleeping apprehension, which
began to wriggle uncomfortably through the cloud of
pastis fumes in his brain. The boulder-stuffed bolster
didn't make him feel any more secure.

Lying in a strange bed in a strange room in a strange
country in the darkness, 'Adrian found all sorts of fears
popped up like charred bread from a toaster.

Maybe I should have drawn a gun from the armoury.

*Bloody hell! Maybe these guys I'm up against are like
the Mafia or something and I'm going to end up wearing
a concrete overcoat.*

'Adrian swallowed and the room danced round a bit. He
waited until it came round again and held it down. Wishing he'd smuggled a bit of Leb in so he could relax, he
had to make do with logic.

Nah, he told himself. *It's just plain, old-fashioned paranoia. They'd never let me anywhere near something seriously serious. Pretend you're a pair of curtains and pull*

*yourself together. Customs men probably go round saying
'Go with God' all the time down here. It's probably just
another quaint old local custom.*

Though 4,000 francs still seemed like an awful lot to
pay for a taxi.

Armies of bell-ringers marching round the inside of his
skull woke 'Adrian at about one. Sharp stripes of hot
sunlight came in through the shutters and razored their
way into his eyes. He could have combed his tongue.
Rags of nightmare fluttered between his ears: something
about Edward G. Robinson yelling at him in garlic-
flavoured foreign, then shooting him with concrete bullets
because he couldn't remember the perfect tense of *être*.

He tried to pretend he wasn't feeling his navel to see if
it belonged to him, but the clamminess was sweat, not
blood. Sighing with relief, he lay back on his bolster.

After that the day got worse.

He discovered why the stupid thing was so lumpy.

His second lot of instructions had been lurking under
his pillow all night.

With a gun in them.

Oh, no.

And orders to be on the docks opposite the oyster
beds by noon at the latest. So he could hide before the
bad guys came to shift the stuff.

Double *oh, no.*

And to take the gun because these yo-yos always went
armed for Iwo Jima.

Oh, no in spades.

He'd drunk half a gallon out of the tap before he remembered all those xenophobic stories about 'don't drink the
water'. Perhaps that was why he was feeling so queasy as
he shimmered furtively along the docks. Then again,

perhaps not. Trafalgar Square in the rush hour would have been quieter.

All around him were boxes and bales and fishermen twiddling their nets between their toes while they shouted at one another. The very unromantic oil terminal near by wouldn't have looked out of place on the Isle of Dogs. Black tobacco scented the salt breeze, which was hideous enough already with fishguts and burnt diesel. Seagulls screamed and engines chugged in French and some idiot almost ran him over in a 2CV; as it rocked past him it made him seasick just to watch its suspension canting it sideways.

Second worst, though, was the sunlight clog-dancing on his head.

And first worst was the fact that he was supposed to find out which of the men lurking around for incomprehensible French purposes were the drug-smugglers. Especially since half the shops in the inhabited universe seemed to be bobbing up and down like people at the last night of the Proms. There were big rusting hulks, trawlers, yachts, catamarans, rowing boats. There were yawls and ketches and a dory with a fringe on top.

There's probably a Roman galley that's been trying to dock for the last two thousand years, Hadrian thought sourly. He was far too depressed to ignore his aitch now. *Only which one of them is the jackpot?*

Knowing my luck, I've probably slept through the whole thing and they've buggered off with the goodies. Graves'll do his nut. He'll have me put in the dungeon in New Scotland Yard and tortured with Andy Stewart tapes. I can't go on any more.

But being Hadrian Rumbold – or indeed Rumbled – he could. And did. On and on and on, chuntering away to himself while flitting conspicuously from heap to heap of dockside junk, his long hair flagellating him in the hot wind as he pulled his frightened head lower between his shoulders like some wimp of an English tortoise.

There seemed to be thousands of men loitering with intent. Any of them could be the good guys. *So where's John Wayne when I need him? And what if I shoot the daft idiot by mistake? Or he shoots me? I can't cope with this at all.* Fear and irritation and hangover seemed to centre on the gun collecting sweat and sticking into his stomach.

Then, by a particularly rancid trawler, his special sense seemed to tighten momentarily.

Hadrian hesitated, his denim flares flapping.

Yes, there it was again! Some psychic muscle contracted almost orgasmically and he homed in on the cause.

Dope! There's dope in them thar bales!

The anticipation of Ecstasy – or marijuana, or any old psychotrope, really – blocked his negative feelings and he reverted to 'Adrian of the derring-do. The stuff was pulling him, reeling him in across the sunny quay. He walked blindly between conversations and over nets, heedless of the curses he couldn't understand anyway. So much for being an ambassador of the good old UK.

There it was. Right at the dockside, hidden in a box of bananas. But not hidden to our hero from the Bureau. Though the trawler's bulwarks were casting a shadow now on the tarmac, some strange quirk of the ship's skyline left the banana-box in a shaft of sunlight. To 'Adrian it was as if the box were haloed.

He knelt by it. He didn't see the two men in tight shiny suits who suddenly peeled themselves off the harbour wall. He didn't see the way their hands went in unison to their arm-pits and came out loaded for bear. He didn't see the tarty transvestite stop haggling with docker, or the way his lipsticked mouth formed a jammy O of horror.

'Adrian tried to open the box. Nailed down. Frustration.

'Adrian pried at it with his fingernails, heedless of splinters. No joy.

The gangsters in their lurex threads started to trot. The transvestite that everyone – except 'Adrian – knew was a cop in drag lurched into a faster totter, cursing his high heels. His wig blew off and his plastic breasts broke their moorings.

'Adrian's crazy-paving eyes never left the object of their desire. He was breathing heavily now, hot with chemical lust. He sent one of his hands on a groping mission and it came back with a strip of metal. It could have been a crowbar or a hockey-stick for all 'Adrian cared.

Two sets of Gucci shoes pounded down the quay, followed by the stuttering click of stumbling stilettos.

'Adrian jemmied up the lid. The squeal of nails leaving wood was like an angel chorus in his ears. As his fingers delved down through the tough bananas to the softness of a package, his mind and soul and groin spasmed on a holy peak of bliss.

The gangsters threw down on him, their guns microseconds from blasting him to oblivion. Metres behind, the cop in drag went for the gun in the top of his tights and couldn't get at it because his plastic breasts were bouncing up and down on his waistband.

But 'Adrian's scream of joy wasn't. For the soft thing he had touched wasn't the package he craved but the soft wriggling shell of a tarantula who wasn't at all happy about the intruder. As the arachnid opened its mandibles, the arachnophobe screamed and threw it away.

It landed on the white V of a mobster's shirt. Horror-stricken, he tried to knock the black octopod off and succeeded only in brushing it on to his mate. He shoved his hands down his front while the first gangster wrenched to get his friend's jacket off. The tottering tart tripped on a rope and fell on the bad guys, his plastic prostheses bursting on impact.

But 'Adrian didn't care. He had found the diamond dust. No matter what Graves said, he had to try this stuff. What was the point of being a drug-tracker if you couldn't sample the merchandise? But a corner of his mind still promised that he'd save enough for evidence. Honestly. This was one time he wouldn't screw up.

Meantime the robber–tart combo fought themselves and each other, with a foreign hand up the policeman's skirt while the frightened spider was who knew where, poor thing, poor thing.

And, reverentially raising the loot above his mouth, 'Adrian opened the packet and closed his eyes.

And then he got a great big surprise.

For just as the first sun-sequinned grains were about to take him to new heights of exaltation, the tangle of law and disorder snared him. All together, they cannoned over the edge and into the rotting fishheads drifting forlornly in the Bien Sûr.

You could have heard Hadrian moaning back in Blighty.

Two days later in foggy London town, Marcia smiled nastily as the intercom spat, 'Tend cat plasted Crumbled bin. Mile till the fun-of-a-stich.'

'But it wasn't my fault!' Hadrian moled.

'Unbelievable!' The Rumbled file skidded across the stack of discards on the occasional table, and fell to the floor beyond, leaving stray sheets of A4 fluttering forlornly in its wake. After a moment they gathered themselves together and floated to their assigned place on top of the heap. 'What am I supposed to tell the Minister about that?'

Why tell him anything? Maybe he hasn't heard.

'Maybe the sky will be green tomorrow. For heaven's sake, Maddie, can you see the French taking the blame for this?'

Why not? They asked for him.

'It won't stop them passing the buck.'

Then pass it back. You're a civil servant. You're supposed to be good at that sort of thing.

'It comes with the job.' Loric sighed and sipped at his tea. 'I'll say we're investigating. Something else is bound to turn up before he remembers it again.'

At least he won't be asking about Philip.

'Well, there is that.' Loric paused and hefted the next file. It was thick, and heavy, somehow menacing; the gnat-like drone from it seemed deeper, more dangerous. It wasn't from the DPR.

Loric opened it, raising an eyebrow. Reports from the Home Office, mostly, with contributions from Scotland Yard's Special Branch and the Anti-Terrorist Squad. Copies to a few of the Gods.

He didn't like the look of it at all.

EL LOBO DORADO IS DEAD, IS DEAD

Liz Holliday

———————

Sarah Gillespie is sitting alone in her room. The blind is closed. The light filtering through it is blood red, as if from a dying sun. In the bay window a half-completed painting stands on an easel. It is a montage: Christ on the cross, a wolf shot by hunters, a young man in a gold leotard being ripped apart by an explosion. The images twist across the canvas and become each other, like a miscegenation Hieronymus Bosch and M. C. Escher.

The radio is on in the next room. It is time for the news. At other times Sarah can ignore it. Not now.

'Turn it off, turn it off, turn it off,' she whispers.

It is no use. The newscaster says: *'The True Human Army have claimed responsibility for the explosion two days ago at Heathrow Airport which claimed three lives. Police are still looking for a young woman seen running from –'*

'Turn it off,' Sarah says again, much louder.

'Meanwhile the siege at the North-western Hotel continues, with Kevin Brigham and several unnamed True Human Army members demanding –'

Sarah does not listen, will not, dare not.

All the time her fingers stroke a newspaper cutting she is holding. Tears fall unwiped down her cheeks and on to a half-healed gash that runs from the ball of her thumb half-way up her left arm.

Once, she begins to rise; stops, as if uncertain, and sits down again

*

From where she stood near the front of the demo, Sarah had a good view of the Talent '92 Roadshow stage. The audience were a mass of colour balanced by the dark piles of the speaker stacks and the ominous mob of Keep Britain Normal thugs on the far side of the display. There's a picture in here somewhere, Sarah thought. But she could not combine the separate elements into a coherent whole.

Captain Croak ran from the stage, and was replaced by another performer. A ripple of applause spread through the audience. Way over on the other side of the park, one of the Keep Britain Normal thugs chucked a full beer can into the audience. A policeman hauled him off in an armlock.

Better them than us, Sarah thought. She wiped the sweat out of her eyes with the back of her hand, while keeping her placard upright with the other. She was suddenly tired and very hungry, shivery despite the heat. What the hell. You had to make some sacrifices. She glanced at Allie, who was speaking to a guy in a Hungry for Change T-shirt.

One of the paranormals – what was her name? Pyro-technique – sent a ball of light up into the sky, and it burst into a shower of red and gold against the clouds. Beautiful, Sarah thought; but she muttered, 'Fascist bitch.'

Allie turned to her, but whatever she said was lost in the roar of approval that went up from the crowd. It was answered on the far side by a howl of outrage from the Keep Britain Normal lot. Sarah suddenly realized that a whole group of them were wearing True Human Army armbands. It was hardly surprising the police were being so ... vigilant.

The THA were a vicious bunch of thugs, she knew: they had been responsible for several bomb alerts at

Department of Paranormal Resources offices. She had been to a talk about them at the Women's Centre: apparently they had neo-nazi connections in France and other European countries.

Someone closer to the front started the chant again:

'WHAT DO WE WANT?'

'NO FREAKS!'

Allie leaned over to her and shouted, 'What's the big difference between this and fireworks? That's what I want to know.'

Sarah shrugged elaborately, *Beats me.* They picked up the chant: 'FREAKS OUT. FREAKS OUT.'

So the afternoon went, with Pyrotechnique handing over to what might have been an acrobat in a circus. He tumbled across the stage, impossibly fast and lithe in his gold leotard. He fought too with assailants in army greens. No one could be that agile, that quick, as if he knew where they would be before they did themselves. Fascist wanker, Sarah thought, as he left the stage and the Roquette came on. He lanced straight up from the stage, then came down beneath a yellow parachute canopy bearing the green Psitroniques International logo. Sarah heard muffled giggles from beside her. She turned to see Allie and Hungry for Change giggling hysterically and clinging to each other.

'What is it?' she asked. Allie looked at her and burst into laughter again. 'What?' Sarah demanded again.

'He can't . . . all he can do . . . he can . . .' Allie said. Her face was pink and her dark hair was plastered against it in little kiss curls.

Hungry for Change took a deep breath. 'All he can do is go up and come down. He'd fall like a dead duck without a 'chute.' He had a nice voice, Sarah thought. Nice voice; nice hands, on Allie's shoulders.

'Let's just hope they don't think to send him up with a bomb,' she said coolly.

'But Sarah,' Allie said, 'all he could do is drop it and fall into the blast zone after it.'

And they were off again, giggling like dopeheads. Sarah turned away. She held her placard up a little higher and joined in with the chanting. They don't understand how important this demo is, she thought. Making sure people realize how dangerous and fascist these paranormals are, what might happen if we let Europe take us the American way; vigilantes prowling the streets would be even worse than the police. At least *they* pretend to obey the rules . . .

Dragons of light and darkness fought their way across the sky. Sarah glimpsed the Greek twins, Hoi Mirzes, on the stage; they were distant figures, insignificant in their black leotards. The publicity said they could only project paired illusions of things fighting: dragons, polecats, Stealth bombers. What does that say about your screwed-up little heads? Sarah thought. Poor little supermen.

And then all hell broke loose.

They came from the sides, from behind. Allie crashed into her. Sarah fell forward. The world slipped sideways in stop-frame motion. Her arms jarred down, folded awkwardly beneath her. Allie was on top of her, and Hungry for Change as well. They were heavy, smelled of garlic and sweat.

Sarah stared into a milling mass of bodies, faces, limbs. A hand with tattoos dancing all over it came towards her. A broken bottle jabbed at her face. She dodged.

A stubbled head turned, split with a blood-red grin.

God-damn police, she thought. Never around when you need them. Her pulse was hammering at her wrists and throat. It had been half a minute, not much more.

She shoved Allie off her, and stared for a fascinated instant at her bloodied hand.

'Come on,' she screamed. She crawled forward, pushing between legs, hardly noticing when she was kicked or punched. And then she was out of the worst of it. She shook off a first aider who tried to put something on her hand. The world seemed very strange, slightly blurry. Her heart was still racing. No problem. She would get the bus home, if the buses were still running. Bloody long walk if not.

She was almost out of the park when she saw them loitering by the gate. There were three of them, looking like refugees from the seventies. Shaved heads that seemed too small for their bodies. Beer bottles in their hands, sweaty faces and arms tattooed AFC.

'Darlin',' the middle one said, opening his arms to her. The one on the end laughed. Sarah stared, realized it was a girl; a girl built like a boy, tattooed with LOVE and HATE across her knuckles, just like one of them. She laughed. The whole damn women's movement comes down to this.

Wrong move. The girl walked up to her. Sarah was suddenly conscious of her Feminists Against Vigilantism T-shirt.

'You on the *march*, then?' said the girl, 'Against the *Talent*?'

Sarah said nothing, tried to go round her. The girl stepped in her way. Sarah tried again.

'Don't you talk then, snob?' the girl said.

'I just want to –'

The girl hit her hard in the stomach. 'Stuck-up bitch.'

Sarah tried to suck in air. Her chest burned. She flailed around with her hands, hoping she would connect, but there was nothing there, nothing there. Something hit her hard on the side of her head. Her vision went crimson. There was laughter.

The girl was in front of her. Sarah tried to grab her.

The girl stepped aside. She grabbed Sarah's hair and pulled her down.

Sarah fell. The girl landed on top of her, still with her hands tangled in her hair. Sarah grunted. Her face was ground into the earth. Stones bit her cheek. A knee drove fiercely into her back. If she could get her arms underneath her, she could get up . . . but they were pinned. Her legs thrashed uselessly. More laughter.

The weight was worse for a moment. Then it was gone. There were shouts. A scream. Thuds. Sarah refused to think about them. When they stopped she counted to ten. Then she pushed herself over and flopped on to her back.

The world came slowly into focus, though her eyes were watering. A hand sheathed in a gold glove presented itself. Sarah took it and allowed herself to be helped up.

He was only a head taller than she was. She let him support her, did not *cling* precisely but held very tightly to his arm. Behind his half-mask his brown eyes were so dark they were almost black, like his hair. His mouth was sensitive. How could someone who went round beating people up have a mouth like a lost child?

She said something to him; she never could remember what afterwards, but she thought it was probably something stupid. Anyway, he shrugged his shoulders as if he did not understand. A moment later he walked away with just a slight swagger.

When he was out of sight, she allowed herself to throw up.

Later, when the room has grown still darker, Sarah stands.

She goes to the wardrobe and stares at her reflection in the mirror there. Her eyes are as dark as bruises against the drawn whiteness of her skin; her lips are cracked and her hand, resting on her green T-shirt, trembles slightly.

Behind her the newspaper cutting lies unheeded on the floor. The dead eyes of El Lobo Dorado stare up at nothing. Above the picture is the headline SPANISH PARANORM SHOT DEAD.

Sarah stumbled up to the front door and managed, somehow, to get the key in the lock. The hall was dim; light and noise bled under the crack of the living-room door. The whole place stank of seaweed and miso, Nina's and Chris's idea of good cooking. She considered going straight to her room. While she was still thinking about it, still wondering if she was going to throw up where she stood, Nina called out to her.

She decided she would have to make the effort. Nina was watching the news. Scenes of the riot faded into the face of Kevin Brigham, leader of the True Human Army.

'Christ,' she said, 'there really was a riot, wasn't there?'

Sarah giggled and sat down abruptly, dropping her bag at the side of the chair. Chris brought the first-aid things and cleaned up her arm and a small cut on her face. The news murmured in the background: *The True Human Army have denied that they masterminded today's riot in Hyde Park. In a statement issued earlier they also claim to have had no contact with their leader Kevin Brigham. Self-styled "General" Brigham is being sought by police in connection with charges of manslaughter, actual bodily harm and incitement to riot –'*

'Looks worse than it is,' Chris said. 'Good job it's not your painting hand.' The antiseptic stung like hell.

'Want to talk about it?' Nina asked.

Sarah did, haltingly at first, then more easily. Why is it, she thought, when she got to the part about the skins, we only ever talk when there's a disaster; like when the water tank flooded, or when Nina's dad showed up and just wouldn't accept her living with Chris?

'. . . so this guy kind of rescued me,' she finished. She saw Nina's eyes go icy. 'Well,' she said defensively, 'someone had to!'

'Maybe you should think about coming to self-defence classes with me after all,' Nina said. She squeezed Sarah's good hand.

Sarah got up and went into the kitchen. The others followed her. She threw together a sandwich. Seeing them watching and feeling defiant, she made it ham and pickle.

'Makes it hard to think of them all as right-wing bastards, you know,' she said, round a mouthful of wholemeal bread.

'Does it?' Chris asked, his Northern Irish accent hard and scornful.

If you feel so strongly, why weren't you at the march? Sarah thought; but she didn't say anything. She just walked back through the living room, picked up her bag and went to her room.

Later, once she was sure they would not come and interrupt her, she pulled the *Evening Standard* out of her bag. She sat on the edge of the bed and unwrapped it carefully. The *Official Talent Roadshow '92 Poster Book* fell out of it.

The regular features of Enrique Garcia Ramirez stared up at her: *El Lobo Dorado*, the Golden Wolf, Spain's premier superhero. Gingerly, as if she thought it might bite her, she opened the magazine and began to read.

Sarah opens the wardrobe. Right at the back there is a pair of black jeans and a black sweatshirt. She takes them out. She undresses, shivering in the cold air. She does not glance again in the mirror, refuses to see the translucent skin, the too thin, almost anorexic arms. She is strong. She is ready.

She pulls on the jeans and T-shirt, follows them with black, rubber-soled plimsolls.

The scissors hissed as they cut through the page of the magazine. Sarah stuck it in the scrapbook, which was nearly full, with Pritt Stick. At first she had collected material about all the Talent who had taken part in the Roadshow. Lately she had realized that she was only interested in El Lobo.

She opened the copy of the *Face*. There was an interview with him. They were claiming it would become a Talent manifesto for the nineties.

'*None of us asked for our powers. I am Spanish and Spain is a Catholic country. I don't deny my faith, but I do question it. If God did not mean us to have these Talents, would he have given them to us? It is my hope people will see how I use my Talent, and say, "Well, yes, this El Lobo, this Enrique Ramirez, he is using his Talent to do God's will." And they will see that this is good –*'

Sarah slammed the flat of her hand down on the magazine. I keep thinking I understand this, she thought, but then I realize I'm making it up as I go along. I thought I knew him, from his pictures, because of the way he turned his head.

But he's *Catholic*. How was he going to be anything else? I was right first time, he's just another fascist, holding his power over normal people, and now he's using religion as an excuse. Just like they all do.

But she could not help reading on. '*But I say, we have our Talents, and it would be possible – as some of our most respected holy fathers have said – to say they come from Satan. We cannot know. We can only say: here I*' *stand, with my power, and I see a wrong thing happening. I can walk away, and the injustice will go on. But then, do you see, I would have to live with it. I would have to live with myself. And I could not. So I take the other road, yes? I take responsibility. I make the intervention, whether it is thieves or terrorista or whatever bad thing. And each night I pray to God it is right, and each Sunday I go to Church and pray for absolution for the violence I do. For to do nothing would be worse. And I, Enrique Garcia Ramirez, I say I cannot live with myself if I do nothing.'*

Sarah smiled. Well, okay, she thought, if he's just saying you have to do the best you can with what you've got. The smile faded from her lips as she thought, but what's the difference between that and bourgeois individualism? If only his personal morality makes him a white hat, isn't that just might is right by any other name? She scowled and started to cut the article out.

Chris banged on the door. Sarah scooped up the pile of magazines and the scrapbook and shoved them under the bed. She grabbed the scissors and glue, but he poked his head round the door before she could hide them.

'Tea?' he asked. 'Coffee?'

Sarah shook her head. He looked round quizzically before he left, and Sarah knew he was wondering what she did in here alone all the time. The empty easel stood in the bay window as if to accuse her.

She went to bed shortly after, staring at its bulk in the moonlight. El Lobo Dorado's voice lulled her to sleep. It sounded velvety brown, the Spanish accent heavy, as she was sure it did. As it must do.

Sarah pulls a duffle bag out of the bottom of the wardrobe. She will use the equipment one last time. Then she will throw it away. She lays the gear out.

There is an ultra-high-power flashlight and the shades that go with it, an electric water-pistol and a coil of fishing line.

She searches around in the piles of photographs and magazines that litter the floor until she finds a glossy folder. She pulls out a sheaf of forms and a laminated card. These she puts in a pocket of the duffle bag, then stows the rest of the gear inside it.

She puts on her old leather jacket, slings the bag over her shoulder, looks at herself in the mirror. She adds the megaflash shades. Just one more almost-Goth going into town on a Saturday night. She won't be stopped.

She smiles. Nothing can stop her now.

Sarah and Allie emerged from the cinema on to the street. Crowds swirled around them and were gone. The sodium streetlights stained the pale summer twilight.

'Thanks,' Sarah said yet again.

'I told you, this one's on me,' Allie said. 'Want a burger?'

'Are you sure?' Sarah asked uncertainly. 'I've still got some of my waitressing money left.'

'Save it. Anyway, tonight I'm celebrating: new bloke, the summer holidays are nigh, what more could a woman want?'

Later, as they went to the tube station, Allie kept up a constant stream of chat. She and Paul were going to see *Romeo and Juliet* at the National on Tuesday. Paul was working on a series of ceramic sculptures at the moment, and his tutors were very enthusiastic. Paul was the guy in the Hungry for Change T-shirt at the demo. Paul was really nice.

'You do think so, don't you?' Allie said.

'What?' Sarah said, surprised at the anxiety in Allie's

voice. She had to think for a second to remember what the conversation was about. 'Yeah. Sure. Better than celibacy, anyway.'

'Good. You okay, Sarah? You seem, I don't know, distracted.'

'It's not that,' she answered. 'I've started painting again, and I've been thinking about it a lot.' The lie startled even her.

On the tube she sat and hugged her bag, in which there was a large scrapbook, and three new *Star Talent* magazines plus a copy of *Hello!*, all bought at Smith's before she met Allie.

At Euston an old man got on. He reeked of meths and sweat and rotting teeth. He started a loud conversation with the Indian woman next to him. She looked away. He got up and reeled down the carriage, letting the motion of the train throw him from side to side.

'Bastards,' he yelled. 'You're all thievin' bastards!'

Allie stared straight ahead of her, as if she could not talk with him there. Sarah held her bag tightly. When the old man came past, she thought of El Lobo, and what he would do.

Allie got off at King's Cross. She glanced at the drunk.

'Take care,' she said and kissed Sarah quickly on the cheek.

He sat down by a young girl. Sarah made her seventeen, probably younger. She twisted away from him in her seat, seemed to be trying to fade into the glass partition. The old man put his hand on her arm.

There were a dozen people in the carriage, all of them sitting very straight. I should do something, Sarah thought. I have to do something or not, take the responsibility one way or the other. El Lobo would.

The train rattled on.

As it pulled in, Sarah got up and walked past the girl.

When she got home, she stuffed the bag under the bed. She could not look at the magazines. Not that night.

Sarah walks down the street. People watch her as she walks by. She is sure they do, but she will not return their stares. The duffle bag is heavy, just as it was that other time, the time when . . .

But she will not think of that, no.

'The True Human Army have admitted responsibility for the bomb threats which closed three Underground stations at the height of this morning's rush hour. Meanwhile their leader Kevin Brigham is believed to have escaped the country. Police are –'

Sarah reached over and turned off the radio. She stared across the room. I can't do anything, she muttered. It isn't my fault.

All she was good for was painting, and she hadn't completed a picture in months.

She got up slowly, and put a piece of hardboard on the easel. She had told Allie she was painting again. It wasn't a lie, Sarah thought. Not really. She had never stopped painting in her mind, making pictures out of the things she saw. It was just that for a long time she had not made marks on paper. Perhaps in painting she would be able to find herself again.

She began to lay down a ground of blue acrylic on the board, sweeping the palette knife across and down. It was to be a scene inspired by the demo. Maybe she could get it out of her system that way. She wanted to show Hoi Mirzes's fighting dragons up for the foolish things they were.

She worked all afternoon and well into the evening. She stopped, finally, when her shoulders were aching with the effort of control, and hunger was a clawing pain in her stomach.

She went to the kitchen and gulped down bread and cheese and most of a pint of milk, then collapsed on her bed.

In the morning she studied the painting. One of the dragons, the green one, had the face of the Keep Britain Normal girl. The other one, the victorious one, was closer to gold than green, and it too had a human face, a face that stared out from under a half-mask.

'Shit,' she muttered; then, 'All right, you bastard, if that's the way you want it.'

She took the board off the easel and stood it against the wall. There was a stack of hardboard offcuts under the bed. She pulled one out at random and put it on the easel. It was already primed, left over from her last productive period. She started with a narrow brush, began dabbing at the board, mixing the paint directly on it. It was going well, she thought. Now if she could just capture the light coming down across him . . .

Half an hour later she stopped. It was crap, sentimental, romanticized crap. She chucked the board across the room. Wet paint spattered the carpet. She would have trouble explaining *that* to Nina and Chris, and they fretted enough about her painting as it was.

The hell with them. She pulled out another board, then stopped. Reference material, she thought. Paint what you know. She grabbed her scrapbooks, and began tearing the pictures back out. There was a packet of Blu-Tack somewhere around. She had promised to use only proper picture hangers. Hell with the walls. What did Nina and Chris know about art? Before very long she had covered the walls in photographs of El Lobo Dorado.

And then she painted.

*

By the time Sarah reaches the hotel, night has fallen, turning every doorway into a dark cavemouth, every window into a mirror.

There are police and reporters everywhere, though by now the siege is old news. She cannot get close, not easily. There are barriers at the ends of the streets. It is, she thinks, very American. She wonders if they have set up a phone line into the building.

She stares up at the blind eyes of the hotel windows, and knows what she must do.

Voices come from outside her room: Nina and Allie. Not to worry. They got on surprisingly well. She would go out in a minute. She wanted to get the section she was working on finished. It would work better if the fist were more menacing, maybe a little larger. But the line was clumsy; maybe the colours were off. She mixed in a little more burnt sienna, a touch of cobalt . . .

'I haven't seen her in ages either,' Allie said from beyond the door. Her voice was raised. Sarah knew Allie was warning her she was there. It was a trick they had developed when they were room-mates at art college. She refused to be distracted and concentrated on the painting.

The door-handle rattled.

'Maybe you can get her to eat something while you're here. I know she doesn't like veggie cooking, but she's even stopped stinking the place out with bacon sandwiches.'

Sarah heard the door open but ignored it as she tried to get the shading on his costume right.

Allie came in. 'What the hell,' her voice said from behind Sarah. 'What on earth have you done to this place?'

Reluctantly Sarah put down her brush and wiped her

hands on her jeans. Allie was staring around at the room. 'What's up?' Sarah asked.

'What in God's name is all this?' Allie said, gesturing around at the room.

'Reference material. You know –'

'Well, yes, but . . .' Allie went over to the wall. 'El Lobo Dorado. Paranorms? For Christ's sake, what's got into you, Sarah?'

'Nothing's *got into me*. I just found a new subject, that's all.'

Allie's gaze shifted from one part of the wall to the next, as if she were trying to see all the photos at once. 'Don't you think you're taking things a little too far?'

'No. It's good. Powerful. You know how they always used to say I was too twee? Well, I reckon I've found the antidote. I thought I might try Chas Loren at the Camera Obscura Gallery again. You remember him? Said I painted like a Sunday-school picnic before. I guess he wouldn't say that now!' She could hardly keep the excitement out of her voice.

'Well, maybe,' Allie said dubiously.

'You don't like it.'

'I think maybe you're taking it a bit too far –'

'But that purity is what makes it so powerful –'

'I don't mean the painting, I mean *you*, damn it! Hiding yourself away like this, what are you – a hermit or something? You haven't called, you haven't been down the pub or the Women's Centre. Wouldn't surprise me if you'd forgotten to sign on. And now Nina says you've been stuck in here, not eating or –'

'Oh, you're a fine one to talk, you with your permanent diet!'

'Have you eaten anything today?'

Sarah stared at the wall. She fought back tears.

'Have you?'

'No!' Sarah shouted. 'I haven't. I've been too busy, all right. Is that allowed? That I should have something important to do?'

'Sarah, for God's sake, that isn't the point and you –'

'You're just jealous, that's what I think. You were the one that was going to be the great artist of our time, and what are you? A primary-school teacher. You can't bear it that you don't have the nerve to take the risks that I'm taking, so you just come round here picking holes –'

'SARAH! For Christ's sake, shut up before you say something you can't take back. Look at yourself. Just take a good look at what you're doing to yourself.'

'Don't patronize me,' Sarah said. 'If you can't be nice to me, just leave me alone.' She closed her eyes against her tears. When she opened them, Allie was still there, watching her.

What must she think of me? Sarah thought. And then it was as if she were seeing the room through Allie's eyes: the walls plastered with pictures of El Lobo Dorado, even a couple of expensive posters; the tatty bits of hardboard stacked everywhere; the paint spattered carpet and closed blind; and in the middle of it she imagined herself, thin to the point of anorexia in her huge jumble-sale shirt and ripped jeans, with her hair unwashed and her face red from anger and crying.

She wanted to say something, but no words would come, only tears. Allie helped her to the bed and sat silently with her until she stopped crying.

'So tell me. Why paranorms? Why this El Lobo Dorado?'

'I don't know. Because he does things? I mean, doesn't just sit back and let stuff happen? He was the one who saved me from those skins at the demo. I told you. It just seemed important to find out about him. Now . . . I don't know. I mean, I never had crushes on pop stars when all the other kids at school did, you know?'

'I know. But I still don't get it. You were so sure of yourself, with the anti-fascist bit and all. I mean, if it hadn't been for you I wouldn't have been on the demo at all.' She grinned. 'And I wouldn't have met Paul. Been meaning to say thank you for that, by the way.'

'There you bloody go again. You and Paul, you and Paul. You and your job and how tough it is and how you should be on a systems analyst's salary, considering how stressful it is.'

'Hey, wait a minute, where did this all come from? One minute we're worrying about you, the next I'm mince-meat?'

'You really don't understand, do you? I'm sick and tired of not being able to do anything. I mean, when you say that, you mean South Africa or Eastern Europe. Me, I can't even afford to buy a newspaper every day. But him, at least he's using what he's got. Doing some good.'

'I don't think you're being terribly logical about this –'

'Don't start.'

'I'm not.' Allie bit her lip. 'I just think if it's so important to you, maybe you should find out more. Really more, not just what the magazines say.'

'Oh, yeah. That'll be dead easy, that will.'

'Sure. Look, there's a DPR office in Wood Green. We could start there. They probably have some kind of publicity office or something.'

'I suppose.'

'I'll go with you if you like. But you have to promise me you'll eat properly too.'

'Okay,' Sarah said, though the thought of food made her feel ill.

'Good. I'll just go and see if there's any bacon left worth eating.'

A uniformed police officer calls out to Sarah. She ignores

106

him. She needs the one in the anorak by the mobile communications unit. She is fairly certain of that. She tries to appear confident. He looks at her.

'Get her out of here,' he shouts to the uniform.

'No, no,' she says quickly, holding out the laminated card. 'You don't understand. I'm with the DPR.'

'Christ on a bicycle, not another one! This is all we bloody need.'

Sarah tucks the card away. 'Policy,' she says. 'Now, if you'll just let me get on and do my job, we can all go home.'

'Not before I've checked this out with your head office. The other one didn't say he was expecting anyone else.'

He turns away. A man in a flak jacket with a radio antenna sticking out of the pocket comes up to him. They begin a heated argument. Snipers are mentioned. Sarah shivers, but this is her job now. She edges round so he is between her and Anorak. The one in the uniform is watching her. She crosses her arms and waits. By the time Flak Jacket has gone and Anorak is on the phone, Uniform's attention has wandered slightly.

It is enough. Sarah sets off across the open expanse of concrete in front of the hotel. Too easy, she thinks. And then: don't knock it. She has her hands wide out in front of her. She forces her mind to go blank. It is that or panic.

There is nothing anyone can do to stop her now. Anything they could do would trigger the bloodbath.

'Take a seat and fill out these forms, please.' The receptionist held clipboards and pens out to Allie and Sarah. Clutter covered the desk, forms and files and empty coffee-cups; a make-up mirror and half a dozen cassette tapes. A notice on the wall behind the desk warned people to stay alert for unattended packages. There had been bomb threats by the True Human Army, among others.

Idly, Sarah picked up one of the forms, an expenses claim.

'Please don't touch that,' the receptionist said primly. 'Authorized personnel only.' She pushed the clipboards at them.

'No, no,' Allie said. 'We aren't here to be tested. We just want some information. We thought you might have a public relations department?'

'Ooh, no,' the receptionist said. 'Nothing like that. This is strictly testing and grading. I don't think there is a PR department.' She rummaged on her desk for a moment. 'I know, though! You can have one of these press information packs. They're left-overs from the Roadshow. I don't suppose we'll be needing them now all the Europeans are going home.'

'Home?' Sarah said sharply. 'Is El Lobo Dorado going as well?'

'Oh, yes. Well, I expect Madrid isn't quite as safe as it used to be without him. Now, are you sure you don't want to be tested? It's quite simple, doesn't take long, and if you want I think I can fit you in this afternoon.'

'Yes!' Sarah said at exactly the moment when Allie said, 'No!'

'Oh, come on, Allie. It'll be fun. Besides, think of the money.'

'No.' She laughed as if to soften it. 'Not even teaching's that badly paid. I'll wait for you outside though – and then we'll go for tea, okay?'

Sarah nodded as Allie left. Then she hurried over to the bench and ripped open the press pack. It was disappointingly bland and rather badly written, though with good pictures. After a while she looked up. The receptionist had gone.

Sarah got up and went over to the desk. As casually as she could manage she slipped as many different forms into the folder as she could find.

By the time the receptionist returned, Sarah was sitting back on the bench, trying to look as if she had never moved.

The receptionist ushered Sarah inside, where she was seen by a rather faded young man in a grey suit. He smiled at her. He really thinks I might have a Talent, Sarah realized. She swallowed hard and sat down.

Fifteen minutes later her test was over. He had asked her a lot of questions, some of them repetitive. Very occasionally he had noted something down. And that was all. He opened the door for her.

'How soon will I know?' Sarah said at the last minute.

'Fairly soon, though I think it's fair to say that it does not look hopeful. We'll let you know.'

There have been death-threats. Sarah knows this. She realizes she has been waiting for the sound of gunfire from the hotel, or perhaps for a body to be thrown out.

Nothing happens. She realizes all she can do is keep walking. The expanse of concrete stretches out in front of her. The hairs on her neck rise every time she thinks of the police marksmen behind her. She can see no movement at the windows of the hotel; they are insane, but they are not fools, these terrorists.

She does not know what she will do when she gets to the hotel. She knew once, but now that plan has gone from her mind. There is only the walking, and the hotel which looms closer by the second, and the heavy weight of the bag on her shoulder.

It happened a few days later. She had gone to sign on. Allie had made her promise, and besides if they stopped her giros she would have no money for paint.

The underpass at Turnpike Lane was dimly lit and stank of urine. An *Evening Standard* advertising flimsy wrapped itself around her feet: PM IN THA DEATH-THREAT SCARE. Sarah kicked the litter away, her mind full of the new painting she was going to start when she got home. Harmonica music drifted on the cold air, amplified by the acoustics of the passage.

There was a loud bang and the music died. Sarah turned a corner. She glanced down one of the other passages and saw two lads in ripped leather jackets standing over a prone man. A microphone was lying across the passage, leads torn from the mini-amp: all of this in a single glance.

She heard El Lobo say in her mind, *I can walk away. And the injustice will go on. But then, do you see, I would have to live with it.* But he had gone back to Spain. It was Sarah who would have to act, or live with the consequences of inaction.

And then she was running down the passageway.

'Get away from him,' she screamed. Her body jolted with the impact of her feet against the ground. Her breath burned in her chest.

One of the youths turned. His eyes widened with shock. She pitched herself at him, but he twisted aside at the last moment. She glanced off his chest. He grabbed her arm and swung her round. Her feet went from under her and she stumbled against the wall. The other one grabbed her from behind, yanked her by her jumper and her hair. Through a blur of tears she saw people walking to and fro across the station, ignoring them.

Number One hit her across the face. The blow jolted her head back. She felt blood spurt from her nose. A tooth impaled itself on the inside of her lip.

'Still wanna play, sweetheart?' Number Two said from behind her. She tried to stamp down on his instep, but

he was wearing army boots and she only had light trainers on. He laughed and pulled her head back further. She
whimpered.

Number One hit her again, in the stomach this time.

'Spoilt our fun, cow,' Number One said. There was
something dead behind his eyes. 'But we could go somewhere, have some other kind of fun. No one need know . . .'

And then, at last, there was the sound of feet running
towards them, and voices shouting. Number Two shoved
her away, almost threw her into the wall. She could not
get her hands up in time. Her head crashed against the
tile, and then the world went red.

She cannot go in the front of the hotel. The terrorists will
be waiting for her. Sarah realizes this belatedly. There is
an alley to the side of the building. She forces herself to
keep walking towards the front entrance until the last
moment. Then she breaks and runs for the alley.

Not even the police arc lights can penetrate the shadows here. They could hide a whole gang of terrorists. She
pulls the megaflash and the electric water-pistol out, then
discards the duffle bag. She puts the flash in her jacket
pocket, tucks the pistol in her waistband and pulls her
T-shirt down to cover it. It is an inadequate disguise, but
the best she can do.

Then she goes to the side door and opens it. Inside
there is complete darkness. Sarah wishes she had an
ordinary torch.

She goes in.

'Just promise me you won't do anything that stupid
again,' Allie said.

Sarah winced. Her head throbbed under the gauze
dressing. She walked a little faster, knowing Allie would
have difficulty keeping up.

'Can't,' she said. 'I can't just stand by and let things happen any more.' She pushed through the crowds of shoppers, swerved to avoid a maniac with a baby-buggy. Her shoulders ached.

'For God's sake, Sarah. Who do you think you are? Carrie Smith? The DPR told you, you don't have any Tale –'

'So what? When did a paranorm last stop anything bad happening to an ordinary person? It's up to people like us to look after ourselves. And since you won't, that just leaves me.' She came to the newsagent's and turned to go inside.

'I'll see you around, Sarah. Take care,' Allie said. She made no move to follow Sarah inside.

'Hey, I thought we were going to go shopping, buy you a pair of shoes?'

'I don't think so. I'll phone you some time.' She turned away, and was lost in the crowd.

Fuck, Sarah whispered to herself. An old lady with a shopping trolley tutted at her. Sarah wiped tears from her eyes with the heel of her hand.

She went to the rack and found the new issue of *Star Talent*. There was nothing in it about El Lobo Dorado. Well, if he would leave them and go back to Spain . . .

On the shelf beneath it there was a magazine called *New Survivalist International*. The cover showed a man aiming a rifle, but it was the blurb that attracted Sarah's attention: *Urban Survival: How to Improve Your Chances – Legally.*

She picked it up and flicked through it. The article was quite long. Some of the things it suggested would have taken too much training, too much time. But it had a list of gear you could buy that would help a lot. She still had a little of her waitressing money left.

When she left the shop with the magazine rolled inside

the copy of *Star Talent*, she was grinning. Let them try to take her on once she had this stuff to help her. Let them try.

Sarah slips through the darkened hallways. Her finger rests gently on the switch of the megaflash. In her other hand she holds the water-pistol.

She expects some of the terrorists will be looking for her downstairs. But the hostages will be in an upstairs room. She finds a door that opens on to a narrow back staircase.

It is very quiet. There is only the padding of her plimsolls on the cord carpet. And the thudding of her heart.

The package, when it came, was smaller than she expected, considering it had taken almost all her savings. She tore open the padded envelope, then the box inside.

The instructions informed her that the *megaflash* generated a microsecond burst of directed light, to an intensity of a quarter million candlepower. It would temporarily blind anyone without proper protection, but without doing any permanent damage. Nevertheless, there were many warnings, about the unit's use and the necessity for wearing the goggles supplied at all times. They were not Ray-Bans, but they would pass.

Sarah grinned. She put the megaflash on the bed, then pulled out her other recent acquisition. It was an electrically powered water-pistol, as recommended by *Survival Today*. When she had bought it in the toy shop, it had been fluorescent pink and yellow. She had sprayed it matt black. Its high-powered water-jet would stop any assailant if it hit him in the face.

Let them try to hurt me now, she thought as she changed into the black T-shirt and jeans she had brought specially. Let them just try.

She got her first real chance to try them out a few days later. The local paper headlined a rape that had taken place in Green Lanes. It was not the first – the police suspected the same man was responsible for this and several others.

That night she wore a short skirt and lace-up shoes with a T-shirt. The goggles were not stylish, but they would have to do. The megaflash itself was a comforting weight in her jacket pocket, but she had to leave the water-pistol in her duffle bag.

Sarah left the glare of the sodium lights on Green Lanes behind her. The dark road stretched out ahead of her. She forced herself to go down it, turn the corner, walk the next one.

Nothing happened that night, or the next. But on the third she heard footsteps behind her.

Sarah speeded up. So did the footsteps behind her. She shoved her hand into her pocket. Her fingers found the switch.

She slowed down. Her mouth was dry, her pulse light and fast.

She might make it into one of the gardens, hammer on the door. Someone might help –

'Hey, chick, got time for me?'

She almost bolted. There was a heavy hand on her shoulder. She shrugged it off. Got to be certain, she thought. Bastard might just be trying his luck. Fingers dug deep into her flesh.

'Go to hell,' she said. He might yet back off. Got to be certain.

He yanked at her and kicked open the nearest garden gate. Sarah went off balance, tried to use the momentum to swing round. He reached for her, his hand going for her breast.

She pulled the megaflash out of her pocket. Without

really aiming it, she flicked the switch. Actinic light flooded the street, bright enough to make Sarah blink, despite the goggles. Then it was gone.

The man screamed and let her go. He stumbled off. Sarah thought, my God, what do I do now? She had thought she knew what to expect; but she had not planned for his pain, or her own pulse-pounding terror.

The man was still stumbling around. She approached him cautiously. He had his hands in front of his eyes. She grabbed one of them and kicked his legs out from under him.

He went down. She pulled out the length of fishing line and tied his hands together behind his back.

Then she ran and did not stop until she found a phone box. She said she had heard screaming, that she thought someone was being attacked.

The police came while she was still waiting for the bus.

The next week the local paper headlined the capture of Sarah's attacker. His description, along with certain un-specified forensic evidence, had resulted in charges being brought against him for a number of previously unsolved crimes. The police were still looking for a young woman seen running from the street where he was found.

At the bottom of the story there was a reminder that vigilantism is illegal in Britain.

The darkness has closed in around Sarah, made deeper by the megaflash shades she is wearing. Her feet, sliding forward, find each riser in turn.

She wonders where they will be. The police all seemed to be staring up at windows at centre-front, but if she were the terrorists she thinks she would have chosen a room towards the back or the sides, perhaps even a corridor away from any windows.

She realizes with horror that they could be waiting for her at the top of the stairs. There might be no time to prepare. But there is no way to retreat. She can only go on.

In the weeks that followed Sarah had a number of successes. She stopped a gang of girls from stealing an old lady's bag. She accidentally barged into a pickpocket operating in Oxford Street. She used the megaflash on a group of Keep Britain Normal thugs who were beating up a paranorm in the park. The poor woman's hair kept changing colour: paprika to cyan to royal blue. Sarah dragged her away while the yobs were still writhing on the ground. She left before the woman recovered, unsure how she would feel about her rescuer.

It was then that she stuck a photo on the blank ID card she had taken – she would not think of it as stealing –from the DPR Office. She wrote a fake name and address. Where it said 'Type of Talent' she put *Girl Wonder*. For grade she put *Totally Dynamic*. She paid a technician at the local Community Centre a fiver to laminate it on the quiet for her.

If she were found with it, she reckoned she could get away with saying it was a practical joke.

She took to wearing black all the time, which seemed appropriate; she always had her duffle bag with her. You never knew when you might need it.

During the Notting Hill Carnival she broke up a fight between two youths carrying knives. That was the first time she used the water-pistol. The water lanced out from it, bright as steel in the afternoon sun. Sarah fought the kickback. She hardly noticed the youth's screaming.

He went down. The other lad ran away. The pistol coughed and died, out of water. Sarah lowered it with aching arms. The boy on the ground coughed and shook.

What now, Sarah thought. Then she noticed the police closing in. She ran. She pushed through the crowds, actually dodged across the parade route. She fell into a doorway and lay there panting. Only when she was sure the police were not following did she allow herself to relax.

She really did not want to try out the new card unless she had to.

At the top of the stairs Sarah pauses.

There are so many rooms, so many corridors. She is suddenly terrified of blundering into something that will get out of control. She will not think of that, will not, will not.

Forcing herself to be still, she hears sounds: muffled thumps, low voices. She starts in their direction.

Sarah picked up the *Evening Standard* from the living-room table. As she was flicking through it, Chris wandered in. He sat down with his cup of tea and turned on the television.

'Allie phoned,' he said. 'Wanted to know if you'll be at the Reclaim the Streets meeting tonight. Said would you phone.'

'I'll do that some time,' Sarah said absently, knowing she did not intend to. Her attention had been caught by a headline in the paper: SPANISH PARANORM ESCORT FOR EXTRADITED KEEP BRITAIN NORMAL LEADER.

She read on, '*Security precautions have been stepped up at Heathrow Airport, where Kevin Brigham is due to arrive tomorrow under paranormal escort. He will face multiple charges of manslaughter, incitement to riot ...*' Sarah grew more excited by the minute. '*... will be accompanied by El Lobo Dorado, Spain's paranorm with the superfast reflexes.*'

This time, she would get to meet him.

Sarah walks quietly down seemingly endless corridors. Somewhere in here there is another paranorm. A real paranorm, she reminds herself sternly.

The voices grow louder. Sarah turns a corner and finds herself facing a man in army fatigues. He has a rifle. Sarah throws herself to one side. As she does so, he brings the weapon up, screams something, fires all in the same instant.

Sarah flicks the switch on the megaflash. Nothing happens. She looks up, sees the man coming towards her. She slams the megaflash with the palm of her hand. There is a faint crackle, and the light kicks in.

The man falls. He screams and brings his arms up to cover his face. Sarah scrambles to her feet. For a split second she considers his rifle, but she knows she does not know how to use it. Besides, she is one of the good guys.

She runs down the corridor. Feet are pounding towards her. She tries one door, then another. Third time lucky. She dives inside.

'Excuse me,' Sarah said. 'Excuse me. Excuse me.' She pushed through the crowds that got thicker the closer she got to the Terminal One arrivals area. She felt like a kid at the fun-fair: stomach queasy, heart pounding, fever-hot despite the air-conditioning.

As she came down the steps into the arrivals lounge, she had a clear view over the heads of the crowd. The police had taped off a corridor from the street exit to the plate-glass windows that led to customs. A three-deep crowd of reporters and photographers and fans jostled along the length of it, while inside a handful of police warned them to keep their distance. Television crews hovered further back, waiting their chance near the exits.

In one corner a group of teenage girls waved banners saying WELCOME BACK EL LOBO DORADO and EL LOBO WE LOVE YOU. A reporter thrust a microphone at one of the girls. She giggled out a few words and obligingly displayed her Talent Roadshow '92 Official Fan Club T-shirt for the photographer.

Children, Sarah thought, though part of her wondered if they had been given any exclusive pictures or information. She jiggled the duffle bag on her shoulder to re-assure herself. The megaflash was in her pocket, where it belonged. He would think she was wonderful. He had to.

As she finished descending the steps, one of the fans on the far side of the barrier pointed at Sarah's side of the lounge.

'There he is,' she screamed and threw herself under the tape.

Sarah looked round. El Lobo Dorado was in the centre of a group of men making their way to the exit. Plain-clothes police she thought, as she recognized Kevin Brigham. He was swaggering slightly, making no effort to conceal the handcuffs that linked him to one of the detectives.

One of the policemen looked over his shoulder. The group broke into a fast trot.

Sarah felt her heart pounding, her mind consumed with joy. The duffle bag jounced on her shoulder. She swerved around a pushchair without apologizing to the woman pushing it: was almost there, almost there –

And then the bomb exploded.

Sarah listens to the sound of retreating feet. When she is sure they have gone, she slips outside. Her feet make no sound on the lush hotel carpet. She runs, knowing there is not much time.

She sees an open door ahead of her. She presses herself to the wall, feeling cold plaster caress her back. She strives for calmness as she edges forward, but does not achieve it.

She has the megaflash in one hand, the water-pistol in the other. It must be enough.

She stops when she can see part of the room. There are three men in army fatigues. All of them stay near the centre of the room. Two of them are armed with rifles. She does not know what kind they are, but she remembers the noise of them, the *smell* of them. She remembers the screaming.

There is a woman slumped against the wall. Her head lolls at an unlikely angle. Her face is puffy, yellow with bruising. Her eyes are closed, her wrists tied behind her.

A man is tied to an upright chair near the window. Sarah believes she understands this. If the police try to snipe at the terrorists, there is a high likelihood they will kill the man. It does not seem likely that they will risk this.

And on the floor lies another man. His ankles and wrists are tied together. He is facing her, and the top of his white robe is soaked in blood from a shoulder wound. A staff lies broken, just out of reach, as if to taunt him. Sarah recognizes him too, from *Star Talent*. He is the Druid, who had – has, she thinks, has – the power of channelling earth energy.

She hears voices behind her. She turns in time to see two men coming round the corner at the far end of the long corridor. One is in paramilitary gear, the other in nondescript casual clothes. There is something tantalizingly familiar about him, but they are too far away for Sarah to make out details.

She must decide what she will do. And now there is no more time.

*

The dull *wumph* of the explosion knocked Sarah off her feet. Something slammed into the back of her head. There was a confusion of screaming, of sirens, of glass and metal hailing down. The lights died and the sprinklers cut in. Within the space of a dozen heartbeats the lounge was full of smoke and steam.

Sarah gagged and tried to sit up. Her eyes were streaming from the smoke despite the megaflash goggles. The room spun round and refused to settle. Her head hurt as if someone had driven a nail into it. Everything was blurry.

An engine roared outside. Glass shattered and metal screamed as it twisted. A lorry with its tailboard down reversed into the terminal.

Christ, Sarah thought. She could barely concentrate. She had to fight to stop the world turning, to force multiple images to come together. She stared blankly, unable to comprehend as several figures in paramilitary gear leaped from the lorry. They had semi-automatic weapons. Kalashnikovs, Sarah wondered, or Uzis? What the hell, they were all dangerous.

The police were hustling Kevin Brigham away, back towards the customs block. They were hampered by the debris that covered the floor, and by Brigham, who struggled and pulled back.

El Lobo Dorado was not with them.

The paramilitaries moved in on the police. With a flash of understanding, Sarah saw the True Human Army patches on their armbands.

A man groaned next to Sarah. He was bleeding from half a dozen shrapnel wounds, and his face was pale with shock. She should help him, put him in the recovery position at least.

'HALT OR WE FIRE. HALT OR WE FIRE.' The voice was electronically distorted. Sarah saw that one of the True Humans had a mike to his mouth.

The police doubled their pace, but the True Humans overtook them easily. One of the terrorists reversed his weapon and clubbed the policeman cuffed to Brigham. The man went down.

Kevin Brigham punched the air in the True Human Army's neo-Nazi salute. He was laughing. The wild sound cut through the wail of the klaxons.

A golden blur moved against the darkness beyond the fight. Lobo! Sarah thought. Got to do something. Got to help him. It was hard to think with the pain in her head.

Brigham ran towards the van, dragging the dead weight of his escort behind him. Two of the terrorists followed, weapons at the ready to cover him. Meanwhile the other True Humans kept the rest of the police busy.

A terrorist climbed into the lorry. Kevin Brigham followed, manhandling his unconscious escort up. The third True Human covered the fight. Light glinted on his gun.

In the other fight one of the terrorists rabbit punched a police officer. The man crumpled. The terrorist slammed the heel of his hand into the man's jaw as he went down.

'THIS IS THE POLICE. WE HAVE THE BUILD-ING SURROUNDED. YOU CANNOT ESCAPE. COME OUT WITH YOUR HANDS IN THE AIR. I REPEAT...'

The remaining terrorists broke off the fight. They ran for the lorry, with the police following. One of the detectives reached the tailboard. He leaped for it and was kicked back.

Kevin Brigham grabbed the rifle from the True Human. His laughter cut the air again as he raised it.

She had to do something. She stood up, swaying. There was a heavy weight in her pocket. Megaflash, she thought. Oh, yes.

The driver gunned the engine. Sarah pulled out the megaflash. Something gold moved in her peripheral vision. El Lobo, she thought. But it was too late. Her finger was already leaving the button and . . .

Sarah slides the water-pistol across the floor. She thrusts the megaflash into her pocket. The two men are some way off still.

She walks into the room, hands held out in front of her. She knows it is her only hope.

'Hold,' she says. 'Hold your fire. I've only come here to talk to you.'

The men turn. Sarah finds herself looking at the barrel of a semi-automatic.

'Who the fuck are you?' one of them says.

'Police negotiator,' Sarah says, hoping they cannot hear her terror. 'I might be able to get you out of this, if you are sensible.'

'We want safe passage out to Singapore. A plane.' He yanks the bound man's head back by the hair. 'That, or these two die. Is that sensible enough for you?'

'You don't have to hurt him,' Sarah says. The man's eyes have rolled up in their sockets. Blood dribbles from his nose. 'Just put your weapons down and I'll see what I can do. There is a chance charges might be dropped.' Tell them anything, she thinks. Just as long as they drop the guns long enough for her to trigger the megaflash safely. 'Especially if you agree to tell what you know about the links between the True Human Army and Keep Britain Normal –'

'We don't inform, girl.' The man who speaks is older, wears his uniform as if he were born to it. Perhaps he was. 'The day will come when Britain will be grateful to us for our great vision, our vision of purity and light. Or it will go down under a sea of blood and the weight of subhuman filth. Do you understand me, girl?' He has gone pale, blue eyes protruding slightly from their sockets.

Perhaps he'll have a stroke, Sarah thinks.

'No one is trying to deny your right to your own politi-cal beliefs,' she says. 'But surely you can see that change must come through Parliament. Britain isn't called the Mother of P –'

'That's the bitch from Heathrow,' Kevin Brigham's voice says from the door.

Sarah turns, sees his raised rifle. And there is no more time.

Actinic light seared the lounge. Screams filled the air. Weapons were dropped or thrown. Bodies slumped to the ground, writhing.

El Lobo Dorado stumbled around, clawing at his eyes. *His hypersensitive vision, hearing and reflexes give him his fighting edge,* Sarah quoted at herself.

As he moved away, she saw that Brigham had held on to his weapon. He had his eyes closed tight against the afterflash, fingers still hooked into the trigger guard. Sarah heard herself screaming.

She had to help, but her gut had turned to water, she would throw up, could not, could not, could not help him.

'This way,' she screamed after what seemed an eternity. It was all she could do. 'For God's sake, towards my voice.'

He turned and stumbled towards her. She saw Brigham's fingers clench spasmodically on the trigger.

'*Stop!*' she screamed. But her words were drowned by the fierce chatter of the rifle.

The bullets laced into El Lobo. His body was thrown up and back, stitched with red, slammed into the plate-glass doors.

'Dear God,' Sarah whispered as she ran back into the anonymity of the carnage. Behind her the engine roared into life, drowning out her words: 'Dear God, it's all my fault.'

'Kill the bitch,' Kevin Brigham says.

Sarah's hand seeks her pocket. She has the megaflash out in one practised movement, finger already on the switch.

Light floods the room.

She turns and sees that Kevin Brigham has his eyes tightly closed. But his gun is raised, fingers squeezing the trigger.

She sees this in a single heartbeat. And she smiles.

'Someone else's problem.' Loric discarded the file with a sense of intense relief. The wretched woman hadn't even been Talented; nothing to do with the Department at all.

Your favourite kind.

'Why not? I've enough of my own.' He yawned again and stretched, considering ways to turn it to his advantage. A Working Party, perhaps; get a little more influence over the Home Office liaison people. It could be done . . .

You should have gone into politics.

'What for?' He was genuinely surprised. Parties and Ministers came and went, but the Civil Service continued to govern unperturbed.

That's what Daddy always said.

'We have to be a bit more subtle about it than he was.' Loric picked up the next file. It was thin and had nothing to show its Department of origin. Just a pair of red rubber-stamped instructions.

EYES ONLY.

DESTROY AFTER READING.

Loric smiled indulgently. The Funny People loved their little games. Maybe it made them feel important.

He shrugged. Might as well see what they'd been up to . . .

PLAYING SAFE

Marcus L. Rowland

———————

That Friday morning I expected to spend a fairly boring day at the office, filling in some reports and fiddling my expenses. A plan that died at nine fifteen, when I was called up to God's fourth-floor office.

'Let me see if I've got this right. Exactly what is it that you want me to do?'

'Discredit Dr Miraculous.'

'Discredit. What the hell does that mean?'

God touched his fingers together, pursed his lips slightly, and said, 'Abase. Degrade. Cast down. Humble. Discredit.' God's name is Dolby, and anyone who makes jokes about stereo should be bloody careful that they don't do it while he's around. The fat bald git is a strong contender for Captain of the All-England Total Bastardy team, and although it didn't officially exist, the organization we both worked for could probably supply most of the other players. He doesn't like me, and the feeling is mutual.

'So you can read a dictionary. Big deal. What the hell has Dr Miraculous done to deserve our attention?'

'The word you were looking for is "thesaurus". A dictionary defines words, a thesaurus provides alternatives. As for Dr Jack Carter, alias Dr Miraculous, he is currently in Britain, and engaged in activities which are contrary to the interests of Her Majesty's Government. He is to be discredited, to the extent of ensuring that his words will

129

not be taken seriously for a few days. He is not to be permanently harmed.'

So what else was new? They'd hardly put us on to him if he was running up a few parking tickets.

'He's an American superhero, a wanker who gets his thrills beating up muggers and running around with his underpants outside his tights. He's got his own TV series, and a bloody comic book. What the hell could he be up to that'll hurt us?'

Dolby dug into a drawer of his desk, pulled out a folder and spent a couple of minutes pointedly ignoring me while he pretended to read it. I looked out of the window, whistling just loud enough to annoy him, and tried to work out if I could justify some leave while the nice weather lasted. Not a hope, I'd already had too much this year. Eventually he decided to acknowledge my presence again.

'As you know, Britain is in the process of finalizing many links with Europe. Dr Carter apparently objects to part of the enabling legislation that will lead to a Common European Policy on Paranorms.'

'He's hardly alone in that. Everyone I know at the DPR reckons that it'll be the biggest cock-up of all time.'

'You talk to the DPR?'

'They're not exactly the KGB, and I was one of the Temps for five years. Why shouldn't I keep in touch with them?'

'And are members of the DPR aware of the function of this office?' Paranoia should be Dolby's middle name. He hated the idea that someone might be talking about him behind his back, and he was terrified that someone might tell the press about our activities.

'Don't be silly. They think I'm working for the Ministry of Agriculture.'

'Why would the Ministry of Agriculture employ anyone with your abilities?'

'I tell them I'm with the corn circle department.'

'Corn circle department . . .? Oh, never mind.' He's slow, but even Dolby eventually notices if you're taking the piss.

'So exactly what has Miraculous been up to?' Second time of asking, maybe this time he'd tell me.

'It appears that he's engaged in political activities. He is lending his name and influence to the, umm' – he glanced down at the file, even though he already knew exactly what it said – 'Paranorm Action Group and making statements to the press. HMG is very disturbed.'

Loosely translated, that means that someone at Number 10 has been on the blower and told him to sort things out or he can forget any chance of a knighthood in the next honours list. Dolby wants a title, and I think he'd strangle his granny to get it.

'What's the Paranorm Action Group? The name rings a vague bell, but I can't place it.'

'The PAG is the organization that fought against compulsory crash helmets for levitating paranorms.'

'Oh, idiots with fractured skulls.'

'Exactly. They claimed that the helmets spoiled their enjoyment and limited visibility.'

'I've never seen the police arrest anyone for breaking that law.'

'I believe that the helmet law is occasionally used to hold suspects when no other charge is available, otherwise it is usually left to the discretion of individual paranorms. Of course, there are only a few levitating policemen, and they do tend to have more important things to do.'

'So why bring it up again now?'

'Apparently there are some objections to the new EEC safety legislation, which will be wider ranging and incorporates stricter penalties.'

'I'd better find out what's going on. It'll be easier to put the boot in if I know exactly why he's interfering. Do you have more details?'

'You'll find everything you need to know at Olympia.'

'What's at Olympia?'

'The annual Health and Safety Exhibition. Here's a pass.'

'Your generosity overwhelms me.'

'Good. Make sure that you keep a record of your expenses.'

He turned to another file. As I was leaving, he looked up and said, 'Oh, by the way, I understand that Carter will be visiting the exhibition this afternoon. Perhaps you could deal with him then. Shut the door as you go out, and don't slam it.'

The DPR has Marcia Jones; we have Mrs Bohl, nicknamed Bohl the Troll, an old bat with a Talent for spotting dodgy receipts. Fortunately there's only one of her, because she makes the Marcias look helpful. As usual she wouldn't let me borrow a car from the pool, and wouldn't issue an advance on expenses, so I ended up taking the train to Olympia.

I popped into a comic shop, picked up the last couple of issues of *Dr Miraculous Monthly* and read them on the tube. They were boring rubbish, with a heavy-handed environmental message in one issue and a totally implausible story about drugs in the other. I'd been wrong about one thing: according to the comic he wore fairly normal clothes, a bit like the uniform the puppets wear in Thunderbirds, and hadn't even got a cloak. Evidently he was a bit of a nonconformist. If the comic wasn't exaggerating his Talent, he was also a tough customer, and I didn't fancy my chances if it came to a direct confrontation.

I reached Olympia just before twelve, and spent a minute watching the crowd outside the exhibition centre. Most looked fairly normal, but a few were wearing costumes, variations on the long underwear and cloaks that most would-be heroes wear. I'd love to know how that style started, it's totally impractical and must be bloody cold nine months out of twelve. I was willing to bet that most of them were unTalented. Someone with a sputtering jetpack flew past, trailing a sign saying END EEC MADNESS NOW. He wasn't wearing a crash helmet. There were a few more pickets on the ground, with signs like PAG NOT EEC and BORN TO BE TALENTED. Their originality underwhelmed me. Someone with a megaphone was shouting, '. . . take away your freedom of choice, your right to decide what to wear. The Eureaocrats want to stifle individualism, and we must stop them now before it's too late. Join the Paranorm Action Group and fight . . .' He turned away from me, and I lost the thread of his message. I had a feeling that I wasn't missing much.

'Oi, you don't want to go in there.' I'd seen the picket before, at a DPR Christmas party, but I couldn't put a name to him. I had a vague idea that his Talent was telepathy with squid, hardly the most useful ability in the middle of Central London. He made a half-hearted effort to stop me going in, but got a nasty shock when he touched my arm. About five thousand volts, to be precise. My Talent is instant static electricity, and it can be useful when people try to crowd me. I can't put out enough power to really hurt anyone, but he lost interest just long enough for me to get through the doors.

The exhibition was fairly full, but not so crowded that I had trouble moving around. I found the government stands on the ground floor. The Health and Safety Executive were there in force, with big displays on chemical safety, waste disposal, groin strain and other exciting topics. When I got there, they were showing a video, a really crappy film about water safety, with someone dressed up as a giant frog pretending to be a paranorm. You'd think they could have found the money to hire the real thing. Never mind, I wasn't there to be a film critic.

The EEC stand was a little smaller. The main exhibit was a row of mannequins festooned with safety equipment; crash helmets, heat-resistant overalls, Kevlar jackets, elaborate visors and goggles, bulky harnesses, and backpacks covered with flashing lights and antennae. There were a lot of people standing around, reading pamphlets and sizing up the equipment, and none of them looked particularly happy. I looked along the rack, picked up one called *Electrical Talents and Safety* and took a quick look. At a first glance it wasn't too unreasonable, though the rubber underwear did sound like it might be a bit uncomfortable and/or extremely kinky.

Something poked me in the back, and an American voice said, 'Sorry, buddy.' I looked around: a cameraman and microphone operator were backing away from one of the displays, too busy filming to notice where they were going. The glare of the lights on the camera hurt my eyes. Under the microphone a uniformed figure was walking along the row of mannequins, looking at the signs and collecting pamphlets. Dr Miraculous. I'd have spotted him earlier if I hadn't been reading. Time to get back to business.

He wasn't quite what I had expected from the magazine pictures. The blond hair was actually light brown, and he looked a little chubbier and a lot shorter. Well under five feet, unless I was mistaken. What the hell was he up to? No one had said anything about cameras.

'Cut.' Another American, this time carrying a clipboard. 'Take ten, while Jack gets changed for the demonstration.'

Miraculous and Mr Clipboard went behind the EEC stand, into a part of the hall that wasn't open to the public. I tried to follow, but yet another American was there to stop me. This one was built like a gorilla, and looked vaguely like one of Miraculous's assistants I'd seen in the comic. If it was the same man, they'd shown him picking up a car, and I didn't fancy trying to get past him.

'Sorry, buddy, the Doc ain't signing no autographs today.'

'What Doc? I'm looking for the bar.' Not the best lie I've ever managed, but it would have to do.

'Sure you are. This part of the hall's closed today, friend. Head down to the left, there's another bar over there.'

'What's going on, then?'

'We're making a documentary.'

'Oh.' I headed off, having seen what I wanted. There was a big van behind the stand, with the CNN news service logo on the sides. It was a complication I could have lived without. I started to look for a phone.

'Well?' asked Dolby.

'Not very. We've got a problem.'

'Go on.' He was using his 'stern but fair' voice, the one that wouldn't fool a five-year-old. Vicious and totally biased is nearer the mark.

'Miraculous is here, all right, but he's got a film crew with him. They're making some sort of news report for satellite TV. Three guesses what it'll be about.'

'I know what it will be about. Why do you think you were sent there? Now, I'm sure that you can arrange for something to go wrong while they are filming; some sort of embarrassing electrical accident, for example –'

'A little static shock isn't going to change anything. Besides, the bastard's probably immune to it.'

'Well I'm sure that you'll think of something.' There was a click as he hung up, and I knew that the unspoken thought was 'You'd better.'

Back at the stand, Miraculous still hadn't emerged. The cameraman was sitting on the edge of the display platform, having a smoke, but the camera was in his lap. I didn't think that there was much chance of getting hold of it for the two or three minutes it would take to fry its electronics. Instead I stood about six feet away, got out a propelling pencil and pretended to make notes on one of the pamphlets, then casually pointed the tip towards the cameraman.

Fortunately the crowd wasn't so dense that anyone was close to me; I had to build up to fifteen or twenty thousand volts for the trick I had in mind. On a damp day it would have been impossible. I could feel my clothes and the hairs on the back of my hands standing out from my skin, repelled by the charge. Little sparks arced between the ends of my eyelashes, but my glasses stopped anyone else from noticing. If I didn't use a little Brylcreem, my hair would have splayed out like a lavatory brush. Meanwhile the sharp metal pencil casing was spraying a stream of ions towards the cameraman. After a while the tiny breeze eddied smoke back into his face, and he started to cough. I'd hoped that he'd end up coughing so badly that he'd drop the camera, but life just doesn't want to co-operate sometimes. He stubbed the fag out and glared at a ventilation fan on a nearby pillar.

Okay, forget that idea. I touched the pencil to a metal waste-bin, to get rid of the charge; two or three people glanced around when they heard the 'crack' as I earthed myself, but so far as I could tell no one noticed that it was me making the noise. It was time to suck a glucose sweet. I burn a lot of calories when I'm working, and that's the quickest way to replace them.

'Look, are you sure I have to wear all this god-damned stuff? It's fucking ridiculous.' Miraculous was back, but he was wearing the silliest outfit I've ever seen. Baggy plastic overalls, a crash helmet, a mirror visor, a big backpack, and thick-soled boots. There was no way I'd get a static charge through that lot.

'It's what the EEC regulations say a guy with your powers should wear,' said Mr Clipboard.

'God-damned assholes. How's a guy supposed tto see where he's going with this crap covering his face?'

'Will you, for Christ's sake, knock it off with the swearing, Jack? This'll be going out on global TV, and they'll refuse to show it if you keep up the bad language.'

'When have I ever let you down, Larry? Just get the fucking camera set up, interview us, then let me get out of this fucking suit before I god-damn melt. And this time I stand on the platform and the EEC guy stands on the floor, he looked about three feet taller than me in the last shot.'

They were setting up for filming again, and I still didn't have any idea what to do about it. Just to add to my woes, a small crowd was forming, attracted by the bright lights and camera; I was near the front, but it wasn't likely that I could stay clear enough to use the pencil trick again. Anything else I tried would have to use low voltages, and that meant very short range.

'Places, everyone.'

Miraculous stepped up on to the stage, next to a bland-looking man wearing an EXHIBITOR badge. They talked for a few seconds, then the exhibitor climbed down, so that his head was only a few inches above the American's. Larry whatever-his-name-was came forward with his clipboard and stood in front of them, facing the camera. 'Olympia, one of London's largest convention centres, is today the scene of an extraordinary dispute between British paranorms and the EEC. It's a dispute that could affect every paranorm who sets foot anywhere in Europe. One American paranorm who is already involved is Dr Jack Carter, better known as Dr Miraculous. With him is Dr Dietrich Gruber of the EEC Paranormal Safety Advisory Committee.'

He stepped back, and the cameraman moved in towards the platform. The sound man swung his microphone over Miraculous, and I realized that I could reach out a hand and touch the end of the metal pole behind his back. I started to build up a quick charge, and lost it as a little boy brushed against my leg. He started crying.

'Cut! Could someone please shut that kid up, we're trying to film here!'

Unfortunately his mother wasn't far away, and a couple of minutes later they were ready to start again. This time I knew roughly what to expect, and had my charge ready as the pole came by. I managed to get in two jolts before he moved away.

'Shit, what the hell was that! Cut it, Larry, I'm getting shocks from the mike, must be a loose connection.' He gingerly put it down and started fiddling with the cables.

'Can we go with radio mikes instead?' Larry asked.

'No, there's too much static in here.'

'Check it out, and for Pete's sake get a move on.'

Miraculous wasn't happy. I could hear mumbles that sounded a lot like swearing. He opened the visor and wiped the sweat from his face with a tissue, then propped himself on the railing around the mannequins.

Hmmm. A chrome railing, but it had clear plastic supports. That meant it wasn't earthed. He was wearing plastic shoes, but his hands were bare and sweaty. One of them was on the railing. Interesting. I moved back a couple of steps and strolled around to the other end of the stand. No one else seemed to be touching the railing, and no one was watching. I put a hand on the rail and tried to build up some voltage, nice and gently. It worked. I must have reached ten thousand volts before I started to feel the charge leaking away, then I just kept it constant until Miraculous got up. He didn't even notice, but I knew that his body had to be charged to five or six thousand volts, and with all the protective gear insulating him the only way to lose the charge was through his hands or his face. Now if he'd only touch something . . . The bastard just stood there with his arms crossed.

Come to think of it, I had a charge of my own to shed. I didn't want to hurt anyone else, especially not where Miraculous might see me. There was no way to get rid of the charge on the railing without someone noticing, but at least I could make myself safe. Fortunately the Olympia halls are steel-framed buildings, and you can always find something earthed if you try. There were too many people near the bin, so I walked further away and touched a fire hydrant. On the way back I got myself an ice-cream.

When I returned, they were just about to start filming again. The sound man had some insulating tape around the pole, so there was no way that I could give him another shock. Dr Miraculous had to be losing charge by the second, and I was out of ideas and feeling lousy. The ice-cream helped a little, and I followed it with another sweet, but I must have shed a lot more energy than I thought when I charged that railing. My Talent wouldn't be good for much for a while.

Larry went through his introduction again, and then went on: 'Dr Miraculous, that isn't your usual costume. Could you tell me why you are wearing all this equipment?'

'I wish I could give you a good reason, but I can't. This junk is what the EEC safety regulations say someone with my powers should be wearing. I don't even know what half of it's for!'

'Dr Gruber,' said Larry, 'we'll get to the doctor's equipment in a moment, but first I'd like you to answer a question that's puzzling me. Your committee is composed entirely of non-paranorms. Why do you feel qualified to advise on their safety?'

'I'm glad you asked me that.' He spoke perfect English, and his smile showed teeth that were a dentist's wet dream. I hated him already. 'We feel that paranorms are too close to their own abilities, too ready to exaggerate their Talents and overlook their human frailties. The committee tries to take a more objective approach, and evaluate risks and the protective equipment needed to handle them safely. After all' – another perfect smile – 'why should someone who fires laser beams from his fingers need less protection than someone who works with an industrial laser system?'

'Couldn't it be argued that you are working from a position of ignorance?'

'It could be argued, but it certainly isn't true.'

'Thank you. Dr Miraculous, you're not an EEC citizen. Why have you become involved in this issue?'

'Well, Larry, I plan to film some episodes of my television series in Europe next year, and by then this equipment may be a legal requirement. I don't accept that it's necessary, I regard it as an infringement of my civil liberties, and I'm not prepared to work under these conditions. If the law changes, we'll have to think about cancelling that part of the series and filming in the USA. I think that I wouldn't be the only American paranorm to pull out of Europe.' He was moving his hands as he talked, but they weren't going near anything that was earthed.

'Dr Gruber, are you concerned about the possibility of a massive withdrawal of American Talents?'

'Europe has its own Talents. While any withdrawal is regrettable, we can undoubtedly manage with our own resources.' He shrugged and spread his hands slightly. And touched Dr Miraculous.

There was a loud crack, and a pretty little blue spark jumped between their hands. The plastic had insulated Miraculous nicely, and he must have still been charged to four or five thousand volts. Gruber was standing on a concrete floor and looked reasonably well earthed. Both of them felt it; Miraculous snatched his hand away, as Gruber shouted, 'Schwein' and punched him on the jaw. It wasn't a particularly hard blow, but Miraculous was off balance and carrying a lot of equipment; he staggered back a couple of paces, then tripped on a wire and fell over. There was a loud hiss, and things started to happen.

They'd certainly given him all the safety gear they could think of. That hiss was air bags inflating, blowing his suit up until he looked like the Michelin Man. Then his backpack got into the act, with flashing strobe lights and the piercing beep-beep noise they use when dust-carts are reversing. There was another hiss, and a cloud of bright green smoke came from a vent. With a loud *whoosh* a couple of signal flares fired from the top of the pack, streaking across the hall and setting fire to a dis-play of overalls. Miraculous lay there, trying to turn over or get up, looking like a tortoise on its back, and swearing so loudly that I could hear him above the noise of the pack. There was another bang, and a panel blew off the pack, turning Miraculous on to his side. A parachute flopped out, and two more flares fired out of the top. I didn't see where they landed.

Gruber ran forward, trying to open a cover on the side of the pack. It squirted him with a stream of fluorescent orange gunge, with a peculiar chemical smell. Shark repel-lent, I think. He reached for the pack again, and finally managed to get the cover open and press a switch. The beeps gurgled and died, the smoke gradually stopped, and the suit started to deflate. Someone in the crowd started to clap, and in a few minutes the hall was echoing to cheers and whistles, and the noise of fire alarms.

Miraculous pulled himself to a sitting position, still swearing, and pulled off the helmet. Larry and Gruber tried to help him up. They got him to his knees, then gorilla-face tried to pull Gruber off. They skidded across the platform, and sprawled in a heap in the puddle of gunge. I couldn't help laughing, and I wasn't alone. All it needed was a custard pie to finish things off, but I didn't have one, and both of them already looked ridiculous enough. There was no way that anyone could take Miraculous seriously after that performance. I edged out of the crowd, out of the hall, and, hopefully, out of the good doctor's life. I'd solved the problem without him even noticing me or having a chance to use his Talents, and that suited me down to the ground.

It wasn't two o'clock yet, and I remembered that there was a reasonably good pub in the neighbourhood, so I had lunch before heading back to the office.

'Okay, I'll accept that you won't pay for ice-cream or the comics. Why the hell can't I have the money for my lunch or the tube fares?'

Bohl the Troll looked smug and said, 'You didn't get a receipt for the tickets, and the receipt you got for the food doesn't give the pub's VAT number.'

'There isn't VAT on food.'

'There is if you eat a prepared meal on restaurant premises.' The cow knew that she had me cold, and there wasn't much that I could do about it. It wasn't really the money, in any case; I just hate to see them get away with anything. She leapt in with the *coup de grâce* before I could think of a reply. 'Oh, I nearly forgot. Mr Dolby said he wanted to see you in his office, as soon as you came in.'

'I've been standing here for fifteen bloody minutes, why the hell didn't you tell me?'

She just sniffed, pressed the intercom button, and said, 'He's on his way up now.'

'Well?' Dolby has never been one to start a conversation by congratulating anyone, no matter how well they've performed.

'Well, what?'

'Well, what? Well, what? Well, what the hell do you think you've been doing?'

'What you bloody told me to do.'

'Really. And how did you accomplish that feat?'

'I made him look like a twit. You should have seen him, lying on his back and wriggling, with all the smoke and fireworks going off around him. It was one of the funniest things I've ever seen.'

'Yes. Very funny. And I'll tell you something even funnier.' He wasn't smiling, and I was starting to get a very bad feeling.

'Yes?'

'He dislocated two intervertebral discs when he fell on the backpack, and he'll be in hospital for at least a week.'

'Great. That ought to keep him out of trouble.'

'Possibly. I should imagine that the lawsuit he's preparing against the Paranormal Safety Advisory Committee will also engage quite a lot of his attention.'

Oops.

'Did it occur to you that you were causing injuries to an internationally famous celebrity on British soil? Did it occur to you that the injuries were a direct result of using EEC equipment, and of a blow struck by an EEC official? Did it occur to you that you have just, single-handedly, put EEC legislation back five years?'

'Oh.'

'You will doubtless be delighted to learn that this operation has not gone unnoticed. I have been ordered to revert to my permanent Civil Service rank, and assigned to one of the Ministries.'

Losing about twenty thousand a year and any hope of a knighthood. What a shame. 'I'm sorry to hear that, sir. We'll all miss you.'

'You won't.'

'I beg your pardon, sir?'

'You're coming with me. The government was not entirely ungrateful for my previous endeavours, and I was given my choice of several assignments. I chose a post at the Ministry of Agriculture. I'm head of the new Crop Damage Investigation Department, and I need a suitable assistant. You've already told me that it's your type of work.'

'I don't quite follow.' Not if I can possibly help it.

'I think you'd better follow, or someone might possibly tell Carter how he came to be electrified. Given the scale of damages he's likely to demand, you'd probably spend the rest of your life paying him off. Then there's the damage to the EEC display, and damage to several other exhibits that were hit by signal flares. I think that the total might reach seven figures.'

'If you put it that way . . . It'll be an honour to carry on working with you, sir.'

'Good. Go down to Mrs Bohl and get her to fill in your transfer form, then report to me on Monday morning with your camping gear.'

'Camping gear?'

'Well, how else are you going to study corn circles? It's not good enough investigating after the event, I want you to be there on the ground when they start to form.'

'But it could take months before I'm in the right place at the right time. Years, even.'

'Yes. It could, couldn't it?' For the first time ever I saw him smile.

The file sailed across the room towards the fireplace, spontaneously combusting as it went. It dropped into the grate like a small stray comet, flared up briefly, then scattered into ash.

Someone else's cock-up. Not immediately useful, Loric thought, but it never hurt to know about them. They could come in handy if you needed a favour. And until he could be sure the Orpington business had blown over for good, he never knew when he might need one in a hurry.

But it wasn't much help in dealing with the Minister tomorrow. He needed something positive to show him. Maybe the next file . . .

He picked it up absently, calling the teapot again. At least this was a DPR file; Marcia's familiar dyslexic typing was on the sticky label, adhering at the usual odd angle to the cover.

Sighing, he tilted his teacup, and turned his attention away from the real world again.

SORTILEGE AND SERENDIPITY

Brian Stableford

Of all the words in all the world, the ones which Simon Sweetland most dreaded to hear were: 'This is Ramsbottom in Accounts. Could you possibly spare me a few minutes to discuss your recent claim for expenses?'

In the eleven years he had worked as a tester for DPR Coventry, Simon had heard those words – *exactly* those words, spoken in exactly the same reedy voice – more than a dozen times, and they had always been a prelude to embarrassment, awkwardness and downright misery. By now he had become conditioned: the moment he heard the fatal syllables, his stomach would contract to the size and texture of a cricket ball, and he would break into a cold sweat.

This time he had known that it was going to happen. In fact he had been apprehensive about the call for two days, since the claim for the Paris trip had gone in. Every time the telephone had rung his symptoms had gone through a rapid ready-steady, poised for 'go', and every time he had heard the soft huskiness of Carol Cloxeter's voice – or even Marcia's petulant whine – instead of the fatal incantation, the abrupt relaxation had left him weak and confused. When he finally heard the words of doom, he was so strung out that he was almost glad to know that the waiting was over.

Almost.

He knew that it was going to be worse this time than

ever before. As he trudged down the stone staircase, wondering at the cruel irony of fate which had located Ramsbottom's lair directly below his own office in the two-storey annexe which Testing and Accounts shared, he wished that he had never accepted the invitation to attend the conference, that the invitation had never been made, that the conference had never been planned, that the United Kingdom had never joined the EEC, that there was no such city as Paris . . .

Ramsbottom was sitting behind his desk as he always was: a tiny ratty little man with an absurd moustache which somehow reminded Simon of Hitler's, H. G. Wells's and Charlie Chaplin's, all rolled into one. When Simon had first seen Ramsbottom many years before, the accountant had been lurking behind massive piles of box-files arrayed like battlements on his desk, but Ramsbottom believed in moving with the times. Nowadays he skulked behind a trio of computer terminals which not only kept the world at bay but bathed his face in an eerie green glow. Although Ramsbottom's office was exactly the same size as Simon's, it seemed much smaller because of the vast stacks of files piled high against every wall; they were all obsolete now that the ingenious Ramsbottom had computerized the entire Midlands Division system (five years ahead of the official time-target), but the DPR, like most branches of the Civil Service, had strong taboos against throwing things away. The hulking masses of ancient paper always made Ramsbottom's den seem dingy and disgusting, although the cleaners presumably went in every morning to give it the despairing stare which was all that NUPE's new demarcation rules permitted them to do.

'Please sit down, Dr Sweetland,' said Ramsbottom. Simon imagined that Torquemada must have used exactly the same tone when inviting his victims to stretch themselves out on the rack.

'There's nothing irregular in our claim,' Simon said pre-emptively, as he took his allotted place. 'All the receipts are there.'

'They are indeed,' Ramsbottom agreed, riffling through the papers in his hand. 'Travel receipts from Thomas Cook, bill for two rooms for five nights at the Hotel Trianon, five restaurant bills, receipts for three journeys by taxi. A very full account of your stay, if I may say so. Very full indeed.'

Simon explained, mostly without being directly asked, why he and Carol had stayed at the Trianon instead of a cheaper hotel (because it was within walking distance of the Sorbonne, where the conference had been held), why he and Carol had taken the taxis instead of using the airport bus or the Métro (problems with timing), and why two of the five restaurant bills were for *à la carte* instead of set meals. He was morally certain that his position was unassailable, and that the very best Ramsbottom could do would be to disqualify a couple of the restaurant bills, but he still felt crushed by the awful pressure of having to justify himself.

'It was an important conference,' he finished lamely. 'The First EC Symposium on Paranormality. It was a great honour to be invited. You must have read the memos London has been sending round about the importance of 1992 and the necessity of thinking European. We were there representing our country.' He threw in the last bit because he suspected that Ramsbottom might be the patriotic type, although it was entirely probable that the accountant's allegiance was to the pound sterling rather than to the Queen. If only Ramsbottom were in charge of the civil list!

'Was it absolutely necessary for Mrs Cloxeter to accompany you to Paris?' Ramsbottom asked, mournfully contemplating the total displayed on his left-hand screen.

'It was a joint paper,' Simon pointed out. 'We were equal co-authors.'

'It may take two people to write a paper,' Ramsbottom observed, lugubriously, 'but it only takes one to read it.'

My God, Simon thought, as the accountant's beady little eyes seared him with disapproval. *He thinks that I took Carol over there for a dirty weekend! He actually thinks we were having it away. And the reason he finds that such an appalling thought is not because Carol's married – it's because he thinks we could have saved on the hotel bill by only booking one room!*

Ramsbottom's suspicion – all the more deadly for being unspoken – made Simon feel horribly guilty, not so much because he and Carol had actually done anything, but rather because he'd spent the greater part of his time in Paris fervently but hopelessly wishing that they might.

'We were both invited,' Simon said as frigidly as he could. 'And we were both given leave to go. I think you'll find that everything is in order.'

Ramsbottom put the receipts down and brought something else out of the mysterious depths behind his high-tech ramparts. Simon recognized it as a copy of the souvenir programme which had been issued to the participants in the conference. It contained heavily abridged versions of all the papers which had been presented – the fuller versions, with the statistical appendices, would appear in a much bulkier volume of *Proceedings* in nine months' time.

'Your contribution to this volume,' said Ramsbottom accusatively, 'is called "Sortilege and Serendipity", I believe.'

'Well,' said Simon warily. 'We actually titled our paper "Experienced Locality Effects and the Inverse Square-law as Key Variables Affecting the Effective Range of Talents for Discovery, and the Significant Differences Pertaining to Sortilege and Serendipity", but the editor felt that the full thing was a bit cumbersome, so he cut it down.'

There was a brief but pregnant silence. It was broken by the sound of a door opening and closing, followed by the sound of footsteps crossing a floor. Simon knew that it was the door to his own office, but curiosity about the identity of the person who had entered (the footfalls had not been those of Carol's high-heeled shoes) was drowned out by painful consciousness of the fact that every day, year in and year out, Ramsbottom could hear every move he made. Simon knew that Ramsbottom *always* stayed late, and therefore always knew to the minute exactly what time he went home. There was no earthly reason why that information should be secret, but somehow it was exceedingly uncomfortable to know that Ramsbottom had it.

'Dr Sweetland,' said Ramsbottom tiredly, 'were you and Mrs Cloxeter *paid* for your contribution to this volume?'

Simon felt his throat go suddenly dry. In all his eleven years with the DPR, it was the first time he had ever been paid for a publication, and he could not help feeling a fit of panic at the horrid thought that he had done something wrong, and that Ramsbottom knew about it. It was pure paranoia, but Ramsbottom always had that effect on him.

'It's allowed,' he said squeakily. 'We don't have to pay it into Department funds. We checked. It's ours. It was only five hundred francs, divided between the two of us.'

'I am aware,' said Ramsbottom frostily, 'that the Department has no *legal* claim on the fee which you and Mrs Cloxeter received for this publication. I merely wondered whether you might not feel a *moral responsibility* to put the fee towards your expenses. As you are well aware, the Department is funded by the *British taxpayers*, and has a *responsibility* to those taxpayers to make absolutely certain that it disperses its funds in an economical and constructive fashion. I merely felt that as a matter of *conscience* and *duty* to the good people of this country that you might feel it *appropriate* to waive a portion of your expenses in recognition of this fee – which you received, after all, as a direct result of your participation in the conference.'

Simon felt that all the slings and arrows of outrageous fortune were being hurled upon him with lethal force and deadly accuracy. Ramsbottom's green-tinged face, with three lighted screens reflected in each dark, accusing eye, seemed absolutely diabolical. He opened his mouth to reply, but no words came.

'Shall I take that as a "yes"?' said Ramsbottom malevolently.

Simon wanted to say 'no'. He wanted to shout, to scream, or to bellow 'no'. He would have given his right arm – or, at any rate, one of his little fingers – for the moral courage to say: 'Damn your eyes, Ramsbottom, if you don't get your sticky sanctimonious paws off my legitimate expenses, I'll feed you feet-first to the shredder.' But it was no good. Even though he was already wondering how he was going to explain it to Carol, he knew that he was beaten. He was not usually an *absolute* coward, but when confronted by Ramsbottom he was a wimp before a weasel, an ant beneath an aardvark's snout.

When he finally managed to persuade his larynx to unfreeze, all that came out was a strangled 'Awk!'

'Thank you, Dr Sweetland,' said Ramsbottom. 'I knew that we could get things straightened out, with a little good will on both sides. At heart, you see, we're both men of good conscience.' The accountant never even smiled. In all the eleven years he had known him, Simon had never once seen Ramsbottom smile, even in victory.

*

When he staggered back into his own office, Simon was momentarily startled to find someone sitting in the chair where loving parents usually sat while watching their offspring strut their stuff. The traumatic effects of Ramsbottom's *coup* had driven the little mystery of who had gone into his office clean out of his mind.

Simon quickly controlled his momentary alarm. The man looked utterly nondescript and quite harmless. His placid, clean-shaven features were far less menacing than Ramsbottom's, and he wore a neat grey gabardine raincoat of a distinctly unfashionable type.

The visitor came swiftly to his feet as Simon crossed to the desk, extending an ID card which he had evidently been holding in readiness for the moment of presentation. Simon took it, read it and gasped. Appearances were, it seemed, deceptive. The ID revealed that his visitor was Inspecteur de la Sûreté Jean Croupion, on secondment to the Marseilles division of Interpol. Simon had never seen an Interpol ID card before, and he was appropriately impressed. He conscientiously checked the photograph to make sure that it fitted the face of the man who stood before him.

'Monsieur Sweetland?' said Croupion in a tone which sounded all the more conspiratorial for being strongly accented.

'I'm Dr Sweetland,' Simon confirmed. The other appeared to be waiting for something, but it took several seconds before the penny dropped. 'Oh, sorry,' he said, fumbling for his wallet, where he kept his own ID. The after-effects of his meeting with Ramsbottom combined with his present embarrassment to make him drop the wallet. His ID card fell out, along with his Access card and his public library borrowers' card. Croupion bent down to recover them for him, glancing at them as he handed them back.

'Is not zat I doubt you,' he said softly. 'But zese days, one 'as to be careful, and zis is a matter of ze utmost delicacy. May I presume zat you 'ave signed what zey call in your country ze Official Secrets Act?'

'Of course I have,' Simon told him. '*Everybody* in the Scientific Civil Service has to sign the Official Secrets Act.'

'Zen I must tell you zat everyzing which passes between us is to be kept in ze strictest confidence. It is not merely ze security of Angleterre which is at stake, but ze security of all Europe. I am investigating a crime of formidable dimension.'

Just as Croupion finished his melodramatic announcement there was a knock on the door, and Simon jumped, almost dropping his wallet for a second time. Carol Cloxeter came in without waiting for an answer, as she always did when she knew that he didn't have any testing appointments. Croupion's right hand made a nervous gesture in the direction of his left armpit, but the move was quickly stilled.

'It's okay,' Simon assured the Interpol man. 'This is my assistant, Carol Cloxeter.' *Who presumably wants to know*, he added silently, *how I got on with the repulsive Ramsbottom.*

'Ah, but of course!' Croupion said. 'The co-author of your excellent paper on sortilege and serendipity!'

Simon blinked, not knowing whether to feel extremely flattered or slightly worried. He and Carol had experienced some difficulty in France because the French language had no word for serendipity, and the French word *sortilège* had such broad connotations that it tended to be almost synonymous with *magic* rather than referring narrowly to Talents for finding things, as it had conventionally come to do in the pages of the British *Journal of Paranormal Studies.* If Croupion was here to find out whether Simon and Carol could help Interpol solve some particularly heinous crime, he might well be labouring under some sort of delusion.

'I'm afraid that the short version isn't as clear as it might be,' Simon said quickly. 'Although the case-studies we cited involved some fairly Talented youngsters, the whole point of our investigation was that they could only find things *in Coventry*. Most of the kids we test can only find things in the street where they live. We really aren't in a position to help track down international jewel-thieves or drug-smugglers. Surely External Relations explained that to you.'

'Monsieur Sweetland,' said the man in the gabardine, putting a reassuring hand on Simon's shoulder, 'I 'ave not talked to your External Relations. I 'ave come straight to you. No one must know I am 'ere, or zat I 'ave been 'ere. Zat is most vital. What I am looking for is in Coventry – I am certain of zat. I 'ave read your paper most carefully, and it 'as given me new 'ope. Zis boy you refer to, 'oom you call *sujet Ash* . . . I zink 'e is perfect for my purpose. I *must* see 'im.'

It took Simon fully ten seconds to works out that *sujet Ash* was French for Subject H. 'But that's young Tommy Ferris,' he blurted out. 'The Phone Freak Kid.' In saying this, he casually broke all the Department's rules about confidentiality and violated all the conventions regarding the use of derogatory nicknames. Tommy Ferris's name had that effect on him – the child was a tester's nightmare, always throwing in fake and supposedly funny answers in order to wind people up. That was hard enough to tolerate in people with Talents which might one day prove useful, but in Tommy's case it was particularly vexing because his Talent had always seemed virtually useless, all the more so because the wild-goose chases on which he delighted to send the people who were sent to check out his claims could be very time-consuming.

Tommy's Talent was one of the silliest Simon had ever encountered. If you gave him the receiver of any telephone in Coventry, and a local street map, he could unerringly find the present location of – but could not actually identify by name – every single person who had used the phone in the previous ten days, provided that they were still in the city. If he had only been able to recall the substance of their conversations, or even if he had been able to operate anywhere outside his home town, there might have been a role for him to play in the Department's activities, but as things stood there seemed little future for the lad except for tracking down the occasional dirty phone-caller. Tommy would probably be taken on to the books when he was old enough, provided that his Talent hadn't vanished with the onset of puberty, but the chances of ever finding him a useful job to do had seemed remote.

'He can't locate the users of *any* telephone,' Simon said, certain that the Interpol man must be labouring under a misapprehension. 'Beyond a seven-mile radius of his home his Talent suffers a steep decline in effectiveness. And the people he locates have to be within the same seven-mile radius. Our paper argues that the seven-mile limit results from a combination of his familiarity with the actual places involved and an inverse-square effect like that governing such field-effects as gravity. Maybe when he's older he can relocate to somewhere more interesting, but transplanted Talents of this general kind don't usually recover their original power and accuracy.'

'Ze man we are after is in Coventry,' said Croupion confidently. 'And we know for a fact that 'e 'as used a particular public telephone. We 'ave traced 'is calls, but 'e is a clever devil – 'e uses ze phone only to emit a signal which triggers . . . but I cannot reveal zat. You must take me to *sujet* Ash wizout delay. It is of ze utmost importance.'

'Well,' said Simon dubiously, wondering what possible interest Interpol could have in phone calls made from a public phone in Coventry. 'Tommy isn't actually a Temp, you know. He's too young. We do call on the services of juvenile Talents when it's absolutely necessary, but the Department rules are very strict about chaperoning.'

'I understand zis,' said Croupion, who was beginning to show distinct signs of exasperation. 'Per'aps you or zis charming lady will volunteer to be *le chaperon*. Zis is a matter of great urgency. More zan life and death is at stake – it is a matter of *international relations*. All Europe will have cause to zank *sujet* Ash, if he can tell us what we need to know, I promise you zat.'

'Will there be any expense involved?' asked Simon warily, with a guilty sidelong glance in Carol's direction.

'Absolutely not,' said the inspector. 'I 'ave 'ired a car. No problem.'

Even Carol had now begun to show signs of impatience. 'I'll do it,' she said. 'I've got no appointments, and I can handle Tommy.'

Simon blushed at the accuracy of her divination. His hatred of practical jokes was such that he would be very happy if he never again clapped eyes on Tommy Ferris as long as he lived. Carol knew that – as, of course, did Tommy, who had naturally added Simon to his list of favourite targets.

'Oh, all right, then,' he said. He added with as much sarcasm as he could muster, 'Give my regards to Tommy.'

'All Europe would zank you, Monsieur Sweetland,' Croupion assured him, 'if zey knew what you 'ad done for zem. If you please, Madame Cloxeter ...' He was already holding the door open for her.

Simon stood still for a while after they had gone,

wondering what on earth was going on. He wished that he could have demanded a fuller explanation, but he knew that it would have been futile. He was used to operating on a 'need-to-know' basis, and what his employers generally felt he needed to know was nothing at all. It was perfectly normal for him to be kept in the dark, and there was no use resenting the fact. But he *did* resent it.

He went to the window and looked out over the car-park. He saw Croupion and Carol get into a big black BMW with a yellow Hertz sticker in the corner of the rear windscreen. Belatedly, he began to wish that he had not allowed the thought of dealing with Tommy Ferris to put him off. An Interpol investigation was probably the most exciting thing which would happen all year.

So far, he thought, *this has been an absolute bitch of a day.*

Absurdly mindful of Ramsbottom's ears, he tiptoed back to his desk. Mercifully, the floors were solid enough to keep his conversations one hundred per cent confidential, and he supposed that had to count as a blessing. He settled back in his chair and unfolded his copy of the *Guardian*, deeply grateful that he had no appointments before lunch-time.

Simon had hardly finished page one when his phone rang. He picked it up with some trepidation, still thinking about the wretched Ramsbottom. But the voice he heard was a booming baritone.

'Sweetland? Tarquin here. I wonder if you could pop over to External Relations for a moment. Got some chaps here from Interpol, no less. Seem to think you might be able to help them.' The voice somehow managed to imply that such a possibility lay far beyond the bounds of plausible imagination. Roland Tarquin, Simon knew, was the Birmingham-based Deputy Director of the entire Midlands Division; he had never met the man and felt slightly needled by the tone of contemptuous familiarity.

'That's okay,' said Simon, languidly exercising the noble art of one-upmanship, 'I've just been chatting with Inspector Croupion. Carol and I were able to steer him in the right direction. Everything's under control.'

There was a momentary silence at the other end, then the dull sound of a hand being placed over the mouth-piece. He heard the Deputy Director speak to someone near by, but couldn't hear what was said. Then the phone went dead. He shrugged his shoulders, replaced his own receiver and picked up the newspaper again.

He was just turning over to page two when the door of his office opened explosively, and two excessively athletic men hurtled in, diving to either side of the door as they did so. Their arms were extended stiffly before them, and in their hands they held automatic pistols.

'Holy shit!' said Simon, dropping the *Guardian* on the floor. He had not intended to say the words aloud, but they seemed to echo from the walls.

Slowly, the two men lowered their guns and raised themselves from the threatening crouches which they had reflexively assumed. They seemed disappointed and faintly disgusted.

'It's all clear, sir!' one of them called out.

After a moment's pause two other men came in. One was short and tubby, and had to be Roland Tarquin. The other was tall and broad and looked as if he could bend iron bars with his teeth. 'Where is he?' asked the big man shortly. He spoke with a faint accent, which seemed to Simon to be German. Simon nearly said 'Who?' but he overcame the reflex, realizing that the answer was obvious. He felt a sudden desperate desire not to look like a fool.

'He's gone,' he said. 'About twenty-five minutes ago. Is something wrong?'

Roland Tarquin looked up at the ceiling, rolled his eyes and groaned theatrically.

'Describe him,' commanded the tall man.

Simon knew by now that he had done something terribly wrong and struggled to make amends. 'Er . . . average height and build,' he stuttered, trying desperately to remember. 'Very noticeable French accent . . . apart from that, rather . . . well, very ordinary.'

The tall man muttered something that sounded like *strunz*. 'Chameleon,' he said to one of the gunmen.

'Dr Sweetland spends his entire life testing for Talents,' said the Deputy Director sarcastically. 'You can't expect him to detect one when he isn't carrying his Zener cards.'

Simon thought that was terribly unfair. The whole point about human chameleons was that they blended in – appearance-wise, at least.

'He was wearing a gabardine raincoat,' he said. 'That won't blend in terribly well with the midday shopping crowd. And he's driving a black BMW with a Hertz sticker in the rear window.'

The tall man raised a half-respectful eyebrow. 'Licence number?' he asked hopefully.

'Didn't notice,' Simon admitted. 'But you can probably get it from Hertz. He's gone to see one of our testees – Tommy Ferris. I take it that he *isn't* from Interpol.'

'You take it right, Dr Sweetland,' said Tarquin, while the tall man gestured to one of his henchmen. The henchman exited, presumably to call Hertz. The tall man turned back, opening his mouth to ask another question, but Tarquin was by now in full theatrical flow: 'You said that you have been – *chatting* was the word, wasn't it? – with this impostor, and that you *steered him in the right direction*?' He seemed to be laying the groundwork for a full-blown scapegoating exercise.

'He showed me his ID,' Simon protested.

The tall man produced an ID card of his own. The photograph was not a good likeness. It identified him as Commander Dieter Lenz. 'Like this?' he asked.

'Pretty much,' said Simon.

'Did you make any attempt to verify it?'

'No. How was I supposed to do that?'

'I suppose, Dr Sweetland,' said Tarquin nastily, 'that it didn't occur to you that an *authentic* Interpol agent would go through the proper channels instead of approaching you directly.'

'Actually,' said Simon defensively, 'no.'

The Director opened his mouth to speak again, but Lenz held up his hand. 'Never mind that,' he said. 'French accent, you say? Genuine, do you think?'

'It sounded genuine,' said Simon, suddenly wondering whether it had been just a little too much like a caricature.

'Probably Union Corse,' said Lenz, speaking to the remaining gunman, who had come forward to stand beside him.

'Or some Mafioso who thinks it's witty to *pretend* to be Union Corse,' said the gunman. 'Or maybe a hitman for the gnomes.'

Simon stared at them, wondering if he had somehow strayed on to the set of a surreal comedy film.

'What exactly did you tell him?' asked Lenz. 'And what's the address he went to?'

'I told him that *sujet Ash* – I mean Subject H – was Tommy Ferris. He went to see Tommy, and Carol went with him to act as chaperone.'

Lenz looked completely blank. 'Subject H?' he repeated uncomprehendingly.

'That's right. In "Sortilege and Serendipity" – our paper.'

'What the hell are sortilege and serendipity?' demanded

Tarquin with unreasonable asperity. The Deputy Director was evidently not academically minded.

'They're the names that British parapsychologists have given to two different sorts of Talent,' Simon explained. 'Sortilege is the class of Talents which involves finding things by some kind of direct association of ideas or goal-orientated searching, while serendipitous Talents are more perverse – people gifted with serendipity can only find things when they're *not* actually looking for them.'

'And you have written a paper on this subject?' asked Lenz.

'That's right. We presented it in Paris a couple of weeks ago at the EEC Symposium.'

'And Subject H?'

'That was one of the case-studies we cited. Tommy Ferris. He has this knack for locating people who've used telephones. Put a receiver in his hand and give him a map, and he's dynamite – provided that the phone and the person he's trying to locate are within seven miles of his home, give or take a few hundred yards.'

While he was speaking, Simon saw looks of comprehension dawn on the four grim faces arrayed before him. 'You *publish* these things?' said the gunman incredulously. 'You shout them from the top of the Eiffel Tower? Are you mad?'

Lenz gestured impatiently. 'We should have known this,' he said. 'We should not have had to rely on good luck – and it *was* good luck, was it not? When I asked your Director and his Mission Controllers whether any of the Temps on your books could help us, they spent fully half an hour making stupid suggestions. If it had not been for that stupid secretary coming in with some irrelevant message about your expenses, it would never have occurred to me to wonder whether your expertise as a tester might be worth consulting. We may have missed this enemy agent, but we must count ourselves lucky that we discovered his existence at all – what was that word again? The word you used to describe such coincidences?'

'Serendipity,' said Simon dully. It had just dawned on him that Carol might be in danger. The man she was with was not an Interpol agent at all, and whatever he was, he was the kind of person that real Interpol agents went after with their guns at the ready.

'We may yet be able to trap him,' said Lenz. 'The address, please, to which he has gone.'

'I can call in the local police,' said Tarquin helpfully, while Simon tapped the keyboard of his desktop terminal, instructing it to call up the Ferris file.

'No,' said Lenz quickly. 'The man is too dangerous, and the matter is too delicate. Special Branch only may be involved, and only on a "need-to-know" basis.'

Simon sighed with relief as the computer displayed Tommy Ferris's record. The system had been remarkably well behaved of late, since the loathsome Ramsbottom had condescended to lend his expertise to the removal of some awkward bugs.

'No. 13 Corporation Road,' he said. 'I'll come with you. I know where it is.'

'No,' said Lenz. 'You stay here. I mean *here*. This office.' He had already turned on his heel, and his remaining henchman hurried to open the door for him.

'But . . .' Simon began.

'No buts, Sweetland,' said Tarquin acidly, remaining where he was while Lenz and his two companions left. 'If this operation goes awry, I want you here for ritual disembowelling.' The voice rose in volume as the three men departed, but once they were out of earshot it sank again to a whisper. 'You'd better pray that your stupidity doesn't land me in hot water, Sweetland,' the Deputy Director said, leaning forward to make his point. 'If there's any comeback on this, from London or Brussels, your neck is the one that's going to be on the chopping block. Savvy?'

'But . . .' Simon began again.

'No buts,' the Director repeated. 'You can consider yourself under office arrest until further notice.' And with that, he turned on his heel and marched out.

Simon knew that there was no use trying to demand an explanation. Even if the Deputy Director knew what was going on, he certainly wouldn't pass on the information. The fact that he would never even be told why his career had gone down the toilet, if indeed that was to be the outcome of his innocent mistake, added an abundance of insult to the probability of injury. For the moment his resentment of Roland Tarquin even outweighed his resentment of the appalling Ramsbottom.

It was not merely a bitch of day, he decided, but an absolute double-dyed bugger of a day – possibly the worst in his entire life. And it wasn't even half past eleven yet.

Staggered by shellshock, and for want of something better to do, he picked up his newspaper. He tried to resume where he'd left off, but his heart simply wasn't in it. He speculated furiously, instead, as to what could possibly be in Coventry that would interest not only Interpol but also the Union Corse – whoever *they* were – and the Mafia. It was obviously something that involved making telephone calls, to *trigger* something . . . and it was apparently something that was important enough to make gnomes hire a hitman . . .

His mind slowly boggled, in its own quiet and relatively dignified fashion.

Then the phone rang again, and when he picked it up

his confusion rapidly increased by several more orders of magnitude.

'Monsieur Sweetland,' said a soft, accented voice which somehow sounded almost reverent. 'Are you playing games wiz me?'

'Certainly,' said Simon bitterly. 'Playing games with fake Interpol operatives is my favourite hobby.' It was not until he had said it that he realized, uncomfortably, that the powers that be might think it very undiplomatic of him to let Croupion know that he had been rumbled. For a moment he felt guilty, but only for a moment. *If they keep me in the dark*, he thought, *they can't expect me to produce the right answers off the cuff.*

'I 'ave to 'and it to you,' said Croupion wonderingly. 'You are ze coolest customer I 'ave ever dealt with. Eizer zat, or ze craziest. Why did you no' place an ad in ze *Times*, hein? Why do you lay down zis silly patchwork of clues? I admit it, I am ver' confused. But now we know one anozer, oui? You want me to make you an offer, n'est-ce pas?'

Simon stared at the receiver, utterly bewildered. 'What kind of offer?' he said, because he simply did not know what else to say.

'Your assistant, she is ver' surprised,' the voice continued. 'Eizer she is great actress, or she 'ad no idea what *sujet Ash* would tell me. She says she is not your accomplice, and I am inclined to believe her . . . but I must keep her wiz me, must I not? Until we can meet, and settle zis matter. I do not understand zis game we are playing, mon ami, but we are ver' reasonable men. We can give you ze protection you need, and anyzing you desire. Zat is what you want, no?'

It dawned on Simon, slowly and painfully, that Tommy Ferris must have told Croupion that he, Simon, was the person that Croupion was trying to identify. It was just the kind of stroke the little bastard would pull. The idea of feeding duff information to a person with a funny accent was exactly the sort of thing that would tickle his fancy, and the idea of fingering Simon Sweetland must have seemed absolutely perfect to the brat. If Carol had tried to explain, the man who wasn't from Interpol had obviously not believed her.

But what on earth was it, Simon wondered, that Croupion thought that he had done? Exactly what sort of skulduggery was involved here? How much trouble was he in? Ought he to try to explain that Tommy was just playing silly buggers, or what?

He decided to play it cool – or, at any rate, as cool as he could. 'Who, exactly, is *we*?' he asked warily.

'Who do you zink?' countered Croupion equally warily.

Simon studied the cracks in his office ceiling, considered the situation as carefully as he was able, then shrugged his shoulders and thought *what the hell*. 'I figure that you're probably Union Corse,' he said casually. 'Unless you're Mafia putting on a funny accent to confuse us all. Or maybe – just maybe – you're a hitman for the gnomes.'

Croupion laughed. 'So you *do* know the score, Monsieur Sweetland – or should I say, *Monsieur Taxman*. Don't worry, mon ami, we always prefer talking to shooting. You 'ave made your point, I zink. Say ze word, an' you are on our team. You must tell me where ze money is, of course ... a matter of good faith, comprenez? An' you must tell me jus' what your Talent *is* ... but then everyzing will be on ze table. You only 'ave to name your terms.'

'Where exactly are you?' Simon asked, trying to sound casually confident, like a man in complete control of his destiny. 'We have to discuss this face to face ... man to man. Do you want to come back here?'

'I don't zink so,' said the man, whose name was presumably not Croupion at all. 'I zink you better come to me, hein? I will meet you in ze Cazedral, if you please. Madame Cloxeter and Tommy will be not with me, so we can 'ave a cosy chat. But if anyzing should go wrong . . . I must 'ave a little insurance, comprenez? If anyzing should happen to me . . . somezing also will happen to zem. We are men of ze world, are we not? We understand zese things?'

It was on the tip of Simon's tongue to blurt out a confession of his complete and utter *lack* of understanding, but he kept himself in check. It was far too late for that.

'I'll be there,' he promised.

He waited to hear the click at the other end before he put his own receiver down. Only then did he permit himself the luxury of panicking at the thought of what he had done.

His first impulse, on realizing that he had thrown himself in at the deep end without knowing whether or not he could swim, was to call the Deputy Director and ask how he could get in touch with Lenz, but he quashed it. It wasn't so much the thought that if Lenz and his friends showed up at the cathedral Croupion would simply fade into the background and might then carry out the threat he had made against Carol, though that was certainly an uncomfortable thought; it was more his resentment of the fact that everyone had been, and still remained, so absolutely determined not to tell him what was going on. He wanted desperately to find out what he'd got caught up in, and he felt that whatever happened from now until midnight, the day couldn't possibly get any worse than it already was.

And when I have found out, he thought, *I'll kill that little bastard Tommy Ferris. I'll teach the little sod not to play his stupid practical jokes on me.*

*

Simon had never liked Coventry Cathedral. In fact he didn't like cathedrals in general. They seemed to him to reek of the Middle Ages: of the burning of witches and the vile tyranny of sanctity. Nor were they particularly convenient as meeting-places. Easy to locate they might be, but once inside there were too many little coverts and too many stone pillars. He wandered round for several minutes, wishing that he had at least the glimmer of a Talent for sortilege, knowing that he had no chance whatsoever of recognizing Croupion's face. After ten minutes of expecting a tap on the shoulder, however, he spotted a gabardine raincoat in a quiet side-chapel.

The chameleon was slumped quietly in one of the stalls in which the landed gentry had once been privileged to sit. At first Simon thought that the Frenchman had simply become tired of waiting and had closed his eyes for a moment, but as soon as he touched the shoulder of the gabardine raincoat he knew that what was beneath it was inert.

Somebody tapped him gently on the back of the neck with something cold and hard and metallic. He had no trouble at all deducing that it must be a gun.

'Lenz?' he said hopefully.

'Not so loud,' whispered a cultured voice, with just the hint of an accent. Simon couldn't quite place it – it wasn't Italian or French, although it just might have been German. Could this, he wondered, be the hitman for the gnomes?

He turned around slowly. The man threatening him with the pistol was not one of Lenz's men, nor was he a chameleon. He was slender, blond and outrageously handsome.

'He's not dead,' said the man with the gun, reaching into Simon's inside jacket pocket in order to remove his wallet. 'Just sleeping. I probably hit him a bit too hard, but one has to be careful.' Simon waited patiently while his Access card, his Switch card, his DPR ID card, his public library borrower's card and his organ-donor's card were carefully inspected. He hoped that he wasn't going to need the last one in the near future.

'A DPR scientist,' mused the blond man. 'It makes sense, I suppose, that the Taxman would hold some such post. Do you work solo, or have you a little team of Talents at your disposal?'

'I have a team of Talents,' Simon said. 'Kids mostly, but top class. A lot of kids have raw Talent in abundance, but they don't have the brains to apply it, so they need a Fagin-figure like me. They're very protective too. Every word we say is being monitored, and I've got PKs with power enough to make you eat that gun. I only pass the duds on to the Temp register, you see – I keep all the best ones for my own private practice, as the Taxman.'

He rather enoyed spinning out the fantasy. Although he was making it up as he went along, it sounded like a really good idea. He wondered why he'd never thought of doing something of the sort. Probably because kids with Talent were mostly a bunch of delinquent no-hopers, like Tommy Ferris.

The blond man put his gun away and looked at Simon quizzically.

'Very good, Dr Sweetland,' he murmured. 'But we live in a world of competing philosophies. Some organizations send out chameleons to do their dirty work, others send out martial arts experts . . . and others send out lie-detectors.'

'Ah,' said Simon, feeling slightly foolish.

'Bruno Wyss,' said the other, holding out his hand to be shaken. 'At least, that's what it says on my passport. Wyss with a *y*, not an *ei*. After the writer, you know.'

Simon inclined his head towards the unconscious

Croupion. 'I suppose you wouldn't care to tell me who he really is?' he asked hopefully.

'He's pretending to be Mafia pretending to be Union Corse,' said Wyss, sitting down in the stall behind Croupion and gesturing an invitation to Simon to join him. 'Actually, it's a double bluff. He really *is* Union Corse.'

'Exactly what *is* the Union Corse?' asked Simon.

Wyss clucked his tongue. 'You really are out of your depth, Dr Sweetland. The Union Corse is a semi-mythical organization, much like the Mafia, which runs all the rackets in the South of France. They supposedly originated in Corsica and now base most of their operations in Marseilles.'

'Semi-mythical?' Simon queried.

Wyss smiled. He had perfect pearly-white teeth. 'Every petty bully-boy from Perpignan to Monaco claims to belong to it in order to make himself seem more dangerous. Because of that, the real members can claim that it's only a legend. But it isn't, as our friend the Taxman clearly knows.'

'You don't happen to know where Carol is, I suppose?' said Simon. 'Carol Cloxeter – my assistant. He . . . sort of kidnapped her. There's a boy with her – I suppose we'd better rescue him too, if we can.'

'All in good time,' said Wyss. 'But I thought sortilege was supposed to be *your* strong point. Isn't that why our friend sought you out? I was following him, as you must have guessed. Such a pity that chameleons can't make their clothes blend in as readily as their faces, isn't it? What exactly are you doing here, Dr Sweetland? Didn't he get enough information from you when he called at your office?'

Simon had met lie-detectors before, and knew that the best way to deal with them was steadfastly to ignore their questions. 'Actually, sortilege is just a sideline,' he said conversationally. 'I only went into it because I got into a bit of trouble with my *last* line of research. Anyway, I just try to make up theories about it. I can't actually *do* it. I thought I couldn't do serendipity either, but serendipity is one of those Cinderella Talents that people don't necessarily notice. Two hours ago I was of the opinion that today's big drama would be losing out on my expenses, but now I seem to have discovered something much more exciting. You *are* the hitman for the gnomes, aren't you, Mr Wyss?'

'That's not the way we do business in Zurich, Dr Sweetland,' Wyss told him, his blue eyes radiating injured innocence. 'We treat all our customers with respect — even the Union Corse. I have not the slightest interest in eliminating the Taxman. Whether he's Talented, or merely talented, he has skills which might be invaluable to us. The best poachers always make the best game-keepers.'

Simon had to remind himself sternly that however personable and amiable Wyss might be, his was not the side of the angels. Dieter Lenz and the men from Interpol were the guys with the badges. But that old cat-killer, curiosity, was still clawing away inside.

'How much has the Taxman managed to rip off?' Simon asked.

'It's not the quantity,' Wyss told him sternly, 'it's the principle. We're supposed to offer total security. Absolute confidence is necessary in our kind of work. It was different in the days when money was yellow metal locked away in iron-clad vaults, ever ready to be weighed and counted. Now it's just data — numbers which change constantly and move around the world in the blink of an eye — the electronic vaults which protect it have to be stronger by far than those old iron-clad monsters. Anyone who can get into our vaults threatens the entire system of world finance, and it doesn't really matter whether he fancies himself as some kind of Robin Hood, stealing from organized criminals and leaving his calling card behind – he has to be stopped. We have to get the money back, and we have to find out how he took it, and we have to make sure that no one else gets in the same way.'

Simon mentally collated this information with the other hints he had already picked up. 'Your thief uses some kind of computer programme – like a virus,' he said. 'You don't know how he gets it into the system, but you know when it's activated. So you were able to find out that the trigger signal came from Coventry.'

'From the central library, to be exact,' said Wyss. 'The real trouble is that we can't figure out where the money *went*. Arranging a transfer is one thing – finding an undetectable hole in which to stash millions is quite another. We really need to know how his clever little programme managed that.'

Simon was still working things out in his head. 'You must have traced at least three calls,' he said. 'That's how Croupion was able to get Tommy to sort out the particular caller he wanted from all the others. Unfortunately, Tommy took it into his head to play one of his little jokes and landed himself – not to mention Carol and me – in deep trouble. Croupion had already checked my ID, exactly as you did – he'd seen my library card, and that had planted the seed which allowed him to believe Tommy's lie.' He stopped abruptly, remembering what he'd scrupulously reminded himself not to do.

'So *that's* why you're here,' said Wyss in a satisfied tone. 'Poor Croupion! So, if we can lay our hands on your small friend, and ask him who *really* made the calls, he can tell us. Fortunately, he won't be able to tell *me* any lies.'

Simon cursed silently, but not because of what he'd

already given away. He felt a sick sensation gripping his stomach. He realized what safety there had been in ignorance, because he also realized that he was no longer ignorant. Now, for the first time, he had a secret to keep – and he was sitting beside a lie-detector who, for all his affability and willingness to chat, was probably not a very nice man.

Wyss moved as if to leave but hesitated. He regarded Simon contemplatively, as if wondering whether to take him along or leave him behind in the same sorry state as Croupion.

'Why do you call him the Taxman?' Simon asked, hoping to gain time to think and consider his own options.

'It's the calling card he leaves,' said the man from Zurich, absent-mindedly. 'Whenever he's moved the money out of an account, our machines – and the customer's – print out a statement which declares the account empty and bears, in ludicrously large letters, the words: YOU HAVE JUST BEEN VISITED BY THE TAXMAN.'

'And you don't actually know whether he's using some kind of Talent, or whether he's just an expert hacker?'

'Talents always seem to lag a little behind the times,' said Wyss philosophically. 'But they catch up, don't they? Now we have computers, those people who have a Talent for messing them up will start to discover the fact. How many people, do you suppose, have lived and died without ever finding out what their Talents were simply because the scope for exercising them wasn't yet there?' While he spoke he leaned forward and started rummaging through Croupion's pockets. Simon guessed that he was looking for the keys to the BMW, which was illicitly parked in a reserved space just outside the cathedral. He wondered whether he dared make a grab for the gun, and decided that he didn't.

'Carol Cloxeter thinks that everybody's Talented,' Simon told him. 'She thinks consciousness itself is a paranormal phenomenon. She thinks the things we call Talents are just idiosyncratic glitches and trivial side effects of a miraculous process that we simply take for granted. She thinks that the natural process of mental evolution will eventually give all our children's children competent powers of telepathy and psychokinesis.'

'And sortilege,' added Wyss, as he discovered the keys in the unconscious man's trousers. 'Don't forget sortilege and serendipity.'

'If we all had that,' Simon said thoughtfully, 'we'd never lose anything, would we? You'd know where all this stolen money had been moved to – we'd *all* know.'

'And we'd be able to find the Taxman just by wondering where he was,' Wyss agreed, standing up to go. 'A dull world, don't you think?'

In front of them Jean Croupion suddenly shifted his position and groaned. The rifling of his pockets had obviously jarred him back to the edge of consciousness.

Wyss seemed momentarily uncertain what to do, but then he took out a second pistol from the pocket of his jacket and handed it to Simon. Simon accepted it, wide-eyed with astonishment. 'Lest you become confused or over-optimistic,' Wyss said, his whisper becoming even more conspiratorial, 'the one you've got is the one I took off *him*, and carefully unloaded. The one I have *is* loaded.' With that parting shot, he slipped out of the stall and moved stealthily into the shadows, leaving Simon face to face with the awakening racketeer.

Simon had only a second or two to think before Croupion fully recovered consciousness, and he spent the time as best he could. By now, thanks to a fortuitous convergence of sortilege and serendipity, he had found out almost everything. He knew who Wyss was and who

Croupion was. He could make a very good guess as to where Carol and Tommy were. Most important of all, he knew who the Taxman was. There was a slight possibility that Dieter Lenz didn't yet know where he and Croupion were, but it was only slight. Even Special Branch, unaided by any particular Talent, ought to be able to locate a car that was parked outside the cathedral.

Croupion looked up at him distastefully. As he raised himself up and straightened the collar of his raincoat, the agent of the Union Corse said: 'You didn't have to 'it me, mon ami. I really wasn't going to kill you.'

'Maybe,' said Simon. 'But when you work for the Union Corse, you have to expect that people will be a little reluctant to trust you.'

'It really doesn't make any difference zat you 'ave ze gun,' said Croupion, probably speaking more truly than he knew. 'You wanted to be found, n'est-ce pas? You knew zat sooner or later you would 'ave to talk to *some-one*.'

'Where's Carol?'

'Who cares? Where is ze money? Zat is what matters.'

'You're wrong,' Simon told him. 'I don't give a damn about the money. The money is irrelevant. But I care about Carol.' It was true – every word. The thought that Wyss, if he were still around, would *know* it was true somehow made him feel proud, though he wasn't sure exactly why.

Croupion was studying him carefully, and Simon felt uncomfortable under the speculative gaze. 'You really 'ave me confused,' the gangster confessed. 'But I don' zink you will shoot.' And with that, he simply reached out and took the gun out of Simon's hand. Simon, not knowing what else to do, let him take it.

'I, on ze ozer 'and,' said Croupion, 'am perfectly 'appy to blow you away. In fact zat is my intention, if we cannot reach a more amicable settlement.'

As Simon looked down the barrel of the unloaded gun, he felt paradoxically brave. He felt as though he were *in control*. Jean Croupion might be one hundred per cent weasel, but the man he was dealing with was not, in his present state of mind, a wimp.

'Carol's locked in the boot of your car, isn't she?' he said calmly. 'Tommy too. You didn't have anywhere else to put them, did you?'

'It's a little cramped,' admitted the Frenchman, 'but zey'll be perfectly all right, even when you and I take ze ride which we must take. You *will* drive carefully, won't you, Monsieur Taxman? You don't want to give your friends a bumpy ride.'

'We're not going anywhere,' Simon told him. 'When I spoke to you on the phone before, I neglected to mention that a posse of real Interpol operatives turned up at my office just after you left. They missed you, but I gave them a description of the BMW. Special Branch have had two hours to find it and stake it out. They'll be waiting patiently for us outside. Being a chameleon, you *might* just slip through the net – but not if you have me with you.' Raising his voice, he added, 'And the same goes for you, Mr Wyss.' He wasn't absolutely sure that Wyss was still listening, but he knew that all lie-detectors were inveterate eavesdroppers.

Croupion looked round, confusion turning to resentment.

Bruno Wyss stepped out of the shadows. He didn't have a gun in his hand.

'You and I are on the same side, Monsieur Croupion,' he said softly. 'We both want the same things: the money returned, the Taxman put out of action.'

Croupion didn't react immediately, but he must have decided that it was true.

'Well,' he said viciously, 'at least we can take care of ze last item.'

He brought the gun up to Simon's forehead and, without the least delay or ceremony, pressed the trigger.

Even though he had every reason to believe that the gun really was unloaded, Simon felt his heart lurch and his bowels quiver – but he didn't faint or suffer any more embarrassing fate, because the silent scream of fear which echoed through his being was drowned by the tide of elation which followed the harmless clicking of the trigger.

Wyss shrugged his shoulders. 'Sorry, mon ami,' he said – addressing Croupion rather than Simon – 'but as the English like to put it, discretion really is the better part of valour. Anyhow, Dr Sweetland is not the Taxman. You found the wrong man.'

Croupion frowned. 'But ze boy ...' he began. Simon was able to watch comprehension dawn in the man's unguarded features, and knew that Croupion had duplicated his own deduction.

He had only a split second in which to act, and he knew that now he *had* to act. Had he been a policeman, or a racketeer, or a film actor, he would probably have been able to move with smooth swift grace to fell Bruno Wyss with a perfect right hook, but knowing his limitations as he did, he simply put his head down and ran full tilt at the blond man, intending to head-butt him squarely in the chest.

His head made painful if muffled contact with the gun in Wyss's shoulder-holster. The blond man let out a howl of outrage and went down like a skittle. Simon ran straight over him, careless of any damage which his size-nine black Oxfords might do to the other's outrageous handsomeness.

Somewhere behind him Simon heard Croupion say 'Merde!' in a half-respectful fashion that was music to his ears. Then he started yelling, at the top of his voice:

'Lenz! Lenz! Get the guy in the gabardine and the blond guy with the gun!'

Mercifully this plea did not fall on deaf ears. With or without the aid of supernatural sortilege, Special Branch *had* found the car. Pretty soon, Simon knew, *everyone* would have figured out who the Taxman was – except, perhaps, for Bruno the Lie-Detector Wyss.

In the confusion which reigned while the men from Interpol and Special Branch overcame the heroic but ultimately ineffectual resistance put up by Croupion and Wyss, Simon had no difficulty in making his way to his own car. He felt slightly guilty about not racing to the side of his newly liberated assistant, but just at that moment the one thing he wanted more than anything else in the world was to be the first person to confront the master-criminal who had ripped off millions from the most secret and most secure bank accounts in all the world.

Marcia was still out to lunch when he got back to the DPR, and the corridors of the annexe were deserted. When Simon entered the office directly beneath his own, Ramsbottom looked up disinterestedly from the screen into which he had been peering. The green glow reflected from his cheeks made him look like something three quarters dead.

'Dr Sweetland,' he said colourlessly. 'How can I help you?'

Simon sat down in the familiar rock-hard chair which Ramsbottom kept for his interrogatees. 'I've got a query about my expenses,' he said, his voice dripping with resolute sarcasm.

'Indeed?' said Ramsbottom, quite unembarrassed. 'I thought that we had settled the matter to our mutual satisfaction.'

'What I want to know,' said Simon grimly, 'is how the hell you have the brass neck to exert every fibre of your scrawny being to the task of screwing me out of a lousy five hundred francs, when you spend your spare time — and, at a guess, a substantial fraction of the DPR's time — stealing millions of francs, deutschmarks, pounds, dollars and every other currency under the sun from numbered Swiss bank accounts operated by the Mafia and the Union Corse? And also how you have the nerve to add insult to injury by proclaiming in your own uniquely mealy-mouthed fashion that screwing me out of my expenses is a matter of bloody *principle*?'

Ramsbottom leaned back slightly in his chair, slightly reducing the greenness of his gills. Simon had hoped to see signs of guilt, alarm, astonishment and disappointment, but there were none in evidence.

'Ah,' said the accountant neutrally.

'Ah!' Simon repeated, injecting as much outrage and disgust into the expostulation as the lone syllable was capable of carrying. 'Is that all you can say? *Ah!* Some slimy French gangster just shoved a gun in my face and tried to blow my bloody head off, under the mistaken impression that I was you, and all you can say is *ah!* Jesus, Ramsbottom, for two pins I'd kick you from here to bloody Wolverhampton.'

'I assumed that I would be found out eventually, of course,' observed Ramsbottom, with just the slightest hint of wonderment in his tone, 'but I must confess that I had never imagined that you would be the one to do it, Dr Sweetland.'

'Well,' said Simon, 'I *was* the one to do it. It was pure serendipity, but I did it. We only have about thirty minutes before the world and his wife catches up with me, but I just wanted you to know that I was the first. And I wanted to ask you my question – which you seem to be ignoring.'

Ramsbottom nodded slowly. 'Well,' he said lugubriously, 'I suppose I owe you that much. But as a matter of interest how, exactly, *did* you find out?'

'Tommy Ferris fingered you,' said Simon curtly. 'He was one of our case-studies. He's a kid who can identify the current whereabouts of people who've used telephone receivers – as you would undoubtedly know if you had bothered to *read* our paper instead of just ripping off our fee. When the people who were trying to track you down traced the source of the calls you were making to trigger your clever electronic thieves, one of them was bright enough to realize that Tommy could locate you. The kid was bang on the button – but he located you on a two-dimensional street map. When he pointed to the vital spot, nobly suppressing his practical-joking tendencies because he was under the mistaken impression that he was helping Interpol, the guy who had been in my office less than an hour before, and had already clocked my library card, promptly jumped to the wrong conclusion. And when the poor puzzled fellow phoned me in order to confirm his suspicions, I contrived, for entirely the wrong reasons, to put the final touches to his delusion. At that point I still hadn't a clue what was going on, but when the gnomes' hitman kindly enlightened me, I was finally able to put two and two together and come up with a Ramsbottom.'

'Ah,' said Ramsbottom.

'Why?' said Simon as softly as he could. 'Just tell me *why*?'

'I'm not sure you'd understand,' said Ramsbottom, with a strange reedy sigh. 'On the other hand, maybe you see it every day of the week, in all those kids you test. Perhaps they all want to be superheroes. Perhaps every single one of them wants, more fervently than anything else in the world, to be the next Sharkman or the new

Lady Wolverene, or Kid Spectrum the Second, or Son of Dr Miraculous. Maybe *everyone* has the same dream, deep down – the dream which says, "What you see isn't the *real* me. It's just a sham, a charade. Inside, my *secret* identity is a million times better, a million times stronger, a million times more enviable." They don't ever tell you that, though, do they, Dr Sweetland? Even kids have to learn to suppress their dreams. They learn that if they say it out loud, people will mock – mock them for not being Talented, or mock them because the Talents they do have are so stupid, so useless, so inadequate. They learn that they have to be ordinary and despicable in other people's eyes.'

Ramsbottom's voice suddenly hardened. 'But *inside*, Dr Sweetland,' he said bitterly, 'it's different. Inside, they're men of steel. They're caped crusaders or hooded avengers, fighting to keep the world safe for justice and democracy. I wonder if you *do* understand, Dr Sweetland. I wonder if even *you* feel like that deep down. Maybe, like me, you've felt that way ever since you realized that bullets wouldn't bounce off you, that you'd never be able to fly, and that you don't have X-ray eyes. How do you *feel*, Dr Sweetland, as you do your job, day in and day out – as you process all those kids, and smash all their dreams?'

Simon blinked when Ramsbottom paused, but he couldn't find anything to say. This wasn't what he'd expected.

'Do you know how people loathe and despise me, Dr Sweetland?' asked Ramsbottom rhetorically. 'Of course you do. You understand completely. But it never occurred to you to wonder, did it, how I might feel about that? I have no Talent, Dr Sweetland – no Talent at all. At least, I didn't have, until the DPR kindly gave me *these*.' He spread his arms wide to indicate his rampart of screens.

'I spent years learning to use these things, finding out what they can do. I don't think there's anything paranormal about my affinity for them, but it doesn't really matter, in the end, whether you get your results by clicking your magic fingers or by sheer hard graft, as long as you get there. I knew, from the moment I made the acquaintance of these machines, that with them I could realize my dreams. I knew that if I worked at it, I could *be* a masked avenger, a man of mystery, a scourge of the underworld. And I knew too – because by then I was no longer a little boy seething with violent resentment against the playground bullies, but an *accountant* – that I could do the job *properly*. I'd learned that violence doesn't solve anything, and that it's utterly beside the point whether you rip criminals to shreds with your bare hands or throw them into overcrowded jails for a hundred years; I knew that the *proper* way to fight cruelty and injustice, the only viable way to make the world honest and good, was to inject some much needed truth into the finest but least convincing motto in the world: CRIME DOESN'T PAY.'

Simon coughed to clear the lump from his throat, impressed in spite of himself. But then he curled his lip and said, 'All very admirable. And I'm sure that the Mafia and the Union Corse have got the message. But *your* crimes seem to have paid off pretty well, don't they?'

Ramsbottom shook his head sorrowfully. 'Oh, Dr Sweetland,' he said, weakly and apparently without an ounce of resentment, 'you still don't see it, do you? I didn't *steal* the money. Why do you think that they couldn't work out where it went, even though they have the entire world financial system at their beck and call? I just *deleted* it. I wiped it out. It doesn't exist any more. That's the DPR philosophy, you see. In America crime-fighting is all fabulous fascists in funny costumes, but we're supposed to be different, aren't we? We're supposed to do things the British way – or, from now on, the *European* way. That's what I've tried to do. No violence; no spectacle; just an educational message, delivered in the only universal language there is: *crime doesn't pay.*'

Simon remembered what Wyss had said about the world having changed. Money wasn't heaps of yellow metal any more. It wasn't solid. It could simply be made to disappear. YOU HAVE JUST BEEN VISITED BY THE TAXMAN. Quicker on the draw than the European Parliament; more deadly than the European Court of Human Rights; less bureaucratic than the Common Agricultural Policy: *The Taxman!* The perfect EEC superhero.

Ramsbottom seemed to have shrunk visibly now that he had got it all off his chest. His fervour had exhausted itself, and he was no longer tautly in control of himself. He seemed nervous, now.

In the distance there was the faint sound of a siren wailing. The people who were coming for Ramsbottom wouldn't be sounding any sirens, of course, but the plaintive whine seemed poignantly symbolic.

'Will they send me to gaol do you think?' asked Ramsbottom plaintively.

Simon looked around the dingy office, reduced to half its natural size by the ancient banks of dead, dusty files. He looked at the desk which Ramsbottom had carefully rebuilt as a fortress in order to keep the world at bay. Finally, he looked at the sallow face and the ridiculous moustache of the absurd little man who never went home until the day's work was completely done.

'Yes, they will,' he said sadly. 'You'll be living in maximum-security luxury for the rest of your life. Your every need will be attended to, if not your every whim. You'll have as many terminals to play with as you can possibly use, and all the time in the world. Everyone who speaks to you will be utterly and absolutely respectful, and they'll toast your every accomplishment in vintage champagne. I don't know whether you'll be in London or Paris or Berlin, but wherever you are, you'll be the greatest treasure in the land, helping to make the world safe for democracy, justice and honest money. And every gnome in Zurich will be weeping and gnashing his teeth over the fact that Switzerland isn't a member of the EEC. It's going to be really tough, Ramsbottom, but you'll just have to take it like a man. Like a true-blue, through-and-through taxman.'

Ramsbottom thought about that for a few seconds, and then he smiled. Perhaps for the first time in his long, arduous and frustrated life, Ramsbottom smiled.

'I hear that you probably saved my life,' said Carol Cloxeter, with just the faintest hint of irony. It was all over, and she had broken the habit of a lifetime by stopping off at his flat for a cup of coffee on the way home.

'Think nothing of it,' said Simon. 'It was the least I could do. After all, it was me who delivered you into the hands of the evil criminal mastermind, so it was down to me to help you out. It's a pity that nobody but Roland Tarquin will ever find out what a hero I was. Anyway, Interpol and Special Branch helped a bit. How was Tommy feeling when you took him home?'

'Over the moon. Not only did his Talent identify the most wanted man in Europe, but he got to be tied up and left in the boot of a BMW for several hours, and he can proudly declare to all his friends that he's been sworn to absolute secrecy about the true nature of the operation, thus conveniently covering up the fact that he doesn't actually know anything at all. Not bad for a kid whose future once seemed to be limited to fingering phone freaks.'

'If I hadn't hated the little brat so much, I might have figured everything out much earlier. It seemed so obvious that he'd dropped me in it. Did you figure out what the true state of play was?'

'I didn't have the chance. I didn't even see where Tommy's finger was pointing – Croupion very carefully blocked my view. I didn't have time to figure out what his stupid questions were getting at before he turned into a human whirlwind and had us both tied up and gagged. You have no idea how uncomfortable it is to lie folded up in the boot of a car, bound and gagged and face to face with an unwashed wriggling child, absolutely bursting to go to the loo. Special Branch got me out just in time. Just my luck to get the damsel-in-distress role. Next time, can I be the one who goes to the secret rendezvous in the cathedral?'

'You wouldn't have liked it,' Simon assured her. 'It was okay until Croupion put the gun to my head, but my insides didn't quite believe Mr Wyss's reassurances about it not being loaded. I wouldn't wish that particular moment on anyone, let alone someone I ... like.' He quickly put his coffee-cup to his lips to hide the slip.

She looked at him rather oddly. 'I ... like ... you too,' she said, in a voice which was perfectly even. She didn't need to add the word *but*, or trail off significantly in a line of imaginary dots; he understood the qualification very well. Its name was Edward Cloxeter.

'Well,' said Simon with a sigh, 'you might change your mind about that when I tell you what happened this morning. You see, I had to go see the amazing Ramsbottom about our expenses claim for the Paris trip, and ...'

He explained, apologetically, why Carol wasn't going to get her half of the fee for the publication of 'Sortilege and Serendipity'.

She took it very well, all things considered. All she said, in the end, was: 'I suppose it just goes to prove that no one *ever* gets the better of a real superhero.'

Was that one any better?

'Possibly.' Loric massaged the back of his neck. 'At least if I slant it right I can make our people look good, instead of just lucky.'

There's no such thing as luck. We make our own.

'Good or bad.'

Tell me about it.

'I don't have to.' He stared at the skull in silence, until the hiss of the logs in the grate filled the room, echoing like the surf on a Caribbean beach he'd never walk again. 'You know I've always blamed myself.'

My eyes were open, Lorrie. I knew the risks as well as you did.

'That doesn't help.'

It never does. Silence, save for the pop and crack of burning. You're just tired. You always get morbid when you're tired.

'I'll go to bed soon.' He fumbled the next file as he picked it up, his fingers slipping a little on the slick cardboard cover. 'Only a few more to go . . .'

PHOTO FINISHED

Molly Brown

———————

'But what's it got to do with us?' the man in grey asked, frowning at the file that had been placed on his desk.

'Quite a lot, sir,' Beresford Huntingdon-Smythe, who was also dressed in grey, replied. 'In a unified European economy, these diamond robberies in Amsterdam –'

'I don't mean what's it got to do with us! I mean what's it got to do with *us*?'

'Ah,' Huntingdon-Smythe said, instantly grasping the distinction. 'If I may, sir.' He picked up the file and rifled through the pages. 'There've been nearly a dozen of these robberies. Here's just one example: a couple of weeks ago a woman stole fifty thousand ecus' worth of diamonds during a guided tour of a polishing factory in Rokin – that's a street in Amsterdam. She ran out into the street, chased by the factory guard, who claims she simply vanished into thin air.'

'That's nothing unusual,' the man in grey interrupted. 'Criminals always, "vanish into thin air". It just means whoever was chasing them was out of shape or over the hill or both.'

'Yes, but there's more to it than that. Both the guard and the woman who conducted the tour insist the thief was a tall, rather heavy middle-aged woman in a raincoat. No one else saw her. Everyone else at the factory that day swears the person they saw running away was a Japanese man in a business suit. There was a similar robbery early this morning, near the railway station. Witnesses can't agree whether they saw an Arab sheikh, a group of skinheads or Arnold Schwarzenegger.'

'Simultaneous illusions, all different?' The grey man shook his head sadly. 'I hate to hear about a paranorm gone bad, it depresses me. Of course, if there's any Talent more likely to go wrong than an illusionist, I don't know what it is. Except telepaths. I've never liked telepaths, nosy buggers, the lot of them.'

'Apparently this paranorm's Talent is strictly limited to illusion, not telepathy, or even fast get-aways. The Dutch police have surrounded a building in the red-light district – the Arnold Schwarzenegger version was seen entering the premises. No one has been allowed to leave – the police have no idea who they're looking for. They don't even know if the illusionist is a man or a woman. That's why they've requested the loan of an exxer.'

'But surely the Dutch have their own people to deal with this sort of thing?'

Huntingdon-Smythe shook his head. 'Less than a dozen registered; apparently their star performer is a man who does something with windmills, but that's hardly what's needed in this case. I might add, sir, the Gods are extremely keen to be seen helping our Dutch friends before the French do. There could be some knighthoods going around.'

'Knighthoods?' The grey man's posture straightened noticeably. 'Then we must do everything we can. The Gods know I'm a dedicated European.'

'Leave it to me, sir. I'll take care of everything.'

'Knighthoods!' the man in grey repeated wistfully.

Alone in his office, Beresford Huntingdon-Smythe placed the Dutch file in the shredder along with the file on Christina Morgan: ex-fashion model, ex-children's television presenter, and DPR Temp, Talent: multiple illusion.

Chas Loren turned his key in the downstairs lock. Mrs Conroy accosted him on the first-floor landing. 'I'll have the rent by Friday,' he told her automatically.

''Ere, some geezer phoned while you were out. I wrote the number down; I had to look everywhere for a pen. I slid the paper under your door.'

It had to be the call he'd been waiting for all week: that private collector who'd read about him in the *South London Advertiser* and been out to see the exhibition on Monday. 'I told you he was bluffing when he said my prices were "overblown".'

'I don't think it was someone wanting a picture,' Mrs Conroy said, following him up the stairs. 'This geezer said something about the DPR. They're that bunch of freaks, ain't they?'

His mouth dropped open. 'The DPR? You sure?'

'That's what he said. What do you want with those weirdos, Chas? I don't want nothing like that going on in my house, you understand?'

'Oh,' Chas said, thinking quickly, 'it couldn't be *that* DPR, it must be DPR the er ... magazine. *Desk-top Publishing Review*. I'll bet it's a photographic assignment. I told you things would start looking up, didn't I?'

'I mean,' the woman went on blithely, 'what you do is weird enough. An art gallery in a bedsit? Leave it out! But that DPR lot, there's no telling what they get up to. Orgies, most like. And look at the state of your boots! You've gone tracking mud all over my nice clean carpet!'

'Someday you'll have one of those blue plaques outside your house: Chas Loren lived here. You won't complain about carpets then, will you?'

'I won't be alive then,' she muttered, turning back down the stairs.

Chas opened the door with the words GALLERY CAMERA OBSCURA written across it in Magic Marker, and looked inside. The scribbled message from Mrs Conroy was on the opposite end of the room, on the counter next to the sink, wedged between the kettle and the Baby Belling hot-plate. Slipped it under the door, did she? Carefully stepping over a reclining nude made from empty lager cans, he made his way to the kettle and plugged it in. He reached over to a section of wall covered in black and white photographs of desolate inner-city landscapes and pulled downwards. Photographic scenes of urban devastation vanished beneath a Murphy bed. He plopped down on the mattress, staring at the tiny piece of paper in his hand. *Someone something hyphen Smythe says phone him urgent. DPR, ext. 4759.*

What did the DPR want with him? He'd never heard a word from them, not since the day he went in to register. They'd hardly been thrilled to see him. The woman behind the desk rolled her eyes and sighed when he told her he'd just found out he had a Talent. She handed him some forms, said, 'Fill these in,' and went back to filing her nails.

He was eventually ushered into an office where a man in a grey suit politely listened to his story (only yawning twice), glanced briefly at the photographs he'd brought along – those photographs from that last assignment for *Vogue* – and told him he didn't think it was enough of a Talent to justify putting him on the register at that time because 'Our budget's been cut by thirty per cent this year, and it's the accountants I have to answer to', but he'd put him in a 'pending' file to be considered for testing in the next fiscal quarter. The man in grey rose, shook Chas's hand, and thanked him for his interest in the DPR. That was five years ago.

His first reaction was to rip the message into tiny pieces; they couldn't be bothered with him for five years – he couldn't be bothered with them now. Then he remembered how desperately he needed money.

He got up and went over to the wardrobe, where eight lurid acrylics depicting various stages in the death and decay of a gold wolf were mounted for display. He'd hoped the damn things would be worth something now that the neurotic wannabee superheroine who'd painted them was dead, but he still hadn't sold a one. He reached inside, past another painting and a multi-media collage, and took a clean shirt off a hanger.

He made the call from a box outside Brixton Station, out of Mrs Conroy's earshot. Then he boarded a bus for Whitehall.

Beresford Huntingdon-Smythe looked up from the file on his desk and nodded. 'Mr Loren,' he said, 'good of you to come. Please have a seat. Tea?' He gestured towards a tin. 'Biscuits?'

'No, thank you.' Chas sat down. A folder was shoved across the desk towards him.

Huntingdon-Smythe tapped the *Vogue* photos with one finger. 'Tell me about these,' he said.

'I explained it to the man I spoke with the last time I was here. He didn't seem very interested.'

Huntingdon-Smythe sighed. 'Why don't you explain it to *me*?'

'Well, I'm a photographer – used to do a lot of fashion, worked for all the big magazines. I was well known, nice flat, red Porsche. I spent every working day and quite a few evenings with the most beautiful women in the world. Now, five years later, I'm two months behind in the rent on a bedsit that's not much bigger than your desk and the social security won't do anything for me because they reckon I'm self-employed and I'm not homeless ... yet. I told them wait another week and I will be, and the bastards said come back next week, then. Now I'm hoping you can spare some change for my bus fare so I don't have to walk back to Brixton; getting here today took my last penny.' He waited for Huntingdon-Smythe's reaction. There wasn't one. He reached for the biscuit tin and shoved one into his mouth. 'Shouldn't have these, really, they bring me out in an awful rash, but what's a painful skin condition when you're starving?' Still no reaction. He emptied the tin into his jacket pocket. 'These'll have to last me for a week.' Huntingdon-Smythe's face was a mask of disinterest. No compassion, Chas thought contemptuously. No compassion.

'Anyway, everything was fine until this assignment for *Vogue*.' He held up one of the photos. 'What's wrong with this picture?'

Huntingdon-Smythe shrugged. 'You tell me.'

'At first glance, nothing. You've got a girl with brown hair and brown eyes smiling into the camera. Only problem is: she was a blue-eyed blonde. The blue eyes came from a pair of tinted contact lenses, the blonde hair came out of a bottle. Still, everyone around her saw a blue-eyed blonde. I saw a blue-eyed blonde. I photographed a brown-eyed brunette.'

He picked up another photo. 'Swimsuit shot. Another model, very well known, very well paid. Can you guess what's missing from this one? I'll give you a clue: they were ninety-five per cent silicone. She threatened to sue.'

'Mr Loren, I'm afraid I still don't understand. What, exactly, is your Talent?'

'The sort of photography I did, it's all about glamour, right? In other words, it's about illusion. I don't know how or why, but one day I woke up and found I couldn't photograph illusion any more. At first I thought there was something wrong with my camera. But it didn't matter what camera I used, what lens, what film. Everyone I photographed came out like they *really* were, so the models stopped speaking to me and the magazines stopped hiring me. They didn't want reality. Most people don't like reality. Reality is ugly. So I've taken to calling it "art", and set myself up as a dealer – I've got a lot of ugly stuff for sale. You ought to come round and have a look some time; I've got a complete set of Sarah Gillespie's acrylics, bound to be worth a fortune some day, and I tell you I'm *giving* 'em away . . .'

Beresford Huntingdon-Smythe interrupted, 'You're an exxer.'

'What?'

'I said you're an exxer. An exxer's Talent is to negate another's Talent.'

'Well, I don't know about that. I don't think I ever met anyone who had a Talent.'

'Oh, haven't you?' Huntingdon-Smythe raised one eyebrow. 'You'd be surprised how many Talented people become models – if their Talent is illusion, that is.' He paused for a moment before asking, 'Did you ever work with a model named Christina Morgan, for example?'

Chas's mouth dropped open. 'I knew her when she was the *Enchantress* perfume girl. She's never a paranorm, is she?'

Huntingdon-Smythe nodded.

'So that's why she would never return my phone calls. But I don't think I could "ex" anybody without a camera, and' – Chas leaned forward with a knowing wink and a leering grin – 'it wasn't photography I had in mind, know what I mean?'

Huntingdon-Smythe did not grin back. 'You're a very

specialized, very low-grade exxer,' he said. 'But we occasionally have need of even the lowest-grade Talents. For one thing, they're cheaper. I'm sorry we didn't get in touch with you sooner, Mr Loren, but I'm afraid your file was temporarily misplaced.'

Five years is this guy's idea of temporarily, Chas thought. Give me strength!

'But I'm pleased to inform you that you will be placed on the register as of now.' Huntingdon-Smythe smiled a practised, professional smile. 'In fact we already have some work for you.'

'Will I get back pay?'

The professional smile disappeared. 'Back pay?'

'Yeah. You pay people just to be on the register, don't you? I reckon I'm owed five years' back pay. You said yourself the only reason I wasn't registered before is because you lost the file.'

The professional smile made a reappearance. 'I think you'll find the subject of back pay covered in the leaflet titled: *Extra Allowances – How to Claim.* I've never known of a precog or a telepath to even bother reading the leaflet, let alone trying to claim – perhaps they know something we don't. Still, one can always get the forms from Marcia, fill them out in triplicate, and live in hope.'

Two hours later Chas was on a plane to Amsterdam. He'd been given an instant camera (on loan – there wasn't time for him to go home and get his own), ten rolls of film, twenty pounds, seven ecus and fourteen pesetas advance against expenses (only after an argument – Huntingdon-Smythe had insisted they *never* pay expenses in advance, Chas had insisted that they bloody well would this time – finally Huntingdon-Smythe gave him the money out of his own pocket, explaining he'd just come back from holiday), and an envelope which he'd been instructed not to open under any circumstances and which was sealed with a big glob of red wax stamped with an official DPR insignia.

He held the envelope up to the light; it was totally opaque. He tried to slide a fingernail underneath the flap; it gave him a paper cut. He was trying to steam the envelope open over a cup of coffee when the announcement came that they would be landing in less than ten minutes and the steward took the cup away. He slumped back in his seat and scowled, thinking over what Huntingdon-Smythe had told him.

He'd said Christina Morgan was a DPR illusionist on special attachment to an EEC commission investigating corruption in local law enforcement. Working undercover, she'd come across something much bigger. 'I can't tell you the details; they're classified,' Huntingdon-Smythe had said earnestly, leaning forward. 'But do the words "international terrorism" and "world domination" mean anything to you, Mr Loren? I can only say this much: it involves a conspiracy going up to the highest levels. Those she sought to expose have framed her for a series of crimes she didn't commit, and she's currently surrounded by marksmen ready to shoot on any pretext.' It was Chas's job to deliver the envelope to her. 'She'll know what to do with the contents – it's the final bit of evidence she needs. You won't just be saving a colleague, Mr Loren. You'll be saving the world.'

Chas shook his head in amazement. He couldn't believe it. Christina Morgan the model, an undercover investigator for the EEC! The last he'd heard of her she had a job on *Blue Peter*.

He remembered her long blonde hair and eyes the colour of emeralds. His mind went back to an afternoon a long time ago when she'd moved sensuously towards him, red lips pursed into a kiss, wind machine fanning her hair. He shot fifteen rolls of film that day, fifteen rolls of red lips and green eyes and flowing hair for *Enchantress*, 'the fragrance that casts a spell no man can resist'.

Then his mind went back to the way she'd treated him, and he made one more attempt to get the envelope open without it showing.

It was a short train ride from the airport to Central Station, Amsterdam. He only had to walk two blocks before he was in the red-light district. There were barricades at the top of O.Z. Voorburgwal, a canalside street of narrow houses with huge picture windows where women sat in various stages of undress. Armed policemen stood guard. Chas flashed the plastic card Huntingdon-Smythe had given him, a policeman shouted something in Dutch, and a woman appeared. She was young and pretty, with spiky brown hair and a leopard-print dress. 'Vicki van Blankert,' she said, shaking Chas's hand. 'PBN.'

'PBN?'

'Paranormal Bureau of the Netherlands.'

'Oh,' Chas said. 'Are you . . . I mean, what's your . . .'

'My Talent?'

Chas nodded.

'I have expanding thighs. Would you like to see?'

'Maybe later.'

Vicki led him down the street to the building where Christina Morgan was hiding. She explained that someone looking like the American actor Arnold Schwarzenegger had been seen entering the house at nine thirty that morning; no one had been allowed out since then. They didn't think many people were inside, maybe five or six, these places usually weren't crowded in the morning. Chas would go in with two armed policemen who would line everyone up. Then Chas would photograph them one by one. Whoever didn't match his photo was the illusion-ist; it was that simple.

'No,' Chas said, 'I'm going in alone.'

A woman in a red négligé leaned back on a divan and lit a cigarette. She said something in Dutch and Chas shook his head. 'English?' Chas nodded, raising his camera. 'Hey!' the woman shouted, 'You want my picture, you pay first! Two hundred guilders, none of your filthy ecus.'

There was a flash and the woman jumped up angrily. The instant picture popped out from a slot in the camera. It wasn't Christina. 'Send me a bill,' he said, pulling a curtain aside and walking through to another room, where he found an old man in a schoolgirl uniform hiding in the wardrobe.

'What do you want with me?' the old man asked. Chas told him he only wanted to photograph him. The old man stared at him in disbelief, then shrugged. 'Hmm,' he said. 'Kinky.'

Chas made his way to the back of the house. A woman stood at the top of a narrow stairway, looking down at him. She was over six feet tall and nearly as wide. Slick black hair was pulled into a severe bun beneath a black leather peaked cap. Small cold eyes glittered above a long, hooked nose and thin, colourless lips. A large mole on her right cheek sprouted three long hairs. Her body overflowed from a black leather basque several sizes too small for her, and she was holding a whip. 'Chas Loren,' she said. 'What the hell are you doing here?'

Alone in a locked room, Chas handed her the envelope. She sat down on a bed, he sat on a chair facing her. Christina was herself now, no make-up, blonde hair tied back in a pony-tail, pink floral-print dress and sandals. She didn't look one day older than the last time he'd seen her, and he hadn't seen her for seven or eight years.

He studied her face as she read the contents of the envelope, wondering what she'd look like if he photographed her now that he had a Talent of his own. Would she still be so young, so breathtakingly beautiful? He decided he'd rather not know.

She looked up and smiled at him. 'Oh, Chas. You have no idea what you've done today. Not for me, but for civilization as we know it.'

'What, Christina? What exactly have I done? Will you please tell me what's going on? This morning I wake up in Brixton – it's like a regular day, everything normal. Then out of the blue the DPR phones up and, next thing I know, I'm in a Dutch knocking shop, surrounded by armed police and loonies with expanding thighs!' He got up and started pacing the room, gesturing wildly. 'Have you seen that girl out there? Her thighs go' – he spread his arms out wide – 'this big! That's what she told me, anyway. And there's some guy says he does something Talented with windmills. God, everything they said about paranormals is true! They're all positively barking! What am I doing here?' He stopped and stood still for a moment, looking at her, a little half-smile on his face. 'But more important . . .' He walked over to the bed, bent over, and placed one hand beneath her chin. She raised her head, eyes half-closed, lips slightly parted. He grabbed her roughly, pinning her arms behind her back. 'Where are the diamonds?'

'I don't know what you're talking about!'

'The ones from the last job, Christina. This morning. They've got to be here somewhere, you never had the chance to dump them.'

'There were never any robberies! That was just a story –'

'Do you think I'm a total idiot? I read the letter, Christina.'

She slumped forward. 'It's not like it seems, Chas. It's not what you think. I wasn't going to set you up; I'd never do a thing like that! You've got to believe me, none of this was my idea. In fact I was just thinking of how I could get us both out of this. Together. There's enough from this morning, we don't need the rest. This last job was the big one! The others were small change, know what I mean? You can have the diamonds, Chas. I'm happy to give them to you. We could go somewhere together, just you and me. I've always fancied you, Chas. You know that?'

His mind went back once more to that afternoon when he was working for *Enchantress*. How at the end of the day he'd asked her if she'd like a cup of coffee – just one cup of coffee – and she'd told him, 'Let's keep this strictly business, darling. There's enough men in my life as it is, and you're really not my type.' So she'd always fancied him, huh?

'Chas, please. You're hurting me.'

He looked down at her tear-streaked face and loosened his grip. So much for my career as a hard man, he thought. 'I'll tell you what. Show me where the diamonds are; consider that my fee for not turning you in. I'll tell that lot outside I couldn't find you. What you do after is your problem, not mine. Got it?'

'Oh, Chas, yes, yes! Anything you say. You're wonderful, you know that?'

'Just take me to the diamonds.'

'I hid them in the basement. Follow me.'

She led him down three flights of stairs, to a dark, damp, windowless cellar with very little air. Chas felt around for the light-switch and found it, illuminating the room in the dim glow of one bare red light-bulb. It looked like a medieval torture chamber. 'What is this?'

'Priciest room in the house,' Christina told him. 'You were always such an innocent, Chas, weren't you?'

'Innocent? Me? Never!'

'Okay, you weren't. If that's how you want it.'

'Stop stalling. Where'd you hide them?'

'Look over there,' Christina said, pointing.

He turned to look where she was pointing. He turned back just in time to see Christina holding an iron bar.

The front door opened and Chas Loren stepped outside. Vicki van Blankert rushed up to meet him. 'We were just about to storm the house. You took an awfully long time.'

Chas coughed and mumbled something about needing time to get it right. Vicki could hardly hear him. 'What?' she said.

'Sore throat,' Chas rasped.

'Did you find the robber?'

'No.'

A group of armed men swept past them and into the building. Vicki swirled around in confusion. Chas seemed to have vanished. She looked up the street just in time to see him getting into a taxi.

'Down here!' someone shouted in Dutch from the back of the house. A dozen armed police stormed down the stairs to the cellar, where Chas Loren was hanging by his ankles from a pair of manacles embedded in the wall. 'You bloody morons!' he shouted. 'She's getting away!'

'Take me to the airport. And hurry.' The taxi pulled away from the kerb, rattling the contents of the camera case. Chas hugged it tightly to his chest, closed his eyes and dreamed of tropical beaches. It was a shame he'd had to leave the camera behind, but he could always buy another one and another and another . . .

*

Several men with hacksaws cut Chas down from the wall. Vicki van Blankert knelt down beside him. 'Mr Loren, are you all right?'

He made an effort to smile weakly. 'I think so,' he croaked. 'But I could use a drink. How about you?' He crooked a finger, motioning her to move closer. 'I'd love to see those thighs expand.'

Vicki giggled and blushed.

A short time later Vicki van Blankert was seen entering a hotel with Chas Loren. Shortly after that she was seen leaving. Alone. She hailed a taxi.

'Take me to the airport. And hurry.'

'Yes, madam,' the driver told the elderly oriental lady he saw in his rear-view mirror.

The old lady smiled and tapped her handbag, which contained a slightly crumpled handwritten note on official DPR stationery which read:

THE DEPARTMENT OF PARANORMAL RESOURCES, WHITEHALL, LONDON SW1

My darling Christina,

By the time you read this I will have been to the rendezvous, picked up the stones from the earlier jobs and taken care of everything. Meet me at the Hotel Brasilia, Room 1514.

The photographer says he's an old friend of yours. You wouldn't believe the story I told him! He thinks you've uncovered an international conspiracy, so play along with it. It should be easy for you to switch places with him. Dispose of him any way you like; there's no record of him at the DPR. Not only have I neglected to register him – I seem to have accidentally dropped his file into the shredder.

But enough about him, from now on it's just you and me and long tropical nights. I burn for you.

Yours for ever,
Your little Squeegee-bum

FROM THE DESK OF BERESFORD HUNTINGDON-SMYTHE

That bastard Chas had stolen the one-way ticket to Rio de Janeiro that had been enclosed with the note, but she'd get to Rio and she'd find him and Chas Loren would learn the real meaning of the word 'revenge'.

The thought of it made her smile.

'Hell and damnation!' The file ended up teetering on the edge of the stack, until Loric herded it back into equilibrium with a passing thought. He couldn't believe it. Another rotten apple in the Department. Orpington's baleful influence, no doubt.

You can't blame Philip for everything.

'Why not? He should have realized what this Huntingdon-Smythe was up to. Probably encouraged him. Someone to throw to the wolves if his own grubby little secrets started coming to light.'

You didn't spot him either.

'That's different. I've been out of the country a lot.' He yawned and drank some more tea. He could feel the fatigue like a physical weight across his shoulders. He flexed them, feeling the muscles crack, and reached out for the next folder.

As his hand neared the blotter, it slowed, as though pushing against some physical resistance. The midge voice from this one was disturbing again; more sun-baked images, probing at memories he'd rather leave buried.

Loric grew irritated. He'd beaten the past once tonight already. He closed his fingers slowly on the file, feeling them strain against an invisible membrane that gave, gradually at first, then abruptly tore. His hand clenched against paper, crushing it; then, without warning, the images rose to engulf him.

MONASTIC LIVES

Graham Joyce

I'd always argued that it wasn't a Talent, it was an exact science. They in turn had always disagreed, and when the new regulations came through from Brussels, that was that and I had to conform. I felt an arrow-shaped directive whizzing across the pond from Belgium, its inked rubber sucker stamping me on the brow: TAL-ENTED. What can you do? They're in charge; they hand out the girocheques.

The lordly Loric was twitching one of his secretive smiles from behind a desk upholstered in green leather, a desk the size of a sports field. He always unnerved me, and my appeal wasn't going well. When the grey folder gently closed itself, and the gold-plated fountain pen fell neatly alongside it, I recognized the signs for *audience over*.

'Why not just send in a medium-grade telepath?' I tried weakly.

'It's been done. We've sent in three telepaths already. That is why we find ourselves in need of your . . . unique talent. Anyway, it's your territory.'

'So what did they find out?'

'If I told you that, your mission would be pointless, now wouldn't it?' Loric stood up. My coat lifted itself from the peg and hovered towards me. The door opened noiselessly. 'Try to think of it as a holiday.'

Then I was out in the corridor. I'd only managed to get

an audience with Loric because of his 'special interest' in my Talent. His special interest, however, was not always an advantage. People regarded you as one of his favourites, but it meant you got all the tail-end jobs, stuff other paranorms had made a hash of. No, Loric's special interest was something you had to tolerate, the way a pet monkey will tolerate wearing an embroidered waistcoat and a tiny fez.

I was passed in the corridors by bureaucrats who averted their faces when they saw me coming, or who affected suddenly to have an itch that needed scratching, a sore eye that needed rubbing. Telepaths they knew how to cope with, but I suppose I unnerve them the way Loric unnerves me. Marcia was the same when I had to sign for my drachmas. She kept her head down throughout the transaction, which at least spared me the toffee-nosed disapproval I attracted before she found out what I did.

Two days later I was set down by military aircraft on the tiny airstrip of Máleme, northern Crete. It was November. I stepped out on to the tarmac and the sun was shining brilliantly.

My objections to returning to the Greek island, even out of season, quickly dissolved in the noon-day sun. I'd hired a clapped-out Suzuki jeep to take me to the monastery at Gouvernéto; half-way there I stopped on a hill and climbed out to look across a broad sweep of bay. The sand was the colour of cinnamon and the water was the colour of a bird's egg; and the events of the past seemed somehow to resolve themselves in the sickle-shaped curve of the bay.

Three years before – almost to the day, as it happened – and in a similar bay to this on the other side of the island, I'd been cheerfully running a rent-a-moped business. There I spent delicious nights stretched out beside Rita, my beautiful German girlfriend; and languid days, either tinkering with poxy moped parts or trying to neutralize my unwanted Talent by injecting myself with venomous quantities of ouzo. The life!

Then, without warning and all on the same day, my business collapsed, my creditors moved in and evicted me, and Rita went back to her secretarial job in Bonn. I recall staring down at bits of moped scattered on the sandy floor, realizing how nature will often find its own way of telling you it's time to go home. And, with a dismantled heart, I did, vowing never to return.

Until Loric had plans for me, that is.

I climbed back into the Suzuki and within half an hour I was rattling down the dirt track towards the monastery. Lizards skittered from the broken stones and smells of sage and other wild herbs scented the warm afternoon air. Yes, I was even glad to be back in the foremost country on earth where if anything can happen, it usually will.

It was my intention to arrive at the monastery about an hour before sundown, so I stopped at a tiny village and sat over coffee for a couple of hours in a cobwebby *kafeneion*. A Cretan shepherd, complete with crook, was the only other customer. When I ordered the owner to give him a *raki*, he accepted it in silence. Like many a Mediterranean peasant, he had a wonderful face of tanned and crumpled soft hide; in fact it was such a good specimen I decided to limber up the Talent there and then. I clipped mirror shades over my spectacles, and I went into his face.

About seventy years old, wife still alive; two sons; one emigrated to Australia and much sadness about that, the other at some distance but near enough to visit occasionally, probably Athens, then; a daughter still on the island;

grandchildren five, should be six but a tragedy there, early, don't go into it. A complaint in the left leg, follow that back, all the way to ... Greece says no! Yes, a soldier, fighting the Italians in the Albanian mountains, Second World War, but strangely no action. Very cold. Long periods of boredom and inaction. Rotting boots. Frost-bite. News of Germans already in Athens. Stuck up here. So why the wound? Ah, here it is ...

'Yamas!'

I came out of his face with a popping of bubbles. The old shepherd slammed his glass of *raki* on the table, raised it aloft and looked across it at me with a glittering eye.

I took off my spectacles. The owner had placed a return glass in front of me. 'Yamas!' I replied, raising the *raki* to my own lips. 'Our health!'

That's my Talent. I am a reader of faces. Or, to be more precise, I can read a personal history etched in the *lines* of a face. Smile lines, frown folds, anxiety creases, crow's feet under the eyes, contours of elation, clefts of despair; to me they're an alphabet, a picture book where all stands revealed and nothing is hidden. In the open, upturned face I see first the innocent flower, and then the serpent beneath.

No, I don't see the future. Only the past.

It's enough.

I didn't return to reading the old shepherd's face. It was already a soul-cycle almost complete, a balance of fault and virtue, at once beautiful and ordinary. Faces are like books. Some bore you by failing to offer anything new; some tire you by detailing everything at wearisome length; and others excite by suggesting more than they express.

Meanwhile I had a job to do. Up at the monastery of Gouvernéto, according to the DPR, an Englishman with a secret was hiding. I had no more idea who he was than I had about his secret. That was the point. My mission was to conduct a ψ reading (DPR-speak for what I prefer to call a mind-map) on any strayed Englishman in the vicinity, then report back. That was it. The DPR rely on my information as corroboration: if the profile fits the DPR identikit, then the subject will be extradited (i.e., bundled in the back of a van and driven at high speed back to London). The DPR operates on a 'need-to-know basis', and I, evidently, need to know nothing. Otherwise a ψ reading might be contaminated by prior information.

I felt a bit wobbly after four glasses of *raki*, but I climbed back into my Suzuki jeep and bounced on down the winding dirt-track. The monastery stood on a headland at the end of rocky peninsula. After two kilometres I stopped to pick up a hitchhiker. It was a young woman in her early twenties, rather scrawny-looking. I suppose you might describe her as some kind of hippy. Anyway, she was heading for the monastery too, and I thought she might provide a bit of cover when we arrived.

She tossed back her long, honey-coloured hair and chatted amiably. I thought her eyes had a rather constipated look which might have been mistaken for lasciviousness – or the other way around.

'Going to spend the season picking oranges and olives,' she shouted above the roar of my gear-crunching. 'Just making the most of the last of the really good weather.'

A tiny crease darted under her eye, like a lizard's tongue; and something like a Greek omega danced briefly above the bridge of her nose. *Liar.* And not a very good one.

'Lucky you!' I shouted, swerving the jeep around a sharp corner while clipping my mirror shades to my glasses. I wanted to take a closer look.

This wasn't a very good idea while driving. I only

learned that Mandy had been or still was a journalist before I struck a boulder with my front offside wheel. The impact nearly pitched her out of the vehicle. The steering was damaged. We managed to limp the last few kilometres, and Mandy showed considerable signs of relief when the bell-tower of the monastery hove into view.

I parked under the whitewashed walls and told her to go on ahead while I inspected the damaged wheel. When she was out of sight, I let the air out of the tyre for good measure.

I followed her through the gates into a courtyard enclosed on all sides by a series of graceful, shady arches supporting a single, interconnecting balcony. The centre-piece of the courtyard was a large four-fruit tree; generations of monks had carefully grafted growths of orange, lemon, lime and grapefruit on to a single citrus trunk. I could hear Mandy talking excitedly in the far corner of the courtyard. The words 'maniac' and 'reckless' came over an octave higher than the rest. A table and chairs were drawn up in the shade, and her audience comprised two figures hunched across it. She laughed nervously as I approached.

The two men at the table seemed utterly baffled by her sudden manifestation; and similarly by mine. Certainly the monastery was too far off the tourist track to receive many visitors, even in high season. They gaped at her as Mandy desperately tried to overlay their silence with an account of our 'accident'. Three empty retsina bottles stood on the table.

'The jeep's in a right state,' I said cheerfully. 'We'll have to get someone out to fix it.' I knew perfectly well that, in Greek terms, rapid deployment of roadside assistance might easily keep us holed up there for a couple of days. The two men looked at each other.

Something about living in Greece prompts Englishmen to favour the growth of ragged, untidy beards. This is a phenomenon I wouldn't care to try to explain, but the point is that it does nothing to assist one's Talent for reading faces. They also wore sunglasses. All I could see was that one of the men, perhaps in his mid sixties, was about twenty years older than his colleague. He was red-haired, the younger man dark.

'It's already late,' Mandy blurted. 'Maybe we'll have to stay the night here.'

'But that won't be possible, you see!' the older of the men shouted suddenly. 'You see, it just won't be possible, you see!' His accent was as Oxbridge as a hired punt. That *you see* came out every time like a sharp little bleat of anguish. 'You see, for one thing, Brother Dimitri would never allow it.'

'Oh, I don't know, Eddie,' droned the second man. He, by contrast, was pure Mancunian. He couldn't keep his eyes off Mandy. 'I don't see what else they can do.'

It was plain they were both tipsy. 'But but but, can't you fix it, you see?' said Eddie, his voice fracturing with irritation.

I smiled oafishly. 'Not mechanically minded, I'm afraid.'

'They can't go anywhere,' said the Mancunian. 'Have some wine. I'll go and fetch another bottle and some glasses. Sit down, go on.'

'Don't mind if I do!' Mandy jumped in the chair he vacated.

'But it won't do, you see!' Eddie shouted after him. I pulled up another chair and he leaned across the table to scrutinize me. 'You must understand, I've no objection. It's Brother Dimitri, you see. He doesn't like it!'

The Mancunian returned, slightly unsteady on his feet. He introduced himself as Spike before splashing retsina into plastic beakers.

'Yamas!' he said. Spike, Mandy and I crashed our plastic cups together. 'Yamas!'

Eddie was looking around wildly for support. 'But, you see, you see . . .'

'Put a sock in it, Eddie, and drink up.'

Surprisingly, Eddie did as he was told and sank into silence. Two bottles later I'd learned that only three monks were dwelling in the monastery. One was very old and on his sickbed; another was in Athens on business; and the third, Brother Dimitri, seemed to spend his time prowling in the shadows, spying on the antics of the two Englishmen. Their presence in the monastery was barely tolerated.

'How long have you both been here?' I asked.

'Questions, you see. You ask a lot of questions, the pair of you.'

'It's my job, in a way,' I said.

'And what exactly is your job?' Eddie demanded to know.

'I'm a writer; you know, always on the look-out for material.' It seemed to be the sort of thing a writer might say. I tried to look slightly pompous and self-satisfied, like a real writer.

Mandy looked at me strangely, as if she suspected I was on to her. Eddie waved a hand through the darkening air. 'There you are, you see,' he said, as if it somehow settled the argument. 'He's a writer.'

Spike became interested, asking me a lot of daft questions, but it was at Mandy he smiled and nodded. Then, with the shadows gathering at our backs, a monk appeared behind us, making everyone jump. We recovered with a surplus of hilarity, in which the monk seemed unwilling to share.

'Oh, come along, Brother Dimitri,' whined Eddie. 'Don't look at us with that cockatrice glare. It's only a bottle of wine. He doesn't speak English, you see, thank God and Kyrie eleison. They've got hundreds of bottles in that cellar. You see.' Eddie was by now practically falling off his chair.

I stood up and formally wished the monk good evening. He regarded me impassively in his black stovepipe hat and robes. He had a black beard, longer and more luxurious than the English imitations. I took him aside and explained our predicament in my best Greek. He listened as though slightly pained by it all. I pointed out that Mandy and I were not 'together', and asked if he would permit us to stay the night in the monastery. It seemed unnecessary to point out that he had about thirty spare rooms.

Brother Dimitri let me finish, and then walked away without saying anything; which is Greek for 'Yes, but I'm not happy with the situation.' I returned to the table and explained I'd negotiated permission to stay. Eddie, however, was leaning across the table, wagging a finger at me.

'You see! You see! He speaks the Greek! He *milates* the ruddy *ellenica*! You see!'

'Oh, shut it!' smiled Spike. 'I'm going to switch the light on and fetch another bottle of retsina.'

'And I,' said Eddie, struggling to his feet, 'am going to take a look at this so-called damaged jeep.' He staggered away, colliding with the four-fruit tree half-way across the courtyard. Brother Dimitri stood at the entrance, watching Eddie bounce off the gates.

Leaving Mandy and I alone. For a moment there was only the unrelenting chatter of the cicadas out there in the night.

'You're a fucking journalist,' she snarled. I shrugged; let her think that. 'How did you get on to him?'

'Who?'

'Don't play games. You know who.'

'Okay. Want to share what we know?'

'You go first.'

'Oh, no. What paper are you with?'

She was about to tell me when an electric light popped on and she changed her mind. Spike came back and she conjured her snarling lips into a smile. For him.

Spike had taken his sunglasses off, and for the first time I had some exposed flesh on which to begin a ψ reading. He was so fascinated by the presence of Mandy that he didn't notice my hard stare.

'So what brought you here, Spike?' she said.

'Don't know. Marriage split up. Lost me job. Found meself wandering. Ended up here about three months ago, trying to get me head together.'

'What about Eddie? How long has he been here?'

'Don't know. Won't say. Guess he's been here a couple of years, though.'

While Mandy pumped him for information about Eddie, I went right into Spike's face.

Within two minutes I had everything I needed to know. Spike only had one history; or rather several histories ending with the same issue. He was not the man the DPR were looking for.

Almost every line on his face led to a different woman. He was a charm-merchant, a radiant con-man, and all his activities in this field were devoted to womanizing. He was an inveterate seducer of female hearts. There was nothing else in his face. I saw three marriages, some producing children, and numerous torrid affairs also resulting in offspring. There were children both sides of the blanket, but they plunged under his beard, as it were. Anyway, I didn't need to see any more. He was only here for the brief sanctuary it afforded from his tempestuous love-life.

What irritated me was how successful he seemed with women. I can only pity a man like that, who has so much success with women; almost as much as I can pity a man like me, who doesn't.

Mandy brought me out of Spike's face. There was a slight popping in the air around me. 'Are you all right?'

'Sorry? Yes! Fine!' I gulped some retsina. 'Yamas!' The trouble with the Talent is that it does trance me, leaving me with my mouth hanging open as I pilot a tiny capsule along the highways and byways of the face in question. When I'm drawn out, it's as though the capsule has been pierced, leaving me momentarily groggy. I got up. 'Just going to stretch my legs.'

Actually I was feeling slightly nauseated by the pace at which their romance was already accelerating. And since Eddie was obviously my man, I decided to go and see what he was up to. As I approached the gates, something made me stop.

It was the monk, Brother Dimitri. He was crouched down by the gates, spying on Eddie. Over the hiss of the cicadas I could hear Eddie groaning softly to himself as he inspected the wheel of my jeep. I saw him kick the flat tyre before making an unsteady path back towards the gates.

At this point the monk got up, turned and blundered straight into me. He gasped in horror, then pointed up at the citrus tree in the centre of the courtyard. 'Four-fruit tree!' he whispered, his black robes flapping as he disappeared in the darkness.

I didn't think anything of it. Greeks, when embarrassed, will tend to point down at something like your shoe and say 'That is a shoe': as if this obvious decoy is somehow marvellous in its subtlety. Anyway, Eddie came back to find me loitering in the passage. 'Don't go away!' I said. I jogged to the jeep, returning with a bottle of best Scotch whisky. 'Present for you.'

I made the amber liquid jiggle in the weak light from the courtyard. I figured a man like Eddie, who liked his grape, might be nostalgic for his grain. I was right. Three minutes later we were back in his cell-room, talking Scotch.

It wasn't much of a room. A pallet-bed, a naked light bulb, a wash-bowl on a table, some magazine pictures taped to the whitewashed wall, and a single aperture-window. A suitcase stood against the back wall, gathering dust. Eddie helped himself to coronary-sized measures of Scotch.

'So Spike's stolen your gel, has he? You see, I told you not to stay here.'

'Such is life. Cheers!'

I'd actually stopped drinking, but Eddie didn't know that. His eyes were already half closed and he started rambling about stills he had known in Scotland and the highlands and the heather. He was out of the game, and I was ready to go into his face.

It was complicated, an ordnance-survey map of a face. Eddie had lived a great deal. There was a miserable childhood, a family bankruptcy, some scandal concerning his mother and a regrettable incident involving a scout-master, all before he was fourteen; then there was a failure at Oxford, some flat business ventures, induction into the British intelligence services, expulsion from same, followed by a great deal of travelling on the Indian subcontinent. Then something popped.

'I say! What the devil are you staring at? Do you mind?'

I apologized and topped up his glass, pretending to have been spirited away by his fascinating discourse. Adopting a different strategy, I plied him with the rest of the Scotch and simply waited.

Eventually his head crashed to the table, and I was

able to carry him over to his pallet-bed, where I laid him out. He was snoring snoutily. His face was unpleasantly pink and sweaty, and I was stroking his hair out of his eyes and bending over to get a good look at his face when I sensed someone watching me. I looked up, and saw Brother Dimitri's face at the tiny aperture-window. Our eyes met briefly before the monk's face disappeared. He'd seen me stroking Eddie and stooping over him. Well, it didn't look good, but I wasn't going to try to explain myself in Greek to an Orthodox monk at that time of night.

I went back into Eddie's face. It was a bit of a nuisance because most of the story plunged under his beard, and all I could do was travel along the available lines. There were several missing years, but what was there gave me a bit of a shock. It seemed to me that Eddie was my father.

Correction. Eddie *thought* he was my father.

Now, this information was complicated by the fact that I was adopted at birth. I was raised by happy, loving adoptive parents who'd brought me up to believe my natural mother was a factory girl and my natural father a Norwegian merchant seaman. The idea that this pink, snorting expatriate dipsomaniac might be my old man was thoroughly distasteful to me. But every line I followed, and every crease or wrinkle of his face I travelled, disappeared under his wretched beard.

There was nothing else for it. I searched his table by the wash-bowl and found a pair of scissors. I ransacked his dusty suitcase to come up with a shaving kit, cut-throat style, long out of commission. I'd fully shaved off the right-hand side of his beard before I abandoned the labour and took another look into his face. It was there, to my relief, I discovered that he didn't just think he was *my* father, he thought he was *everyone's* father. Then I realized who he was. Not only was he a psychotic, he was an infamous one.

His name wasn't Eddie at all. It was Roland Tansley, one-time leader of a right-wing religious sect and owner of a huge estate near Inverness. He'd made himself a fortune by converting and seducing a few impressionable spinsters and upper-crust neurotics. He persuaded them to call him father, took all their money and installed them, in appallingly spartan conditions, in his Scottish mansion while he lived it up elsewhere. He'd flown the coop – and the wrath of his followers – a few years back when his embezzlements were exposed by the tabloid press.

But this revelation only baffled me. This wasn't my man. The Department wouldn't have any interest in Tansley. The Inland Revenue possibly, but not the DPR. I sat there for a while, twiddling the still-soapy razor. If it wasn't Tansley I was after, and it wasn't Spike, then who was it? Finally it occurred to me, if we could have fathers who were not fathers, could we not also have brothers who were not brothers?

Brother Dimitri! I could have kicked myself! He wasn't a monk at all, wasn't even Greek: he was an Englishman dressed up to fit the part. What better disguise? That would explain why he hadn't spoken a single word earlier when I'd told him, in Greek, about my predicament with the jeep! And the nonsense about 'four-fruit tree': a bit of pidgin-Greek to try and protect his disguise. No wonder he was spying on everyone!

My immediate problem concerned his unmasking. He certainly wasn't going to stand still for me while I went into his face and completed a ψ reading; and neither was he going to let me get him brainless on Scotch whisky.

I switched the light off on the snoring Tansley and

sneaked out to the jeep, wishing I could remember the training I'd been given at Tintern House. Was it two drops at ten seconds or four drops at thirty seconds, or three minutes or what? I couldn't remember. I rooted around in my bag for the chloroform pad and went back inside, looking for Brother Dimitri.

Eddie, or rather Tansley, was still snoring loudly as I passed his cell. I tiptoed along the balcony, drawn by grunts issuing from the cell in the far corner. It was the sound of the passionate embraces of Mandy and Spike. Obviously they hadn't wasted much time in the two hours since I'd left them. And I didn't have to look much further for Brother Dimitri. I practically stumbled over him in the balcony shadows. He was listening at Spike's door, muttering and shaking his head.

I jumped on his back and let him have it with the chloroform pad. I don't know why I'd expected him to go under in ten seconds, but a full minute later we were still rolling around on the balcony, the pad muffling his shouts as Spike and Mandy nudged towards a crescendo in the adjacent cell. His black hat went spinning over the balcony as we struggled, his elbows crashing wildly into my ribs, the racket of our violent embrace obliterated by the cries of the lovers. It was like wrestling with a stuck pig. Finally he succumbed to the chloroform, going under in impressive symphony with the activities on the other side of the door.

I sat on the floor, recovering my breath. Then I dragged him by his feet into a nearby cell and set to work with the razor. Once again I'd got half a beard off when I realized I'd made a terrible mistake.

I did a quick read. A mummy's boy; very fond of pasta; growing up in an Orthodox Church school in Herakleion; university in Athens; seminary in Thessaloniki. Shit. Brother Dimitri was as Greek as a plate of *tzatziki*. He started to come round, so I gave him another dose of chloroform and closed the door on him.

Out on the balcony, Mandy was smoking a cigarette. Spike was still inside, no doubt feeling pleased with himself.

'Can I have one of those?' I asked.

She flipped me a smoke. 'Are you all right? You look a bit rough.'

'So do you,' I snapped. I suppose I did look a bit dusty, and I still hadn't found what I'd come for. We smoked in silence. When I got to the end of my cigarette, I said, 'You went for the wrong man. Tansley is the other one.'

'So I just realized. How did you know what I'm after?'

'You're a journalist. After the Tansley story.'

'You too? Which paper are you with?'

'I'm not a journalist. I'm a paranorm. DPR.'

She stiffened, sensing a story. Then I had an idea. 'Mandy, I'll tell you all about it. Everything I've found out about Tansley, plus what I'm doing here. You can have the full story, subject to DPR clearance. But I'm going to need your co-operation.'

She didn't need much persuasion before going back inside with Spike. I found her some equipment, then I gave her about half an hour in the dark with him before I went in and turned the light on them.

Spike was naked, strapped to the four corners of the pallet-bed, with a stupid grin on his face. The grin evaporated when he saw me standing there with a razor, and Mandy squeezing back into her clothes.

'What's this?' he said. 'What's going on?'

'Calm down!' I told him. 'I only want half of it.'

I was lathering Spike's face for a shave when the door crashed open and Brother Dimitri staggered into the cell. He looked dreadful. His face was white, his eyes were puffy and bloodshot, and his black robes were torn and powdered with white dust. He looked first at the naked man strapped to the bed, then at Mandy wriggling into her jeans, and finally at me kneeling ritualistically across Spike, wielding a razor. He backed slowly out of the room. Then we heard him run along the balcony, down the steps and across the courtyard to the gates, shouting something incomprehensible in Greek.

I ignored it, and started on Spike's beard.

'Good work,' Loric told me back in London. 'Well, your ψ reading confirms our suspicions. The profile fits. Spike was our man all along.'

It was the children. Spike's children. The ones hiding under his beard, as it were. I found four lurking there when I shaved off half of his facial hair. The point was, all four of his children were paranorms and known to the DPR. Since they had different mothers, Spike himself was of enormous interest to the Department. They wanted to take a peek at his DNA. What for, I can't say. That's their business.

What had confused the telepaths was that Spike himself didn't know exactly how many children he'd fathered; and those born in wedlock he'd not seen often enough to recognize their paranormal abilities. The telepaths had anyway been drawn to Tansley, whose psychotic predisposition made him rather skilful at misleading even the top-grade telepaths sent out there by the Department. Meanwhile Mandy got her story and a generous by-line. A picture of the half-bearded Tansley appeared in all the Sunday papers the following week.

Loric's only complaint was the fuss caused by the Greek government about our working methods. The Greek Orthodox Church had issued some kind of angry statement which was relayed to us via the Foreign Office. Loric let me see the memo.

For one of the Gods, he looked quite puzzled. 'Do you think it lost something in the translation?' he asked.

I made a timeless Mediterranean gesture, indicating we'd never know. Loric let the matter drop. After all, he'd lived there once too, and I knew he could see the funny side of things. It was written all over his face.

Are you all right?

'I think so.' His hand shook slightly as he raised it to his face. The file, crumpled, a perfect palm print outlined in sweat, lay unheeded beneath his chair. 'It was Crete . . .'

And the memories wouldn't stay buried. Kaleidoscopic flashes of the year Madeline died, and he'd fled there in search of solitude. Months of mourning under a sun he'd hated for its brightness, but which had never reached or lightened the shadows inside him. Eventually he'd learned to contain them, ignore them, but the shadows still seeped out in his dreams, or whenever memory gave them way.

He stared at her photograph, hair flowing back in the wind, teeth sharply defined against the dark planes of her face as she half turned to laugh at some long-forgotten jest. He could recall the sound even now: a rich, throaty chuckle, welling up from deep in her chest. It echoed inside his head, thin and attenuated.

You old romantic. She laughed again.

'I miss you,' he said.

I know. There was a pause, while the logs hissed in the grate. But I'm still here in spirit.

'It's not the same,' he said.

Don't knock it till you've tried it.

'I'll get round to it.' He felt the stirring of a smile, in spite of himself.

Before you finish those bloody files, probably.
'Nearly finished.' He picked up the next one.

THE FOREIGN POST

Colin Greenland

———————

Thanks, very nice, I don't mind if I do. Cheers. Do you smoke? Do you mind? It's a nice place here, isn't it? A world of its own. Don't you think? Is this your first time in Brussels? I've been here since February, actually. Yes, a while. It's all a bit strange to me still, it's not really my sort of place. I'd never been out of England until they sent me here.

I'm with the DPR, that's what we call – Yes, that's right. I'm only seconded to the Commission. It's not so bad, it's a doddle, very easy, actually, the work. Compared to what I'm used to. I never expected to end up here. What happened was, one day Loric called me at work and asked me to go to London. When he said it was him, you could have knocked me down with a feather. You've heard of him, Loric, have you, where you come from? Where is it you're from again?

Yes, he phoned me up himself and asked me to come to DPR head office. Took me out to lunch. To this big French restaurant. I thought he was going to introduce me to somebody because he wouldn't let me have a drink, in case it interfered with me. I don't think it does, actually. Yes, another drop of that would be very nice, thank you very much.

To tell you the truth, I'd never had any time for them. Paranorms. I spent a lot of my life trying to think I wasn't one, that I wasn't any different from everyone else, that it was normal to get stuff like that through your letter-box every day. I was never going to register, there's a lot of people don't, I expect it's the same for you. No, this recruiter came round the office and some-body must have said something. I know the women don't like me, a lot of them. And the men are all jealous, if you can believe that. That or they think it's funny.

So I had to go to the interview, they couldn't test me, exactly, I just had to take along my post for two weeks. Then there was basic training, that was only like Boy Scouts, really, projects and PE, except there was a lot more paperwork, I can tell you! Well, I'm used to that. Accounts processing. That's what I do normally. That's what I'll do when they send me home. If I can get a job.

For a long while after that I thought they'd forgotten me. Then they sent me this stuff I had to spray on every day, three times a day, like a deodorant. Well, that's one thing it wasn't. It made me smell awful, like sweaty cheese. People stood upwind of me for weeks. I nearly gave it the elbow, but frankly I was grateful for the giro. Anyway you can't cheat them, they've got telepathic in-spectors, have you heard that?

Well, I don't want to bore you, but I had to use the spray for a month, you see, then I had to go to Robinson Heath, I don't know if you'll have heard of that. Yes, the nuclear-weapon place, that's right, the DPR have got a place there. No, I don't know either. I didn't like the thought of it, to tell you the truth. Anyway, I looked on the map and it was miles away, the other side of Reading. They said there'd be an extra giro, and it was a day off work, so I didn't mind, really, even though I don't much like doctors, hospitals, all that. I was hoping if I asked, they might give me something to take the smell away.

A policeman met me off the train. He had an unmarked car. I didn't know why, but when we got there, there were these protestors at the gate. Not about the department, you understand, about the missiles. They were all women, as far as I could see, they were all bundled up in duffle-coats and woolly scarves. They looked depressed, well, you could imagine, out there in all weathers with the guards passing comments. They were sitting on torn-up plastic bags and chanting. As we went in, a woman threw something at us, I won't say what, but they all laughed and cheered when it hit the window.

Anyway, I'm sorry, you don't want to know that.

In the lab they took my temperature and blood pressure and put me in a waiting room with this kid, about seventeen he was, I'd say. Well, of course, as soon as I walk in, he says: '*Phwor*, what's that, mate, killer sweat?'

I said, 'Ha ha, very funny,' but there again, I suppose it might have been. I suppose there are Talents like that, aren't there? I gave him a fag, cigarette, I used to smoke a lot more then, I thought it might help with the smell.

He wanted me to tell him what I did. Kept on at me. I reminded him we weren't supposed to tell people. I said, 'Didn't they make you sign the declaration?' He was getting on my nerves. In the end I said, 'I don't do anything, it just happens to me.'

Well, he wouldn't let me alone after that, and of course then he started guessing, I bet this and I bet that, and he got so close I ended up telling him. I didn't see any point in trying to hide it; not there. I did tell him one lie: I said I hadn't got any of the letters with me. And I didn't tell him much, anyway, not like I'm telling you. I'm glad you don't mind me telling you.

'Course, the kid's eyes nearly popped out of his head when I told him. Then he grinned and said, 'That's a bit of all right, then, innit?' His voice had gone all hushed and high, and he even started to go a bit pink around the cheeks. Very quietly, he said, 'How many of them have you had, the birds, I mean?'

Well, I told him. 'None,' I said.

He didn't believe me. 'You what?' he said. 'Why not? Go on, why not?' And he kept on at me, why not, why not, so I told him it just doesn't work like that.

He said, 'Go on, I bet you –' Well, you can imagine what he said. I just said 'No.'

I'd rather not see them. I've seen some of them, well, I *know* some of them, of course. One of them's this secretary you always see at the DPR. Another one works in the supermarket where I go. She won't talk to me when I'm in there. They don't really want to see me, when it comes to it. Some of them think they do, they come round and they get all confused; 'I don't know what I'm doing here,' you know. Sit there shivering. All they want is literally just to write to me. They hate themselves for it, a lot of them. A lot of them hate me, obviously, I can't blame them.

I have to have met them. That's all. Only once. Then they start any time after that. Years after, some of them. A woman I knew when we were six suddenly started writing to me from Halifax. She said – well, you don't want to know what she said. Do you? Well, she said she thought about us in a balloon together, over the Alps, we started losing height and had to throw out all our clothes. That was a weird one.

The kid at the lab didn't understand, really. He said, 'You mean they don't really want it, they only think they do?'

'Sort of,' I said.

He sniffed. He said, 'That's birds all over, innit? That's nothing to do with you, is it?' He seemed to want to reassure me.

To change the subject I asked what he did. Do you know what he said? He said he can see black and white TV, black and white films, in colour. He said he always knows when they're black and white, right, but he can see what colour everything really is. He told me he was a parasensitive, grade two. Oh, he knew all about it, the ways they classify you, all the technical stuff. I couldn't be bothered. Luckily some more people turned up then, and the kid talked to them. He tried to get me to tell them too, but I wasn't having any. I was wasting time when I should have been at work, I was going to have a lot of catching up to do before Friday.

I was the first one they called. A man took me to a room. He asked me some questions, then he said he was going to bring in three women. He told me we were to say hello and our names, nothing else. They were all about my age. One of them shook my hand, the next one stood a little way away from me, about as far as you are now, and the third didn't come in, she just stood in the doorway. One of them was really gorgeous, but I wasn't allowed to say anything except 'Hello, Barry Bennett.' They they took my blood pressure again, and then they said I could go.

Well, I don't know what you think but I've thought about it. I think maybe the idea was that the spray would stop it happening. It didn't prove anything, though, except that I was telling the truth, because over the next fortnight I got letters from all three, and another one that said, 'I only saw you for a second, in the back of that car, but I think about you all the time. I left my husband when I came here. A lot of the women here are lesbians, I thought I might be one until I saw you.' She said – are you sure? She said, 'I want you here, now, on the ground, with all the others watching.'

I don't even know how they get my address, some of them.

It was a few weeks after that I got called to London, and Loric took me out to lunch. During lunch I had to do the talking. I don't know what he had me telling him. He just sat there smiling, hardly touching his food, and I had to talk to him the whole time. Then he stopped me suddenly and said, 'Oh, look, over there, isn't that, ah –'

He was looking at a woman who'd just come in, with a man following her, writing down what she was saying. Loric was pretending he'd forgotten her name. He pointed at her.

Suddenly she stopped talking and came towards us. She left the man standing there and walked straight over to us, she was gazing into space, not looking where she was going, I thought she was going to walk right into our table. At the last second she swerved and came round my side, and she put her hand on my chair to steady herself, as though she felt she was going to fall over. She stumbled on the heel of her shoe and stared down at me and said, 'Ah, sorry!' She stared at me as if I puzzled her, she wouldn't stop staring.

Do you know who it was? It was Sandra Taggart. Have you heard of her? She was a British MP. Mrs Thatcher used to hate her. She was the one who tabled that Freedom of Information bill, and almost got it through. She'd been on *Wogan*, on this TV chat show, and she'd accused him of sexism and had a big argument with him. They liked her for that, even the blokes at work thought she was all right.

I'm not interested in politics. I don't trust any of them, they're all out for number one, aren't they? Oh, ours are, anyway, they must be. I mean, Europe, you can see the sense of this, everybody sitting down together and trying to sort things out. But it's all over my head. I don't have anything to do with that side of it. All I have to do is read some of the publications that come in, press releases mostly, Xerox some of them, mark them up to file or post. The DPR want copies of anything that mentions paranorms specifically. I don't have to go into the library much, a couple of times a week. I don't go out at all, much, well, it's safer all round, isn't it? I stay in my room most of the time, watch the cable.

I suppose you know I shouldn't really be telling you this. I have got to tell you, though. I think you understand that, don't you? I thought you did. What about finishing this bottle? Shall we? Here, let me.

A lot of them never write again after the first time. It depends. Some of them write twice, three times, some of them keep writing, even though they say they must never see me again. They say things like: 'Dear Barry, you will see I have moved away, I'm not going to tell you my new address.' They always say they think it will be best for both of us.

Then they say: 'It doesn't matter, though. I can still write to you. I think about you all the time now that I can't see you.' What they think about me is the usual. My arms around them, and then the rest.

Oh, yes. I do, I read them all, or look at them all, anyway. The Department asked me to log them, and I did make the effort, but I could tell they weren't really interested, so I let it slide. Yes, you'd have to have had a computer to do it properly. I did cut off the postmarks for a while, though, oh, years ago now, that was quite fun. Got all these maps of Britain and drew rings all over them. I think it definitely gets weaker over distance; but then there's this woman in the West Country who's been writing to me since we were at school.

She's funny. She says things like, 'I wonder if you ever think about those days, Barry. At school, I mean. I remember you in your football clothes, all muddy and sweaty. I imagine you coming in the girls' changing rooms by mistake. Sometimes I imagine you come in on purpose, because you know I'm there.'

The others? Well, one kind says, 'You won't remember me but.' They usually sign them, those ones, Mary, Siobhan, Caroline, just the first name. Most of them are anonymous, they could be from anybody, it could be men, really, for all I know. Some are really bold and crude, I suppose that excites them. I think some of them are very young, they don't seem to know very much. They talk about 'your hard steaming thing'. Well; I suppose if it's very cold, it might. But you wouldn't be out in the cold, would you? You'd find somewhere warm. I mean, you'd go to bed, wouldn't you? I don't know, perhaps some people like it in the cold, do you think? I'm sure some people like to *think* about doing it outside in the cold, well, I know they do. I don't mind what they think. I just wish they didn't have to tell me about it.

I hadn't heard from the Department for months when I stopped doing my log. I hoped I might have slipped their minds, though by then I knew I couldn't ever get away from them. Well, some of the letters I handed over, right at the beginning, I mean, I never thought. Letters where they'd signed their full names. Letters with addresses, or PO boxes, some of them do that, when they think they want me to write back. Letters that could be very nasty for the women who wrote them. Break up homes. Ruin marriages. Push people, you know – over the edge. It's frightening how many of them say I am depressed, I take valium, I think all the time about killing myself. Ones like that I used to send to the Samaritans. Do you know –? I don't know if they did anything with them or not. I used to cut my name off. I couldn't stand it if I heard one of them did, you see. Do herself in, I mean.

One woman wrote some desperate stuff. 'My womb aches with loneliness. The sun is too bright, I want you here in the dark pit with me.' 'I am the rose under your foot,' one of them said, I don't know if that was her or another one. 'You must crush me, yet I will sting you and make you bleed.' Something like that. Very poetic, some of them.

Mostly, though, they say, oh, you know. I have bouncing 42-inch boobs. My thighs are wet for you. Can you fill me, my husband cannot. Fill me with your manhood: that's the sort of thing. I want to play with your soldier, one of them said. I liked that, it made me laugh.

You don't know what it means to me, telling you all this. You don't know how much you've helped me already.

They tell me about their dreams. 'In my dreams you come into the room, undress completely without saying a word, then crawl to me on your belly. You beg me for mercy.' Or the other way round. 'I wear my chains in your name. You hold the key.'

A lot of 'prisoners', I get. One woman signed herself the Lady of Shalott. It's this old poem. Knights in armour; you know? She said she saw me every day in her mirror. 'I am making a picture of you naked,' she said. 'I want you to help me with the colours.'

Sandra Taggart started writing straight away. No, she didn't sign it, but she didn't have to. She said in the House the men see her as an enemy, or an ally not to be trusted, she said that. She said, 'I know you would not be like that. I know you would not be afraid of my body. I want to feel your body against mine.' Oh, that wasn't the worst of it.

What did I do with it? I burnt it. Well, of course I did. I set fire to it there and then, I do that with a lot of them, most of them, in fact. I got this fire bucket from a junk shop, red with white letters on it that say FIRE, I keep it outside the back door. I put them in there and drop a match in. Envelopes and all. Cut the stamps off first, for charity.

Some of them I keep. No, of course I don't write back, never. But some of them are quite sweet, if you know what I mean. Some of them, a few of them, do get me going, I can't pretend they don't. I won't tell you about them, but I do want to be honest with you. You want me to tell you? No, no.

All right. The only ones I keep are a few when I know who they're from, and I know no harm could possibly come from my keeping them. They're ones from women like, oh, women at work; or the daughter of a landlady in the house I lived in when I left home; barmaids in a couple of pubs we used to go in. The ones from women I actually fancied, ones I might have asked out, even, if it hadn't been for the letters. It's like I told the kid at the lab, they don't really want me. They can be quite friendly, oh, yes, some of them, we get on all right; but not in that way.

No, I've never had a proper girlfriend. Well, how can I?

Sandra Taggart started writing the end of November, I think it was, then they sent me here, that was in the February. They only gave me a couple of days' notice. There's a plane, you will be on it. That sort of thing. They put me in a hotel, like you, no, I'd better not tell you which one. I reckon the Department did a good job on my mum and dad, I haven't heard from them all the time I've been here. Not that they ever thought much of me. They forward the rest of my post.

One of the blokes at work, it was, that sent me the *Sun*. He'd written on it, next to the picture, 'No wonder you can afford to bugger off to Frogland', with all these exclamation marks. It was part of a photocopy of her letter. He must have thought I'd sent them it. It said experts had authenticated her handwriting. I don't suppose they'd even had that done, really, they just liked the story.

The DPR kept their name well away from it, of course they did. They left my name out too, but all my mates at the office knew. They'd suggested the same thing themselves, some of the ones that like to think they're hard. The paper said it was concealing my identity because I was in danger. That might have been true, I've had some threats in my time. Yes, I've been knocked silly a few times. I can look after myself. You have to, really.

Well, I phoned Whitehall from the library, and I kept phoning until I got Loric himself. 'It's bedlam here today,' he said. 'What do you want?' He sounded as if he was annoyed I'd phoned.

So I told him.

'Beastly nuisance,' he said. 'Beastly. They get their inky little fingers in everywhere, don't they? The gutter press.'

I said, 'I burnt that letter.'

'Oh, come on,' he said. He said it as if he was tired, as if he was doing his best for me, but, you know, couldn't give a toss, basically. Couldn't be bothered. 'My dear chap,' he said. 'We read all your correspondence. We always have. Didn't they tell you?'

I was gripping the phone like fury. I could see red spots in front of my eyes. All I could think of to say back was, 'Isn't that a bit expensive, for the old DPR?'

Loric laughed. It sounded metallic down the phone, like something nasty running out of the receiver. He said, 'You must be joking, old man. They'd pay us to read your stuff. Oh, dear me, yes, we've got them queueing up for Barry Bennett duty.'

I wanted to hang up, but he was still gassing. He said, 'We only give you to good little boys and girls. They've all got fan clubs, you know, all your regulars. Pity about Ms Taggart, though, I do agree. Somebody slipped up somewhere. Good thing for you that you were out of the country when it broke, really. Of course we're doing everything we can to protect you. Keep your head down, that's the best advice I can offer you.

'I hope you're happy over there, Barry,' he said. 'We may be wanting you to stay over there just a little longer.'

Well, it's all right here, isn't it? I don't mind. I do what I'm told. I don't push it. To tell you the truth, it's been quite nice to have a fresh start, with people who don't know me from Adam. I try not to meet many people. Even I can't turn down a direct invitation, though! When you said I'm the first Talented person you've ever met, well.

I suppose I ought to go back to my hotel now, though, didn't I? Is that really the time?

Well. Helena. Thank you for a lovely evening. I hope you didn't mind me going on and on like that. You understand I don't usually tell people. Especially not women. I mean, I think you should either tell all of them or none of them, and I couldn't stand it. I really couldn't. But I wanted to tell you.

I mean, just in case.

Very slick. *Daddy always said you had hidden depths.*

'We're not allowed to run death squads in this country. We just have to make do with the tabloid press.' Loric yawned and threw the folder aside.

Temper, temper. Conscience a little tender about this, is it?

'I had to do something.' Loric yawned again and massaged his temples. 'I mean, that Freedom of Information nonsense is dangerous enough at the best of times. But now we've really got something to hide . . .'

So it all comes back to Philip again.

'Of course. What dirty work doesn't, these days?'

This, for a start. His attention slowly focused on the next file. The mosquito voice had a raw, eldritch edge to it. *Threatening, and somehow familiar. And images of bloody Greece again . . .*

'I think you're right,' he said.

A PROBLEM SHARED

Tina Anghelatos

I have never liked the smell of hospitals, the air always seems tinged with disinfectant. This one in particular was giving me the creeps, a special house deep in the heart of Surrey put aside for paranorms who had had 'accidents'. Or, to put it another way, for whom something had gone badly wrong. However, at the DPR's request, I stood at the bedside of a middle-aged man, looking down.

'What's wrong with him?' I asked the staff nurse.

She gave me the long-suffering look of a professional forced to deal with an amateur. 'He's catatonic, in a total state of shock. We're still trying to determine exactly what happened.'

'Which is why,' a smooth male voice came from behind me, 'they need me.'

I turned round to meet the self-assured stare of a young man. Well, one about my own age, mid twenties. A tweed jacket was flung casually over one arm, his designer shirt was open at its crisply ironed collar. 'I'm Simon,' he said, taking my hand firmly. 'You must be Kathy. We're going to be partners on this one.'

'Oh, really?' was all I could think of to say. It was the first I had heard of a partner on this assignment. My Talent is, as I say to the inquisitive, a seasonal one with limited appeal. Around December the ability to create the illusion of a small dancing Christmas fairy has its uses.

At other times of the year it has far less value as a Talent. Once, just once, as a child I had managed to produce something else: a brown teddy bear I saw in a shop and dearly wanted. My mother's subsequent threats after an uncomfortable half hour with the store detective still rang in my mind. Since then it has been the Christmas fairies only.

Simon nodded and eyed the patient. 'I read thoughts,' he commented. 'Don't worry, my dear, not extensively, just the basic, most powerful ones.'

It was the 'my dear' in those upper-class tones. He had to be Eton or Harrow; I have always hated the type that those places produce. They seem to think the world owes them something for existing. He must have caught my thought, because a slight flush rose to his cheeks and he moved to the bed.

I watched him work, his face intent. After a few moments he looked up and pushed back his fair hair. 'I can only get one thought, "I CAN FLY!" And I assure you, he's shouting it. What was his Talent?' He cocked his head at the nurse.

She rustled her starch. 'He could levitate himself. About three inches, no more.'

'And now he thinks he can fly. An interesting delusion, wouldn't you say, Kathy?'

'Very,' I snapped back, embarrassed that he had so easily picked up my dislike. 'But what's that got to do with me?'

A slight smile. 'Well, Kathy, let's go and sit somewhere quiet and I'll explain.' He led me outside the room to a small lobby, set to one side of the corridor. 'I work for MI6.'

'MI6? You're a spy?' I tailed off.

The aristocratic cheek bones didn't move. 'National security is a necessary part of the government; my section is concerned with the protection and safety of our para-norms in the EEC. I was at a ... particular university and naturally got recruited. It's a new section, of course, set up because of our recent EEC commitments, so we're still in the development stages. Now' – and he dropped his voice confidentially – 'some of our Talents have been murdered.'

'Murdered?' My heart beat faster. 'Who? Where? How?'

'One Glaswegian and a Londoner. Oh, and an Italian; at least I think he was. How, we don't know, we were trying to get some clues from this chap here. He was another attempt, British again. A passing tourist found him staggering out of a small alley-way one night. We think the murderer must have been disturbed. We only just saved him as it is.' A certain tone of offence had filled his voice at the idea one would murder an English-man. 'They all had one thing in common: they were on holiday in Athens.' A pause. 'You do speak Greek, don't you?'

Which was how I came be in Athens, showing my Talent off, trying to attract a murderer. I had found a small café to operate from, a short walk up the road from my hotel. It was just far enough away from the crowds, and was cool and green, set in a small square surrounded by trees. I had discovered it after I had been in Athens a couple of days and decided I liked its ambience. Quiet but busy. I visited it every day at some time, drawn back to its padded chairs and paper-clothed tables.

Today the waiter smiled knowingly at me, white teeth flashing in the sunbrown face as he attempted for the umpteenth time to look down my shirt. Visions of Theo came back to me, a similar bearded face, clear eyes.

'A beer, please.' I still felt hassled by his memory and in times of stress, my Greek deserts me.

'Of course.' He paused a second and then swung away, hips flaunted provocatively. A Greek male's game, I recalled from Theo. Theo, that last time, standing half naked at the door of my bedsit. His handsome face forced into a smile as he tried to conceal the woman inside the room. Never come back a day early from a weekend away without telling your Greek boyfriend. I shut my eyes for an instant and put my thoughts away with a sigh.

I waited until a fair number of people were sitting at the other tables, most sipping cold drinks. Time for the dancing fairy. I eyed them as they began to gather round. Out there amongst them, well to the back, was the detestable Simon. My perpetual shadow, I would see him occasionally behind me, dressed in crease-free beige shorts and floral shirt. Watching me follow my orders. 'Make your Talent obvious,' he had said, 'we want to attract the killer. Don't worry, I'll protect you. MI6 trains us very well.' Somehow he did not totally reassure me. I had encouraged myself with the thought that I was there for a cause, to help protect other Talents. Not only, as a sneaking little voice in my mind suggested, for the money.

The fairy did her tricks. Some of the customers I was beginning to recognize now as regulars. There was an old man, sitting bathing in the sun, drinking ouzo. Next to him a group of flamboyant youths who watched through glances and concealed stares. Quite near me a well-dressed woman who drank coffee and gazed with amusement at the fairy. I sent it pirouetting near her and she caressed it with a slight smile.

Quite soon after that I ran out of steam and the fairy vanished. With it went most of my admirers, until only the regulars remained. I heaved a sigh, sat back and took a long drink of beer.

'You want postcard?' A small boy approached me.

'*Ochi.*' No.

'Souvenir?' Beads on a frayed leather string.

'*Ochi.*'

'Sweets?'

'*Ochi.*' I wished Theo had taught me something stronger.

He waved to an older youth and said something too fast for me to translate. The other approached me. 'You speak Greek? You want to go to nightclub?'

'No.' I felt his appraising eyes and decided it was time to leave.

I made for the Acropolis, the entrance a short walk up through the narrow streets and then along Apostle Paul Street. Simon followed. I hoped he was getting heartily sick of the ancient sites I visited; he had already made a few comments to that end on one occasion when we had met 'for a briefing'. With that in mind, I had made a list of all the others I could find to visit.

I found the way in along with a host of other tourists and began to climb the hill. A long flight of marble steps, worn smooth by thousands of years and many visitors. At the top I paused for breath and looked around; I had seen the Acropolis in the brochures, I knew what it ought to look like. A marble white city would be shining under a cloudless blue sky, with a cool breeze that carried the rumour of antiquity and the exotic. A few dedicated people, scholars like myself, would be wandering idly round the tall columns of the Parthenon, constructing its past glories, the gold crowned statues and heroic friezes. Across the city there would be other temples, the Sacred Way glistening and the tree-lined hill of Lycavitos. The smells would be spiced and foreign, a hint of the orient and maybe romance. That was how Theo had promised me it would be in the hours when he had described Athens, the 'city of the violet crown'.

Maybe it had been once. Maybe it was because I was nervous, kept thinking I saw people following me, kept glimpsing Simon wandering aimlessly behind me. Maybe it was really the absence of Theo. Theo, who had taught me Greek, been delighted when he found I'd studied the classics, and who had so much charm I'd have died for him. Until that last day. Now, as I gazed around, I felt loss and disappointment. In the distance famed Lycavitos was wreathed in mist; a smog that obscured my vision, I could smell it here and all over the city. The oriental smells of my dreams had been replaced by one of smoke, flavoured gently with drains. Behind me the Temple of Athena was full of tourists and scaffolding. Artistically placed between the iron bars and ancient pillars were wooden boards, designed to keep both visitors and smog away from the sacred stones. A half-covered sign read THE GREEK GOVERNMENT REGRETS ... I heaved a sigh of relief that the Elgin Marbles were still safe in the British Museum and wished I was similarly back in London. It was hot and sweaty, and I wanted to go home.

I considered a dancing fairy here and wondered if the killer had already noticed me – that is, if there really was a killer and it was not all coincidental murder. After all, violent death happens in every city, and not just to Talents on holiday. I leant back against the cold marble and decided it was time to take a break. I had done one fairy today. I would walk slowly back to my hotel, change and then return to my café. I could order another beer, sit quietly at the back and relax for a while.

I set off back down Apostle Paul Street and into the Plaka, the slightly down-at-heel area of Athens. Hidden up here in the narrow streets was the Hotel Aphrodite, close enough to Syntagma to be called central, far enough away to be cheap. More people surrounded me, men pressing over close, women pushing past laden with huge baskets from the market. I sought the relative safety of the tourist shops, at least all I could be offered there was dubious silver, brittle statues and imitation pottery. Eventually, exhausted by the process and tired of looking over my shoulder, I made for home.

Some hours later I found myself drawn back to my café. It was growing dark, and I felt rested enough to go out. A quiet evening in the café should help to restore me; with luck, most of the self-conscious males would have left for the dubious discos that blared out loud Top 40 music. I debated visiting the discos with the fairy and decided that I could wait a while until I felt more confident. A happy thought crossed my mind: it was possible that Simon might well be uncomfortable shadowing me in those places. I chuckled to myself as I made my way through the Plaka and resolved that there would be other nights for the nightclubs. Tonight, however, the café suddenly had a multitude of attractions: it was familiar territory and provided food.

The sun was sinking as I sat down and waved at the waiter. Inside I winced; he did look disturbingly like Theo. He cocked an eyebrow in an intimate way as I discovered I was ravenous and ordered Greek salad and beer. I stretched out and relaxed in the warm summer air.

Click. The sound of wood rolling on wood. Softly in the background. I ignored it until it came again. Curiously I squinted in the direction of the sound. At a table opposite a Greek woman was sitting, a backgammon board in front of her. She was setting out the pieces, rolling the dice occasionally. I remembered her fine dress and striking face from earlier in the day. She had played with my illusion as it had danced in front of her. Now she sat at the table next to me, and I watched covertly as she positioned the board and started the game. First black, then white; she was playing herself. Fascinated, I stared as her gold-ringed hands moved the pieces.

Warm brown eyes regarded me suddenly and then the full red lips curved into a gentle smile. An invitation. 'Do you play?' The slight accent of one who has been taught by an American, a lazy drawl of a voice. Hopeful too, I guessed.

Reluctantly, I shook my head. 'I don't know how to, I'm afraid.'

'Ah, English.' A faint pout of the lips and a half wink. She made us conspirators together. 'Would you like to learn? Backgammon is the only game in the world to play.'

An open café and a sleepy evening, why not? I stood up. 'If you're patient.'

'Of course.' An expansive shrug of her black draped shoulders, a wide spreading of the hands. 'What is the hurry when we have this evening?' She sipped from the small coffee-cup, leaving a slight red gloss on the china. 'You like Greek coffee?'

I had always called it Turkish, it had driven Theo mad. 'Not much, it's too sweet.'

'You should order it half sugar.'

'*Metrio?*'

'You speak Greek?' She appeared delighted that I should speak her tongue.

'A little. I had a Greek boyfriend.'

'Ah, men! Yes.' She patted her stomach and I noticed that she was bulging slightly. 'This one, he makes me with baby, then leaves.'

'Leaves?' I was horrified, 'After getting you pregnant?'

She shrugged slightly again. 'It's common here. And now, who knows where he is? Hades, perhaps. You know the Greek underworld?'

I recalled my studies, *The Odyssey*. 'I know.'

'Well.' Her face darkened visibly and she leant across the table, the brown eyes widening dramatically. The scent of perfume assailed me. 'I tell you, I would leave the body for the dogs to find. In a small dark place.' Simon's descriptions of the last failed murder sprang to mind and I shivered. As if she noticed, she smiled again and the storm was gone. 'So you are here alone? Or do you have another boyfriend?'

'No, I'm just alone. I want to see the sites here.'

'The Parthenon, the Theseion, so far from what they were.' She gazed distantly as if she could see their glories. 'And all gone. Still, that is the nature of things.' She rolled the dice in one hand. 'Now, I shall teach you to play, my own style of backgammon.'

We spent the rest of the evening together, bent over the board, punctuated with cries of *Kala!* and *Malaka!* when she lost a piece. And I watched her, the board and my pieces, and forgot the others who might be watching me. In the end she took my final piece with a feral smile. 'You should never leave them unguarded, that's the way you lose.'

I shrugged, her own gesture returned to her. 'Next time.'

The brown eyes sparkled. 'You will come again?'

'Why not? I'm in Athens for a while.'

'*Kala!* Most afternoons or evenings I'm here, but if I don't play here, in the Kerameikos.'

'The Kerameikos?'

'The old walls and gates of Athens. You can enter free on Thursdays and it is near my home. It is very beautiful there, there are statues and few tourists.' She began to pack the board away. 'Do you stay near here?'

'Just up the road, near the cathedral.'

'So, that is not so far. You can walk up Mitropoleos to get there. Oof.' She looked up at the night sky. 'It is getting late. I will go home.'

'I'm sorry, I never asked your name,' I said, sad to see her leave me.

She fitted the dice into their home. 'Olympia,' her mouth dimpled, 'I was born there.'

I tried to imagine being named after an exhibition hall or, worse, Birmingham. 'Oh, I'm Kathy. Do you often call people after places?'

'Sometimes, but sometimes after the gods.' She chuckled. 'I could introduce you to an Aphrodite.'

'Aphrodite. Poor girl.'

'Indeed. You haven't seen her.' A flash of malicious pleasure, I thought. My Greek lady was very human. 'She's more like a Medusa, ugly enough to kill.' A nod of acceptance to me. 'Maybe I'll see you again, then, Kathy.' She was gone with swift pace down the street, long skirts flowing around her.

I considered and looked around. I could see the floral of Simon's shirt and I signalled to him. We could get our briefing out of the way here. All this cloak-and-dagger stuff he insisted on was simply increasing my nervousness. He frowned slightly but came over.

'May I join you?' His cultured British tones came loud enough for the waiters to hear.

I smiled. 'Of course.'

He sat down and lowered his voice. 'What the hell? We're not supposed to meet in public.' His eyes were fixed on her departing back, enthralled by its sway.

I snapped at him. 'Come on, Simon, it's convenient here. Did you get anything from anyone?'

He sighed, obviously irritated with me. 'No, nothing from anyone. And your lady had only a very keen interest in the game. It took all her attention. And yours.'

'Have you been reading my thoughts?' I nearly forgot to keep my voice down.

He gave me a teasing glance. 'Not really. I just picked it up. You were both absorbed. And I did have to monitor the situation. After all, Kathy, you have been to this café every day and used your, er, Talent. You'd be easy to track.'

Relieved by his information, I suddenly felt the need to defend Olympia. Especially after the way his eyes followed her. 'That's what I'm supposed to do, isn't it? Be noticeable. Are you suggesting that Olympia is something to do with you-know-what?' I felt angry at his intrusion on my thoughts. 'She just wants to play backgammon. She's also pregnant and probably wants some company.'

He narrowed his eyes. 'Exactly so. But we do have to check these things, you know. As you say, you're supposed to be noticed.' A superior smile. 'I'm here to protect you, make sure nothing happens to you. And to solve our problem. So you don't have to panic.' Like this, his voice indicated. 'But there's no need for you to actually get friendly with the natives.'

'"Get friendly with the natives"? God-damn it all, it's their country. What happened to the EEC?'

'Economic necessity, that's all.' He flicked his shorts. 'They're still foreign in the end. No genuine British spirit. Still' – he grinned slightly and appeared younger – 'she was very, ah, alluring.'

I made no attempt to conceal my disgust, taking pleasure in the fact he could feel it, and left, leaving him to pay the bill.

I decided after that to give Simon a run for his money. I visited every site at least twice, I took the bus to Eleusis, the train to Corinth. Whenever I could, in the afternoons and late into the evenings, I went to meet Olympia to play backgammon. I found myself beginning to win; I spent some nights working out strange variations to entertain and confound her. I still did my job: I showed her my Talent and attracted a crowd. She seemed delighted, and my other observers fascinated by the little rotating figure. I danced it towards Olympia's face and she prodded it; I made it leap back and disappear with the brightest spark my Talent could produce. Behind me I could feel Simon's tacit reluctant acknowledgement that I was doing as instructed. In all that time there was no sign of a murderer; I began to think the paranorm deaths more accident than design on the part of a Talent hater.

About a week after we had met, Olympia asked me, 'Do you like the theatre? It's the Athens Festival and they are doing the ancient plays in the theatre below the Acropolis.' She moved a piece to take one of mine.

I had noticed and had meant to go before, but, with all my running around the countryside and time spent in backgammon, I'd been preoccupied. 'What's playing?' I considered my pieces.

She smiled gently. 'One of my favourites, the *Agamemnon* of Aeschylus. Do you know it?'

'Vaguely. It's about his return from Troy?'

'That's it, he gets killed by his wife Clytemnestra for bringing another woman home.'

She couldn't have chosen something that would have appealed to me more at that time. Visions of Theo with the woman filled me. 'Sounds fun, let's go.' I moved to block her piece.

She looked at me, amused. 'Very well. I will meet you by the theatre, then.'

I considered trying to give Simon the slip to irritate him but decided against it; after all there had been someone murdering paranorms here. A guard was a guard, whatever I thought of him and the manner in which he eyed my Greek lady. So I went and he followed, a yellow floral shirt today.

After the performance Olympia yawned slightly. 'Would you like coffee? In our taverna?'

I nodded and we walked through the narrow deserted streets of the Plaka, with the shops boarded up on both sides. She moved close to me as if for comfort, feeling her swollen stomach slightly.

'Are you all right?' I asked.

'The child is beginning to stir,' she began.

Behind us came sounds and then a pattering. 'What's that?' I asked her sharply.

She looked back and took my arm in a firm grasp. 'Only a cat, Kathy. They're all over the city. Don't be afraid.'

Our eyes met, hers that warm embracing brown, mine blue like the skies above Olympus, as Theo on one of his more poetic days had told me. Regret was in her gaze as she looked away. She pulled at my sleeve. 'This way, there's a short cut. Up behind the Kerameikos.'

I followed her in the moonlight along the shadowed streets, stumbling on the cracked pavement. She stopped at an iron railing and pointed. 'It was the old cemetery of Athens, you know. The ancients buried their dead here. You can see the tombs.'

I stared through the bars, across the fallen stones and along the Street of the Dead. Dimly in the night, I could see statues erected to honour the dead, reliefs raised of white marble depicting the farewell ceremonies. A warm breeze blew towards us, carrying the sounds of the trees moving, the only guardians of the dead that remained.

'A peaceful place to be buried.' Her voice came softly as she touched my hand. I felt a sudden weariness, like that of falling asleep and shook myself. Olympia's face was turned to me, half shrouded by the dark. 'I liked you, Kathy, I really did.' She gazed at me and those brown eyes became wells of darkness, consuming my soul. I stepped back, hit the railing and screamed.

Olympia's voice again, full of sadness. 'I bear you Talented no ill will, Kathy, but I am driven on by my nature. I always attract Talents; I do try not to call them, really I do, but in one way or another they come to me. I have always needed to consume Talent to live myself, you see. And I found out years ago that I could enthral them with a focus.' A pause and I felt her mind touch me. 'Like backgammon.' Mesmerizing tones. 'I need to feed so much more at present. It is for the child, you must understand that. She is getting hungry.' I began to sink forward.

A voice from behind us. 'Kathy? What's happening?' Simon.

The draining sensation lessened as Olympia swung round, her hand still tight on my arm. 'You. In the café. I thought you were there too much. And *you are* Talented.'

He took a step back. 'My God. Hunger.'

She reached out and grabbed him, pulling him against me. His thoughts, his voice in my head. 'KATHY, SHE'S DRAINING MY TALENT. VAMPIRE. RAVENOUS. OH, MY GOD. SO HUNGRY. I CAN READ HER MIND.' Pictures of what he read filled my mind, images of darkness, of victims slowly dying.

Simon again, excited, loud in my mind: 'I CAN READ HER MIND. NOT JUST ONE THOUGHT.' Another image from Simon, of the vampire bent over the last victim she had drained. The hospital case.

My own Talent started inflating as she began to drink it again, growing it as much as she could, making it all it would ever, could ever, have been. Desperation filled me as horrifying flickers came from the weakening Simon. Beginning to die. I was starting to panic as the vampire gave me her gift; she expanded my Talent so I could make any illusion I wanted, be it teddy bear or aeroplane. I could have this for a few seconds, my full Talent, just before she drained it from me. The knowledge of what could have been a real Talent filled my mind. I wanted it and I wanted to live. Then I was caught with Simon once more, inside the vampire's thoughts.

Simon pushed me into her mind, shouting for help. He read her inmost thoughts and showed them to me. The strong desire for food and survival. Then below it all, a fear. Something that she had once barely escaped, a terror of long ago: the gorgon Medusa who turned her victims to stone. He gave it to me, showed me the image as the vampire remembered it. A tall body in robes of black, gliding over the old Temple stones towards the hidden watchers. The hiss of the snakes and face hidden in the dark. A glint of eyes and turning of the dark head. The deliberate way the Medusa had lifted the torch to light her face and how the vampire had fled, leaving her companions behind.

A distant echo of her words came to me: 'like a Medusa, ugly enough to kill'. In despair, I started to create a Medusa, an illusion that would stand between us and the vampire. With my back pushed against the bars of the old graveyard of Athens, I used the vampire's memory and made a Medusa, the horror of the past that had killed with a look. I turned the illusion on the vampire, and heard the whisper of the snakes and shrill scream as the gorgon rushed towards her.

Silence. The sound of night birds. There was a harsh breathing next to me and Simon drew close, leaning against the stones. There was a body in front of us and he bent down to it, feeling the pulse. Awed for a second, he looked at me. 'You killed her.' He breathed deeply again. 'With an illusion.'

In the hush that followed, I felt a strange sadness for

the woman Olympia. Then, more than anything else in the world, I wanted all the Talent I had known so briefly before the vampire had died. I knew now what I could have been, and that is the cruellest thing that can happen to anyone. I would never be so Talented again. Simon must have felt it also. A genuine sympathy showed in his eyes as he rested next to her body.

'It would have been nice,' he commented. 'To have a large Talent. I never guessed. I could have done so much.'

We called the police. Simon flashed an ID card at them and they let us go with a promise to return in the morning. We went to the nearest café, not the one Olympia had drawn me to, and sat there drinking black coffee. He leant over for the sugar and our hands brushed. I leapt away as an electric shock ran through me. Talent, power.

We stared at each other as a small illusion appeared before us. A woman, in a stage of undress. I eyed it and then Simon.

He blushed and said quickly, 'Talent! Kathy, we've got full Talent. Look, you're making an illusion of what I'm reading.'

I rubbed my head; it was true, I felt my Talent expand again to be all it had been with the vampire. From his face, he was finding the same with his. I shook off his touch and my Talent faded.

His eyes shone. 'Kathy, it's when we're together! We can do anything. She must have fused our Talents in some way.'

My jaw dropped. 'You're joking! I'm not staying near you. You mean I can only have my true Talent if I'm with you?'

He beamed at me. 'And touching. So I'm afraid, sweetheart, it looks like it's me or the Christmas fairy.'

I didn't know there were any of them left.

'Me neither. Not after Prague.' He shuddered. 'But they've had plenty of time to spread out. If this wasn't just a single rogue Talent, or some straggler we missed.'

We'll have to do something. Make sure . . .

'I'll spread the word.' But that was a job for the Gods; nothing to concern the Minister, whose only Talent was the ability to look calm and confident on television when the autocue broke down. What would concern him, Loric knew, with the absolute certainty of the precognitive, was the content of the file now uppermost on the blotter.

Reluctantly, he hefted it.

TOTALLY TRASHED

Roz Kaveney

'Well, in the first place, you're exaggerating about the cat litter, damn it,' Leonora said, tapping, with exaggerated care, the ash of her cigarette into one of Michael's horrid pentagonal crystal ashtrays.

When you are having a row about basic attitudes to life with your lover of six weeks, it would be dumb to desecrate his snowy carpet any more than you can help in the general run of things. Particularly when you bummed the cigarette in the first place, knowing that you would need it as a prop in the row that had seemed to be brewing from the moment you walked in.

'I am not exaggerating at all,' Michael said in a hurt voice, turning from his desk chair to turn down that crappy Dire Straits album he insisted on playing all the time – supposed to be the Best Of, but how could they tell? – and posing himself against the window so as to appear to the best advantage against the sunset and the northern curve of the river.

'Yes, you are,' she said. 'You're always doing it, pushing things to extremes in order to put other people in the wrong.'

'Sometimes I wonder about you,' Michael said. 'You have this paranormal ability.'

Leonora winced.

'Leonora Norton,' he went on. 'Captain Conscience, the girl who almost makes men feel guilty.'

In between embarrassment, irritation, and relief that he obviously knew nothing, she wondered whether he realized that, in order to get the full effect of his beauty, she was having to squint as she looked at him, and whether this was the object of the exercise, to make her the less devastating of the pair of them. Her eyes were her best feature, she had always thought, even through thick glasses, and not at their best, squinting.

'What's worse,' he said, 'is that you make people feel guilty for your faults, not theirs, so that they don't notice what a leech you are.'

Bum a cigarette, she thought, and the next thing is they complain about feeling drained, poor babies.

'It is not possible, in logic,' she said, 'that you can actually believe that somehow particles of cat litter adhere to my person for the whole of a working day, only to dislodge themselves the moment I get into your flat. Or is the theory that I bring them round specially, in a small paper bag, and spread them when you are fixing drinks, in order to cause you grief, or remind myself of home?'

There was no point, she thought, in pushing her luck and trying to reduce the real explanation to absurdity before it could occur to him.

'I don't talk about your faults,' she said, looking at his desk and the three monitors whose dead screens glared across the room at her. 'I mean, I know you love your silly old computers more than you love me.'

'I don't,' he said unconvincingly.

'Yes, you do,' she said. 'You talk baby-talk to them when you think I'm asleep.'

To her surprise, he blushed.

'It's just a way of encouraging them,' he said, 'a way of getting results. You don't mock people for talking to their house-plants.'

'I do,' she said. 'And you don't have any plants.'

She looked around the vast bare expanse of his living room. What is the point, she reflected, of having all this money if you don't spend it on any furniture worth having, or of living in a spacious apartment if you don't fill it up with things?

Mind you, he works so hard, poor lamb, that he's never free when furniture shops are open; and he lives out here, where there're probably no shops anyway except for garden centres. That probably explains why his chairs and sofa aspire to the conditions of raffia and wrought-iron respectively.

'I don't know how or why you bring all the mess into my flat,' Michael said. 'And I don't much care. It's disgusting, that's all. I do like you; but I can't bear the squalor you live in, and I can't bear the idea of your importing it into my space. What's the point of my not coming round to your flat and protecting our relationship from my natural distaste, if it's just going to mean that my flat inexorably turns into the kitchen midden you inhabit? It has got to stop now, and if it doesn't, we will.'

Leonora was starting to become mildly irritated. Why should she put up with this anal little twerp just because he had a niceish body and a slightly interesting mind and lots of money to spend in over-priced restaurants? How dare he think that gave him the right to lecture her on hygiene? She was so angry that she almost did not notice a sharp pain in her left buttock.

She jumped up, having noticed it.

'You can't bear the truth, can you?' he said.

'Truth is the one important thing in my life,' she said.

'Oh, no, it isn't,' he said. 'One reference to the appalling mess you have made of your life, and your flat, and your pathetic little articles on history, and you run screaming from the room.'

There was no point in explaining that she had merely

stood up to get away from the jabbing of his rotten straw chairs, and so she headed for the door. The relationship was probably time-expired at this point, and there is such a thing as dignity.

'You know nothing about my life,' she said. 'Fucking is not expertise.'

As she walked towards the front door, pausing only to grab her bag and her coat, two large broken paper-clips and a torn-off piece of newspaper fell out of the bottom of the left leg of her Calvin Kleins.

'See,' Michael said, 'bloody see. You spread rubbish wherever you go. It just falls off you, like dandruff.'

She paused and picked up the rubbish, walked over, dumped it in the ashtray and continued to leave.

'Fuck off, pencil dick,' she said. There is no point in being verbally elegant at such moments.

There is a time when the important thing is just to leave. It is part of such times that you honour custom and slam the door; when she did so, something detached itself from the inside of the door frame and fell to earth with a gratifying set of clinks. He never did fix the security chain properly.

As Leonora turned from the door, she more or less collided with two men in grey suits, who stood outside poised, as if to knock. The younger man was Sharpe, an obnoxious young man from the Department of Paranormal Resources who, she remembered, thought he was cleverer than he was.

'I have nothing to say to you people,' she said. 'As you yourself said, Sharpe, last time we met, the Department generate enough crap of their own already, without needing me.'

'Hello, Miss Norton,' said the older of the two men, flashing a folder that contained a police warrant card, but that also identified him as working for the DPR.

'How convenient. We were going to have to come and see you later.'

'But I just said –' Leonora said.

'Later, I said,' the policeman continued, 'after we speak to Mr Sinden. Nothing you need worry about, Miss Norton; just one or two minor questions. It's Chummy we need to talk to. There's just a few facts I'd like clarified.'

'We have an interesting proposition to put to him,' Sharpe said.

'He's in trouble, then,' she said, reining her mild interest back from the point of tottering into glee.

'I really couldn't say, Miss Norton,' the elder said. 'That hasn't been established.'

'Tell me, miss,' he continued. 'Has he given you any very expensive presents lately? Or proposed extended stays in exotic locations?'

Leonora looked at him, baffled.

'I see,' he said.

'I don't,' she said. 'What's going on?'

'Oh,' he said. 'Nothing you need worry about. It's just one of those things that happen sometimes, in the City, that we and the Department get called in on. Nothing anyone need worry about.'

'Oh,' she said. 'You don't mean Michael is a paranormal too. You know, I'd never thought of there being paranormals in the City; one thinks of us as being either wonderfully useless or highly decorative, not as men in suits shouting into phones and staring into computer screens and boring themselves into hypnotic trances.'

'Well,' said Sharpe, 'actually, that doesn't seem to be the problem at all. Rather the reverse, actually.'

'Interesting case,' the older man said. 'Don't know whether he even knows he does it.'

'Gosh,' she said. 'He did say that it was like talking to plants to make them grow. Surely that's impossible,

though. I mean, there has to be a mind for you to hypno-
tize, doesn't there?'

'Well, that's another thing,' Sharpe said.

'I can tell you this, Miss Norton,' the older man said,
'because you're practically family, as far as the Department is concerned. And you signed the Official Secrets
Act back when you registered. Besides, you are his girlfriend.'

'I am afraid,' said Leonora, 'that you are under a misapprehension. Mr Sinden and I have parted company.'

'What was it?' Sharpe said. 'The state of your flat? Or
those idiotic articles you write in *History Today*?'

Leonora looked at him.

'Shut up, Sharpe,' said the older man.

'Oh, don't worry,' she said. 'Sharpe came around to my
flat in the old days, trying to sniff his way into the family
mystique, and, if he has been there more recently, well, I
take it for granted that people like you enter flats illegally
as a matter of course. And I have nothing to hide.'

'Whatever government or the police do, miss,' said the
older man, 'is no business of yours, and he has no business talking about it.'

'Well, I'm sorry,' Sharpe said. 'But you've never had to
go in there. There's the stuff you get on your shoes –
stains the leather, you never get it off. And those cats,
they're feral. Or psychotic.'

'No,' Leonora said, 'they're just not very used to strange
men.'

'Unlike their mistress,' Sharpe said.

'Good enough for you,' said Leonora. 'In your time.
And what's wrong with my articles?'

'I think they're dead offensive, particularly that last
review,' said Sharpe. 'Paranormals need their history –
you of all people should know that.'

'My dear little man,' she said. 'I have no objection at all

to our having as much history as we can possibly handle. I just insist that it be real history, and not all this Guy de Horvendile stuff.'

'I had a poster of Guy de Horvendile on my wall, when I was a kid,' he said. 'He was a gallant knight, a crusader.'

'Nonsense,' she said, 'he was a colonialist, and probably a racist. But he wasn't a paranormal. If paranormals have to have their own history, it should not be all this heritage crap that they keep making up to pretty up a shameful history of exploitation and oppression.'

'But what about your grandparents?' Sharpe said.

'Classic case,' Leonora said. 'They practically bred them when they were at Ditchley – then Orpington sacrificed her on some hare-brained scheme and put my grandfather to work on horror weapons until he went completely dotty and blew himself to offal. No heroism there, Mr Sharpe, and only an idiot would call it glamour.'

'You only take that attitude because you're practically unTalented yourself,' he said. 'A systematic definition of Talent would leave you out altogether.'

'Define away as you please,' Leonora said. 'I prefer to consider myself impractically Talented. Which keeps me out of the grips of people like you.'

She stalked away. So Michael was a paranormal, was he? And if it were true about the computers, well, at the very least, he'd be in endless demand; work the little so-and-so even further into the ground than he is already. After all, we're all Europeans now. They'll probably make him move to Strasburg and sit in boring meetings, where they probably have even more uncomfortable chairs, and they serve stinking cabbage in all the wine bars.

She called the lift and got into it. She was still angry, but there is a time for swearing and walking out, and there is a time for calm reflection; he hadn't asked her for his keys back, and that should be worth dinner at least by the time he has had to conquer his embarrassment about having to ask for them other than in the heat of the moment.

And she had had a chance to sneer back at the awful Sharpe; it wasn't her bloody fault she could never control her power.

Honestly, these flats really are not worth the money they make you pay to live in them – there were dust rolls all over the corridor, fluttering off the floor like clumsy birds. Or maybe they were hers.

When she got out of the lift, she had to stop and take an insole out of her shoe – there seemed to be an extra one. Funny how they manage to get two stuck together and then one peels off and comes loose and gets all crumpled and uncomfortable suddenly under your foot.

As she stood up straight again, she nearly twisted her ankle on a half-brick she had not noticed on the pavement. Honestly, this great ugly pseudo-ziggurat of a building – no class, no style and falling to pieces already.

She looked up in an attempt to see whence it had fallen – she really did hope it had fallen – and noticed one of the two men on Michael's balcony, waving to her.

She waved back. No point in being totally rude; if they have seen the contents of your knicker drawer, well, like the man said, they're practically family.

When she got to the local station, she had to wait for the silly little bus they have when the trains aren't running, which would be too much to expect, of course. Still, at least you're safe from muggers, because they're too smart to be here; yupps like Michael drive everywhere – he'd drive to the toilet if they let him have a car indoors – so it is only discarded girlfriends that are ever waiting for the bus. Or presumably boyfriends, if there are women or gay yupps, which there must be, logically. All human life is here in Yupptown; just no bloody buses.

She pulled up the collar of her coat against the wind and reached in her pocket for a scarf. Then she thought better of putting it on, and used it to wipe her glasses instead.

'Sorry to trouble you, Miss Norton.' It was the policeman. People always jump out at you when you're not looking.

'What is it now?' she asked, putting her glasses back on, decisively. 'Any chance of getting this over before I end up missing the bus?'

'Probably not, miss,' he said. 'It seems like you may have to help us with one or two inquiries of your own, after all. I'd wanted to speak to you, anyway – I knew your mother, you know, oh, years ago.'

He opened the briefcase he was carrying and displayed its contents. There were, all carefully bagged and numbered, a half-brick, a crumpled insole, some dust-bunnies, a quantity of what appeared to be cat litter, two broken paper-clips and the corner of what appeared to be a page of the *Guardian*.

'Could you explain these, miss?' he said. 'I read your old file, when it became clear you were involved in the case. Sharpe said the matter was closed, but, from what the records say, you really do generate an awful lot of power for someone who is supposed to be completely useless. So I had a look around Chummy's apartment. And guess what I found.'

'I've no idea, officer,' Leonora said. 'It is officer, isn't it?'

'Yes, miss,' he said. 'Inspector Smithers to you. Late chief forensic divvy of the Art Squad, currently on secondment to the Spoonbenders. What with the Cranston business and the Marcias and all.'

'How nice,' she said, 'and you fly as well. In your spare time?'

'No, miss,' he said. 'I can't fly. Line of sight teleportation, if I've got a head wind.'

'Anyway,' she said, 'what has all this to do with me? And why are you showing me all this perfectly ordinary rubbish? As your friend so politely pointed out, I've got plenty of that sort of thing at home. I'm famous for it. As you know. Presumably the story from the *Sun* is in my file.'

'Excuse me, miss,' Smithers said, with dignity and not at all apologetically. 'That was nothing to do with me. I wasn't at the DPR back then.'

'Sharpe was,' Leonora said. 'And Lord Orpington.'

'Yes,' Smithers said. 'But the story in the *Sun* had nothing to do with them either. Hackforth-Fford was running the PR campaign then, and they were giving him a free hand.'

'Oh, yes,' Leonora said. 'And that story was entirely his decision, of course. Improve the DPR's image by getting everyone to laugh at the comic lefty paranorm with her silly power, while, brackets, reminding everyone of her heroic grandparents and what they gave for the nation, close brackets. Don't tell me Hackforth-Fford went into all that without Orpington's approval.'

'It's all very regrettable, in hindsight,' Smithers said, 'but he did a lot of far more unpleasant things to people he didn't like.'

'To women he didn't like,' Leonora said.

'Well, yes,' said Smithers. 'But you've lived it down, haven't you?'

'It has not helped me find academic jobs in the middle of a recession,' said Leonora, 'to be notorious as Captain Kipple, the paranormal garbage lady.'

'Anyway,' Smithers said. 'I know you're an historian, studied for years, but you are not, forgive me, an expert. Whereas I am an expert. Didn't have to study, of course, nice thing about being a divvy.'

She looked at him, and he took it as encouragement.

'I mean, ordinary household rubbish. I don't think so, pardon me. This brick – take that – that's not brick, anyone can see that – rose marble, that is. And that insole – kid leather that is, seventeenth-century Venetian, with gold thread in it. I mean, that's rare – they didn't hardly use insoles in the seventeenth century. And the hairs in those dust-bunnies – mammoth, those are.'

'Awfully small for mammoth, wouldn't you say?'

'Eyelashes, miss,' he said. 'See for yourself.'

He closed the case so only a slit was open; grudgingly, Leonora was unable to ignore the extent to which the paper-clips glowed in the dark.

'And take the newspaper. Go on, look at it.'

She looked at it through its baggie for some time, and then realized that the typography was slightly different, and it was called *Le Gradien*, *Gardien* surely, and the date was the 7th of Fructidor.

'Very interesting Talent, you've got there, I'd say, miss, even if it is completely useless,' he said. 'Really sloppy of them to miss the implications. I really should have gone down to your flat with Sharpe. Of course, we've got you registered from last time, so just pop round. Any time.'

When she got home, her cats were sitting on the doorstep, looking depressed, and her flat was preternaturally empty. They'd left her furniture and her books, but the comfortable odds and ends that always seemed to accumulate there, no matter how often she cleaned up, were missing.

Her neighbour, the one who sometimes complained, said that men from the government had been round in a van and taken everything away in bin-liners. Leonora sat around being annoyed for several minutes, and noticed, to her not especial surprise, that the flat was half-an-inch deep already. She picked up the cork that had appeared by her left foot and sniffed. Not a good year.

*

The good thing about having had the DPR runaround before was that you knew to bring a good book along.

'Interesting, is it?' said Marcia the receptionist. 'Gavin never leaves me alone for five minutes at home, so I don't do much reading myself.'

'I would have thought,' Leonora said, 'that you could probably manage the odd page or two at the office. When you're not filing your nails or talking to yourself.'

'I do not talk to myself,' said Marcia.

'Yes, you do,' Leonora said, 'I've been listening to you do it all morning.'

'I never did,' Marcia said.

'On the telephone.'

'That's different,' Marcia said. 'You'd talk to yourself a lot if there were a lot of you.'

'You know,' Leonora said reflectively, 'I don't think I would. I think you probably like yourself more than I do.'

'If you'll pardon my saying so, Miss Norton,' Marcia said, 'you might like yourself more if you could try being less of a stuck-up cow, Miss Norton.'

'What do you mean?' Leonora said.

'Well, honestly,' Marcia said. 'You've been sitting here all morning, and this is the first word I've heard out of you apart from saying you were here for an appointment. You used to come round all the time, back in Peckham; I thought we knew each other enough to have a natter. I was quite looking forward to it.'

'Sorry,' Leonora said. 'I didn't realize you were that Marcia. I thought you were some other Marcia.'

'It really annoys me,' Marcia said. 'Ever since all that got out, in that magazine, no one treats any of us properly any more. We're not numbers, you know. It's not fair, really it isn't. I don't even think we look that much like each other. I was saying so to Gavin only the other night when we were over there.'

'I thought Gavin was your husband,' Leonora said.

'No, silly, not my Gavin,' said Marcia. '*Marcia's* Gavin, him that's the brother of Marcia's Nigel.'

'So you're not all married to men called Gavin?' Leonora said.

'No, of course not,' Marcia said. 'Like I said, we're individuals. Seven of us are married to men called Justin.'

'Makes all the difference,' Leonora said.

'But of course we talk to each other a bit,' Marcia went on, genetically impervious to irony. 'I mean, wouldn't you? After what happened to Marcia, and to Marcia.'

'What happened to Marcia, and Marcia?' Leonora asked.

'That's just what we don't know,' Smithers said, as he came through into the reception area.

'Someone hit Marcia in Batley over the head,' Marcia said.

'And someone tried to throttle Marcia in the Chelmsford office,' Smithers said. 'And they're both lying in hospital beds, gibbering with fear. Both of them managed to scrape cheap chromium plating under their nails in the course of the struggle. You don't see that sort of chrome finish any more, thank God; went out with tail fins.'

'I don't understand it, really I don't,' Marcia said. 'I mean, who could want to try to kill Marcia, or Marcia?'

Leonora did not feel called upon to say anything.

'Yes, well,' Smithers said. 'To other matters, miss. We don't actually need to talk to you about Mr Sinden. He owned up to everything.'

'I'd been meaning to ask you about that,' said Leonora. 'How did you get on to him in the first place?'

'It's the old story, miss,' Smithers said. 'His Psion organizer got jealous of his Filofax, and she grassed him up.'

'Well,' Leonora said. 'If you don't need me, I'll be off, then.'

'Oh, no, miss,' Smithers said, 'I'm sorry, but we really need more from you than that. After all, you are registered, and you have been getting our allowance, and there are those implications.'

The chair in the lead-glass isolation chamber was fairly uncomfortable, and the sense of being watched and measured was oppressive. There were cameras, and thermometers, and barometers, and all sorts of sophisticated machines whose purpose she could not begin to imagine. Several of them appeared to have stopped working, however. A discussion was proceeding outside; it was not clear that they meant the internal speakers to be on.

'Very interesting,' said the scientific evaluator, Jenkins. 'Hard to know what it is, though.'

'I'd have thought it very simple,' said Fredericks of the Department. 'Whenever she is upset, she generates rubbish. But we knew that years ago.'

'Yes, yes,' said Jenkins. 'But you don't understand. Smithers was quite right to go over your head and call us in. That's the trouble when you let bureaucrats decide what is useful and what isn't; God knows what it will be like when Brussels starts telling us who is Talented and who is merely paranormal. Merely, I ask you?'

'Absolute chaos,' Fredericks said, 'particularly if the Germans get their way, or the Italians. Hard to know which would be worse. The Germans want to derecognize anyone whose Talents aren't useful, and the Italians want to include people who can wiggle their ears or memorize Dante.'

'I mean, take Norton here,' Jenkins said. 'She isn't *useful*, never leaps buildings or anything, but she's fascinating. Look at her.'

Fredericks declined this invitation, so Leonora stuck out her tongue.

Jenkins went on. 'Is it rubbish she takes from places all over the planet, adjusting their inertia in the process, or is it rubbish she steals from alternate universes, proving that they exist, by the way, or does she actually create matter? I can tell you that, apart from the massive display of psychic force Sharpe and Hackforth-Fford mentioned, there is absolutely no visible energy loss or gain in the area.'

'Until your monitors went down,' Fredericks said. 'What about after that?'

'They went down,' said Jenkins, 'because they are dust-sensitive. And so dust had to be being produced before they went down. And if no energy was lost or produced before the dust reached a concentration such that they went down, it is not likely it suddenly came into play afterwards. Think logically, man.'

'Actually,' said Fredericks, 'I'm more worried about the effect on the budget. Some of those monitors come dear.'

'Listen,' Jenkins said. 'This is the big time. Unless she is just shifting stuff round the world, which seems unlikely given the bits of newspaper, but would be a space drive, properly harnessed, she proves either alternate universes or continuous creation. That should be worth a Nobel or two, in anyone's money. That girl is gold dust, cosmologically speaking.'

'That's all very well,' Fredericks said. 'But my masters need something practical to interest them.'

'I'll tell you one thing,' Jenkins said. 'I wouldn't be at all surprised if this had something to do with the Cranston effect.'

'That's entirely different,' Fredericks said. 'You're only saying it because she's his granddaughter and because you got that memorandum about the thefts.'

'No, look,' Jenkins said. 'He made machines that couldn't possibly work in our universe but did anyway; she generates, as rubbish, artefacts that shouldn't exist in our history.'

Leonora got out of the chair and pushed open the door of the isolation chamber.

'What's all this about Cranston, and thefts?' she said.

The phone rang. Jenkins lifted it up, listened a second and handed it to Leonora.

'It's only bloody Marcia,' he said.

'Just putting you through, Miss Norton,' Marcia said.

'When they've finished, miss,' Smithers said, 'we'd like you to come back over here. At once.'

'At once', in DPR speak, did not, of course, oblige anyone to pay any attention to Leonora. And she had left her book back in the isolation chamber. There was always Marcia; better her than the *Reader's Digest* for October 1973.

'They really won't be a minute, Miss Norton,' Marcia said.

'Oh, call me Leonora.'

'Can I?' said Marcia. 'That'll be nice.'

A silence fell.

'Do you enjoy being a receptionist?' Leonora asked.

'Not much,' Marcia said. 'But it gets me out of the house, is what Gavin says. Besides, they went to all that trouble, sending us to school. And to secretarial college; only fair we should contribute, isn't it?'

Leonora didn't think it was fair at all, but who was she to spread social unrest?

'Tell me,' said Marcia, 'I don't mean to pry . . .'

Anyone who says that, thought Leonora, always does mean to pry.

'But have you got any kiddies?'

'No,' Leonora said. 'Have you?'

'Well, no,' Marcia said. 'I'd quite like to. Gavin worried it might not be a good idea.'

'Do you always do what Gavin says?' Leonora asked.

'Yes,' Marcia said. 'I don't believe in all this feminism; Marcia down on the switchboard does, even since Gavin tried to set her straight. Stuck-up cow — not surprising she never married. Anyway, Gavin did suggest we think about adopting, but it's not the same is it?'

'But why shouldn't you have a child, if you want one?'

'When we got married,' Marcia said, 'Lord Orpington gave us away, each of us, and he had a little word with Gavin, or Nigel, or Justin. They just don't want to take any chances.'

'I think that's outrageous,' Leonora said. 'Why on earth shouldn't you have a child?'

'Well,' Marcia said. 'You never know how they'd turn out. Suppose there was something wrong with Her, and they're not telling me.'

'Her?' Leonora said. 'Who?'

'The one Mr Cranston started from,' Marcia said.

'You know,' Leonora said. 'Even though I'm his grand-daughter, I never thought of that. Obvious, really. He had to get the cells from somewhere.'

As she spoke, there were heavy footsteps in the corridor and a vague smell of motor-oil. The door opened a crack, and a chrome nozzle poked through it. It wavered momentarily towards Leonora, and then jerked decisively towards the receptionist's desk.

'Duck,' Leonora said.

Marcia hurled herself sideways from the chair, and a streak of energy, whose afterglare left lurid green patches floating in front of Leonora's eyes for the next five minutes, left a patch of char on the institutional paint behind Marcia's chair. Outside there was metallic clattering, and something vaguely gun-like, with lenses, sights and several kinds of trigger, fell through the half-open doorway to the floor, where it fizzed away in a wasp-swarm of sparks. As Leonora rushed across the room, to check that Marcia was all right, she heard footsteps clunk limpingly away down the corridor.

'Help,' she said, on the general principle of the thing.

The door from the inner office opened and Sharpe came out. He glanced at Marcia, who was picking herself up; he kicked the gun out of his way, winced at the additional sparks that resulted, and then peered gingerly out into the corridor.

Almost at once Smithers entered, pushing past him. He was holding something that looked a bit like a dustbin lid with its handle on the wrong side.

'You two all right?' he said brusquely.

'Yes,' Marcia said.

'Did you catch him?' Leonora said.

'Chummy out there, you mean?' Smithers said. 'No, all I saw was a trilby hat and a trenchcoat and a noise as if he was carrying old iron along with him. And he seemed to be limping. You caught him nicely, miss.'

'I didn't do anything,' Leonora said, as everyone looked at her.

'I'm sorry, miss,' Smithers said. 'But this is obviously yours.'

'But it's a dustbin lid.'

'No, it isn't,' Smithers said. 'It's a Mycenean shield.'

'But I only generate rubbish,' said Leonora.

'I didn't say,' Smithers said, 'that it was a good Mycenean shield. Royal armourers have their off-days, same as anyone else.'

'Aren't you going to go after him?' Marcia said.

'He's probably miles away, by now,' Sharpe said.

'And I thought I'd better find out whether we were

talking serious massacre,' said Smithers, 'or merely damage to the paintwork.'

'You could have looked out of the window,' Leonora said, 'and teleported out after him.'

'Ah,' said Smithers. 'I should have explained. Line of sight. Through open windows.'

'I think,' said Leonora, 'that you were scared of him, and that means you are not telling me everything. And I think that I will become very unhappy if you don't tell me everything very soon. I just want the truth. You wouldn't like it if I got very unhappy.'

As she spoke, slowly but surely, the institutional grey carpet started to disappear under wind-battered crisp packets, most of them Lark Tongues in Aspic flavour.

'Why is everyone in the DPR suddenly going on about my grandfather?' she said.

'Well,' said Sharpe. 'At first we thought it was ordinary criminals, because there were signs of a break-in.'

'Not the papers,' Leonora said. 'I told my great-aunt not to let you get your hands on the papers, but I was only the great man's bastard granddaughter, so she wasn't going to listen to me.'

'It wasn't the papers; they're still in the library,' Smithers said. 'It was the collection. From the Museum. You've seen that gun before, and you know as well as we do where it came from; and you probably noticed that Chummy clunked as he walked. I wasn't going to follow him by myself down a badly lit staircase.'

'You can't mean that ridiculous robot my grandfather made,' she said. 'The one with huge screws in the ball-joints. It never worked; I remember Mother telling me so when I was scared when I was little.'

'That's as may be, miss,' Smithers said, 'but it wasn't a break-in to the collection. It was a break-out.

'It feels very strange,' he went on, 'to have appreciated

something for years as a classic piece of awful period design, and then have to worry about whether it is going to swivel on its chromium-plated sockets and try to kill you.'

'My God,' Marcia said. 'It went down the staircase. The switchboard is down there, and Marcia.'

Leonora and Smithers dashed down the corridor and the staircase. The door of the switchboard room was off its hinges, but a Marcia with rather short hair was standing in the doorway with a fire-extinguisher. Behind her the switchboard glowed and clicked and buzzed; it seemed unnecessarily bulky and complex, though what did Leonora know? All the ugly redundancy of superannuated high technology.

'Took your time, didn't you?' Marcia said.

'Did he come down here, miss?' Smithers said.

'Of course he did,' said Switchboard Marcia. 'Great ugly clanking thing; I heard footsteps so I shut the door and got the fire-extinguisher. And it said "Prepare to meet your doom" and I said "Make my day" and it whirred a bit and then it said "I'm going out now. I may be gone some time".'

Smithers stood around making fatherly consoling noises, and Leonora decided to make herself useful and made everyone a cup of tea. Marcia was grateful, though whether for the noises or the tea remained obscure.

The switchboard continued to make odd noises, even when no one was ringing in.

'That is a peculiarly horrible object,' Leonora said. 'I know the Department are broke, but can't they afford anything better?'

'I know,' Marcia said. 'I think it's horrible too; I don't know why every DPR branch in the country has reasonable equipment and I am stuck with this. It's so embarrassing when Marcia from Birmingham comes round –

she's got a really lovely switchboard, with a computer and everything. But it's his Nibs upstairs, Lord Orpington. Won't hear of changing it. Says it feels like an old friend.'

'That reminds me, miss,' said Smithers. 'That's why I called you. His Nibs wants to talk to you; didn't say why.'

'Shocking business,' Lord Orpington said, getting up from his armchair to welcome her into his office. 'Would you like milk or lemon, Miss Norton? Or may I call you Leonora?'

'Oh, why not,' Leonora said. The office was a museum of late Empire – assegais, maps, Purdey shotguns and the glassily staring heads of beasts.

'After all,' Orpington said, 'I was your mother's god-father. And at Ditchley we were all in love with your grandmother. Makes us practically family, doesn't it?'

'You may call me by my first name,' Leonora said. 'But do not presume on that. You sent my grandmother to her death, all of you. And when my mother turned out not to be anything very special, none of you had any time for her at all. She died when I was seven, but I can remember standing in the rain by my great-aunt and there were none of you at her grave. Just Loric. And he wasn't even with the Department then.'

'I'm sorry about your mother,' Orpington said. 'But she didn't want anything to do with us, even when she was a child, after Cranston died.'

He was an immortal, or something like it, she knew, but he was clearly actually sorry, because he suddenly looked old.

'You can't get off the hook,' she said. 'Not with her, or with me. I've looked at my grandfather's journals, some of them, when I was little and my great-aunt still had them; even when I was little, I could tell that he was barking mad. And you used him.'

'It was different then,' Orpington said. 'There was an empire. And a war. We were making serious decisions then, about serious things.'

'And that,' Leonora said, 'is why you encouraged him to make ray-guns that shot fluorescent beams. And robots with exterior springs. Really serious things.'

'You don't understand,' Orpington said. 'I was hoping you would. The whole thing might have worked. I was hoping there would be some loyalty. You young people don't understand loyalty.'

'When I was doing my doctorate, in Berlin,' Leonora said, 'I got them to show me where my grandmother died. It was just an ordinary wall, round the back of a building, and the bullet holes were near the ground, because she could no longer stand up. I think I understand very well what you people mean by loyalty. All one needs to understand that is to be a fatherless girl with a Talent you people can't use.'

A janitor came into the office with a large black plastic bag, and quietly removed paper and fluff-balls from the carpet.

'You can leave that a second,' Orpington said. 'Miss Norton will be leaving. And I have to go to the House for the debate on the Definition.'

'I need some answers,' Leonora said. 'And my guess is that you know what the answers are. What did my grand-father make that robot for? And why have you stopped poor old Marcia having babies?'

'The robot was for a good and sufficient purpose,' Orpington said, 'and I shouldn't concern yourself with the Marcia girls. Hardly your preferred companions, I'd have thought.'

'Ghastly woman,' he added, enunciating unusually clearly and staring fixedly at his telephone.

'I want to know,' Leonora said. 'I'm a trained historian, and I smell a large rat. It has whiskers and a long tail, and little beady eyes, just like yours.'

'I couldn't possibly tell you,' Orpington said. 'There is no need for you to know, and no need for you to concern yourself with the matter. When I was younger, you could tell people that things were in the national interest and they would actually listen to you.'

'And that's how you got my grandparents to commit suicide, and why my mother died young.'

'Your grandmother died for her country,' Orpington said. 'Sometimes you have to put out a goat for the tiger. I know that sacrifice isn't fashionable nowadays. So did your grandfather, more or less. He made us the things we needed him to make, even though his sanity was tottering. I remember the day he went off to do the experiment that killed him – you know I think he had a premonition. He said, "Someday soon I will be able to say to myself 'now you can rest'."'

'And what about my mother?' Leonora said.

'Your mother killed herself,' Orpington said. 'She was mad. And no better than she should have been.'

'And whose fault was that?' Leonora said. 'At the end of the day? You drove my grandfather off the edge, and she followed after him. It wasn't fair. Whoever my father was, she had lost him for good. And my great-aunt would not even let me have a photograph of her – worried I'd be contaminated by immorality and madness. You know, I hardly even remember what she looked like; just the feel of the touch of her hand.'

When Leonora went to the Manuscript Reading Room, they told her that the Cranston papers were not currently available to readers.

'But my family donated them,' she said.

'I'm sorry,' the clerk at the desk said. 'But they came in a van and they took them away. I was here when he signed for them.'

'He,' she said. 'Not a tall gent with a limp and a trench-coat and a hat pulled down over his face?'

'Oh, no, miss,' the clerk said. 'No one like that. It was Lord Orpington. Are you Miss Norton?'

There was a note for her, on House of Lords stationery. It said

I told you to let the matter rest – O.

Leonora left hurriedly – no point in making the reading-room staff clear up after other people's behaviour.

But there were still the letters on display in the main gallery. Grandmother's last journal and letters had always stuck in Leonora's gullet – they were the sort of historical document earnest mistresses went on about fervently to the Fifth Form, a sort of cross between Anne Frank, Edith Cavell and Mrs Miniver. Cranston's letters, on the other hand . . .

The last of them said, 'Honestly, Philip. Just how much more do you want of me. First I make them, poor little things, because you say the country might need them, and then you ask me to make the other damn things. Just in case. And now there's the Egypt business, and you want me to put something cheap together for that; I can't go on, you know, old chap, I really can't. Not without Leonora.'

And then it tailed off in maunderings about his dead wife. Leonora wondered what had been in the collection apart from the robot, and whether it was a damned thing, or a poor little thing. She really must check it out in the biographies, not that any of them were much good.

When she got back to her flat, it was dark and raining,

but the cats would not come in off the steps. They hissed and arched as if she had done something wrong.

'Suit yourself,' Leonora said, continuing to swig from the bottle of milk she had bought to pour out for them, and let herself into the building. Her flat door had a large hole in it and so she turned to tiptoe back to the front door and let herself out.

It was behind her, as such things usually are. It was tall, and it smelled slightly of motor-oil, and it had springs in tubes all the way up its legs and down its arms; the tubes were filled with some sort of gloop that bubbled gently as the thing walked ponderously towards her. It had placed its trenchcoat and its hat on the hat-stand in the hall; you can tell it was designed in the fifties, she thought, it has bourgeois manners.

It stood, looming shinily in the light of the forty-watt hall bulb; it had what might as well be called a head, which it put to one side, considering her. Leonora realized with some concern that she was too scared to be angry.

'Sorry to have troubled you,' it remarked conversationally. 'We all make mistakes.'

'What the bloody hell?' she said.

'No need for language,' it said. 'You are not the one. Sorry to have troubled you. Unavoidable confusion.'

It was the way it whirred between sentences, like a jukebox with rheumatism, that really irritated her. Quite suddenly a chaise longue, with one of its legs missing, but covered in some rather nice purple and gilt brocade, materialized six inches above its head and dropped neatly down on it, knocking it to its knees and leaving its head and torso poking through the horse-hair and torn fabric.

It looked at her with what was almost reproach, the needle of its speech centre stuck on the last phrase.

'Unavoidable confusion. Click. Unavoidable confusion.'

It pulled one of its hands free and tapped itself sharply on the side of the head.

'No need to take it like that,' it said, as Leonora turned and bolted for the back door.

When she came back with the police, there was nothing there except some bits of horse-hair.

Neither Sharpe nor Smithers was taking her calls. Marcia on the switchboard gave her a phone number for Hackforth-Fford, but it proved to be that of a very exclusive hospital for the well-connected deranged. Orpington, needless to say, had told his flunkeys to keep her out of his office, and his club; she checked in Hansard, and he only ever went to the Lords when they were discussing the Department.

'I think you should probably all flee the country,' she told Marcia in Sharpe's office over the phone. 'After all, the robot would never get itself through customs. It would make all their little bells go ding.'

'You're just being hysterical,' Marcia said. 'Your friend, Lord Orpington, sent us a memo and told us so. After all, the robot hasn't really hurt any of us; I was visiting Marcia and Marcia only the other day, and Marcia seemed to recognize me, and Marcia even ate three of the grapes.'

'Lord Orpington,' Leonora said, 'is no friend of mine. And no friend of yours either.'

'Lord Orpington,' Marcia said, 'gave me away at my wedding. He is practically one of the family.'

Finally, Leonora decided to humble herself and rang Michael Sinden; he had left his job in the City, and when she rang the flat, his answering machine said that it had never liked her and hung up on her. Luckily, she remembered that she had been very complimentary about his cellular phone once and rang him on that number instead – actually she had been being ironic, but even Michael was unlikely to have managed to endow a phone with much in the way of perceptiveness.

'I've got your keys,' she said. Having agreed to meet him on neutral territory, she arrived sufficiently late for him to have got the hint and bought her a drink.

'I've changed the locks,' he said unpromisingly.

'You didn't need to,' she said. 'I have some manners, after all. In the matter of going where I'm not wanted, at least.'

'Well, that's it, isn't it?' he said. 'You have been meddling, from what I hear. And not even very effectively. You really might show the Department a bit more loyalty, after all the crap they've put up with from you over the years.'

'It seems to me that loyalty is what it's all about,' she said. 'Poor old Marcia nearly got fried, and no one seems to take it seriously.'

'Ghastly women, Marcia,' Michael said. 'I'm sure none of them are in any real danger. Lord Orpington told me the whole story.'

'I doubt that very much indeed,' Leonora said. 'He may, however, have told you a selection of the facts, pleasingly arranged.'

'But that's all you do,' Michael said, 'and you call the result history.'

'No,' Leonora said, 'I arrange facts so that they will produce the truth, and I call that history, and I don't care whether it pleases anyone or not.'

'You never told me the truth,' Michael said. 'I could have done with your telling me that you were a paranormal; it would have made me feel less like a wally when I found out.'

'The thing is,' Leonora said, 'that I worry about whether I feel like a fool or not; this is an operation that takes too much time for me to worry all that much about people who have half the computers in London to boost their egos.'

'You don't understand,' Michael said, 'they aren't exactly company – just pleasantly babbling idiots, most of them.'

'But they don't answer back,' Leonora said.

'No,' said Michael, 'they don't.'

'Sounds ideal for you.'

'Honestly,' Michael said, 'he was right. There really is no point even talking to you once you've got annoyed with a chap.'

'Who said that? You've been discussing our relationship with Orpington?'

'No,' Michael said, 'of course not. No, I had a drink with Sharpe.'

'So that's all right, then; just two of my former boyfriends sitting around discussing how impossible I am.'

'No,' Michael said. 'Actually we'd just both been getting our expenses processed and we were discussing how impossible Marcia is. You just came in as a sort of after-thought.'

Sometimes there is just no point talking to boys, Leonora thought as she silently drained her glass, filled it again from the bottle, drained it again, and left Michael to cope with an irate manager and several leaking crates of past-the-use-by-date Persian caviare.

It was a long wet autumn. Leonora got on with an essay provisionally entitled 'Galton, Orpington and Himmler – Three Studies in Eugenics', but it never got very far before there was too much fluff in her typewriter to continue. Luckily, the Department were sending her a very generous cheque every month, just for going round to see Jenkins, and have him measure things for an hour or two.

'I forgot,' he said. 'You left your book.'

'So I did,' she said. 'Nothing like being shot at to make you forget things.'

'I wouldn't know,' he said. 'No one's ever shot at me.'

'Try it some time,' she said, and left.

Leonora did not usually travel on the Underground, except when she was feeling especially calm; it was quite grubby enough, without her adding to it. Still, today she was in a hurry. Inevitably her tube train was delayed outside Bank, and so she opened her book to avoid getting anxious. On the old envelope she had been using as a bookmark, someone had scrawled 'Alternate Tuesdays. 4.30 p.m. Parliament Hill Fields. Cricket pavilion if wet.'

It was Tuesday, and 3 p.m. and how do you know which Tuesday is the alternate unless you waste your time going both weeks? She changed at Bank and got on the train for Hampstead; Smithers was sitting directly opposite her in the carriage and trying to avoid her gaze.

'Either it's you,' she said, 'or you're following them. And if you're following them, you know where we're going. And if they're following you, they know you've been going there. And if they're following me, they're on to you already now.'

Smithers looked annoyed.

'There's no use your looking at me like that,' she said, holding up the envelope.

He nodded, reluctantly.

'Only,' she said, 'since it's you, we can get off at Camden. I don't see walking round the Heath in the rain, and I can go round Sainsbury's while you talk.'

Smithers got off with her, but he tried to stay ahead of her on the escalator; poor man had obviously done a course on being followed at some time. In Sainsbury's he insisted on getting a trolley of his own, even though Leonora had to lend him a pound to put in the lock, and wandered round after her, buying one pot of apricot yoghurt and a corned beef and coleslaw sandwich.

Once they got into the queue for the delicatessen, he grabbed her by the sleeve.

'We can talk now,' he said. 'Clear view from all sides.'

'It's all very odd,' he continued. 'Chummy hasn't been seen since he came to your flat. No attacks. Nothing. Maybe you really hurt him.'

'I doubt it,' Leonora said. 'Grandfather's designs are not noted for their fragility. And it was a fairly flimsy chaise longue that fell on it.'

'Orpington's up to something,' Smithers went on. 'Keeps giving little pep talks to senior staff about rationalizations and cuts. And talking about the War. Don't you hate it when they go on about the War?'

'I hate it,' Leonora said, 'when people like Orpington go on about the weather, or the price of sprouts. There's always an agenda, whatever it is. But yes, when they start talking about the War, it usually means that there is something particularly smelly that they want to justify.'

'I mean,' Smithers said. 'I don't care very much about politics or science. But Marcia on the switchboard is a nice plucky girl; the others are all right, really, come to that. And someone tried to hurt them. I'm just an ordinary thief-taker, when it comes down to it, and I don't think that's right.'

'What else has been going on?' Leonora said. 'I used to be able to get hold of some of the gossip, if I wanted to, but Orpington's frozen me right out.'

'Nothing much,' Smithers said. 'Orpington pulled Sharpe off liaison with me; he's spending all his time at the EEC lobbying for the German Definition. All very boring. Your friend Sinden – well, he seems to be well in; Orpington likes him. And otherwise nothing much; I've had nothing to do since the trail on Chummy went dead. I ended up volunteering to help with the Christmas party.'

Leonora turned from being served six ounces of black pitted olives, four ounces of thin-sliced pastrami and half a pound of particularly runny Brie.

'What Christmas party?' she said.

'Well,' Smithers said, moving his trolley out of the way of the queue behind them, 'they've always had a party at the DPR offices in London. And at some of the larger out-stations. Orpington says that he has to cut costs, and it makes more sense to have one big party, and bus people in for it. I don't see how it works, unless he has some deal with the coach people, but that's not my side of things.'

'My God,' Leonora said, as they wheeled to a confidential halt beside the soap powders, 'that old bastard.'

'No need for you to talk like that, miss,' Smithers said. 'Even if he is.'

'But don't you see,' Leonora said. 'Staff from all the out-stations. That means just about all of the Marcias. And they'll all be in one place at the same time.'

'Chummy,' Smithers breathed.

'He said that sometimes you have to put out a goat for the tiger,' Leonora said. 'He doesn't care about Marcia; just about getting the robot back. Some sort of crack-brained scheme to use it for defence or something. He's using them as bait.'

'The old bastard,' said Smithers.

'I've not been asked,' Leonora said. 'But I've got to be there. He's used up two generations of my family, one way or another, and I'm not letting him use anyone else.'

'I knew your mother, you know,' Smithers said. 'Long time ago – we'd just done A-levels. She was a lady, Albertine; she was really nice.'

'And,' Leonora said, 'she let them break her when she was half the age I am now. You must have known her then – where were you?'

'I was on National Service,' Smithers said. 'I had to go away. She sent my letters back, or her aunt did. I knew better than be where I wasn't wanted.'

'She went mad,' Leonora said, 'or maybe she was mad then. You'd know.'

'She never seemed mad to me,' Smithers said.

'And she killed herself,' Leonora said.

'I heard,' Smithers said. 'Years later. It was Loric. He thought I ought to know.'

'What about him?' Leonora said. 'Where would he stand on all this?'

'Dunno,' Smithers said. 'He's out of the country, anyway. Off in Brussels; has been for weeks. Same thing as Sharpe – this bloody EEC Definition thing. Nothing to do with all this.'

'How am I going to get into the party?' Leonora said.

'Well,' Smithers said, 'I appointed myself Father Christmas, being as Loric was in Brussels – he usually does it, way of keeping his finger on the pulse, common touch sort of thing, he says. I'll have loads of sacks, and I could get you in in one of those.'

'I refuse,' Leonora said, 'to crash a party and then spend the whole of it hiding in a sack, peering out in case something happens, getting irritated and having to share my sack with the expensive detritus of eternity, in imminent danger of having someone try Lucky Dip on me.'

'You know,' Smithers said, 'I wonder. Take off your glasses a second.'

'If you tell me I'm lovely,' Leonora said, 'I shall reach into your trolley, take yoghurt and pour it over your head.'

She took her glasses off.

'You know,' Smithers said, 'if you did your hair and wore different clothes, you'd look quite like her.'

'Who?' Leonora said. 'My mother?'

'No,' Smithers said. 'Not a bit like her. She was only a kid. No, like Marcia.'

'Nothing on earth,' Leonora said, 'would make me dye my hair blonde and have it cut like Princess Di. Nothing on earth would make me wear a Benetton jogging suit.'

'Orpington,' Smithers said. 'Chummy.'

Leonora looked stubborn.

'Finding out what's going on,' he continued. 'I thought you believed in the truth. I thought you wanted what was fair.'

It was very crowded and very smoky and very noisy. Parts of the floor, down at the other end of the hall, were already awash with spilled drink, and the buffet table had not lasted more than about fifteen minutes; a little man had decided that he liked the sausage rolls and then turned into a giant frog so that he could increase his capacity for them. Now he was leading a conga-line, splashing his way through the puddles of booze; paranormals are just as noisy as everyone else, except that they have more ways of making noise.

No one talked to Marcia at parties, Leonora discovered, and the Marcias, or should she think of them as the other Marcias, were all at the bar, getting in pints of real ale for their husbands and Camparis for themselves and each other, and groping Father Christmas. Leonora was carrying a Campari as cover, but was at no risk of getting drunk on anything that tasted that horrid; it was hard enough to see straight without her glasses, without getting rat-arsed.

She stood against a wall in a remote part of the room –

Orpington had threatened to have the party in the Department itself, but the logistics had made that impossible, and Smithers had been able to get hold of a hall through chums in the police. Chums with funny handshakes, no doubt. It was years since she had been at a party – she always hated them, though they were one of the places where small amounts of rubbish were assumed to be part of the environment. People could always ensure you had a good time; less to clear up if they did.

'Told you it would work,' said Smithers from behind his beard.

'I wish you wouldn't do that,' Leonora said, removing, from under her jogging-suit top, two specimens of the Great Auk, imperfectly stuffed. 'You know what happens when people surprise or annoy me, and you persist in teleporting behind my back.'

'No, I don't,' Smithers said. 'I just got here, through the door, from the Gents, where I've been changing.'

'Well,' Leonora said, 'don't look now, but there is someone in a Father Christmas outfit making a fool of himself at the bar, going ho ho ho a lot.'

'You don't suppose?' Smithers said.

'It is a disguise, after all,' Leonora said. 'And I'm sure robots are not good actors, and no one expects Father Christmas to be convincing.'

They edged through the crowd towards the bar.

'Excuse me,' Smithers said, taking the other Father Christmas by the elbow and steering him towards a quiet patch of wall.

'Ho ho ho,' the other Father Christmas said, for the benefit of those around them, then turned and glared at Smithers once they had got away from the crowd.

'I thought I told you that you could go and change and enjoy the rest of the party. I always do this – moving among my people sort of thing.'

'Loric, sir,' Smithers said, slightly flustered. 'I thought you were in Brussels still, doing the Definition.'

'I already told you,' Loric said. 'I came back after lunch. A large lunch, with lots of toasts. They accepted the Italians' draft, worse luck – Orpington always thought they might, must settle my bet with him. Now go and change, you silly little man, like I told you. Can't have two Father Christmases, you know, spoils the mystery.'

'Loric,' Leonora said.

'Hello, Marcia,' Loric said in a tone that combined resignation with a vaguely drunken benevolence. 'Nice to see you all, sort of thing, but I'm busy right now. Private Father Christmas business, sort of thing.'

Leonora glared at him and a single strand of unravelled Bokhara carpet appeared in his beard.

'I say,' Loric said. 'It's Kipple. What're you doing dressed up as Marcia, Kipple? Not a fancy-dress party, you know, except for Father Christmases.'

'Leonora, to you,' Leonora said, putting her glasses back on. A pool of some sort of industrial effluent appeared under Loric's left boot.

'Calm down, miss,' Smithers said. 'Look, sir, it's the whole business with the robot.'

'Lot of nonsense,' Loric said. 'Thing never worked, wasn't good for anything. I told Philip Orpington so.'

'It works,' said Leonora, 'believe me.'

'Hang on,' she said, 'if you just got here, Smithers, who was it Loric told to go and change into civvies?'

'Don't know,' Loric said, 'but he did an awfully good ho ho ho. Then he said he was going out and would be gone some time.'

From the other end of the room there came a very loud, and indeed very effective ho ho ho and the double doors flew open and in came a very large Father Christmas that still limped slightly, dragging a very large sack that dragged along the floor.

'Ho ho ho,' said the Father Christmas, with a small whir between each ho.

The assorted bureaucrats and paranormals stepped back, except for a couple of children, who wandered over to the Father Christmas and looked up at him.

'Are you Father Christmas?' one of them said. 'Proper Father Christmas.'

'Not like him at the bar,' the other said. 'Proper Father Christmas doesn't smell of beer.'

'Yes, he does,' the first said. 'He does in Selfridges. And he does when he comes to our house.'

'That's your dad,' the second said.

'No, it's not. My dad's over there, with my mum. My dad makes lightning come out of the sky.'

'My dad can beat your dad.'

'I like children. Ho ho ho,' said Father Christmas, bending down to pat one of them on the head with a heavily mittened hand. The child promptly pulled at his beard, which twanged off its elastic.

The two children walked away.

'Snot Father Christmas,' one of them said. 'It's the Terminator.'

'It never is,' the other said. 'It's some other dopey robot.'

The robot creaked up to its full height, threw back its hood and elegantly eased off its mittens. No one spoke – it has the timing that goes with real star quality, Leonora thought to herself.

It looked round, confidently.

'I suppose you're wondering,' it said, 'why I've called you all here together.'

No one felt the need to interrupt.

'I was created to put an end to an experiment gone

wrong,' it continued without any whirring and without the slight scratchiness that occurred in more commonly used sentences. 'An experiment that has become a menace to the United Nations, the Commonwealth and Her Majesty the Queen. I refer of course to the evil women known as –'

'Maggie Thatcher,' shouted someone in the crowd.

'Marcia,' said another voice from inside the sack.

'You are the best and brightest,' said the robot, 'but even you have been unable to deal with this menace. Luckily, the far-sighted genius, whose unfortunate mistake has caused you to bear such terrible consequences, created me and my companion to set things right.'

Out of the sack there crawled a thing which looked a little like a turtle and a lot more like the DPR Central Office telephone exchange, except that bits of it had folded out and bits of it had folded in.

'She is judged by the verdict of you all,' said the robot.

'What do you mean?' Smithers said, stepping out of the crowd. He had disposed of his Father Christmas outfit and was pointing at the robot a lethal-looking machine-pistol that he had had strapped to the pillow round his stomach. An arm came out of the second robot, the one on the floor, and took the pistol away from him with a precise force that left Smithers clutching his wrist.

'She is judged by the verdict of you all,' the robot said with even more emphasis. 'We have weighed her in the balance and found her wanting. I call the witnesses for the prosecution.'

From a hatch on top of the second robot there appeared a very ancient reel-to-reel tape recorder, with very large reels.

'Horrid woman . . . ghastly woman . . . absolute menace . . .' it started, and continued with minor variations for what seemed like hours. Each phrase was in a different voice and each was full of what sounded like hatred; many of the people in the crowd recognized their own voices and some of them had the grace to blush.

After a while it stopped. The crowd looked embarrassed, and several of the Marcias were sobbing into their handkerchiefs or being poured restorative snifters from their Gavins' hip-flasks.

The robot reached beneath its robe and produced a terribly modern Minimi.

'Come and take your medicine, evil women,' it said. 'Justice must be served. Come and take your medicine.'

Leonora stepped forward and the robot raised its gun. Then it paused.

'You are not the one,' it said. 'Unavoidable confusion.'

'You know,' Leonora said, 'you really piss me off.'

A 1923 Hispano-Suiza and a 1963 Silver Ghost, their radiators and fenders inextricably entwined, and their internal upholstery horribly stained, appeared above the robots and smashed down on them. The small robot, with the tape recorder, was instantly reduced to scrap, but a blue glare appeared around the other and the cars just bounced off it. Leonora was knocked to the ground by a detached hub-cap.

Several of the paranormals present chose this moment to try and do something on their own account. Bolts of a variety of forces blazed against the blue glare and were effortlessly absorbed by it; one of the Gavins took a swing at the robot and jumped back with a stinging hand and his hair sticking out at right angles from his head.

One of the telekineticists, the one who worked in Virgin Records, up-ended all the ice-buckets in the room over the robot in an attempt to short out the force-field; all that happened was that the robot got soaking wet and glistened, menacingly. The nearest Marcia, the one from the former switchboard, who had been fussing over Smithers's wrist, eased through the crowd and reached down and helped Leonora to stand up.

Michael Sinden pushed his way through the crowd. He stared hard at the robot's skull.

'Itchy-titchy-coo,' he said. 'Diddums-want-hurt-Nice-Marcia. Bad Robot.'

The robot stared at him with the cybernetic equivalent of incredulity.

'It usually works,' Sinden said defensively.

'It doesn't have that kind of brain,' Orpington said smugly from the chair at the side of the room where he was sitting with a brandy and soda. 'Cranston never liked Turing, you know, and he based his robot on entirely different principles.'

'You're behind this,' Leonora said, still clinging like grim death to Marcia's hand.

'And why on earth would I have anything to do with it?' Orpington said. 'Blame your grandfather, if you must blame someone. Poor mad fool. Since there is nothing to be done, I suggest you let well alone. It is expedient that the Marcias die for the common good.'

'Shut up,' Leonora said. 'I'm trying to think things out.'

'Prepare to meet your doom,' said the robot, pointing its gun at Marcia from the switchboard.

'I'm trying to think,' shrieked Leonora. 'Bloody shut up.'

Inside the blue glare there suddenly appeared a myriad of tiny squares of paper, which settled on the robot like adhesive butterflies; layer after layer of them, building outwards. The robot tried to move forward, but they were in all its joints, bandaging it like a papier mâché mummy. Everyone stared in fascination as it became ever more encased – the layer of paper thickened until it reached the boundary of the force-field, which promptly winked out.

Smithers reached down and picked up a loose one.

'Penny black,' he said. 'With three misprints.'

Leonora looked down at her hand, holding Marcia's, and a long, slow smile crept over her face. She walked towards Orpington and the few people who had been sycophantically hovering around him drew back.

'You old bastard,' she said. 'I remember now. The feel of the touch of her hand, I said, didn't I? And you looked as smug as you do now. But that's it, isn't it? That's who he used, wasn't it? His daughter, his only daughter.'

'I hardly think so,' Orpington said. 'Your mother, like your grandmother and even yourself, was, after all, a lady. The Marcia sluts are just middle-class nobodies with vulgar manners.'

'And who picked their school and oversaw their upbringing?' Leonora said. 'You hated my grandfather because my grandmother preferred him. And you sent her off to her death for it; and you worried him into his grave; and you hated my mother because she was their child. You got Grandfather to produce the Marcias because you assumed the daughter of two powerful paranorms would be so powerful you could rule the world with two hundred of them. You sent them to some mediocre little dame school so that they would be passive and obedient. But mother wasn't paranormal, and neither are they. And my Talent is wild and inexplicable, so you didn't want any of them to have children, in case there were hundreds of children you couldn't control.'

'Such a clever girl,' breathed Marcia from just behind her, and Leonora looked round to face four hundred proudly maternal eyes.

'This is all a nonsense,' Orpington said. 'Loric, old chap, you can't possibly believe all this. I knew the girl

300

was unstable, runs in the family, poor thing. Unhinged neurotic paranoid fantasy.'

'I can believe it, Philip,' Loric said. He had sobered up entirely. 'I most certainly can believe it. You had access to the Museum and you were the last person Cranston talked to. Who else could have woken the damn thing up, and who kept the other thing buzzing away in place over at the DPR when everyone else wanted to modernize it – we all thought it was sentimentality and let you get away with it. Cranston's oldest friend and all that. Who could have persuaded him the Marcia girls might be a threat one day and who but an immortal could he guarantee to be around to wake the thing up when necessary?'

'This is the real world,' Orpington said. 'People don't do such things, not over a woman who died fifty years ago.'

'No,' Loric said. 'They do them for money.'

Michael Sinden said, 'I used to handle Lord Orpington's money – there really isn't anything fishy about him, you know, Leonora. His finances are perfectly straightforward – his inheritance, his rents, his shares, his salary, his trust fund.'

'What trust fund is that?' Loric said. 'Who on earth would set up a trust fund for an immortal? Bloody silly idea, if you ask me.'

'Only a madman,' Leonora said. 'Only a man mad enough to trust his best friend with the money to bring up his daughters, and give them a proper education, all of them, all two hundred and one of them.'

'That's plausible,' Loric said, 'up to a point. But what was enough to send even two hundred and one girls to public school in the 1950s would hardly be enough for a man like Orpington to kill over?'

Sharpe looked a good deal more hungover and travel-worn than Loric, as he joined the crowd that was standing accusingly round Orpington.

'It's the Italian Definition, I think,' he said. 'And the rest of the new regulations. The ones making all monies disbursed to paranormals working for the government retrospectively a matter of public record; they were worried about all the paranormals in the Eastern Bloc. There were paranormals in the Securitate, after all.'

'But Marcia isn't a paranormal,' Leonora said.

'According to the Italian Definition,' Sharpe said, 'paranormal includes anyone with any Talent, active or latent, or any other unusual genetic capability considered to be of public use by the government concerned. I think a clone would be included in that, particularly one we hired for being a clone.'

Leonora looked on both him and Michael with a degree more benevolence; she was almost not sorry to have slept with them.

'Besides,' Fredericks said, joining them, 'I've never seen what the fuss was about. We accepted the idea back in the seventies, when the Italians first raised it – part of the idea of hiring Marcia in the first place was to give them all a regular gratuity, encourage them to stay. Provide continuity.'

'What regular gratuity?' shouted all the Marcias in genuine indignation.

'The one the Department pays into your trust fund,' Fredericks said.

'What trust fund?'

Marcia from the switchboard walked up and threw her Campari in Orpington's face.

'Oh, Philip,' Loric said, 'I really did think of you as better than a common embezzler, fiddling the petty cash and worried about people asking to see the books.'

From the almost forgotten robot there came ominous creakings – the stamps had dried into a hard brittle shell, which started to crackle and shift.

'Prepare to meet your doom,' it said muffledly.

'At least I have some satisfaction,' Orpington said. 'It'll get them, you know. The thing is unstoppable.'

'My grandfather was mad,' Leonora said, 'but he was not completely stupid. There has to be some way of turning the damn thing off.'

'It's usually a code word,' Loric said. 'Don't know why. I suppose people who build things like this subconsciously think that they're golems. I'm an expert on golems, you know. It's usually a code word.'

'Death, Sleep, Lie Down, Fall Over,' he added sternly and inconsequentially as the robot continued to creak its way out of the shell. 'It's all in the tone of voice. Show it who's master. Die for your country, boy.'

'Rumpelstiltskin,' someone added unhelpfully.

'It is a password, of course,' Orpington said. 'But I'll never tell you. And my mind block is much too good for those of you who are telepaths, so there.'

'But you did tell me,' Leonora said. 'Honestly, you are so smug and so infantile. You told me what my grandfather said, just before he managed to kill himself.'

She turned to the robot. 'You can rest now,' she said. 'You really must get out of the habit, Orpington, of thinking other people are entirely stupid.'

The robot was free of its case and striding forward across the room, but suddenly it froze.

'I can rest,' it said.

'Yes,' said Leonora.

It lay down on the ground and the lights on its face dimmed. Everyone breathed a sigh of relief.

Then it sat up again.

'I sleep,' it said, 'for now, but I shall return. In our country's hour of greatest need. Farewell.'

Then it slumped to the ground with a particularly final clang.

Two hundred Marcias converged on Orpington.

'We want our money,' they said. Two hundred people saying the same thing very quietly is very loud.

'Arrest me, Smithers,' Orpington said. 'It is, as they say, a fair cop. And before you think you're so clever, Miss Norton, remember that your family is dead, and you're still the garbage lady.'

'Don't see the point, really,' Smithers said, turning to Leonora and to Marcia from the switchboard. 'He'll get off with six months in some open prison – I don't think you can conspire with a machine, and he knows all the judges. Bet you he's back at the DPR in a decade or two. People like him always get a second chance.'

'Oh, go on,' Leonora said. 'You might as well. Just for the record. Go on, dad, book him.'

Smithers smiled at her shyly.

'What do you think?' he asked Marcia.

'Arrest him, Mr Smithers,' Marcia said.

'Oh, Marcia,' he said, 'don't call me Mr Smithers. Call me Gavin.'

'Oh,' she said. 'Oh, yes, Gavin. I will. But, Gavin.'

'Yes, Marcia,' Smithers said.

'We'll have to wait until after I've been to university. I'm not going to run a switchboard all my life, you know.'

Leonora looked at them, and smiled. All over the room Marcias were explaining to Gavins and Justins and Nigels that the extra money wouldn't be going on the car, that they were going to need it for themselves.

Sometimes a second chance is not a bad thing.

Quite suddenly it rained bits of wrapping paper and oranges and nuts and squeakers and cracker mottos and slightly misshapen liqueur chocolates.

A child tugged on Leonora's elbow and said, 'Now that's what I call proper Father Christmas.'

*

Leonora went back to her flat that night, late and slightly drunk. The cats glowered at her, and she showered them with fish-heads. The cat litter stank, and the room was full of odds and ends of stuff, and so she shut one eye and stared at it really hard with the other, and then suddenly it went away, most of it.

'Ha,' she said. 'Take that, Orpington. Revenge of the garbage lady.'

She was feeling altogether cheerful as she took the cover off her typewriter and, just to get herself committed, typed a little page.

'Leonora Hughes, Thomas Cranston and Albertine and Marcia Hughes-Cranston – A Paranormal Family and the British State 1940–1992, by Leonora Cranston-Smithers.'

And then she smiled.

'I fail,' Loric said, 'to see what's so amusing.'

I was thinking about Philip.

'So was I. If the Minister has even the faintest idea of what's been going on in this Department . . .'

Evanescent laughter interrupted him again.

But you know how fastidious he is. Can't you just picture his face when that woman pulled her party trick?

Loric thought about it, the corner of his mouth beginning to quirk, despite his fatigue and irritation.

'It is rather appealing, isn't it?'

Couldn't have happened to a nicer guy.

Abruptly, Loric found himself laughing. He sprawled back in the swivel chair, feeling the tension dissipate. Maybe Maddie was right, he was getting things out of proportion. They always looked better after a good night's sleep.

That's my boy. Only one more to go too.

Encouraged, he drank the rest of his tea and picked it up.

THE LAW OF BEING

Storm Constantine

To the House which none leave who have entered it
To the Road from which there is no way back . . .

from an Assyrio-Babylonian stone tablet recounting the
myth of Ishtar and Tammuz

It was the biggest Transmission of Future Light Convention ever. Held in Amsterdam, thousands of followers from all over Europe had flocked to see its luminary, Emory Patrick, in person. The diversions on offer included a week of rock concerts by over a dozen well-known bands, theatrical productions with a spiritual theme, and panel talks by eminent New Agers, occultists, writers and media stars. There would be group rituals, workshops, meditations and dances; parties at night by communal fires. Everyone had the intention of drinking and doping themselves into cheerful oblivion. To the many thousands of Future Lighters (as members of the movement liked to call themselves), Emory Patrick, rock star, philosopher and healer, was the new messiah.

Patrick had risen to prominence two years ago. TOFL had been established round about the same time as the band, which was also named Future Light. Patrick was the singer and motivating force behind both the music and the movement, although he was assisted by two close friends and business partners, Linford Brown and Iliana Forsyth. Transmission of Future Light attracted the young. It was a beacon which shone relentlessly through the dusty, mildewed catacombs that orthodox belief systems had become, being youth-orientated, uncompromisingly modern, aggressively forward-thinking, and, perhaps most potently, largely free from dogma. Patrick himself was the creed, simply by example: you can live like me, be like me. He was incredibly successful, and did not make any attempt to conceal the more commercial aspects of his movement, boldly asserting that there was no shame in having money or earning money, as long as you didn't attempt to rip people off. Thus, the books, T-shirts, badges and magazines were plentiful (the merchandise sheets alone were virtually a magazine) but reasonably priced and made of quality materials. They were fun too. Future Light was not po-faced; its slogans sometimes included swear words and buzz words from youth culture. Its image was bright and vigorous, and its philosophy did not appear to carry any great threat to the establishment, even though the young flocked to Emory's camp in droves.

On the day before the convention started, Future Lighters from nearly a dozen European countries were setting up their stalls around the edge of the site. The high, razor-topped wire fences had already been erected, and TOFL security were patrolling with walkie-talkies and dogs. Beyond the wire, as the followers arrived in vans or on foot, brightly coloured tents were sprouting up into a sprawling and lively temporary community. There was an atmosphere of expectancy and excitement. Emory Patrick himself appeared around noon, in the kind of long black limo stars were expected to travel in. He was accompanied by his band, their dancers and the inevitable presence of Iliana Forsyth and Linford Brown.

Leaving Emory to meditate in his bungalow-sized cara-van, and Iliana to supervise the last details of the cater-ing, Linford wandered off to inspect the enormous, cano-pied stage. It too was in the last stages of completion, with only a few more adjustments being required to the lighting rig. Linford wandered on to the stage and stared out over the vast space that would, by tomorrow, be filled with adoring Patrick devotees. He was a spare, angular man in his late thirties, who had perhaps lived a little too hard, but who had found, in Future Light, a comfortable niche in which to exercise his talents, which had been forged in the music industry. Emory Patrick was an easy person to work with and for. He was genu-ine. Although Linford was not at all religious, and grinned at the most avid followers who declared Emory was undoubtedly the New Son of God, he believed in Emory's power as an individual. He believed Emory really did have the capacity to change the world in a positive way because, in loving people, he gave them courage and confidence in themselves. There were no tricks and no bullshit.

Linford was just in the act of reflecting how perfect his life was when something large and dark hurtled past the edge of his vision and hit the stage with a sickening, liquid crack. Immediately there were shouts and the sound of running feet. Linford blinked and stared at the object lying very close to his feet. It was the body of a man; very decidedly a body, rather than just a man, because the neck and limbs were all contorted into highly unusual angles and blood had begun to pool across the stage. Linford was stunned. He couldn't move. Someone was shouting, 'Get an ambulance, get an ambulance!' and someone else was shoving Linford out of the way.

'Fucking hell, he's dead, man, he's dead!'

People in Emory Patrick T-shirts were swarming all

over the stage. The corpse was one of the lighting technicians, Linford realized. Must have fallen. Oh, God! He turned away, collapsed on to his belly and vomited over the edge of the stage. Wiping his mouth, numb in the midst of confusion and panic, he looked up and saw Emory walking towards him, obviously having been disturbed from his trance by the shouting.

'What's going on?' Emory asked. For a brief moment Linford was filled with the blinding realization that everything he had worked for was about to be demolished. He did not want to tell Emory what had happened, didn't want him to see the hideous broken flesh, which was screened by the frantic huddle of people on the stage. He wanted to lead Emory away, because then nothing would change. Linford, though imaginative, was also something of a sceptic. He rarely heeded his instincts.

'An accident,' he said. 'Terrible accident.'

Emory climbed nimbly up on to the stage. He looked vulnerable and fragile and young, his long hair tied back, his eyes wide and curious. Struggling into a kneeling position, Linford put out his hand to grab hold of Emory's shirt.

'Leave it, Mori. There's nothing we can do . . .'

Emory looked down at him. He didn't say anything, but something in his almost vacant expression rekindled Linford's bone-deep apprehension.

'Mori . . .'

Emory was pushing through the crowd. Linford followed. People had instinctively drawn back as Emory approached, allowing him to squat beside the corpse. Emory's face was still expressionless. Squatting in the pool of blood, he methodically straightened the limbs and head of the dead man.

'Mori, don't,' Linford said in a soft voice. He couldn't bear to look at the corpse again, but rested a hand on

Emory's shoulder. Surely, the body should be left alone until the proper authorities had arrived? Ignoring Linford's plea, Emory lightly placed both of his hands on the dead man's chest. His head drooped forward. Linford could see that Emory was shaking. He wished the ambulance would come. Emory himself would need treatment for shock. The onlookers were observing Emory's behaviour in wide-eyed silence. Some appeared awed, which was typical of TOFL people when Emory did *anything*, while others looked a little embarrassed. Seconds passed.

When the dead man twitched and uttered a groan, three of the people watching fainted immediately.

Linford swayed and stepped away from Emory Patrick. He felt bile rise in his throat again. *This isn't real. Can't be. No, the guy wasn't dead. Stunned. He was just stunned! Yes.* The rationalizing thoughts gushed through Linford's mind. Around him people were moaning or weeping, while others were muttering grateful prayers. Yet, beyond the circle of their bodies, the silence of the day was immaculate.

Ignoring the spectators, Emory helped the lighting technician to sit up. The two men embraced and Emory kissed the resurrectee on his bloodied mouth. Watching, Linford bit through the edge of his tongue.

The doctors who would later examine the man who fell to his death would find no trace of a fracture, nor even a bruise.

Nina Vivian was a very disgruntled woman. Primarily because she could not believe the Department of Paranormal Resources was taking this business seriously, and secondly because she had bad feelings about getting involved in it. Call it guts, call it instinct, or good old Mother Goddess, she wasn't interested. The DPR unfortunately *were* interested, and, as she was one of their Temps, and a very special one at that, their interests were inevitably hers to share.

'Of course, there is always the possibility this guy is not a fake, not even Talented, but exactly what his followers claim he is?' She only said it to provoke her companion, but still twisted the rather emotive statement into a question, before laying the print-out she'd been given down on the desk in front of her. The high-ceilinged office was bathed in the muted light of a single desk lamp. Outside rain patted at the windows. It was very late.

The man seated behind the desk in partial shadow was swivelling gently in his plush executive chair. With his fingers steepled against his chin, he raised one immaculately curved eyebrow. 'That cannot be ruled out completely yet, but personally I find it hard to convince myself it might be the explanation. My dear Nina, as an experienced member of the DPR yourself, I am sure you must feel, as I do, this man has to be one of ours.'

Nina grimaced. She didn't really believe Emory Patrick was a paranorm or a messiah. 'It's a stunt,' she said. 'Has to be.'

The man's eyebrow lifted again. 'Well, whatever your opinion, because of the enormity of what Patrick *appears* to have done, coupled with his considerable influence, it is imperative we establish whether he's paranormal or simply a cheap magician. If it's the former, then we'll have to have a little chat with him.'

Nina wrinkled her nose and peered at the black and white digitized photograph on the polished mahogany. What looked back at her was a prime and immaculate specimen of masculinity. 'He looks like a rock star to me, nothing more.'

The man smiled tolerantly. 'The media seem to concur

with you. However, some of the individuals who witnessed the event were not connected to the organization – caterers and so on – and Patrick's people have been insisting they be given lie-detector tests to prove their man's a miracle worker.' He rolled his eyes in exasperated scorn. 'Although Patrick himself has refused to discuss the subject, several of his staff have appeared on TV earnestly insisting the resurrection was genuine.'

'Great media stuff!' Nina said.

'Quite.'

Nina grinned. 'Personally, I think it's a great stunt!' She gestured at the print-out. 'Come on, Gervase, your initial research doesn't seem to have thrown up anything damning. This guy's clean. He's just a showman.'

The man shrugged. 'I don't believe anyone making that much money from such a project can possibly be clean, but then I am not a spiritual person. Perhaps I'm too cynical.'

Nina pushed her fingers through her hair. It felt lank. She'd been called from her bed in the middle of the night before what promised to be an excellent shoot in the morning. The DPR didn't call her out at any time unless something big was going down. Nina Vivian only did 'big stuff'. She leaned back in her chair, sending a hopeful message to the Receiver she knew was sitting out in the next office that yes, she was rather in need of a large coffee. 'So, spit it out, Gervase, what d'you want, or expect, me to do with this?' She flicked her nails against the photograph.

He spread out his hands. 'Do what you do best, my dear, in your expert inimitable way. Investigate . . . bring him in, if necessary.'

She sighed. 'I hope you're not going to say anything like I'm booked on a flight to Amsterdam in the morning, because that will annoy me intensely. I have Sable Grant up before my lenses first thing, and believe me, I can't and won't miss that.'

Gervase Allerby closed his eyes and laughed silently, throwing back his head. 'No, Ms Vivian, your flight is booked for early afternoon. That should give you enough time. I tuned in to your schedule before I woke you.'

'Efficient. So what was I dreaming?'

'My dear, I never pry.' He grinned.

Sable Grant proved more tractable than Nina would dared have hoped for, which at one time would have been an unusual trait in an up-and-coming starlet. Not so nowadays. The image had changed. The New Age had bit deep into Hollywood flesh, and everything was mellow. Nina still couldn't help wondering how much of the girl's perfect bone structure and flawless configuration was indebted to the surgeon's cosmetic knife. Perhaps America bred these lissom creatures as a kind of subspecies, whose natural habitat was the film industry. Even though Nina was aware that all self-respecting stars made a point of discussing in their interviews how much they shunned the prima donna temperament nowadays, she still wouldn't have believed it until she'd met Sable. Everything was natural, everything was relaxed. Only desperately insecure people possessed painful egos to inflict on others. Sable was well at home in her skin. She was charming.

During a break, while Viennese coffee and wafer-thin continental chocolate biscuits were handed round by attentive film company personnel, Sable Grant hunkered down beside Nina, who was sitting on a pile of packing cases, fiddling with her equipment. She didn't need to fiddle with her equipment, but it prevented her having to make conversation. There was nobody there Nina thought it was worth talking to. Just the girl and her entourage. She didn't imagine the girl would want to speak to her.

'You're good,' Sable said. 'You make me feel so tranquil.'

Nina smiled. She didn't think Ms Grant would ever be anything other than tranquil in front of a camera. 'That's kind of you. Thanks.' Was she supposed to deliver a compliment back now?

'I really wanted to come to England. I love it. I love the history.'

Don't they always, Nina thought. 'Yeah ... there's plenty of that.'

'And you have Emory Patrick over here too. That's wild.'

Nina looked up sharply, far too sharply. It was her DPR persona look, not the habitual laid-back expression of Nina Vivian, photographer.

'What is it?' Sable asked quickly, eyes wide.

Nina shook her head. These New Age techniques the stars were getting into made them too damn sensitive for her liking. 'Oh, coincidence, you know. I was just thinking about him. I have to photograph him tomorrow.'

Sable's eyes widened. 'Really! Wow, I mean, how lucky for you.' She laid a beautiful, long-fingered hand on Nina's knee and lowered her voice. 'Hey, I know this might be a heavy question, but is there any chance I could get to meet him? Could you, like, arrange that for me?'

Nina smiled. 'I'm sorry. The shoot's in Amsterdam, not London. I wish I could oblige but ...' She gestured helplessly.

'That's okay. I understand. I would have liked to meet him, though. Just to see whether he's on the level.'

Nina was surprised. 'Think he's a fake, then?' she asked.

'No, not exactly. I think I'm scared he might be all that his people claim he is. It's strange, but in a way I think that would be worse.'

'Yeah,' Nina said. 'I suppose it would.'

Linford Brown was worried. Since the incident at the convention, everyone had thought it best if Emory moved to a hotel, rather than stay in the caravan on site. The place was crawling with media scum. Emory had seemed dazed, as if he'd been severely drained of energy after the lighting guy had done the sit-up-and-walk gig. Emory had passively submitted to Linford's and Iliana's suggestion of privacy, only now he wouldn't come out of the hotel room at all, and wasn't taking calls. He was still eating, but refused to see anyone other than hotel staff. Now, Linford was standing outside the door to Room 223, trying to address the person inside, getting more and more wound up by the fact that people kept walking by and giving him strange looks. The TOFL security man on duty outside Emory's door studiously ignored the proceedings.

The convention had been limping along since the incident at the site, but the atmosphere seemed flat without Emory there. People were understandably disappointed. After all, they'd paid a large fee for the privilege of seeing him. The band performances, sideshows and panel talks had continued as planned, but the audiences only wanted to talk about and hear about Emory's healing miracle. All other subjects seemed to have lost their appeal. This obsession was beginning to frustrate the official convention guests. Several of them had left after the first day, mainly writers and scholars who claimed they found the publicity associated with the event somewhat distasteful. It was fortunate the musicians and actors had taken an opposite stance and were unashamedly lapping the publicity up. What worried Linford more than absconding guests was the amount of people who were turning up at the site gates demanding entrance. None of these newcomers had tickets (the event had sold out months ago), and they were either invalids or accompanied by invalids. They had come to see the master. They wanted his healing power. Despite being kept outside the site, they would not go away.

Linford himself was feeling dazed and drained of energy. He'd always been behind Emory a hundred per cent, had believed without reservation in the man's sincerity and convictions, had basked in the Apollo glow of Emory's charisma. Only he hadn't believed in miracles. This was spooky shit. Future Light was meant to be about finding yourself in a world gone crazy, and using that self-knowledge to enlighten others, thereby helping the world to heal. Now the whole movement was poised on the brink of zipping back to the Dark Ages as fast as it could. Just as Emory did the one thing that perhaps proved his followers' claim that he was the New Son of God beyond all doubt, an immovable host of doubts was cast over the organization. It was all too weird. It didn't fit into Linford's scheme. Now the man himself was acting crazy.

'Look, Mori, I have to talk to you. Don't do this to me, man. Let me in!' Normally Linford would not raise his voice to Emory, but perhaps a little uncharacteristic aggression might produce results that habitual serenity would not. 'I'm not taking any more of this shit! If this door doesn't open right now, I'm out of here. For good. I mean it!' He thumped the door with a closed fist and then kicked it. He heard the lock rattle.

'They'll charge us for the paintwork.' Emory said, opening the door. 'You'd better come in.'

Linford felt embarrassed. He'd never behaved like that before, never threatened or used emotional blackmail. The feeling of powerlessness, of regression, was crippling. Emory was wearing a long dark-blue robe which hung open. He was naked beneath it. Some cans of beer were chilling in a bucket of ice. He tossed one to Linford. 'I expect you need this.'

Linford wondered whether Emory was drunk. He never shunned alcohol but his intake was always moderate. 'I'm sorry. I . . .'

Emory waved a hand at him. He was standing at the window, staring out through the floor-length nets. ''S okay. Forget it.'

'Are you all right?'

Emory looked at Linford over his shoulder. 'Fine. Why shouldn't I be?'

Because you were virtually catatonic when we brought you back from the site; because you've been incommunicado for nearly two days; because you've shut both Iliana and myself out, that's why, Linford thought, but said nothing. His burst of anger had passed. He shrugged. 'We were worried about you,' he said.

Emory turned away from the window and flung himself into a large white overstuffed chair, one leg hung over the arm. 'I know what you and Iliana have been thinking. You're thinking I shouldn't have done it, right?'

Linford sighed and sat down on the edge of the bed, which appeared unslept in, but of course the maids come around regularly. He wondered whether Emory displayed himself to them so blatantly. 'You know I wouldn't judge you,' he said. 'You did what you felt at the time.'

'Which was perhaps the wrong time. I know.' Emory closed his eyes and rested his head against the back of the chair.

'Mori,' Linford ventured timidly. 'What exactly *did* you do?'

Emory swallowed, the small convulsion shivering down his long throat. 'Something natural,' he said. 'That's all. It wasn't that guy's time to buy it. It was an accident.'

There are no accidents. There are no coincidences. Those were two of Emory's maxims. Linford felt uncomfortable. He couldn't quite rid himself of the suspicion that Emory had done what he'd done simply to display his power. Linford had not imagined that Emory's powers might encompass anything so potent.

'Was he really dead?' Linford asked. He had to. Even though he'd seen the body, that broken scrap so evidently vacated by anything resembling human life, and had spent the last two days trying to convince himself he hadn't.

Emory gave him a withering glance. 'You want me to say "no", don't you? You want me to come clean and admit it was all some kind of sick stunt. It wasn't. I'm sorry. You'll have to live with that.'

'Mori . . .'

Emory sat upright, suddenly animated by a spasm of emotion, which looked very like rage. 'Isn't this what you all wanted?' he asked. 'Haven't you marketed me as the great saviour of the world? I can't understand why you're so pissed off about this.'

'Emory,' Linford said, hands extended. 'I've said nothing. How could I? You've refused to see me since the incident.'

'You don't have to say anything.' Emory stared at him balefully.

He can't read my mind, Linford told himself firmly. 'All I'm worried about at the moment is the way this business has affected you,' he said, trying to sound calm and reasonable. 'It's obviously upset you, otherwise you wouldn't have hidden yourself away like this.'

'I'm not upset. I needed to think, that's all. I needed to think clearly. Much as I love you both, you and Iliana are distractions.' Emory got up out of the chair and wandered back to the window.

Linford cleared his throat. 'Well, anyway, I'll call the promotion people and go over to the site today. We'll have to wind it down . . .'

'No!' Emory turned round in a whirl of blue cloth.

'What do you mean, "no"? The followers want you, Emory, nobody else. And you're here, shut in this damned room. The site is surrounded by weirdos, who are also all crying for you. It's got out of hand. We have to fold the show.'

'You won't close the site, Linford. It's not finished.'

'What isn't?'

Emory threw up his hands. 'I don't know! I don't know!'

'Talk to me!' Linford cried. 'What is going on, Mori? Everything's changing, isn't it? What's happening?'

Emory curled his lips into a sneer. 'You don't want me to talk, you just want reassurance!'

This is like an argument, Linford thought. This is like trouble. He and Emory had never exchanged angry words before, or experienced an uncomfortable atmosphere between them.

Emory leaned against the wall, rubbing his face vigorously, as if to massage something away. Then he dropped his hands and laughed. 'Shit,' he said. 'I'm terrible for you, so much hassle . . . I know. Come here.' He opened his arms and Linford walked into the embrace, because he hadn't the will or desire to refuse. The blue robe enclosed him like a shroud. It felt like goodbye.

Nina read through her notes again on the plane. No flimsy print-out this time but a bound booklet of laser-printed information, complete with comprehensive illustrations and photographs. It was the biography of Emory Patrick's life. Her job was to fill in the blanks. According to the DPR data, Patrick's parents had died in the famous

Milton Keynes murders, when he'd been only five, gunned down by a psychotic member of the Pro-Life group, who'd freaked out in a hypermall. Following that undoubtedly traumatic incident, Emory had been entrusted to the care of his Aunt Mary, who had been a devout Christian of the Women's Institute persuasion. There was no evidence to suggest the woman had forced her own beliefs upon the boy, but Nina envisaged a childhood surrounded by garish representations of nearly naked crucified men and white-robed limpid saviours that might well have had some influence on Emory's development. He appeared to have enjoyed an unsurpassingly normal childhood in his aunt's care, although once he went to university, his personality had evidently blossomed. He'd studied psychology and embraced the teachings of some of the wackiest gurus available to the student population at the time. As well as joining a student band, through which he could exercise a previously unglimpsed musical talent, Patrick had initiated consciousness-raising meetings. By the time he'd achieved his degree, with honours, he was a hero of the social scene and the hub of a thriving self-awareness group. Information had been collected from individuals who'd known Patrick at the time, who claimed he'd had a certain magic, that his touch was healing, that he could influence reality with a single thought. After leaving university, close friends had encouraged Patrick to expand his self-awareness group into the organization now known as Transmission of Future Light, and he'd eventually met up with Brown and Forsyth, who'd since steered his career in an upwards direction. It had been Brown who'd brought the band to prominence, realizing it was the ideal medium through which to reach the youth culture. Patrick's physical attractiveness obviously contributed to his success. Although his religious beliefs were fairly unstructured and subject to

change, and certainly estranged from the established pa-
triarchal Church, many people believed he really was the
New Son of God. Patrick did not publicly concur with
this idea, but neither did he deny it.

After a last look at one of the photographs – Patrick on-
stage, his shirt falling off one shoulder, hair all over the
place, mmmm – Nina closed the binder. She felt a little
dazed. That part about Patrick being brought up by his
Aunt Mary was just too much, and what percentage of
the anecdotes about his college years, gleaned from old
friends and acquaintances, was reliable data? Not a great
deal, Nina suspected. She was also sure most of the
information had been gathered from the newspapers. Although they scanned the media and culture for potential
paranorms, both directly and psychically, the DPR had
probably thought Patrick was a money-making joke, like
all the other New Age manias, until the Amsterdam gig.
They hadn't thought him paranormal until now, because
he hadn't really done anything to suggest that. Nina took
another look at the photographs: Emory Patrick talking
to crowds of adoring devotees, Emory Patrick singing
with his band, Emory Patrick holding group meditation
sessions. His charisma shone from the frames; he was
indisputably star material. People fell for that; they loved
heroes, but only unTalented ones. So, Mr Patrick, what
now? she wondered. The Dutch authorities were freaked
– understandably so – and because Patrick was British,
it had fallen to the DPR to investigate and presumably
shuffle the New Son of God off the continent and back to
the UK. And, she had to admit with a private smile, it
would be kind of weird having the New Son of God on
the Temps list. What would they call him in for? Divine
retribution, when it was needed? Nina still didn't believe
Patrick was paranormal. Despite her earlier misgivings,

she had become intrigued by the Amsterdam affair and was looking forward to delving into it, but somehow the thought that a Talent had been responsible seemed unreal. In her experience paranorms spent their lives trying to live down their differences, hide them and apologize for them. They did not veer toward flamboyance. Still, if Patrick was a Talent, his days as guru were numbered. Once the public found out, his movement would be history. Paranorms had never been popular, a circumstance initiated by fear and ignorance more than anything. Nina herself never divulged her Talent. It was fortunately easy to conceal, and certainly in the DPR's interest to keep it under wraps. Even the DPR branch she worked for was a highly secret operation that only a very few people knew existed. Should she ever be unveiled, the DPR would probably deny all knowledge of her. Her name would not be found on any DPR file, and the office she was called to visit in the middle of the night would be as empty and dusty as if it hadn't been used for years.

Her camera case lay on the rack overhead. The camera was a prop for her Talent but not essential. It disguised what she could do, just as much as it had revealed what she could do. The memory was mercifully fading with the years, but that time on the shoot in the Lake District still festered darkly in the depths of Nina's heart. They'd told her to confront it, wear it out by becoming familiar with it. *That bitch who tried to ruin my life! God, I have no regrets!* But she did. She had so many regrets that she'd nearly lost her sanity. It had been the DPR who'd picked up the pieces after the incident, called in by frantic onlookers who'd realized what was happening. Gervase Allerby had been the suave, dark angel who'd glued Nina back together. She felt he now held the keys to her soul even though she sailed through her glitteringly successful professional and social life as if she hadn't a care in the world. In reality she felt she belonged to the DPR alone, the unacknowledged underworld of the DPR that no one knew about, the truth beneath the bureaucracy and red tape above ground. She had no complaints. Without them, she'd be locked up in one institution or another. So, she did the job, and sometimes the job was tame. She hoped this one would be. Still, the DPR must be frightened of Emory Patrick, very frightened, to put Nina Vivian on his case.

Nina was due to meet a Dutch telepath at the airport who'd been doing some preliminary work on the Patrick situation. The two of them would work in concert until they'd managed to ascertain whether Emory Patrick was Talented or not. Presumably, once that was established, the telepath would butt out and leave Nina to do what was necessary, if anything *was* necessary.

The telepath was named Chantal, a skinny, dark-haired gamine, who looked like a refugee from a Delacorta novel. Like most young Dutch people, she spoke flawless, idiomatic English. 'You're French?' Nina asked, as they shook hands.

The girl wrinkled her nose. 'Yah, sort of. Mother was. Lived here all my life, though.'

Chantal took Nina through the beautifully clean streets of the city to a cool, dark bar, where they sipped champagne, courtesy of Chantal's agency's expense account, and swapped gossip about other paranorms they knew. Nina was beginning to feel muzzily philanthropic by the time the subject of Emory Patrick was introduced. Chantal had lit a slim cigar and leaned conspiratorily over the table.

'I've been sniffing round the convention site,' she said, 'but the man has gone underground since the incident.'

Nina had lifted her camera out of its case and now

peered through the viewfinder at her companion. 'I expect there are quite a few people sniffing about,' she said. 'I'm not surprised you didn't come up with anything. Patrick's people must be feeling very paranoid right now, and don't paranoid people have a tendency to erect their own unconscious mind blocks?'

'Oh, I found out enough,' Chantal said. 'Enough to tell me the Future Lighters are as stunned by Patrick's Jesus trick as much as everyone else. He's never pulled a stunt like this before.'

'There's mention of healing sessions in the briefing notes I've got,' Nina said.

'Yeah, but Patrick never claimed responsibility for that. Always said the people concerned had healed themselves through their belief. Nothing paranormal about that. Even your family doctor will prescribe a little positive thinking to kick out the blues nowadays.'

'That's true. It's crazy, isn't it, along comes someone who might genuinely have the most awesome Talent and the authorities are terrified of him. From what I've read, he seems a genuine guy, not even particularly power-hungry. I wonder why the DPR are so nervous about him? Why not just let him get on with what he's doing, which is basically cheering people up in this god-damned shit of a mess we call a world?'

Chantal shrugged and pulled a face. 'Perhaps it's because he's genuine and not power-hungry that makes your DPR nervous. My lot are the same. Let's face it, a religious leader who isn't a bone-deep self-aggrandizing bastard and a Talent who isn't ashamed of his powers makes for one poky individual. Think about it. I reckon if we do find out Patrick is a paranorm and he decides to come out about it, he wouldn't lose any popularity at all.'

'Oh, he would! Certainly in the UK anyway. I know what people are like about paranorms there.'

Chantal shook her head. 'No, Emory Patrick is different. You don't understand what he does to people. His followers really *love* him. Desperately. Wouldn't make any difference to them what he is. If he confessed he'd killed his parents or a thousand babies, they'd forgive him.'

'How can you be so sure?'

Grinning, Chantal turned the collar of her leather jacket around to display an Emory Patrick badge. 'I've been close, very close, to members of the Patrick following,' she said.

'Wow, paid-up member!' Nina said. 'Hope your agency picked up the tab.'

'Naturally. Anyway, it's up to you to get us close to the man himself now.'

'Thought it might.'

'I picked up which hotel he's staying in from someone at the convention site. We're booked in there too now.'

Nina lifted her camera to her eye. 'I'm impressed!' Then she winked around the camera's body at Chantal. 'Take me to your leader,' she said.

Iliana, lying on one of the two beds in the hotel room she was sharing with Linford, bit through another of her lovingly manicured nails with an audible snap. Linford jerked in irritation, lying on the other bed. Air-conditioning hummed into the summer afternoon. Everything was very still in the microcosm of the room. Outside the city buzzed faintly, as if the sounds came to them through a virtually impenetrable shield.

'Maybe we should go back to England,' Iliana said, and then spat, expelling a sliver of fingernail.

'We can't leave him!' Linford snapped.

'I meant we could take him with us,' Iliana replied in a flat voice. 'Those were your thoughts speaking, honey, not mine.'

She shifted restlessly on to her side, a shapely odalisque in turquoise leggings and an Emory Patrick T-shirt, silky blonde hair falling over her coquettishly frowning face. Appearances were deceptive, Linford thought. He'd always considered she looked like a mindless tart, but the brain inside that cover-girl body was as sharp as a hypodermic and capable of injecting equally subcutaneous poisons. It was she who held the business side of the Future Light together; a cage around the men that kept predators away from their meat. Iliana: metal and sharpness. You should listen to her, Linford thought, and then remembered the promise he'd made to Emory earlier, a promise he'd been almost physically coerced into making.

'The convention's only half-way through,' he said. 'People have paid.'

'People can be refunded, for God's sake! We can mail them all a Care package as well, if that's what it takes! This is a mess. I'm confused. I can't think. We need to lie low for a while, re-evaluate our set-up. Anyway, I can't see Mori coming out of his room to address the crowds in the near future, can you?'

Linford sighed. 'I don't know what he's thinking. His mood is . . . strange. He's shut off from me.'

'Idiot!' Iliana exclaimed and thumped the duvet. 'Idiot! Idiot! Idiot! Why the hell did he have to go and do that?' She'd already asked this question about a hundred times over the last few days. Linford had run out of answers.

'I'm going to have to say something I've been putting off saying,' Iliana said into the silence that had followed her outburst.

'What?' Linford was apprehensive of her tone of voice.

Iliana sat up on the side of the bed, legs apart, hands dangling between her knees. Linford noticed, for the first time, how tired she looked. She almost looked her age, which was unusual. Although he was unsure what her true age was, she generally looked about twenty-five, but he'd known her too long for that to be the case. 'There's something I haven't been confronting in my head, Lin. Emory really did it, didn't he? He really brought someone back from the dead. What does that mean?'

'Something we've always believed. That he's no bull-shitter.'

Iliana closed her eyes and shook her head. 'No, my darling, it does not. What it means is that our beloved Mori has . . . powers. Magical powers? Spiritual powers or even . . . paranormal powers?'

Linford sat up. 'No! You can't mean that! He's no freak!'

'Now don't get hysterical on me,' Iliana said in a low, deadly voice. 'We've no time for that. This is serious.'

'Yeah. I'd say so! It'd be the end of us!'

'That's not quite what I meant,' Iliana said. 'It's going to open a whole can of worms, don't you see? The implications are awesome. Tie in the religious aspect with paranormality, and you get a nasty mess of quandaries regarding faith-healers, psychics, my God, perhaps even people like tarot-readers, I don't know! Unwittingly, Emory Patrick might redefine the whole concept of what paranormality is and where its boundaries lie.'

'How can that affect us?' Linford regretted the question even before he'd finished speaking, aware of its selfish tone.

'The DPR will be interested in Emory, Lin. They might already be here.'

'So what? They're just a bunch of clerks!' Linford couldn't help laughing. The DPR! Yeah, terrifying, really terrifying.

'Don't be pathetic,' Iliana said. 'They'll be wondering what other little surprises Mori might have up his sleeve. They could just snatch him.'

'That's illegal.'

'Grow up, Linford!' Iliana stood up.

'Jesus, Illa, you've been watching too many spy movies,' Linford said. 'This is the real world, with formal procedures, etc. No one can just snatch someone like that. Not officially.'

Iliana turned, one hand on her hip and sneered at him. 'Despite the vast experience you claim to have, you're really such a child, Linford! Emory has power, real power. Thousands belong to TOFL, every one of them prepared to stand by their Great Man. If that Great Man turns out to be a paranorm, things could get nasty. How will the great general public react, for example, knowing a paranorm has so much influence, that their sons and daughters flock to his concerts and talks? The DPR would *have* to do something. They'd have no choice.'

'But Emory might not be a paranorm,' Linford said.

Iliana snorted. 'Don't be ridiculous! What else could he be?'

'But . . .'

She threw her hands up over her head in a dramatic gesture, stalking towards the window. 'Oh, Linford, face reality, will you? There's no messiah, no Second Coming, there's only hope. That's what Emory is: hope. Nothing more, in a spiritual sense.'

'Then what can we do?'

For a moment the pair of them swapped the most naked glance that it is possible for two people to share. They knew that as survivors, which they undoubtedly were, they should leave Emory Patrick to his destiny, they should run while they still could.

Then Iliana visibly steeled herself. 'He's not losing it, Linford, he really isn't. I don't quite know what he *is* doing at the moment, but Emory is no fool. All I have to suggest is that we go back to England. The rest is up to him. We'll have to trust him.'

'You mean, you think his powers are strong enough to protect him from ... well, anything? Strong enough to protect us?'

Iliana grinned a crooked grin. 'Doesn't he say you only have to believe in something to make it real?'

'It's a risk, Illa.'

'Sure, and I'll be watching his back like a god-damned hawk-lady until he's got his act together again.'

The hotel lobby was full of people wearing Emory Patrick T-shirts and little identification clips. They all appeared to be scurrying around doing nothing very much except scurrying. Nina had brought only her camera case with her, plus a hold-all containing a change of jeans, cosmetics and a toothbrush. Chantal appeared to have brought nothing, but of course she would have checked in earlier. Nina noticed the Dutch girl nodding hello to quite a few of the Patrick people.

'Any of these the ones you got close to, like really close?' Nina teased.

Chantal pulled a face, and then pantomimed a demure voice. 'I believe you misunderstood my meaning, or perhaps my grasp of language was in error.'

'Your grasp of language seems sweetly accurate to me, lady!'

Chantal shrugged. 'Well, some of the guys are cute.'

They went into the lift. 'Our room is as close to Patrick's as I could get,' Chantal said. 'Fortunately, the hotel staff are not paranoid and therefore as easy to read as a cereal box.'

'Does he have security?'

''Course. They have a few heavies – you know, concerned *brothers*, to keep the hordes from the big man.'

'He's not doing interviews, I take it?'

Chantal rolled her eyes. 'No, not exactly. I reckon you

should get to Forsyth or Brown to get to Patrick. If not directly, then through the merchandising staff or something.'

'You mean I might have to buy a T-shirt?'

'It may come to that. Can't your expense account take it?'

'You kidding? I'm a Temp for the DPR. Whatever I buy on expenses has to have about six invoices, a signature in blood, ten good reasons why I bought it . . .'

Chantal groaned. 'Oh, grim! Well, here's our floor. We should make dinner if we hurry. Perhaps that'll give us our first contact.'

'Damn, I knew I should have brought a posh frock with me!' Nina said.

Chantal put a hand on her arm. 'Nina Vivian, this is Amsterdam. Anything goes here. Relax.'

Linford did not feel like eating. He felt hyped up, excited. Iliana glanced pointedly at his glass every time he summoned the waiter to refill it with Scotch, but she said nothing, eating her seafood like a cat, in a dainty yet macabre manner, and betraying no sign of unease other than her nibbled fingernails. She'd been to see Emory before coming down to dinner and had not yet divulged the outcome of the interview. Linford felt she was tormenting him deliberately by her silence, but he shrank from asking her outright.

'I shall miss this food,' she said, clawing the flesh from her last monster prawn. They'd eaten out at Indonesian restaurants every night before this, but tonight some instinct prevented them from straying into the city. Both of them wanted to stay near Emory. Iliana had said earlier she was sure Emory 'wasn't losing it', but just the fact she had spoken those words suggested she was worried he might be. Eventually Linford could stand it no longer and shouldered his pride aside.

'How did he seem tonight?' he asked.

Iliana licked her lips. 'Wired, I'd say. He's suffering, Lin, I know he is. Kicking himself, I think, but he won't talk about it.'

'I told you,' Linford replied.

Iliana ignored the remark. 'I suggested England and he was vague about committing himself. But I reckon if I just book the tickets and pack, he'll comply.'

'God, I do hope so. I've started getting really jumpy since you put that thought into my head about DPR creeps. I'm seeing men in grey everywhere! Do you know . . .' Linford noticed he no longer had the shred of Iliana's attention he'd had before. She was looking up expectantly, a welcoming smile spreading across her face. For a moment, before he followed the direction of her gaze, Linford thought Emory himself had shown up for dinner. But what he saw first was a large expensive camera, and then the tall, lanky woman who was holding it up to her face. He stood up, extending his arms, fingers spread.

'No pictures!'

'Oh, sorry!' The woman lowered the camera, revealing a strong attractive face with little make-up. She pushed back her long, straight brown hair behind one ear.

Iliana put a restraining hand on Linford's arm and said, 'It's all right, quite all right.'

The woman came right up to their table, the camera dangling heavily against her chest. She wore a faded T-shirt with a badly screened fractal print on it, her leather jacket was scuffed and her jeans were ripped, but something about her presence spoke comfortable affluence. 'I hope you don't mind,' she said, beaming at Iliana. 'I realize now who you are, but – you won't believe this – when I saw you sitting there I thought you were someone else, a Hollywood someone else, as it happens. I do apologize. You must be going through hell with photographers at the moment. I was well out of order, pointing a lens at you like that. I am sorry.'

Iliana would normally crush such an approach with a blast of well-delivered verbal cruelty, but tonight she was obviously prepared to be magnanimous. 'Oh, as I said, it's quite all right. You staying here, or just passing through with your recording eye?'

God, she's flirting! Linford thought, aghast.

The photographer grinned. 'Staying here, actually. I was just about to sample the cuisine of this establishment with my colleague.' She gestured towards another jeans-and-leather-clad female hanging back by the door with folded arms.

'Really? Well, please, join us!'

Linford was astonished.

Iliana extended a hand, which the photographer shook vigorously. 'I'm Iliana Forsyth and this is Linford Brown.'

'Pleased to meet you,' the woman said. 'I'm Hazel Rose.' She beamed at Linford and indicated the seat by him. 'Can I sit here?'

'Nina, you are brilliant, absolutely brilliant!' Chantal leaned against the side of the lift, her grinning, slightly intoxicated face reflected in the shiny doors opposite.

'Hazel, please, not Nina!' Nina said, giggling. They had spent a very pleasant evening in the company of Iliana and Linford, being heaped with delicacies both culinary and alcoholic, all of which had been paid for by the Transmission of Future Light.

'I could get into religion if it's this well paid!' Nina had whispered to Chantal as they'd left the restaurant. Now they were on their way to a meeting with Emory Patrick himself.

'I don't know how you did it,' Chantal said. 'It looked so natural.'

Nina rearranged her hair, peering at the misty reflection of herself in the doors. 'It *was* natural,' she replied. 'Anyway, we've got a few minutes alone together, so tell me what was on their minds.'

Chantal wrinkled her nose. 'They're planning on leaving soon. Iliana couldn't stop thinking about it. She was also quite surprised at herself when she asked us up to meet Emory. As for Linford, he nearly had a cerebral haemorrhage when Iliana came out with the invitation. Still, they don't suspect we're anything but what we claimed to be.'

As far as the Future Lighters were concerned, Hazel Rose and her assistant were in the city to photograph a local rock star's wedding.

'Your Department certainly sent the right woman for the job,' Chantal said. 'You have one amazing Talent for coercion.'

'Yeah.' Nina didn't mention the rest of it. She already liked Chantal a lot and didn't want to lose her friendship. They'd just kind of clicked together, made a good team. If Chantal knew the rest, she'd back off. It didn't take telepathy to work that one out.

Linford and Iliana had gone back to their room and had arranged for Chantal and Nina to meet them there in ten minutes or so. Enough time for Nina to drop off her camera – Linford had insisted on that – and for Chantal to roll a joint of the excellent grass she'd insouciantly ordered from over the counter in the bar they'd visited earlier. As they sat on Chantal's bed, smoking together, Nina was aware of a certain tightness in the fibres of her body, and consciously regulated her breathing. Was that fear or excitement? 'Read me,' she said to Chantal.

Chantal frowned. 'Don't have to. It's radiating off you, like you're just about to go on your first date. Palpitations! He freaks you, this guy, doesn't he?'

Words flashed through Nina's brain, almost as if she could hear them, but she didn't recognize the voice. *Sometimes, it's like a premonition.* She stood up, swaying a little on her feet. 'Come on, let's get this over with.'

Iliana was putting down the phone after speaking to Emory, Linford hopping around uncomfortably behind her, between the beds. 'Well, what did he say, apart from "go to hell"? We don't know these women, Illa. What are you playing at?'

Iliana straightened up and turned round slowly. She looked like an ice goddess, all stretched white satin and glittering paste jewellery, statuesque neck and coiled hair. Her expression, however, was strangely vague.

'Linford, you know me as well as anyone. I don't know why I invited the Rose woman and her friend up here. I just felt compelled to. I still do. That's not like me, but in a way, I'm not worried about it.'

'What's going on, Illa? This sounds weird.'

'Gets weirder.' She sat down on the bed, leaning back on straight arms. 'Emory knows, Lin. I'm sure he does. He knew what I was going to say before I spoke. Oh, he let me say the words, but he could have stopped me at any time and finished my little speech. All he said was "I'll be ready". Just that. No argument. Nothing. There's something special about that woman . . .'

Linford's mouth dropped open. 'Oh, my God!'

'What?'

'She couldn't be . . . well, connected with what we spoke about earlier, could she? A woman in grey?'

Iliana laughed. 'Don't be ridiculous! No. I have a nose for officials and Hazel Rose doesn't have the right smell. She's poky in her own right, but I strongly feel she's independent. Good God, Linford, you really are seeing grey shadows in every corner, aren't you!'

'Remember you're the hawk-lady.'

Iliana nodded. 'I know. But Hazel Rose isn't prey, isn't vermin. She's another hawk.'

'Jesus, she's really made an impression on you, hasn't she!'

Iliana shrugged. 'She picked me out. I'm not stupid.'

The atmosphere in Linford and Iliana's room was electric when Chantal and Nina arrived. Nina had to escape to the bathroom, where she sat on the toilet with her head in her hands, trying to collect her thoughts. Why did she feel like this? It was just a job like any other. Her stomach churned with pain as if her guts were twisting into knots. Was she genuinely ill or something? This was terrible. She'd have to be in peak form to handle the next stage of the operation. One moment of lost concentration and the whole fragile structure of coercion she'd erected around Iliana – and hoped to extend to Patrick – could crumble. Iliana came and knocked on the door. 'Are you ready? Emory's expecting us.' Nina flushed the chain and came out. Iliana put a hand on her arm. 'Are you all right, Hazel? You look very white.'

Nina raised a hand. 'Yeah, I'm fine. Had a busy, busy day, that's all, and a little overindulgence. Got a bit of a headache.'

'Would you like something for that?'

Nina shook her head. 'No, really. I'll be fine. Just don't offer me another drink.'

Walking the short distance up the corridor to Emory's room, Nina felt as if she might faint at any time. Chantal, picking up the way she was feeling, linked her arm through Nina's to give her some support, both physical and emotional. Nina was thinking, this is a gruesome parody of sociability. We all feel as if we're going to our deaths, yet we're still walking, still smiling at each other.

It's a sham. Are you in control of this, Nina Vivian, are you?

A tall, well-muscled individual, obviously a bodyguard, stood outside the door to Emory Patrick's room. Two young girls were sitting on the floor against the wall. They had a large ghetto-blaster between them, which filled the corridor with raucous music. The enormous, half-empty bottle of wine sitting on the carpet indicated the girls were entertaining the bodyguard during what must be the loneliest watch of the night. Both the girls wore identification clips which proclaimed they were Future Light merchandising staff. They peered curiously at Nina and Chantal as Iliana addressed the muscle-man.

'Hey, I've seen you,' one of the girls said to Nina. 'Weren't you in *I-D* magazine last month? Aren't you that photographer ... er ... sorry, forgotten your name – what was it?'

Iliana glared frostily at the girls, as she opened the door. 'Come along, Hazel.' Clearly she disapproved of mixing with the menial staff. As Nina went through the door, she heard the girl's lowered voice say, '*Sure the name wasn't Hazel* ...'

Linford was relieved to see that Emory had dressed and shaved himself for the occasion. He was looking splendid in tight black leather with a loose red shirt, his hair hanging round his shoulders and back. Iliana busied herself with the introductions, as she poured everyone a drink.

'Emory, this is Hazel Rose, and her assistant Felice.'

Emory smiled at Nina. 'Ms ... *Rose*, pleased to meet you.' He held out his hand to be shaken. Nina hesitated, prompting Chantal to take hold of the hand herself.

'Hazel isn't feeling too well,' Iliana said brightly. 'Have you any Perrier, Mori?'

'No, but we could ring for some.'

Nina sat down in one of the white overstuffed chairs. She flapped her hands at them. 'Oh, please don't make a fuss. I'll be okay in a minute.' Chantal sat down beside her on the arm of the chair. Nina was grateful for her support. The initial sensation of being in Emory Patrick's presence had been like standing too close to the lip of a volcano. One false step and she'd fall, to a death by either broken neck or incineration. Yet that feeling had only lasted brief seconds, and she felt it might have been self-induced. She'd hyped herself up for this meeting far too much.

'I'm very pleased to meet you, Hazel Rose,' Emory said. 'I'm familiar with your work.'

The room bucked before Nina's eyes. 'Are you?' she managed to say. 'I'm surprised.'

'Why? You're fairly well known, aren't you? I've seen your stuff in all the glossy magazines.'

He knows who I am, she thought. He knows everything about me. And yet she was sure that, for whatever reason, he wasn't going to expose her to his colleagues. He probably thought she was a scheming little paparazzo, angling to get some sensational pictures, and had decided to play along for a while. The indignation she felt at that revelation cleared away some of her confusion. She sat upright. 'So, are you going to let me photograph you when you get back to England, then?'

He shrugged. 'Perhaps, *if* I go back.'

'I thought we'd decided that earlier,' Iliana said sharply.

Emory looked at her. 'Had we? The convention's only half-way through, Illa. I shall be returning to the site to-morrow.'

'What? Are you mad?' Iliana appeared to have forgotten there were strangers present. 'You can't! Your stupid stunt has probably drawn crazies from half the known world! It's too dangerous for you to go back there.'

'Iliana, there is no danger.'

'Well, you might have had the decency to mention this earlier!'

'I hadn't decided earlier.'

Nina hoped Chantal was busy using her Talent on Patrick. She herself didn't feel it was the right time to bring hers into play. Not yet. Some part of her still believed it wouldn't be needed, and she hoped Chantal's probing would back that conviction up. Her initial impression was of a man who was clearly used to adulation, but nevertheless did not take himself too seriously. Like Sable Grant, he was comfortable in his skin. He had a confident performer's compelling eyes, but the charisma was just part of the act. This was a showman, not a messiah, she was sure of it. She could not imagine him raising somebody from the dead.

'How's your headache?' he asked her.

She shrugged. 'Manageable.'

'Give me your hand.' Aha, it was show-time. With a cynical smile, Nina extended her arm. He took her hand in his. The skin was warm and dry, but there was no electric jolt. He's not Talented, she thought. He's not. Emory closed his eyes briefly and squeezed her fingers.

'Stress,' he said.

'You don't say.'

He let her go and pulled a wry grin. 'I can tell you're not a believer.'

She shrugged again. 'Well . . .'

'It doesn't matter,' he said. 'You clearly have your own belief system that works for you pretty well.'

'Not as well as yours. I'm sure.'

He grimaced. 'Some people might say mine isn't working too well at the moment. Strange, isn't it? You give people what they want and it scares them.'

'Like raising the dead?'

Linford cleared his throat loudly and interjected, 'I don't think we should discuss that now, Emory.'

'Why not?' Emory asked in a reasonable voice. 'I'm not ashamed or embarrassed about it.'

'Look, neither am I . . .' Linford blathered. 'But . . .'

Emory turned away from him. 'You're sceptical about that, aren't you?' he said to Nina.

She nodded. 'Do it again in front of me, and I might not be.'

'Is that a challenge?' Emory laughed.

She raised her hands. 'If you want it to be.'

'Part of being what I am precludes rising to challenges.'

'Oh, well, never mind.'

Emory smiled. 'Ms Rose. I might not be able to provide the hard evidence you so obviously want, but what do you say to accompanying me to the site tomorrow? You could get some good pictures there, at least, and a ringside view.'

He was making it too easy for her. Nina felt edgy. 'Er . . . yeah, thanks.'

'That'd be marvellous!' Chantal said.

'I hope you're doing the right thing, Emory,' Iliana said.

'I'm just doing what comes next,' he answered.

On the way back to their room an hour or so later, Chantal said, 'Well, how's your headache? Did the Great Man heal you or what?'

Nina smiled. 'The headache – and the gut ache which I didn't mention – have gone, but they were caused by stress, being too tired and having drunk and smoked too much. I don't think Emory was responsible for getting rid of them. I just sobered up and relaxed, that's all.'

'You really are too sceptical, Ms Rose!'

'So enlighten me otherwise. What did you pick up?'

Chantal pulled a face. 'You won't like it.'

'What won't I like?'

'I couldn't read him at all. He'd protected himself.'

'Are you telling me he protected himself in a Talented way? Now that I really won't like!'

Chantal shrugged. 'Non-paranorms can't generally screen themselves, and when they do it's reflexive. Otherwise, it registers as a Talent, I'm afraid. Anyway, why are you so anxious to prove Patrick isn't a paranorm?'

Nina couldn't tell her, partly because she didn't know, and partly because once that fact had been proved, she would have to call the DPR for further instructions and she knew what they'd be. Since she'd become familiar with her Talent, she had never doubted it for an instant, but she still shrank from confronting Emory Patrick if he was Talented himself. It wasn't that she felt she'd fail, or that he'd be more powerful than her; it was something else, something buried or undefined, something she didn't want to know. 'I suppose I don't want to spoil his party, in a way. He's not doing any harm.'

'Well,' Chantal said. 'I'm sorry, but tomorrow I've got to phone in my report, and it will have to include the fact that Emory managed to block me tonight.'

'We have no real proof yet. He might just be strong-minded. Can you delay reporting in until after we've been to the convention site?'

Chantal didn't look too happy about the request. 'Okay but this is thin ice, Nina. If anything happens, and things get out of control at the site, my withholding information might incur disciplinary penalties.'

'Look, I can use my Talent to make sure things don't get out of control. Trust me.'

Chantal sighed. 'Well, as the lady said to our friend Mr Patrick, I hope you know what you're doing.'

*

In the morning Nina woke up with a tense headache. She knew the DPR would want evidence that Patrick's 'miracle' had been faked, and although she was sure it had been faked, she felt that Emory himself didn't realize it. She was honest with herself enough to see that she wanted his image of sincerity and concern to be a true one. Had she dreamed about him? Chantal was a little surly with her.

'You fancy him, don't you!' she accused.

'He's a stunner,' Nina admitted, 'but my guts are telling me he's not Talented. That's all there is to it.'

'Yeah, course!'

The two women went down to the lobby in uncomfortable silence.

Accompanied by the triumvirate of Future Light, Nina and Chantal rode to the site in a hired limousine. Emory seemed calm and at ease, although his colleagues were rather antsy. Iliana flipped through a sheaf of schedule notes, while Linford fiddled with a pocket computer. Emory sat between them, hands comfortably laced, smiling gently to himself and not catching anybody's eye. Nina didn't want to look at him, but her eyes were continually drawn to his face. Wonderful bones! She chastised herself silently. Remember, this is a job, a *job*. The words became a mantra long before they approached the site.

Chantal sat beside Nina, staring out of a side window. She was sullen and twitchy because Nina had repeated her request about not phoning in the report that morning. 'I don't want to contravene the rules!' Chantal had said. Nina was surprised by that; she hadn't thought Chantal the sort of person to care about rules particularly.

The silence in the car was oppressive. Its cold, purified air was sickly with vehicle deodorant.

It was easy to tell when they were nearing the convention site, because there were so many people milling around wearing Emory Patrick T-shirts. Many of them wore backpacks. Even through the polarized, security windows of the limo, the pumping sound of loud music could be heard. The car glided forward, as noticeable as a hearse, but, although people turned their heads to glance at it, no one appeared to realize it might contain the sacred presence of their Great Man. Nina wondered how Emory was feeling, knowing all these people were his, disciples of the pop Messiah. Her camera case felt heavy upon her knees. She noticed Emory looking at it. She smiled at him. He blinked at her, turned away.

'Thank God they haven't realized who's in this car,' Iliana said, shuffling her notes into a neat pile and inserting them into a briefcase. With her action, a sense of movement and communication came into the car. Linford put away his computer.

'What are you going to do today?' Nina asked Emory.

'Talk to them,' he replied. 'Perform. Do what I'm here to do.' His voice was almost cold. Nina felt as if he'd slapped her.

'I called the band,' Linford said. 'They're ready for you.'

Emory nodded, distracted. He's worried, Nina thought. He's trying to hide it, but he's worried.

Having skirted the main entrance, they were now approaching a smaller gate in the high fence that led to the performers' enclosure. Here, the crowds were pressing up against the site boundary, and the TOFL security staff were augmented by local police. The day was going to be hot. The police looked cheerful in shirt-sleeves. Then, Nina noticed Chantal press her fingers against the car window. 'Look at that. Shit, look at that.'

Nina looked. Hot glint of chrome against the fence. She saw wheelchairs, hundreds of them, people with other people carried in their arms, children lolling mindless and drooling against desperate breasts. She saw bodies without limbs, and limbs in plaster, atrophied, deformed.

'Oh . . . my . . . God!' Iliana looked disgusted. She turned away from the window.

'Aren't you used to this?' Nina asked. 'Isn't this part of the show?'

Emory gave her what she supposed amounted to a hard look.

Linford said, 'No, no, it isn't.'

'You brought this to us,' Iliana said, not looking at Emory. 'By Christ, you brought this to us!'

People had stuck things to the wire fence; messages, entreaties, petitions, ribbons, baby clothes, photographs. Overhead, helicopters whirred like carrion birds.

'They can't get in, those people,' Iliana said. 'It's tickets only.'

'Fortunate for you,' Nina said.

Emory Patrick said nothing.

The car swept round behind the enormous canopied stage and parked among a cluster of marquees and caravans. The flattened grass was damp underfoot, squeezed of its juice, and strewn with sand in places. The air smelled of hot rubber and electricity. People were milling everywhere, all wearing identification clips. Security was heavy. Dour men were marching around, speaking into walkie-talkies. Photographers and video crews, who were either Future Light employees or people who'd paid their way in somehow, were weighed down with equipment, the majority of which was pointed at the car. Everyone had been informed Emory Patrick was going to make an appearance. Getting out of the car, Nina sensed the atmosphere immediately, like that of a huge, hungry beast that, scenting meat near by, was straining to be let out of its cage. The crowd beyond the stage, hidden from this area, was a gigantic muted roar, the buzz of the helicopters an almost insignificant guttural whine above it. Word was being passed around already, perhaps a wordless telepathic message: Emory Patrick is here. They must have sensed his presence.

'This is freaky,' Chantal whispered to Nina. 'Too powerful. I wish you'd have let me phone in.'

'I didn't physically stop you,' Nina hissed back waspishly. 'I only asked a favour. You didn't have to agree.'

Chantal shrugged and moved away.

Emory Patrick was last out of the car. As soon as he set foot on the ground, flanked by Linford and Iliana, the crowd of officials and Future Light personnel swooped on him in a twittering, sycophantic flock. He smiled affably, nodded and raised his hands, Linford and Iliana clearing a path ahead of him. Iliana, dressed in black leather, her hair piled high, her eyes hidden behind huge shades, looked mean. People skittered out of her path. Nina and Chantal, already apart in feeling, were separated by the milling bodies, shunted away from the star.

Everyone converged on one of the marquees, where wine and beer were being served on trays. Nina, remaining near the entrance, helped herself to a beer and took her camera out of its case. Linford came over. 'He's going on stage in ten minutes to address the crowd,' he said.

'Doesn't waste any time, does he!'

'Er . . . no. You can follow us up. He's asked you to.'

Nina nodded. 'Okay . . . Is this anything like you expected?'

Linford pulled a sour face. 'Emory's appearances are always a powerful event, but this is different. Kind of hysterical.' He shook his head. 'I wouldn't have asked you here, but Emory was insistent. Seems like he and Iliana have both taken a fancy to you.'

'Oh.' She'd certainly influenced Iliana, but was unconvinced her Talent had swayed Emory Patrick in her favour. Neither had she sensed any evidence of it.

'I don't think he should be doing this,' Linford said suddenly.

'I know. I think you're probably right.'

He smiled gratefully. 'The crowds at the fence are causing a problem. We've been told the riot-control squads might have to be called in.'

'God! Didn't realize it was that bad. How awful.'

'It's worse at the main entrance, apparently. They're all sick. They've come from everywhere. Seems like thousands of them. Where have they come from?' Linford shook his head in despair. Nina felt an unexpected stab of sympathy.

'Riot squads to control sick people?' she asked. 'Seems a bit extreme.'

'There's so many of them. They're all trying to get in, to get at Emory. They want him to heal them.'

'Like Lourdes or something,' Nina said.

'No, not like that,' Linford replied. 'It's fevered, desperate ... they're like animals. One of the video crews has been filming it all. I've seen the footage. They're running it on a VCR back there.' He gestured behind him and then shook his head again. 'I wish we could go back to England this minute. Perhaps you can use your influence on Emory. He likes you.'

How ironic, Nina thought. That's probably exactly what I'm here to do. 'I've hardly met him, Linford,' she said. 'I really don't think I can get involved.'

He shrugged. 'Oh, well. You'd better come with me now. Where's your assistant?'

'Oh, she's around. It's okay. I can manage by myself for this.'

*

The view from the side of the stage was breathtaking. Before Emory or any of his musicians and dancers appeared, Nina climbed up the speaker stacks and took a few shots of the crowd, using her most powerful lens to take a look at the distant boundary fence, the thousands of desperate faces pressed up against it, the desperate fingers hooked through the wire. The audience itself was a swaying, colourful monster, arms rising and falling in some sort of cult dance. Voices ululated into the summer morning, a crooning chant that held an undeniable note of threat in its depths. Overhead, police helicopters were weaving their own frantic dance, back and forth, back and forth, as if they were concerned about what was happening, but unsure what to do. An enormous security man wearing an old ripped Emory Patrick T-shirt came and shouted at Nina to get down. Reluctantly – because although the crowd alarmed her slightly, she found the sight of it compelling – Nina scrambled down and allowed the man to direct her, none too gently, to where Linford and Iliana, along with a group of Future Light satellites, were standing in a raised enclosure to the right of the stage.

Even before Nina reached them, the crowd began to scream. She turned around, fighting away from the security man's insistent hold on her arm. Everyone in the vast audience was rising to their feet. The colourful, hungry monster was flexing its spine. The hairs rose reflexively on Nina's neck and arms. She didn't even have to look to know that Emory Patrick had just walked on stage.

Iliana, nervous and tense, pulled Nina towards her. 'What do you think?' she asked in a desperate, brittle voice.

Nina shook her head. 'Awesome,' she said.

'I've never seen anything like this,' Iliana replied. 'Don't know if it's good or bad yet.'

Emory Patrick's voice came over the PA, almost drowned out by the baying of his devotees. He greeted them, made a few jokes about remarks the media had printed recently, and then called for silence.

Never! Nina thought. He's got to be kidding.

The crowd fell silent.

'Now we shall breathe together!' Emory told them.

Nina's own breath was caught in her throat. She was aware of Iliana's fingers digging into her arm through her leather jacket. She was aware of many thousands of chests aligning themselves into a single organ. 'Oh, God,' she said weakly.

It the planet itself could sigh, it would sound like this, she thought.

Tranquillity fell over the crowd like narcotic dust. Emory breathed. The crowd breathed. Emory's arms swayed. The crowd swayed.

Is this a Talent at work, Nina thought. Is it? She was unsure.

Then, the music started up, faintly and slowly at first, and a line of dancers whirled on to the stage. Emory dropped his arms, dropped his head on to his chest.

He's left us, Nina thought. He's no longer here. He's *somewhere else*.

The reality Emory Patrick inhabited was that of his own power, his own universe. A great crashing of drums came through the PA. Emory raised his head and roared. The crowd went wild.

Nina lifted her camera and began to take shots automatically, her lens pointed at Emory Patrick. He was in her sights. She could act now, couldn't she? Somehow, she hadn't the will. She just kept firing the shutter, again and again. He turned his head. Had he sensed her? Had he seen her? No, his eyes were closed. The music swelled around her, a cushion for the power of Emory's voice as he hurled his philosophy at the crowd. The words meant nothing to her. Drained, Nina patted Iliana's hand and indicated she wanted to go and sit on the steps that led down to the ground. Iliana, thinking this was an invitation, followed. The steps were like a small pocket of no-time, where the sound of the music and the crowd was muted.

'He's really on form,' Iliana said. 'Brilliantly so. Perhaps this fiasco will turn out for the best after all.'

'I hope so,' Nina said.

I've seen nothing that indicates paranormal activity, she thought. I've seen a star, a hero, nothing else. No matter what Chantal thought, no matter what she said in her report, Nina intended to phone the DPR shortly and tell them Emory Patrick was clear. Powerful and charismatic as an individual, yes; a little crazy, quite possibly; but in all other respects completely normal. If he was a threat to the authorities because of his influence, it was not a problem that fell under the DPR's sphere of activity. Let someone else deal with it. Let someone else uncover the charade that had made a man appear to rise from the dead.

Then Linford Brown came charging towards them, and Nina's world tilted on its axis, never to right itself again.

'Illa, there's trouble!' he gasped.

'What? What trouble?' Iliana was high on the power Emory had invoked. She didn't stop smiling.

'The crowds at the fence. They're going berserk. Breaking down the wire. There's riot squads homing in. We've got to get Emory off stage and out of here!'

Iliana seemed dazed. 'Are you sure?'

'Yes! For God's sake, prepare yourself. I'm going to get the power cut!'

He leapt off the steps and disappeared. Iliana and Nina stared at each other for a few moments.

'Is this real?' Nina asked.

Iliana stood up. 'Come on.'

They sprinted back up the steps and Iliana, with her official capacity, got them past the security men to the very edge of the stage. At that moment the music stopped dead.

There was a moment's stasis. The band looked surprised, confused, while the crowd poised open-mouthed, arms raised, bodies contorted in mid-dervish chaos. In that moment of utter silence, horrendous sounds could be discerned coming from the boundary fence.

'Emory!' Iliana yelled.

He seemed dazed, and she had to shout twice more to get his attention.

'Come here!'

The crowd had now started to yell and jump around, still good-natured, because they believed this to be a temporary halt to the proceedings. Their ears were buzzing. They had not yet deciphered the sounds rising behind them.

Emory paused to adjust his mike stand and then sauntered over, ignoring Iliana's frantic gestures for him to hurry. 'What's happened?' he asked. 'Can they get it fixed?'

Iliana shook her head. 'No. It's not fixable. The people at the fence are rioting. It's all very ugly. You'll have to leave now.'

He smiled. 'No, Iliana.'

'Emory, I know you're enjoying yourself, but this is a dangerous situation.' She grabbed his arm. 'Come along. We'll go to the car quickly. We'll be out of here before anyone realizes you've gone.'

Emory stared at her for a moment and then addressed Nina. 'What's happening?'

Nina shrugged helplessly. 'Exactly what she said.'

'Mori, please, let's go!' Iliana's voice had become desperate. She was afraid.

'I can't,' Emory said. He glanced back over his shoulder.

Linford Brown came hurrying towards them, his habitually pale face quite red. 'Water cannon!' he gasped. 'It's on the video monitors. It's like a fucking massacre!'

'What?' Emory roared.

Linford pointed at the distant fence. 'Police everywhere, shields, horses, the lot. And water cannon. They're firing on the cripples.'

'I don't believe it,' Iliana said in a restrained voice, as if to refute a small piece of scandal.

At that moment the convention of Future Light transformed into pandemonium. Having broken through the fence, all the non-paying spectators, able-bodied and otherwise, poured into the site, followed by the riot squads, who'd been trying to drive them in the opposite direction. Even from this distance, Nina could see the high, razor-topped fences falling like the walls of Jericho. An ugly surge was spreading down towards the stage, as panic was kindled among the crowd. Police horses were cantering into the mêlée. Nina's camera was to her face, the shutter firing, film winding, too slow to capture what she was seeing. It was so medieval, like a scene from hell. Terrified people were struggling to find safety, clawing at each other, trampling each other underfoot. Some were trying to break through the security barrier in front of the stage in an instinctive attempt to be on higher ground. Nina caught the image in her viewfinder of a lone wailing child, seconds before the child disappeared in a jumble of panicking bodies. She took another shot of two teenage girls, weeping and clutching each other, a senseless third lolling between them, blood on her face. They were tiny images, picked out and magnified by her camera, in a landscape of insanity too big to take in as a complete picture. Nina could hear the sound of cars, four-wheeled-drive vehicles and limos, starting up from behind the stage as staff tried to make an exit.

'Emory, let's get of here,' Linford pleaded. 'Now!'

Emory did not answer.

He glanced coldly at Nina, who had lowered her camera. The glance went on too long, and there was certainly a message in it, but not an obvious one.

Emory tried to pull away from Iliana, failed, and was therefore obliged to drag her with him as he strode back to the microphone. The band and dancers, more sensible, had vanished.

'The mike's dead,' Linford said to Nina. 'What's he fucking playing at? They won't hear him.'

A high-pitched whistle filled the air.

'Enough!' roared Emory Patrick. 'Enough! Enough!' His arms were raised. His voice, amplified a thousand times, boomed out like the cry of a god.

Nina fell to her knees, as a sour wind knocked the breath from her belly. She felt Linford drop down and huddle against her. Her hair was whipping across her face, her eyes were stinging, but she could just see the statuesque shape of Emory Patrick looming on the stage, Iliana crumpled at his feet. The air was a seething mass of dust motes that writhed like a leviathan over the crowd.

Emory screamed.

The helicopters, careening overhead, were suddenly flung aside, not crashing, not falling, not bursting into flames, but simple blown away to new skies. Nina saw them go. Emory gestured wildly, as if he were throwing power outwards. Nina could hardly breathe. Everything was too confused. It was like a nightmare. And then time froze. Nina closed her eyes. She was alone in a desolate place, completely alone. A wind was blowing from far away, carrying memories, fragments of dreams. She had always been alone, for eternity. Alone with her purpose, her secret, shameful purpose.

Then a warm, living hand touched her face. 'Hazel!' She opened her eyes. Linford was staring at her, wide-eyed, strings of hair hanging over his eyes. 'Help me,' he said. 'Help me get him out of here.'

'Can we move?'

'Try!'

They could move, but only sluggishly.

Hanging on to each other, as if fighting against a gale, Nina and Linford stood up and struggled on to the stage. The crowd was, once again, held in stasis. Nina wanted to look, to understand, but Linford dragged her forwards relentlessly. But in one glance, she had witnessed enough. What had she seen? Horses frozen in mid-air, people in mid-fall. Limbs tangled and rigid like the limbs of trees. A thousand expressions of dismay, terror and bewilderment caricatured in a complete lack of animation. A cataract of water turned into a shining bridge. Debris thrown into the air and caught there as if held in rock. A multitude of agonized individuals, the component parts of the hungry beast, were caught in freeze-frame. Reality had become a tableau, a single frame of a movie. It was a power that spread out from Emory Patrick's staring eyes, Emory Patrick's outflung arms. Everyone who'd been standing behind him had been unaffected, and the majority of them had fled the scene.

Iliana was kneeling on all fours, blinking through her dishevelled hair, a shunned handmaiden at the feet of a manic deity. Emory Patrick's body was rigid, his arms held above his head, his dark eyes round and wild.

Somehow, and later the memory would be incomplete and fragmented, Nina and Linford manhandled Emory

Patrick towards the side of the stage. Iliana tried to assist, but was too shocked and confused to be of much help. Nina did remember, and would always remember, having the courage to look into Emory's eyes and say, 'You're coming with me.' She had projected her Talent, but only slightly, terrified that in some way it might rebound on her from the face of Emory Patrick. He returned her gaze, only half aware, only one foot in this world. Then, his body went limp and they could take him, drag him away. Simultaneously, a tide of movement and hysteria swept back over the crowd. Nina did not turn to see it.

Only one car was left back-stage. It might have been the one they arrived in, but there was no driver with it now. Everywhere was eerily deserted. Litter blew along the ground. Nina remembered Chantal and, with a twinge of guilt, hoped she had got away all right. She shut off her mind to the sounds of terror and panic that had once again come to dominate the day.

Linford climbed behind the wheel of the car. Fortunately, the keys were still in the ignition. Future Lighters were trusting; they did not steal from one another. Iliana and Nina shoved Emory into the back seat and sat on either side of him, gripping his arms. He did not speak or move, did not even blink. Iliana was weeping. Her forehead was cut but not badly. Blood had stained the ash blonde waves hanging over her eyes. Linford cursed as the car refused to start. Perhaps that was why it had been left behind, abandoned in favour of more reliable transport, like feet. Then, the vehicle roared into life and shot forward with a jolt, catching the guy ropes of a nearby marquee and nearly dragging it behind. Both women buried their faces against Emory's shoulders as Linford put his foot down and accelerated forward through what was left of the fence. Things bumped the car. Nina dared not look. Things were under the wheels. She dared not even think.

After a nightmare journey, as Linford tried in vain to remember the route, they eventually arrived back at the hotel, through sheer luck rather than strategy. They clambered dazedly out of the car, leaving the doors hanging open, and ran into the lobby, dragging Emory between them. Nina was alert for the presence of police, but it seemed all efforts must still be concentrated on the convention site. Other Future Light personnel, who'd fled the site earlier, were hanging round the reception desk. Some appeared to be checking out hurriedly.

Linford wanted Nina to come up to their room. He implied they'd need help with Emory, who had still not spoken.

'I'll be there,' Nina said. 'I will. Soon. Just let me check to see if Chantal made it back. Okay?' There was a call she had to make first.

Even before she'd unlocked the door, Nina knew Chantal would not be inside. The Dutch girl's clothes were still thrown over her bed, a pair of sneakers lay on their side in the middle of the floor. Nina did not look at them too long. She sat down on her own bed and picked up the phone, requesting the secure emergency line to the DPR. She stared at her hands while she waited for the connection, the phone jammed between shoulder and jaw. Her hands were shaking. They were bloodstained. She'd lost her camera, her purse. Oh, God!

'Nina?'

'Gervase? Gervase?' She could only say his name.

'It's all right,' he said. His voice was low and soothing. 'We've seen the bulletins. Are you hurt?'

'No. . .' The sound of concern over the line seemed to burst the shield she'd constructed around her emotions.

She began to cry, her chest convulsing in great heaving sobs. Allerby let her weep, making appropriate comforting sounds down the phone.

'You're so far away,' Nina said. 'So far.'

'Nina, remember the Dallywell shoot.'

She held her breath, even her sobs cut short. It was a code between them, a slap in the face.

'I'm sorry,' Allerby said. 'But it's imperative you regain control. You can regain control. You know you can.'

She laughed shakily. 'Thanks for the cold shower.'

'That's better. Now listen to me. Other personnel are already on their way. Loric himself will be with you shortly.'

'You want us to get Patrick out, right?' She wiped her face, wishing she could light a cigarette, even though she'd given up smoking three years previously.

'Nina . . . Events have progressed in a direction everyone hoped they wouldn't. This is too big. Too . . . *awkward*. We're really concerned about it, Nina. Very concerned. Therefore, we feel it is necessary for you to bring us a picture of Mr Patrick.' He didn't say anything more, but she could feel him in her mind. Remember the Dallywell shoot. Remember your training. Now, you are machine. Nothing more. She glanced towards the chair under the window where her other camera lay, its lens reflecting the sun. Too hot for it there. Stupid. Should have moved it.

'Okay,' she said and hung up.

Iliana answered Nina's knock on the door. She enfolded Nina in a close embrace, pressing her wet bloodied face against Nina's cheek. Nina raised one arm half-heartedly.

'Oh, this is terrible, terrible,' Iliana said, dragging Nina into the room. It appeared to be packed out with a confused and terrified bunch of Future Light personnel.

Some of them were suffering from minor injuries, patching each other up from a ridiculously small first-aid case. 'We'll probably be thrown in jail!' Iliana cried. 'Linford is trying to make reservations on the next available flight. Oh, Hazel, I'm scared, actually scared. I'm wondering if we'll ever get home.'

'How's Emory?'

Iliana shook her head. 'He's gone to his room to pack. Linford's with him. He's making the calls from there. I don't know how Emory's feeling. He's calm, but he hasn't said much. I'm just thankful he's doing what I tell him. Do you think we'll get out of here, Hazel?'

'I don't know.'

Iliana clutched at Nina's arm. 'Thank you for what you did. I'll never be able to repay you.'

'It's okay. Don't worry about it. Can I see Emory?'

Iliana shrugged. 'That's up to him.'

'Right. I'll go see, then.'

'I'll come with you.'

Nina looked into Iliana's eyes. 'No.' Iliana dropped her arms, flinched.

Then Nina walked out of the door.

Emory Patrick's room was full of peace. There was no other way to describe it. Linford Brown's voice was an insistent whisper against the phone, but had little effect on the atmosphere. Emory himself was carefully folding shirts and putting them into a case. Nina had simply knocked on the door and walked right in.

'I was waiting for you,' Emory said.

Nina shrugged and touched the camera hanging round her neck.

'Linford, could you conclude your business elsewhere?' Emory asked.

'I've finished,' Linford said, putting down the phone.

'If all goes well, we should be out of here by tonight. Took some doing, but . . .'

'Thank you, Linford.' Emory's soft remark was a dismissal. Linford fled.

Emory and Nina faced each other across a small space. He folded his arms. 'Why are you so afraid?' he asked.

Nina said nothing. She knew she shouldn't speak. She raised the camera to her eyes.

'So it's come to this,' Emory said. He turned his back on her, walked away, began packing again.

'Emory.' He did not look up. 'Emory, look at me.'

He paused, then did so. She began to raise the camera again.

'You don't need that,' he said. 'Or is that your shield, the shield across your perception? Can't you bear to see what you do? It's like shooting me in the back.'

Ignore it, she thought. Don't listen. She summoned her Talent, projected it into the viewfinder, felt it slide off the mirror inside the camera, slither into the lens itself.

'They made a monster of you,' Emory said, still packing. 'So much so, you don't even have the capacity to think about it any more.'

She felt the power go, felt it sizzle like a laser from her mind. Emory looked up at her. She felt her power enter his body, felt the resistance of muscle and bone giving way. He walked towards her and tore the camera from her neck. She cried out and stumbled, momentarily stunned, the breath squeezed from her throat. Her neck was burning.

'At least have the decency to return the look you demand of me!' he said.

She shook her head to clear it, rubbing the skin of her neck. Very well, if that was the way he wanted it. She raised her chin. If it was to be a contest, then so be it. He folded his arms and smiled. His eyes were as dark as infinity, unfathomable. And suddenly, she was not seeing him at all. She was peering through a long lens at a woman posturing for the camera. She hated that woman. It was the person who had tried to destroy her, undermine her career with lies, steal her lover. Simone Dallywell. As she pressed the shutter, she was thinking, 'Die, you bitch, die!' And then there was blood everywhere, blood from the eyes and nose, and a strangled croak. There was death. It had been the first time.

'Coercion,' said the voice of Emory Patrick, 'to the point where you can order a person's own nervous system to destroy the body it services. No trace of murder. That's some Talent, Nina Vivian.'

She blinked, and the image of Emory Patrick swam back into her field of vision.

'I just wanted you to know I'm aware of the truth,' he said in a gentle voice. 'That's all. What happened with the Dallywell woman was an accident, Nina. Everyone has murderous thoughts like that sometimes. You were not to know you could make them real. Neither are you to blame for what you are now, but the people who fucked your head over after the Dallywell incident certainly are!'

Nina could not speak. The image of the Dallywell shoot was still too strong in her mind.

'I knew why you were here even before you did,' Emory said. 'But, I feel there is one thing you should know. Your instincts were right: I'm not one of your kind.'

'You are,' Nina said, speaking in spite of the unwritten rule she had created for herself never to converse with her subjects once the process had begun. 'I saw what happened at the site, and you've just proved you're a telepath. My instincts were wrong, maybe, but I know a Talent at work when I see one.'

He shook his head. 'No. Not quite.'

'What are you, then? Really the Son of God?'

He smiled. 'There is no God, Nina, not in the sense people understand it, but then you know that, don't you? There are chances, though, chances for the future. Sometimes the universe creates such chances, such hopes. But it is futile. People aren't conscious enough. I love them all, but I know they're not conscious.'

'Tell me,' she said. 'Tell me what you are.'

'I am shattered hope,' he said. 'And you must do what you came here to do. I realize now I've had my chance. You are my reward.'

'You're a liar,' Nina cried. 'You're a paranorm.'

'Then kill me like you've been ordered to!' he shouted. 'Go on, do it!'

She turned away. *Can't do it. Can't.* 'Get out of here, Emory Patrick. Get out now. Run anywhere. There's not much time.'

She heard him laughing. 'Beautiful,' he said. 'What a beautiful ending.'

'I mean it!'

'I know you do. You have fought against this so painfully, haven't you? You have been dreading it. But it's inevitable. Now . . . turn around.'

She could not disobey the order. Even as she was turning, with agonizing slowness, she was remembering the words of Sable Grant. *If he is what people claim he is, it would be worse.* Yes. Worse, because the world can't handle it, doesn't want it, not even the so-called enlightened New Agers, such as Sable herself. The world destroys things it can't understand. *Don't make me do this. Don't!*

She was facing him now, and he was holding her Talent in the depth of his eyes. He held her in stasis, as he'd held the entire convention site before him in stasis earlier. He directed her will.

'No,' she said, but the word never made a sound.

'I felt you coming yesterday,' he said. 'And some part of me welcomed it. I can't let you deny me now. It's over, Nina. I screwed up. Now it's time for me to go.' He grinned wearily. 'Let's just say I have better things to do. I'm sorry. I hope you'll forgive me one day.' Inexorably, he drew her Talent out of her, focused it on himself. Her eyes were streaming. She could taste blood in her mouth. It was as if her hands were around his heart, crushing it to a pulp. He was too strong to resist. There was no contest. Her Talent was tiny in comparison to his. In the end, she let go, and let him have it all.

Soon, he was lying back on the bed, and a single fly was buzzing round the otherwise silent room. His eyes were open and he looked slightly surprised but not afraid. Nina stood over him swaying, one hand forced between her teeth. She was biting hard, but could feel no pain. She felt drained of all feeling. Ultimately, it had been just another job. She'd deceived herself, believing the thing she'd become would have it any other way.

'You're so beautiful,' she said in a thick voice, mumbling around the obstruction of her hand. 'I don't have to forgive you, because there's nothing to forgive. This is just what I do. Sometimes.'

Then she sat down beside him to keep the vigil, until the others came.

By the time the final file joined the heap on the occasional table, Loric's sense of well-being had completely evaporated.

'We'll have to talk to the others. As soon as possible.'
And get hold of this Allerby's file as well. That might take some doing; he belonged to the Funny People more than to the DPR.

Why? It seems to me he's solved a potentially messy problem for you. Neatly, and discreetly.

'Oh, yes. I'm sure Daddy would have approved wholeheartedly.' Loric stood, and walked around the desk. His neck refused to flex, however much he massaged it. 'All he's bloody done is approve the assassination of a God.'

You think this Patrick really was the Messiah, then?

'Don't be facetious. This is too serious,' He paced the room, agitating the spiders in their glass tank. 'You remember what I told Carrie Smith. We've worked on the myth of our invulnerability to protect the weaker paranorms. The normals are afraid of us, and they laugh at Captain Croak, and we all survive. What happens if they find out one of my own subordinates killed a bloody God?'

Oh.

'Precisely.' He paced the room, until the ormolu mantel clock chimed apologetically. 'Half past two. Jesus.'

Go to bed, Lorrie. You're too tired to think straight anyway.

'I know. You're right. I need to sleep on it.' He yawned again and headed for the door.

But sleep was a long time coming.

ABOUT THE EDITORS

Alex Stewart's fiction, articles and comic strips have appeared in a wide variety of publications, some of which he is prepared to admit to. As well as the *Temps* series, he edited the critically acclaimed anthology *Arrows of Eros*, from which two stories were later selected for Best of Year collections.

In his spare time he practises martial arts and worries about his overdraft.

Neil Gaiman is co-author of the best-selling apocalyptic fantasy *Good Omens*, with Terry Pratchett, but is better known for his work in the comics medium, particularly for his ongoing dark fantasy *Sandman*, which has won lots of awards. He comes up with quite a few of the ideas for Midnight Rose, while other people do the real work: Alex Stewart did all the heavy lifting on *Temps* (also published in ROC), and Mary Gentle and Roz Kaveney had to get their hands dirty with *The Weerde* and the forthcoming ROC anthology *Villains!*

Alex Stewart and Neil Gaiman also collaborated on *Temps*.

**Exploring New Realms
in Science Fiction/Fantasy Adventure**

The Soul Rider Saga
by Jack Chalker

Titles already published or in preparation:

Book One: Spirits of Flux and Anchor

Book Two: Empires of Flux and Anchor

Book Three: Masters of Flux and Anchor

Book Four: The Birth of Flux and Anchor

Book Five: Children of Flux and Anchor

Cassie did not feel the Soul Rider enter her body ... but suddenly she knew that Anchor was corrupt. Knew that the Flux beyond Anchor was no formless void, from which could issue only mutant changelings and evil wizards ... Flux was the source of Anchor's existence! The price of her knowledge is exile – the first confrontation with the Seven Who Wait for the redemption of World ...

**Exploring New Realms
in Science Fiction/Fantasy Adventure**

SHADOWRUN™

Titles already published or in preparation:

Volume 1: Never Deal with a Dragon
Robert N. Charrette

In the year 2050, the power of magic has returned to the earth. Elves, Mages and lethal Dragons find a home where technology and human flesh have melded into deadly urban predators.

Volume 2: Choose Your Enemies Carefully
Robert N. Charrette

As Sam searches for his sister, he realizes that only when he accepts his destiny as a shaman can he embrace the power he needs for what waits for him in the final confrontation...

Volume 3: Find Your Own Truth
Robert N. Charrette

A young shaman unwittingly releases a terror from the ancient reign of magic.

Volume 4: 2XS
Nigel Findley

Dirk thought he knew all about the dark side of the streets ... until 2XS became the new hallucinogenic chip of choice.

Volume 5: Changeling
Chris Kubasik

In a dangerous future magic transforms a young man into a creature from the mythical past.

**Exploring New Realms
in Science Fiction/Fantasy Adventure**

BATMAN™ IS BACK IN ACTION!

Batman™: To Stalk a Specter
by Simon Hawke

Gotham City Blackmailed!

Drug Lord Caught by U.S. Commandos! Desiderio Garcia to
Stand Trial in the U.S.! The headlines – and the authorities – are
jubilant, but not for long. For Garcia has a deadly would-be
rescuer: the superassassin known as Specter. And Specter's reign
of havoc and horror has already begun. The people of Gotham City
are held hostage and destined to die by the thousands unless
Garcia is freed. The people's only hope lies with Batman's bold
and dangerous plan. In a war with only one winner and one
survivor, he's going to make himself the archkiller's target,
matching his enemy weapon for weapon, deception for deception
– and with good for evil!

BATMAN™ CREATED BY BOB KANE

**Exploring New Realms
in Science Fiction/Fantasy Adventure**

BATTLETECH®

Titles already published or in preparation:

Volume 1: Way of the Clans
Robert Thurston

It is the 31st century where the BattleMech is the ultimate war machine ... where the Clans are the ultimate warriors ... and where a man called Aidan must succeed in trials that will forge him into one of the best warriors in the galaxy.

Volume 2: Bloodname
Robert Thurston

The star captain locks in deadly combat on the eve of the invasion of the inner sphere

Volume 3: Falcon Guard
Robert Thurston

A clash of empires ... a clash of armies ... a clash of cultures ... the fate of the Clan Jade Falcon rests in Star Colonel Aidan's hands.

Volume 4: Wolf Pack
Robert N. Charrette

The Dragoons are five regiments of battle-toughened Mech Warriors and their services are on offer to the highest bidder. Whoever that might be...

Volume 5: Natural Selection
Michael A. Stackpole

A terrible secret threatens to begin the violence anew – in the bloodiest civil war man has ever known.

**Exploring New Realms
in Science Fiction/Fantasy Adventure**

Villains!
Devised by Mary Gentle
and Neil Gaiman

Who needs heroes anyway?

These are the untold stories – the other side of the Legend. For in the Twenty Four Kingdoms lie those dark and dangerous places inhabited by halfling assassins, corrupt warriors and necromancers, evil princesses, and wickedly clever orcs ... the world of sword and sorcery as it really is!

At last the time has come to enter in their company the slums, mountains, cities and wilderness; to cross the boundaries of the Dark Land itself – and hear the *real* truth.

Because just for once the Dark Lords, mercenaries, money-grubbing dwarves and monsters are the stars of these new tales from Mary Gentle, Storm Constantine, Stephen Baxter, Keith Brooke, David Langford, Charles Stross, Alex Stewart, James Wallis, Roz Kaveney, Paula Wakefield, Molly Brown and Graham Higgins.

And just for once – the bad guys may even win!

**Exploring New Realms
in Science Fiction/Fantasy Adventure**

The Weerde
Devised by Neil Gaiman, Mary Gentle and Roz Kaveney

They are among us...

In the Library of the Conspiracy many theories are pursued in rare books and documents supplied by a caste of white-gloved librarians. Many wild-eyed researchers piece together their elaborate nonsenses of Templars, Vampires and Illuminati.

But one such theory weaves like a constant thread of darkness through human history. The rumour of an ancient race, more powerful than we are: elusive, terrifying, offering sexual frenzy but bringing madness and early death.

These are the tales of the Weerde. They gather at the edges of our settlements, they appear nightly on TV. They are not werewolves. But they are the shape-shifting predators of which occult legend speaks. They are plausible, charming, different ... and very, very dangerous.

The Weerde contains eleven chilling stories that expose the terrifying truth behind the conspiracy. Their authors are Storm Constantine, Mary Gentle, Colin Greenland, Brian Stableford, Josephine Saxton, Charles Stross, Roz Kaveney, Paul Cornell, Chris Amies, Michael Fearn and Liz Holliday.

**Exploring New Realms
in Science Fiction/Fantasy Adventure**

Temps
Devised by Neil Gaiman and
Alex Stewart

At last, the cutting-edge of Superhero fantasy!

Danger: Talent at work

To the tabloid press the Department of Paranormal Resources is
a scroungers' paradise, issuing regular girocheques to a motley
collection of talents with questionable results.

But for the 'Temps' who place their bizarre abilities at the service
of the State in exchange for a miserly stipend and a demob suit,
life with a very British League of Superheroes leaves everything
to be desired . . .

Temps begins a startling new series in which a team of gifted Psi-
fi writers explore a strangely familiar world of empaths, precogs
and telepaths – with hilarious and terrifying results.

Contributors include: Storm Constantine, Colin Greenland,
Graham Higgins, Liz Holliday, Roz Kaveney, David Langford,
Brian Stableford . . . and many more.